THE
SLEEP
WALKER

Lars Kepler is a No.1 bestselling international sensation, whose Killer Instinct thrillers have sold more than 17 million copies in 40 languages. The first book in the series, *The Hypnotist*, was selected for the 2012 Richard and Judy Book Club. The most recent, *The Sleepwalker*, went straight to No.1 in Sweden, Norway, Finland and the Czech Republic, and was the most sold fiction title in Sweden in 2024. Lars Kepler is the pseudonym for writing duo Alexander and Alexandra Ahndoril. They live with their family in Sweden.

Also by Lars Kepler

The Killer Instinct Series
The Hypnotist
The Nightmare
The Fire Witness
The Sandman
Stalker
The Rabbit Hunter
Lazarus
The Mirror Man
The Spider

THE SLEEP WALKER

LARS KEPLER

ZAFFRE

Originally published in Sweden by Albert Bonniers Förlag in 2024
First published in the UK in 2025 by
ZAFFRE
An imprint of Bonnier Books UK
5th Floor, HYLO, 105 Bunhill Row,
London, EC1Y 8LZ

Published by agreement with Salomonsson Agency

A CIP catalogue record for this book is
available from the British Library.

Hardback ISBN: 978-1-83877-790-6
Trade paperback ISBN: 978-1-83877-791-3

Also available as an ebook and an audiobook

1 3 5 7 9 10 8 6 4 2

Typeset by IDSUK (Data Connection) Ltd
Printed and bound in Great Britain by Clays Ltd, Elcograf S.p.A.

FSC
www.fsc.org

MIX
Paper | Supporting
responsible forestry
FSC® C018072

The authorised representative in the EEA is Bonnier Books
UK (Ireland) Limited.
Registered office address: Floor 3, Block 3, Miesian Plaza,
Dublin 2, D02 Y754, Ireland
compliance@bonnierbooks.ie
www.bonnierbooks.co.uk

Sleep and dreams have always fascinated mankind, walking by our side like a couple of enigmatic companions.

In Greek mythology, Hypnos was the god of sleep. He lived in a dark cave by the river of forgetfulness, and his son Morpheus – the god of dreams – watched over him while he slept.

Nowadays, science recognises two key phases of sleep: deep sleep and REM sleep. During the deep sleep phase, the electrical waves in the cerebral cortex are long and slow. Several times a night, however, the waves become shorter and more frequent, resembling those seen in waking people. This phase is known as REM sleep because of the rapid eye movements behind the sleeper's closed eyelids.

Parasomnia is the umbrella term for a group of disorders in which the brain is partially asleep and partially awake.

The well-documented disorder of sleepwalking, or somnambulism, occurs in roughly five per cent of all children, but it is much less common among adults.

As with the majority of parasomnias, almost all sleepwalking occurs during the deep sleep phase, and only lasts a few minutes, but there are also those who sleepwalk during REM sleep. For them, it is their dreams that trigger physical activities such as getting dressed, unlocking the door and leaving the house.

Prologue

The silvery light from the heavy sky shimmers in the restless rings on the puddles, in the water dripping from the roof and the overflowing zinc washtub.

Mother is standing in the middle of the yard, between Grandpa's rusty old car and the woodshed. Her blonde hair is sopping wet, her bra and jeans soaked through.

The pouring rain mixes with the fresh blood still weeping from her wounds, rinsing it away almost as quickly as it appears.

That morning, she grabbed a knife and slashed herself all over, then tossed the blade to the floor and left the house barefoot.

The boy peers out onto the porch and studies the bloody door knob, the peeling wallpaper, the knife and the empty bottle of vodka between his father's rubber boots.

Mother spent all night talking to the jerry can in the car and the axe in the woodshed, screaming at them and pleading with the heavens to send his father home.

The boy turns back into his room and watches her through the window. The rain is now lashing down on the tin roof and the window ledge in front of him.

The gutters are clogged with old leaves, and they quickly overflow.

The plastic-coated cable around the boy's left wrist is attached to a handrail that has been screwed to the ceiling, allowing him to move freely around his room. He can lie down in bed, stand by the window and play with his toys on the floor.

He has a troll with bright orange hair, pointed like a flame, a bendy Pink Panther and an American police car with lights that flashed blue the week he first got it.

With the cable around his wrist, he can go out onto the porch and use the toilet, but he can't reach the front door. If he stretches as far as he can, until his wrist burns and his shoulder aches, he can see the broken floor in the kitchen.

His mother disappears into the woodshed and re-emerges with the axe. She stands still for a moment beside the heap of old tyres and rusty engines, head bowed. The glow of the neon Ford sign illuminates the raindrops behind her.

She lifts her chin and slowly turns around. She points at him in the window, then starts striding towards the house.

Introduction

The *Razor Crest* spaceship hovers in the darkness. The woman smiles as she looks down at her son. His face is pale in the moonlight spilling in through the locked window, a slight crease between his brows.

His chest and stomach rise and fall with each steady breath.

After his evening bath and snack, he brushed his teeth and took the fifteen milligrams of promethazine she gave him, and he is now sleeping soundly.

She still feels flustered that Robert arrived while the boy was awake, meaning she had to lie and say he was a delivery man dropping off some papers.

The baby monitor is focused on his sleeping body.

She gets up as slowly as she can, but her movements still set the big Lego spacecraft swaying on its nylon cords.

The woman tiptoes out into the hallway, closes the door and has just started to turn the key in the lock when something thuds to the floor on the other side.

Holding her breath, she presses her ear to the wood.

He doesn't seem to have woken.

She told Robert not to make a sound, but she can hear soft music from her bedroom. She turns the key, smooths her dress and walks down the hall, through the door with the window in it and past the top of the stairs.

Robert is sitting in the dark with his phone in his hand. He whispers sorry, and she can't help but smile when she meets his eye.

With his short, curly hair, the silver coin he wears on a chain and his bare chest, he looks like a young Roman emperor.

'He's asleep,' she says.

'OK, so what are we waiting for?'

'The answer's always you, if you ask me.'

'I'm here. I came,' he says, getting up.

You came, you saw, you conquered, she thinks as she moves over to the window and pushes back the curtain, overcome by a sudden rush of anxiety. The heavy full moon is low above the treetops, silver and scarred. Down on the driveway, Robert's rusty car is parked in the shadow of the maple.

'Has he ever come home early?' he asks.

'That doesn't stop me worrying,' she replies, turning to him.

'Come on, I grabbed a bottle of fizz from—'

'Hang on,' she cuts him off, raising a hand to her mouth.

'What's wrong?'

'Nothing, I just realised I turned the key twice.'

'Why does that matter?'

'It doesn't, it's just me. It's . . . you know, a habit. I want to be able to get in there quickly if I need to,' she says as she leaves the room.

The hallway is cool and dark.

The vacuum cleaner has been left up against the wall, its cord wrapped around the cylinder.

When she reaches her son's room, she can't help but glance back over her shoulder. Robert is in the doorway, and he holds up the bottle of sparkling rosé wine he found in the kitchen. Always so eager. She smiles, gives him a thumbs up and then turns the key counter-clockwise.

The mechanism clicks.

She is just about to press her ear to the door when she hears a low pop from her bedroom.

Robert is standing in a pool of moonlight when she gets back, two full glasses in his hands. He passes one to her and looks deep into her eyes.

They toast, kiss and sip, their shadows dancing eerily over the old communion bell on the wall above the double bed.

'Mmm,' she says, sitting down on the edge of the mattress.

On the screen of the baby monitor, the boy's face is calm, his chest rising and falling beneath the blue covers. The speaker crackles as he moves his hand in his sleep.

Robert drains his glass, sets it down beside the bottle on the chest of drawers and moves over to her. He leans in and gives her a light peck on the lips.

She lowers her glass to the bedside table, puts her hands on his hips and looks up into his intense eyes.

'What are you thinking about?' she asks, unable to hide her smile.

'What do you think?'

Lowering her eyes, she sees that his jeans have started to strain. She kisses the fly softly several times, making him harden even more. The denim is now so taut that the zip is visible.

'Come on, then,' she murmurs.

She shuffles back on the bed, pushing a cushion out of the way and lying down with a quick glance at the monitor. In the cold moonlight, her son's face resembles a leaden egg. Robert undoes his jeans and sways as he kicks them off. He crawls towards her and kisses her pubic mound, his hot breath filtering through her clothes.

She feels a flutter in her stomach as he reaches beneath her dress, pulls down her knickers and parts her thighs.

'Come here,' she whispers, eyes darting over to the dark doorway.

He climbs on top of her and kisses her with a smile, and she pants softly as he slowly enters her. Her legs are forced apart, and for a brief, quiet moment, she completely envelops him.

Her nipples harden against the smooth fabric of her bra.

He pulls back and begins thrusting rhythmically, with growing intensity. The headboard knocks against the wall, making the communion bell ring.

In her mind's eye, she sees a lost boy walking through a forest with a bell around his neck.

She turns to the monitor, trying to push back those thoughts, and closes her eyes in an attempt to focus on the moment, the pleasure. Her breasts sway with each thrust, and she tenses her thighs and pelvic floor, clutching his arched back. She is getting close, and she relaxes for a few seconds, panting, before tensing her muscles again in a powerful orgasm.

She tries to keep quiet as her toes curl and sweat prickles on her scalp. On the street outside, she hears a car pull up.

Robert is still going, pumping harder and harder. He climaxes with a low sigh and then slumps on top of her, breathing heavily. His semen spills out of her, coating her thighs.

She can feel his heart pounding against her chest, against her own heart.

One beat after another, she thinks. A countdown.

For a while, they lie quietly, limbs still entwined. They should finish their wine, she thinks. Talk about their future together.

A heavy thud causes her to wake with a start in the darkness. The bedroom window is wide open.

There is a crash as one of the roof tiles breaks on the lawn, and then she hears a terrible scream.

1

The November sky above Vårberg centrum is the colour of cast iron. It is almost three in the morning, and the streets are deserted.

A police car cruises slowly past a shuttered beauty salon.

John Jakobsson and Einar Bofors sit in silence as they drive. The two officers stopped speaking almost a year ago, and neither says a word unless they absolutely have to.

The bag of leftovers from the fast food kiosk is on the floor by Einar's feet, and the smell of grease fills the car.

John drums the wheel, thinking – as he so often does – about his older brother's lifeless face as he stares out through the windscreen.

The lights from the entrance to the metro station are reflected in dusty window displays, and the ground between the pillars in the arcade is littered with rubbish, leaves and broken glass. Outside the charity shop, there are a couple of discarded spray cans, plastic bags and flattened cardboard boxes.

The two police officers are both lost in thought as they pass the parking area and turn right at the Ethiopian church.

Heavy snowflakes have begun to dance through the air in the light from the streetlamps, making the area look like something out of a fairytale.

To John, it feels like an unwelcome reminder of his childhood.

The milky glow from the touchscreen of the mobile data terminal illuminates his tight grip on the wheel.

Einar has just taken out a pot of snus when a call comes in from regional command.

A break-in has been reported at the campsite in Bredäng.

Einar responds to the call as John turns off behind the supermarket, drives around the green recycling bins and pulls back out onto the road.

'The campsite's closed for the season, and the owner's in Florida,' the dispatcher explains. 'But the security cameras are linked to his phone, and he can see a light in one of the caravans.'

Without turning on the siren or blue lights, John accelerates along the empty road, passing apartment blocks and the old power station.

The wipers sweep the snowflakes from the windscreen.

Neither officer says anything, but they both know that the break-in is probably just someone trying to avoid freezing to death. Someone without a home or papers, an addict or someone with mental health issues.

The usual.

They pass the Scandic hotel and turn off onto Skärholmsvägen.

Almost five years ago, John picked the lock on his older brother's room and found Luke slumped on the floor beside his bed, his lips blue. The yellowed rubber tie was slack around his arm, and the blood-stained cotton ball had stuck to his Nirvana T-shirt.

John will never forget his brother's pupils in his wide eyes. They were impossibly small, like they had been drawn in with the tip of a needle.

Since he first started going out on patrol, John has always carried three doses of Naloxone with him, despite the fact that it isn't required kit. It isn't something he ever talks about, but so far he has managed to save eight lives using the nasal spray.

They drive past the dark football field, through the industrial area and into Sätraskogen nature reserve.

By the time they pull up outside the gates to the campsite, eight minutes have passed since they responded to the dispatch call.

The shop, office and Thai restaurant are all shuttered.

Heavy snowflakes fall slowly through the air, landing on the tarmac in front of them.

Without a word, John and Einar get out of the car and climb the gate. They check the site map, locate pitch G and start walking.

The vast campsite feels strangely desolate without any cars, tents or people milling around.

They cross an area of dead grass criss-crossed by roads as they make their way over to the caravan section.

To the right, the trees on the hill are all bare. Snowflakes sail down between their sprawling black branches.

They pass a small playground and the septic tank before turning off between the static caravans. The acoustics change, and the sound of their footsteps echo back at them.

The windows are dark, the flags on the tall TV aerials slack and the cramped patio areas empty.

John finds himself thinking about how afraid he was for his brother during the last year of his life. How angry Luke got sometimes, how reckless, like the time John asked him to pay back the money he had lent him.

They spot the light in one of the caravans from a way off, and as they approach, they see that it is coming from a lamp behind the curtains in one of the windows.

John stops and fills his lungs with cool air. He draws his gun, climbs the metal steps, knocks loudly and opens the door.

'Police! We're coming in,' he shouts without any real weight to his voice.

He steps forward into the gloomy caravan and sees dark footprints leading in both directions on the wood-effect vinyl. His eyes scan the hallway to the right, past two closed doors and the cramped bathroom.

Everything is quiet.

With his gun lowered, he starts moving towards the brightly lit living area. The walls and ceiling creak with every step he takes.

All he can see up ahead is the dining table and four chairs. The indirect glow from the lamp further back gleams softly on the scratched surfaces.

John stops dead when he hears a woman's hushed voice somewhere in front of him.

'Pick up, stud. Pick up,' she says playfully. 'Pick up, stud . . .'

'Police, I'm coming in!' John shouts. The adrenaline coursing through his veins has made the hairs on his arms stand on end.

'Pick up, stud. Pick up, stud. Pick up, stu—'

The woman's voice stops abruptly, and John moves forward with his pistol raised.

The stale air is heavy with a metallic scent that reminds him of a damp whetstone.

He feels the floor shake as Einar enters the caravan, and he pauses, breathing raggedly through his nose. John listens for a second, then steps into the kitchen, swings round to the right and whimpers.

On the stainless-steel drainer, there is a human leg, complete with a plaster on its knee and a black sock on its foot. The muscles and tendons have all been crudely severed.

The hip bone has been torn out of its socket and looks glaringly white against the dark red tissue.

'What the fuck . . .'

The walls, ceiling and floor are all drenched in blood.

On the coffee table, between two fake plants, John notices a head. The chin and jaw are both missing, but it is clear that the victim is a man with straggly black hair with bleached tips.

The surface of the table beneath it is slick with blood, dripping down into a large pool on the floor.

On the sofa, the screen of a mobile phone lights up with the name Anna, and the strange ringtone starts blaring again:

'Pick up, stud. Pick up . . . Pick up, stud . . .'

At the other end of the caravan, Einar has just opened the door to the main bedroom. His torch beam swings across the double bed, illuminating a limbless torso. The wounds are ragged and crude, revealing pale cartilage and sharp bone.

He stares down at the dismembered man's hairy stomach, limp penis and muscular, tattooed chest. At his throat and the lower section of his head.

The blood has soaked into the mattress, and the entire torso glistens in the light from the torch.

Einar feels his pistol trembling in his hand, as though an electric current is surging through him. The sight is so shocking that his legs feel like jelly.

He shoves the torch beneath his arm and claps a hand to his mouth. The lingering smell of ketchup on his fingers mixes with the stench of fresh blood, and his stomach turns.

John hears his heavy footsteps, and he glances down the hallway and sees Einar backing out of the bedroom. His colleague drops his torch as he fumbles with his radio, rushes out of the caravan and throws up.

John has just started making his way back towards the door when he stops. As he strains to listen, a shiver passes down his spine. He can hear an oddly relaxed, yet robotic laugh through the walls.

Maybe it's coming from outside, he thinks, right as the laughter gives way to a wailing sound. A moment later, it stops.

Heart racing, he approaches the last closed door.

Out of nowhere, he imagines finding his brother Luke standing on the other side, with blue lips, pinprick pupils and a bloody machete resting over one shoulder.

He can hear Einar talking to command outside. His colleague sounds shocked and incoherent.

John turns the handle, pushes the door open and aims his pistol at the darkness beyond.

Mounted to the wall beneath the window, there is an unplugged radiator. The white surface is flecked with blood.

The hinges creak softly as the door comes to a halt, and John reaches out to open it the rest of the way, then steps inside.

On the floor beside the bunkbed, a young man is lying on his side with a severed arm beneath his head.

His pale face is calm, his eyes closed. He is wearing jeans, trainers and a moss green sweater.

John moves towards him to check his pulse.

There is an axe on the lower bunk, he notices.

Outside, Einar shouts something.

The floor creaks beneath John's feet as he leans forward.

Right then, with his eyes still tightly shut, the boy laughs. His white teeth flash brightly against his bloody face.

John stumbles back, fumbling with his pistol. He flicks off the safety catch, slips in a pool of blood and crashes against the wall. His gun goes off, hitting the floor.

The boy wakes with a start and sits up. He blinks a few times, staring at John in confusion as he pushes back his fringe with a bloody hand and licks his lips.

'Where am I?' he asks in a frightened voice. 'What's going on?'

2

Bernard Sand is in the kitchen, preparing an extravagant breakfast. He whistles to himself as he fries two potato cakes on a high heat. It is quarter past seven in the morning, and he is wearing a burgundy dressing gown. His salt-and-pepper hair is still tousled after a good night's sleep.

Before he made the transition to becoming a full-time author, he was a professor of the History of Ideas at Stockholm University. Bernard writes romance novels, and has enjoyed international success with his series about the DeVille siblings.

After six books, he is ready to try something new.

It isn't that he is bored, but he has started to worry that he is getting too comfortable as a writer.

He is currently working on his seventh book, and also writes a relationship column for one of the Sunday papers, answering reader questions.

The romance novels are how he makes a living, but they also generate a lot of work alongside the actual writing.

Yesterday, for example, he had to pore over a couple of contracts from his Dutch and Polish publishers. He then spent an hour talking to his Japanese translator. He has three email interviews he still hasn't tackled, and a long list of requests for author visits and video messages from his agent.

Bernard is fifty-two, and has been living with his partner Agneta for the past eight years. He has a seventeen-year-old son called Hugo from a previous relationship.

He is a tall, slim man with a pale face, intensely blue eyes and thick brows that need trimming every week.

The potato cakes sizzle in the pan, and he feels a sharp pain as a few droplets of melted butter hit the back of his hand.

Bernard serves the crispy cakes onto two plates and adds a dollop of crème fraîche whipped with lemon zest, dill and pepper.

The sun still hasn't risen, and the kitchen is reflected in the dark windows like some sort of brightly lit theatre stage.

Agneta comes into the room with a subtle waft of perfume. She has just completed her morning breathing exercises, showered and pulled on a pair of jeans and a knitted sweater.

'I need to be in the car in sixteen minutes,' she says.

Her face is still flushed, her skin shimmering like bronze and tiny beads of water clinging to her short black hair.

'New lipstick,' says Bernard.

'Well spotted.'

'It's very nice.'

'Thank you, but if you think that's all it takes for me to throw my arms around your neck and kiss you, then—'

'Do it.'

'You think so, do you?' She smiles, but her face quickly turns serious. 'God . . . I'm so impressionable. It's just so easy to forgive you because—'

'Sorry.'

'Because my heart . . . my idiotic heart loves you,' she says, taking a seat at the table.

'I love you, too.'

She sighs and looks up at him with a frown. 'I think you really do mean that . . . but as an author, you should know that it's not enough just to *say* you love someone. You have to actually show it, too.'

'I agree.'

Agneta Nkomo is thirty-seven and works as a freelance culture writer. She regularly reviews dance performances for *Svenska Dagbladet*, writes reports for a local news site and also carries out research for a popular true crime podcast.

She has lost count of the number of times she has asked the producer for a real part in the show, a chance to get behind the mic and discuss new theories and mistakes in the police investigations. She knows she could be great, but so far her requests have been met by polite surprise and hollow words about keeping her in mind.

Agneta met Bernard when she was commissioned to interview him about the film adaptation of his first book about the DeVille siblings. He was so busy that she had only thirty minutes with him, but that was all it took for them to fall in love.

Bernard's hand starts to shake, and he waits a few seconds for it to settle before adding a heaped spoon of roe and some finely chopped chives to both potato cakes. He then carries the two plates over to the table and pours a couple of glasses of champagne, though he knows Agneta won't touch hers.

'I really wanted to talk to you yesterday, but you fell asleep,' she says quietly, picking up her knife and fork.

'I may sleep from time to time, but I'm never tired,' he replies, taking a seat opposite her. 'Venus, our mistress, turns nights of bitterness against me, and Amor never fails to be found wanting.'

'Very passionate,' she says with a sigh as she starts to eat.

'I'd give my right leg to have written that,' he says, knocking back her champagne.

'You're a brilliant writer.'

'I can be.'

Agneta dabs her mouth with a napkin and checks her emails on her phone as Bernard gets up to serve their next course: steak tartare with capers and Dijon mustard.

'Bernard, honestly, this is all very nice,' she says, trying to meet his eye. 'I love steak tartare, but I don't want fancy food. I want you to talk to Hugo like you said you would.'

'Yesterday was a mistake,' he says, pouring two small glasses of Czech beer.

'Yesterday, the day before yesterday, every day . . .'

'Yes,' he whispers.

'What would you tell yourself if you had your advice column hat on?' she asks.

'"Grab a shotgun and open your mouth."'

'I'm serious.'

He sighs and sits down.

'"Bernard, making Agneta a lavish breakfast won't cut it,"' he says.

'And?'

'"I don't think she expects you to change overnight, but she needs to see you take a first step in the right direction before you start buying roses and champagne."'

'Because that's your way of running away from things,' she adds. 'Even though Agneta does like being given flowers, et cetera, et cetera.'

'"She needs to see that your words about love are backed up by genuine emotion, that you're loyal and take her side when your son acts up . . . in order for her to feel like an equal member of the family."'

Agneta puts in her earrings and thinks back to their dinner last night. She had taken ten milligrams of Propranolol to calm her nerves. Bernard knows that she occasionally uses beta blockers ahead of important meetings, but not that she has started resorting to them whenever Hugo eats at home.

The teenager was hunched over his plate, holding back his messy hair with his left hand as he shovelled food into his mouth.

'I applied for that job at *KULT* magazine, by the way,' Hugo said with his mouth full. 'I'm going to Uppsala to see the editor tomorrow lunchtime.'

'Bravo! This will open doors for you, I'm sure of it,' said Bernard.

'I dunno. It feels a bit . . . self-absorbed to sit there, spewing a bunch of clichés . . .'

'Just be yourself,' Agneta told him. 'You can do this. You love reading, so show them that. That's all they need to see.'

'It's not like I'll get it anyway,' he sighed, turning his attention to his phone.

'You can only do your best,' said Bernard.

'It doesn't even pay much, either . . . I dunno if I can be bothered,' Hugo muttered.

'I'm sure you'll be fine as long as you don't stay up too late tonight,' said Agneta.

'You're not my mum.'

'No, but—'

'You act like you are, but you're not.'

'You don't need to remind me constantly,' she said.

'Would it make any difference if I stopped?' he asked, turning to look at her.

'I'm not your mum, but I do live here and I care about you,' she replied, unable to stop her eyes from welling up.

'Seriously? You're doing the whole crying thing? What, so Dad feels sorry for you? So . . .'

Hugo trailed off when his phone pinged, and he glanced down at the screen and then left the table without clearing his plate away. Bernard sat quietly with his head bowed, refusing to meet Agneta's eye. The teenager's footsteps faded down the hallway, and Agneta heard the front door open, followed by a woman's voice.

'Guess the cougar is here,' she mumbled.

Hugo is in a relationship with a woman called Olga, who is almost twice his age. Agneta has always thought she is beautiful – striking, even – but she has also started to notice a certain steeliness beneath the surface. As though Olga is trying to hide the fact that she is actually a mercenary with her glittery makeup and youthful clothing.

Olga followed Hugo to his room without coming into the kitchen to say hello, and the pair then locked the door and put on loud music.

Agneta has no idea whether Olga stayed over or not, because she took a sleeping pill in order to get some rest. His room is now quiet, in any case, and Hugo likely won't be out of bed before midday unless someone wakes him.

Bernard has been filled with a strange energy all morning, dancing around their bedroom, folding back the duvet at the end of the bed and kissing each of her toes before hurrying down to the kitchen to make breakfast while she worked on her breathing.

'Aren't you going to try the steak?' he asks.

'I'm honestly too upset to eat,' she says, carrying her plate over to the counter.

Agneta goes out into the hallway and puts on her coat. She has just started buttoning it when Bernard appears with a small princess cake and a cup of strong black coffee.

She can't help but smile as he tries to feed her while she pulls on her boots. He even follows her out to the car in his dressing gown and slippers. It is so cold that the snow that fell overnight will probably linger until the sun rises at around eight thirty.

'I wouldn't have to keep going on about this if I thought you were listening . . . but could you please tell Hugo that I'm not trying to be his mum?' she asks, taking the cup. 'I just want to have a good relationship with him, and that means I need to be treated like a member of the family.'

'You're right. I agree.'

'But you never do anything about it,' she says, sipping the coffee before handing the cup back to him.

'I've tried, but I suppose I don't fully know what you actually expect me to do. He's seventeen . . .'

'Christ,' she says, taking a deep breath. 'I hope you can see that this isn't working, at the very least . . . mostly because you aren't showing me any loyalty.'

'I want to . . .'

'Bernard,' she says softly. 'I need you to be on my side. Not always, but at least some of the time.'

'Sorry.'

'I need your love,' she continues, wiping the tears from her cheeks. 'I love being with you, talking books and philosophy . . .'

'The best.'

'But it's not enough, that's what I'm trying to say. I can't do this anymore. I'm going to ask Mum if I can go and stay with her.'

'You're leaving?'

'I think I just need some space,' she says as she gets into the car, slams the door and starts the engine.

Bernard watches Agneta's Lexus pull away with a racing heart. He then finishes off her coffee and sets the cup down on the charging post.

He has just decided that he will wake Hugo in good time ahead of his meeting with the *KULT* team in Uppsala when a police car turns off onto the driveway and comes to a halt.

Bernard tightens the belt of his dressing gown as an officer gets out of the car and walks towards him with a serious look on her face.

'Bernard Sand?'

'Yes . . .'

'A young man claiming to be your son was arrested last night.'

'Hold on a second.'

'He didn't have any ID on him, so we need you to confirm his identity.'

'I'm not sure I understand.'

'Is your son Hugo Sand?'

'Yes, but he's asleep . . . I'm going to wake him at nine.'

'When did you last see him?'

'Yesterday evening.'

She sighs and takes out a phone, then makes a brief call to the prosecutor to ask for the images from the booking following the arrest in Bredäng.

'Could you tell me what happened?' Bernard asks with a rising sense of panic.

'I'm afraid I can't go into any more detail before you—'

'Is he hurt?'

The woman doesn't speak, just stands quietly with the phone in her hand. After a moment or two, it pings, and she opens the message and holds it up to him with a neutral expression on her face.

It feels as though a jet of hot air has just blown straight through Bernard's skull. He fumbles for something to lean against and knocks the cup from the charging post.

Hugo's frightened, dirty face is pale in the harsh glare of the flash. He has his mother's delicate features, but his shoulder-length hair is knotted. The police must have confiscated his nose and lip rings, his earring and necklace. In the image, his tattoos make it look like he has dipped both arms in clay.

A board has been placed in front of him, the spaces for his name and ID number left empty. The only information provided is his height, the image number, the district ID and the date.

'That's him, that's my son . . .' Bernard says, clutching his stomach with a trembling hand. 'But I don't understand, there must be some sort of misunderstanding . . . I'm sure you've heard that before, but I . . . I . . .'

'Is there anyone else in your house at the moment?'

'No, I don't think so. I—'

'You don't *know*?'

'I thought Hugo was in his room, but if he's not . . . then no, I'm the only one.'

'OK, thank you.'

'I can go in and check?'

'We'll need you to stay out here until forensics arrive, but if you're cold, you're welcome to wait in our car,' says the officer.

'I'm not cold, I can't even think about that right now. Sorry, but I need to know what's going on,' Bernard says, his voice faltering.

'Forensics will be here soon, and they'll take you inside and help you find some clothes and gather up everything you might need before we cordon off the house.'

'Do I need to speak to a lawyer? Hugo is only seventeen. I assume that means I have a right to know why he was arrested.'

'He's being held on suspicion of murder,' the police officer replies.

3

Joona fires two shots in close succession, and the double recoil reverberates through him like an extra heartbeat.

He sees both bullets strike the target's forehead, sending fragments of cardboard flying through the air.

Joona ducks as he runs, passing a plywood screen. He spots the next target behind an orange net, drops to one knee and pulls the trigger. His shot hits the red circle in the middle of the cardboard figure's chest.

The ground is damp in the shade behind the rusty shipping container, and spent cartridges shimmer on the gravel.

Joona follows the painted route, rounding two plastic drums full of sand, dragging a heavy dummy to safety behind a police car and hitting the last target square in the forehead.

A cloud of dust hovers in the sunlight as Joona secures his weapon and pushes it into his holster.

For some reason, his thoughts turn to his father, himself a police officer, killed in the line of duty. Joona was only eleven when he died, but the loss was like a prism, bending the light and – in all likelihood – guiding him to become the person he is today.

He has spent his entire adult life trying to make the world a better place, first in the military and later as a police officer. Without a single thought about what the job was doing to him, he forged ahead for years on end.

He doesn't need to look back to know that he has left a trail of death behind him. A battlefield on which more and more vultures have begun to gather to peck at the bodies.

Joona has often been told that looking back is futile, but it has become increasingly difficult to avoid it when he is alone.

I can't handle the loneliness anymore, he thinks. Not in my private life, and not at work.

He already misses Valeria, and he longs to see his daughter, Lumi.

In the past, he always insisted that he preferred to work alone, but he has begun to realise that he needs someone by his side.

He wishes Saga Bauer could be that person. They would complement each other perfectly.

Saga feels like a sister. A brilliant but complex woman who needs him, too – though she would never admit that, even to herself.

She is too proud, too stubborn.

Joona is stubborn, too.

When he knows he is right about something, he is incapable of giving in, of backing down. It doesn't matter what it costs him.

Joona brushes himself off, checks his time for the range and has just started making his way over to the next one when his phone rings.

The call is from Lisette Josephson, the prosecutor, and they talk briefly as he heads back to the parking area.

Five minutes later, Joona drives away from the National Tactical Unit's training centre in Sörentorp. He tries to come out to the dynamic shooting range as often as he can.

During the call, the prosecutor explained that she had taken the decision to remand a seventeen-year-old male in custody overnight, citing article twenty-four, paragraph two of the Code of Judicial Procedure because they had been unable to establish his identity.

That morning, they had determined that the teenager's name is Hugo Sand, and that he is registered at an address in Hägersten. He doesn't crop up in any police or social services databases, but he is suspected of having carried out a violent axe murder.

The dismembered victim found in the caravan has also been identified as Josef Lindgren, a thirty-one-year-old teacher who lived in Tumba with his wife Jasmin and their young child.

Lisette Josephson asked Joona to assist her in the first interview with Hugo Sand, conducted in the presence of his guardian and solicitor.

Joona Linna is a detective superintendent with the National Crime Unit in Stockholm. He is an expert on serial killers and has solved more complex murder cases than anyone else in Scandinavia. Before he joined the police force, he was a member of the military's special operations unit, training in unconventional close combat and innovative weapons under Lieutenant Rinus Advocaat in the Netherlands.

* * *

The suspect's father and solicitor have taken their seats on one side of the varnished pine table in the windowless interrogation room.

Bernard Sand seems calm and composed, sitting tall with his hands folded in his lap. He is clean-shaven, and his thick, greying hair is neatly combed back, his eyes watchful.

Joona and Lisette Josephson are sitting opposite them. Lisette has sleek blonde hair, a slight underbite and a stern gaze. She is wearing a pair of chestnut brown leather trousers and a nougat-coloured cashmere sweater. Her coat is draped over the arm of her chair.

Joona flicks through the forensic technicians' photographs from the static caravan for the second time, pausing to study the image from the bedroom where the teenager was found.

The axe is on the bed, the gleaming blade resting on the pillow, almost as though it had tossed the young man to the floor and then lain down to sleep.

There are bloody hand- and footprints everywhere, bright spatters high up the walls, smeared blood and a large pool around a severed arm on the vinyl floor.

The clear impression of a shoulder is visible in the middle of the pool.

There is a curt knock at the door, and Hugo Sand is led into the room by a guard who takes a seat by the wall.

Hugo sits down between his father and solicitor.

His green custody tracksuit makes his skin look pale and sickly, emphasising the dark circles beneath his eyes.

He immediately starts chewing on his thumb nail, and his father reaches out and gently pulls his hand away from his mouth.

After the usual formalities, the prosecutor welcomes everyone and explains that they will be following the national guidelines for the handling of cases involving minors.

'That's why we've held off on interviewing you so far, Hugo – until your solicitor could be here,' Lisette continues.

'OK,' he mumbles.

A waft of the solicitor's aftershave drifts through the air as he pours some water into the paper cups and loosens his tie slightly.

'Right, shall we get started?' Lisette asks, briefly reading from the files in front of her before she looks up. 'Following a call reporting a possible break-in at Bredäng Campsite, Hugo Sand was arrested by the responding officers at quarter past three this morning. Forensics found blood belonging to the victim on Hugo, and his fingerprints and DNA were also found at the crime scene.'

The solicitor leans forward and clears his throat. 'My client doesn't deny having been in the caravan when—'

'His fingerprints are on the murder weapon,' the prosecutor cuts him off.

'Wait,' says Hugo, his voice barely holding. 'I don't know what happened. I woke up when one of the cops shot the floor in front of me, but I had no idea what I was doing there.'

'My client is a sleepwalker, clinically diagnosed and very well documented,' the solicitor says, opening his briefcase.

'A sleepwalker?' Lisette asks, blushing slightly.

'Here is a list of places where Hugo has previously woken up, including but not limited to a metro car, a rowing boat on Lake Mälaren, a Thai massage parlour—'

'Joona, perhaps you could take over?' Lisette says, her voice faltering.

'What did you do yesterday evening?' Joona asks, fixing his eyes on the boy.

Hugo turns to his representative, who gives him a near-imperceptible nod in response, and then looks up at Joona.

'Nothing.'

'We ate dinner together around seven,' says Bernard.

'And after that?'

'I hung out in my room with my girlfriend,' Hugo says with a shrug.

'How long did she stay?'

'Till eleven.'

'And what time did you go to bed?'

'I don't really know. I listened to some music, then fell asleep. Probably around twelve.'

Hugo tugs at the neck of his sweatshirt.

'How often do you sleepwalk?' asks Joona.

'About once a month, I guess . . . Except when I'm having a bad episode. It happens pretty much every night then.'

'And how often do these bad episodes occur?'

'Not very often these days. Maybe every other year,' Hugo replies, taking a sip of water.

Joona hears Lisette jot something down.

'How long do the episodes last?'

'Three months, max . . . I don't know, it's always pretty tough – for everyone around me.'

'Do you know what triggers your sleepwalking?' Joona continues.

'If you mean the episodes, we haven't managed to detect any concrete patterns,' the father replies.

'I've got a kind of parasomnia called RBD, which stands for REM-sleep behaviour disorder,' Hugo explains.

'You dream while you're sleepwalking, in other words,' says Joona.

Hugo nods and pushes his long hair back from his eyes. He has a number of small piercing holes in his lower lip, nostril and down the ridge of one ear.

'My doctor calls them catastrophic dreams,' he says.

'What sort of catastrophes do they involve?' Joona asks, leaning forward.

'I dunno, I never really remember anything . . . But I'm always scared, and I usually have to run or hide.'

'Who is your doctor?'

'Lars Grind at the Sleep Science Lab in Uppsala,' Bernard replies.

Joona turns back to Hugo. The teenager is slim and pale, with the face of a young fairy-tale prince – albeit with tired, bloodshot eyes and chapped lips.

'Would you say that you're capable of doing the same things as someone who is awake while you're sleepwalking?'

'You don't have to answer that,' the solicitor interjects.

'It's OK, I can explain what it's like. What difference does it make?' says Hugo, turning to Joona. 'So, for example . . . when I'm sleep-walking, I can unlock my phone and call people without any problem, but when they pick up apparently I don't make any sense.'

'When did you first start sleepwalking?' asks Joona.

'I'm not sure, I was little.'

'He's always done it, but we sought help for the first time when he was six,' Bernard says quietly.

'Why?'

'Hugo woke in the middle of a road with a lorry blasting its horn and slamming the brakes on . . . He'd got out of bed, gone down the stairs, unlocked the front door and walked almost two kilometres.'

Hugo smiles apologetically, but his face turns serious when he notices Joona's eyes on him.

'How often do you wake up in other places?'

'Pretty often.'

'And do you know where you are when you wake up?'

'It varies.'

'Have you ever been to Bredäng Campsite before?' Joona holds Hugo's eye.

'Yeah . . . I used to go there all the time with my friends. I've taken girls there, too, smoked hash.'

'You never mentioned that,' says Bernard.

'Wonder why . . .' Hugo mumbles.

'As I understand it, sleepwalkers often have their eyes open. Is that the case for you?' asks Joona.

'Yes, he does,' Bernard replies on his son's behalf.

'Do you remember any of what you see?'

'Nope.'

'So you have no idea whether you murdered the man in the caravan?'

4

Tiny snowflakes swirl across the tarmac in the half light on Göran Greiders väg, giving Joona the sense of slowly driving a motorboat down a grey canal.

He is thinking about the fact that it isn't unusual for killers to be found at the scene of the crime, drunk or on drugs, regretful or paralysed by their deeds. But Hugo Sand was fast asleep on the bloody floor with a severed arm beneath his head.

Joona passes the Department of Neuroscience and turns off towards the National Board of Forensic Medicine, where electric Advent candles glow in every window. Nils Åhlén's white Porsche is parked a few metres from a slanting charging post surrounded by shards of red plastic from a broken taillight.

He parks, gets out of the car and fills his lungs with the cool air.

A sudden rush of anxiety for Valeria washes over him, and he takes out his phone and dials her number, but the call goes straight to voicemail.

She has gone to Brazil to be with her mother. Her father's death didn't come as a surprise to anyone, but her mother has really been struggling with the loss.

Joona makes his way up the steps into the building and finds Lisette Josephson waiting on one of the sofas in reception.

Following a request from the Prosecution Authority, Joona is here to support her. At present, the focus of the preliminary investigation is to find sufficient grounds to charge Hugo Sand, and to do so as quickly as possible.

Joona says hello and sits down opposite her. Lisette glances at the clock on her phone and says that she has time to take him through the latest developments before they go in.

'You asked about CCTV, but it doesn't look like it's going to be that easy this time,' she says in a weary tone. 'The owner of the campsite managed to wipe the entire hard drive while he was trying to save the footage.'

'Can it be recovered?'

'Apparently not, according to our IT guys.'

'OK.'

Muffled rock music drifts through to them from the autopsy room. Drums, bass and rhythm guitar.

'We've spoken to Jasmin, the victim's wife. She says she has no idea what Josef was doing at the campsite . . . but his computer was *full* of cookies from a forum used by people buying sex – before someone told him to download Tor and switch to the Darknet.'

'And that's where the trail goes cold,' says Joona.

'Aside from the fact that Hugo Sand also uses Tor, so it's possible we'll find some sort of correspondence between them.'

Lisette reaches into her briefcase, pulls out a thick ream of paper and puts it down on the table in front of her.

'Printouts of Hugo's text messages, social media posts, call logs, et cetera,' she says.

'Have you read through everything?'

'Of course.'

'So what are you thinking? Who is Hugo?' asks Joona.

'I see a young man . . . Articulate, self-absorbed and pretty irresponsible,' Lisette begins. 'He lives at home with his father Bernard and Bernard's partner, Agneta Nkomo . . . He's had a number of brief, casual relationships with various women . . . but his current girlfriend is called Olga, and they've been planning a trip together, trying to save up money. Hugo's name doesn't crop up on any of our databases. Some drug use, but no serious criminal activity. No history of violence, no extremism . . . We found traces of benzodiazepine in his blood, but nowhere near enough to have made him fall asleep at the crime scene.'

'What possible motive could he have?'

'That's not exactly clear, but I'm going to pursue the theory that it was a homophobic hate crime,' she replies. 'Hugo arranged to meet the victim, possibly with the view to sell sex or rob him . . . They met at the caravan, and either it happened right away or the man's approach acted as a kind of trigger, unleashing some sort of uncontrollable rage in Hugo.'

'Is there anything to indicate homophobia here?' Joona asks, pointing to the printouts.

'No, but we'll keep looking.'

Nils Åhlén's assistant, Chaya Aboulela, comes through to reception, says a quick hello and shakes their hands.

Chaya has a narrow, somewhat stern face, with arched black brows, pale brown irises and full lips. Her hair is covered by a pale-yellow hijab, and she is wearing an open doctor's coat over an embroidered blouse and a pair of low-cut jeans.

'The maestro will see you now,' she says with a wry smile.

Joona and Lisette follow her down the corridor.

'I'm assuming you've seen a dead body before,' Chaya says to the prosecutor. 'But I should probably warn you that this one is particularly grizzly.'

'I see corpses more often than my own kids,' Lisette mutters.

Chaya opens the heavy doors to the autopsy room. The lighting is harsh, gleaming on the stainless-steel table, sink, taps and strainers.

Nils Åhlén is waiting in the middle of the room in his white coat. He has a narrow, crooked nose and thin lips. The lights on the ceiling look like a bright pearl necklace in the lenses of his aviator glasses.

Åhlén is a professor at the Karolinska Institute and considered one of the world's leading experts in forensic autopsy.

On the bench in front of him, Josef Lindgren's remains have been laid out and numbered.

Joona and Lisette slowly make their way forward and study the dead man.

It is a classic – if chaotic – case of dismemberment, with the arms, legs and head severed from the torso. Unfortunately for Josef Lindgren, the process was also carried out in an extremely aggressive manner, starting while he was still alive and thus forming part of the murder itself.

Half of his head is still connected to his neck, his right arm has been severed just beneath the shoulder, his left arm at the elbow, and both legs have been cut off.

'Just to explain what you're looking at: we've laid out the bigger pieces separately, as you can see, and we've tried to arrange the smaller body parts in a kind of anatomical order,' Chaya explains to Lisette. 'We've got his right hand and the tip of his index finger here, some loose teeth and fragments of jawbone here . . .'

Joona hears her voice fade as he sinks into a relaxed state of hyper-focus in an attempt to take in every detail, studying the wounds on the man's torso.

He takes in the stump of Lindgren's arm and the gash on his ribs, the man's throat and the ragged edges where his thigh has been severed.

One of his legs is intact, his foot still wearing a sock, but the other has been hacked into five pieces.

A section of Lindgren's head, complete with hair, has a visible blunt force injury to the temple. The majority of his face has been laid out beside a piece of his skull, still attached to ragged scraps of neck muscle.

Centimetre by centimetre, Joona works through the incomplete cuts, the superficial injuries and scrapes. There is a short, diagonal wound on one side of Josef Lindgren's stomach and another on his shoulder.

'I'm guessing you'd like to know how our victim died?' he hears Åhlén say.

'Yes,' Lisette replies with a nod.

'Which was the first wound, which killed him,' Åhlén continues. 'The sequence and number of injuries . . .'

Joona's eyes linger on every little bruise, on the faint patches of livor mortis beneath the skin that was touching the floor.

'Do you have any working theories yet?' Lisette asks, looking up at Åhlén.

LARS KEPLER

'Of course . . . But I know by now to let Joona go first,' he replies.

'Sorry, but you know that Joona has access to fewer facts than I do.'

'This isn't a competition . . . It's just that Joona has a very good eye,' Åhlén explains, pushing his glasses back onto the bridge of his nose.

'OK, be my guest.' The prosecutor gives him a forced smile and gestures to Joona.

'It's clear that the victim and whoever killed him saw each other before the attack,' he begins.

'And you're sure of that?' asks Lisette.

'They were standing face to face.'

'How do you know?'

'Because the first blow came from directly in front of Lindgren,' he says. 'The axe was probably concealed before it swung upwards and hit him square on the left temple, side-on . . . It was powerful enough to knock him down, and he collapsed onto his side . . . He was likely pretty groggy when the killer chopped off his right leg on the floor.'

Lisette shakes her head.

'There's no way you can know that,' she says.

'Using the pictures you sent me from the crime scene, I can,' Joona replies. 'Judging by the marks on the floor and the angle of the wounds, I'm guessing it took at least five strokes to separate his leg from his body. The blood was pumping out of his artery at full pressure – that's what caused the spatter marks right up the wall in the main bedroom.'

'Annoying, isn't he?' Chaya mutters to the prosecutor.

'That injury to his leg was probably fatal,' Joona continues. 'But in this particular case, it's not what actually killed him, because it all happened so quickly.'

'Bravo,' whispers Åhlén.

'The victim shuffled back, trying to get away and stem the bleeding with both hands. It was the next blow, through his skull, that killed him . . . Strictly speaking, the rest of the injuries were just part of the dismemberment process.'

For a few seconds, silence fills the room.

'Who needs a professor of forensic pathology?' Åhlén says with a smile.

'You know it,' Joona replies.

'OK . . . With the proviso that we haven't even started the autopsy yet, I'd say we're looking at a total of eighty-three major wounds, plus a couple of minor cuts. Some of the injuries would have taken multiple strokes – cleaving his head, for example. As Joona says, it was the second blow to the skull that killed Josef Lindgren, but it took another four to separate the top of his head from his body.'

'Some didn't go all the way through . . . like this one, on his left thigh,' Chaya points out.

'Is there anything missing?' asks Joona.

'Yes . . . oddly enough, we're short of two teeth,' Åhlén replies, scratching his temple.

'The whole campsite is cordoned off, and we're bringing in sniffer dogs tomorrow,' says Lisette.

'Shall we flip him over?' asks Åhlén.

'Please,' says Joona.

Chaya and Åhlén lift the sturdy torso and gently turn it onto its front.

'You haven't said when you think he died,' says Lisette.

'Judging by the temperature of the body and the extent of the livor mortis, I'd say he'd been dead for almost an hour when the first officers arrived.'

'Around two in the morning, in other words,' says Joona.

'Yes.'

They study Josef Lindgren's exposed spine.

'Who did this?' asks Lisette. 'What sort of killer are we looking for?'

'It wouldn't require a huge amount of physical strength,' says Åhlén, 'but whoever it was would need to be in fairly good shape.'

'Could a young man have done this?'

'Sure.'

'In his sleep?'

5

Hugo wakes with a start, filled with a sense of unease. It is the middle of the night, and he isn't sure what roused him. For a moment, he lies perfectly still, listening intently. He hears a faint knocking sound through the wall, but it stops suddenly.

He opens his eyes and stares up at his lampshade in the darkness. A white rice paper orb, stretched over rings of thin bamboo.

There have been a number of violent robberies to the south of Stockholm recently. The police have issued warnings, and there is talk that the perpetrators are a group of career criminals with military backgrounds and equipment. They let themselves into people's homes during the night and force them to make large bank transfers, leaving a trail of dead, mutilated and raped family members in their wake.

Social media is rife with rumours that the group's commander looks like a skeleton. A man who kills his prisoners with a spade before burning their houses to the ground.

The slow knocking sound starts and stops again.

Hugo turns his head and focuses on the closed blind, hovering like a grey rectangle in the darkness. The lights are on in the garden, and the shadows cast by the bare branches of the lilac are like cracks on the smooth fabric.

He closes his weary eyes, relaxes and hears a car pass by on the street. He should check the time, he thinks, see whether Olga has sent any more weird pictures, but he doesn't have the energy.

All he wants is to go back to sleep, but he hears something that leaves him wide awake. The soft crunch of footsteps on the frosty grass outside.

The shadow of a person darts across the blind.

A moment later, several windows break at the rear of the house.

Hugo hears a series of dull bangs, and the house itself seems to groan. A light sprinkling of dust falls from the lampshade.

The blood in Hugo's veins runs cold as he gets out of bed as quietly as he can.

His body starts shaking as the front door is forced open and shards of glass, wood and bits of metal crash to the tiled floor.

Through the walls, he hears a muffled voice bark an order, followed by the thudding of boots on the stairs.

Hugo tiptoes over to the window, carefully opens the blind and tries to see if he can make anything out in the dark garden.

He needs to get out, run away and call the police. His hands grope the window frame, but the latch has been removed.

The aggressive shouts of the men reach him through the ceiling, and there is a loud crash as the carafe breaks on the floor.

The smell of smoke drifts through the house.

Hugo tries pulling on the window frame, but it won't budge, seems to have been screwed shut from the outside.

He hears gunfire, two salvos of three shots, followed by a woman screaming. It must be Agneta, but her voice sounds so panicked that he barely recognises it.

Hugo's father shouts, 'Don't touch her!' and more gunshots ring out.

In the room above, shattered glass crashes to the floor. Agneta screams again, and Hugo hears her being dragged out of bed and away.

Heart racing, he starts hitting the windowpane with both hands. Despite the darkness, he realises that there is some sort of solid material covering the glass. Beneath a small hatch with horizontal metal slats, there is also – oddly enough – a laminated notice about evacuation in case of fire.

Hugo hears quick footsteps coming down the stairs, someone shouts a command, and door after door is kicked in along the hallway.

Trying not to make a sound, he tiptoes back over to his bed. His hands shake as he plumps up his pillows to make them look like a body beneath the covers.

They will be here any minute now.

He crawls beneath the bed, right up against the wall, and holds his breath as his door is kicked open.

* * *

It is light when Hugo wakes beneath the bed, and he feels a rush of anxiety when he remembers where he is. His body aches as he crawls out and straightens up. The yellow blanket he was given the night before is rolled up on his bed. He sits down on the edge of the mattress and stares at his hands. One of his knuckles is caked in dried blood, the bruises like dark clouds beneath his skin.

Hugo realises he must have been sleepwalking again, but he remembers only fragments of his nightmare.

Shouting and shots from the floor above.

His remand hearing took place yesterday afternoon, and the prosecutor cited the 'special grounds' covered by paragraph twenty-three of the Young Offenders (Special Provisions) Act in her argument for keeping him in custody.

When the district court ruled that they agreed with the prosecutor, Hugo turned to look at his father. Bernard's eyes had welled up, and his chin was trembling with repressed emotion.

Hugo was remanded in custody on suspicion of murder and transferred to Kronoberg Prison.

Because he is not yet eighteen, he cannot be held for any longer than three months before charges are brought against him.

His first night in detention is now over, and he feels a rising sense of panic.

Hugo tucks a lock of hair back behind his ear and takes in his cramped cell. His eyes wander over the wall-mounted bed, the shelf, the chair and dented pine desk.

He doesn't have a toilet, but can always pee in the sink if necessary.

There are five thick horizontal bars over the window. Behind that, there is a dusty void, then another pane of glass.

The sky is dark above the rooftops.

Hugo is still wearing the soft green sweatpants and T-shirt he was given in custody, and he catches a strong whiff of sweat from himself. The white slippers are on the flecked grey floor.

This is already unbearable.

He missed his meeting with the *KULT* editorial team yesterday.

Makes no difference, he tells himself. The job wouldn't have suited him anyway. His life will be way too unstructured before he goes on his big trip.

Hugo was only seven when his parents split up. Claire had never been happy in Sweden, and she got hooked on synthetic opioids and moved back to Québec. At first, she wrote to him every week, but as the years passed their correspondence became increasingly infrequent, and she began to forget his birthdays. After Bernard met Agneta, virtually all contact with Claire stopped, and it has now been two years since he last heard from her. For all he knows, she could be in rehab, or maybe she just moved.

It wasn't until Hugo met Olga nine months ago that he began to understand just how much he had missed his mother. He found he could talk to her about Claire, and he was taken aback by how emotional it made him, realising for the first time that the loss of her had shaped his entire life.

It had been Olga's idea for them to travel to Canada together over the summer, to track down Claire.

'But you have to be prepared for the possibility that she might still be stuck in the same place she was when she left, and everything that goes along with that,' Olga had warned him as she lit a cigarette.

'I'm not expecting some happy-ever-after reunion. I just want to see her, to say hello and look her in the eye . . . You know, it makes me feel physically sick when I think about how I've almost completely forgotten her.'

Four months ago, he and Olga opened a joint account to save up for their trip. Olga has paid in three times as much as him so far, but he plans to work over the Christmas break, maybe even ask his dad for a loan.

Olga speaks French and has a driving licence, and she has promised to help him in his search.

Hugo likes to imagine his mother living alone in her parents' dilapidated old house in Le Grand-Village, with nothing but her dog, plants and hens for company. She has been clean for several years, drives a rusty Ford pickup and works part-time with pre-school children in Cap-Rouge.

In this fantasy, he stays with Claire once Olga goes home, spends the summer with her, and before he too flies back to Sweden, he takes his mother out to a nice restaurant with white tablecloths and colourful lanterns hanging from the ceiling.

They get dressed up and spend hours eating. Claire says, 'I'm sorry I couldn't be your mother until now,' and he gives her his silver dinar.

Hugo has no idea where the coin came from. All he knows is that it was in his hand when he woke in the forest after sleepwalking as a child. Since that day, he has worn it as a kind of amulet on a thin chain, telling himself that it protects him.

The coin is incredibly thin, made from dented silver, and it features an image of a dog or a wolf surrounded by what looks like Arabic text.

When he told Olga about his fantasy, she pinched his cheek as though he were a child and said that he was a silly little cutie pie.

Hugo gets to his feet and runs a hand through his hair. His stomach is aching, and he hopes it might be time for breakfast soon.

Someone walks by in the corridor outside, the wheels of a trolley squeaking.

Through the thick walls, he hears one of the other men shouting.

He realises he must have tried to get out of the cell in his sleep when he sees the blood on the door, on the bars over the hatch and on the little sign telling him what to do in case of fire.

6

Agneta wakes at six thirty to the sound of Bernard's electric razor through the closed bathroom door.

It takes her a few seconds to remember where she is.

While the police search their home, she and Bernard have decided to make the best of a bad situation by checking in to the Grand Hôtel in central Stockholm.

Her plan was to enjoy a lie-in while he set an alarm and drove back to the house to welcome the police and prove himself cooperative.

Agneta dozes off again, noticing little more than a faint waft of toothpaste as he kisses her on the forehead and leaves the room.

At eight o'clock, she gets up to open the door for her breakfast trolley, pours herself a coffee and eats a plate of scrambled eggs and toast in bed.

The sky grows bright above the green copper roof of the palace on the other side of the water.

Agneta doesn't have to be at the newsroom by Telefonplan for another two hours, and she drinks a little more coffee and thinks back to dinner last night.

She had changed into a black crochet skirt woven with shimmering gold thread, a yellow silk blouse that hugged her chest and a pair of gold sandals with a stiletto heel.

'Spare me, Aphrodite,' Bernard said as he held the heavy door for her.

She walked down the quiet hotel corridor ahead of him, swaying her hips from side to side.

'I'm on my knees,' he called after her, tucking the key card into his breast pocket.

She had laughed and continued over to the lifts, pressed the button and heard the whirr of machinery on the other side of the brass doors.

Bernard checked his phone for what felt like the hundredth time. He was worried, and had been trying in vain to get hold of both Hugo and his solicitor all evening.

They left the lift and made their way down the stairs to the restaurant, where they were shown to a small table at the very back of the room and immediately ordered two glasses of champagne.

They tried to have a nice time while they ate, with Bernard telling the story of when he found himself sitting beside Salman Rushdie on a small plane on the way to a literary festival.

'So, you know, with my fear of flying and the fatwa against him . . . Selfishly, all I could think about was myself, and I was completely panic-stricken. Still, we had a good chat and became friends during the flight.'

Agneta had heard the story before, but she laughed all the same. His fear of flying probably stemmed from the bus crash he survived as a child, she thought.

She had felt the scar beneath the hairs on his chest the first time they had sex, and had asked him about it later, while they smoked a joint together in bed. Bernard had told her all about the accident, saying that it had attracted a lot of press coverage and that it was one of the reasons why seatbelts were now required by law in all buses. It was also the reason he drove so slowly, with traffic building up behind him.

Agneta put down her cutlery, sipped her wine, leaned forward and took a deep breath.

She decided to revisit their earlier conversation about Hugo, explaining that she felt they were stuck in a rut as a family and that that was why she had said she was thinking of going to stay with her mother.

'It's just . . . I don't really know. At first – when Hugo was younger, I mean – it was all quite easy . . . but as he got older, he started to pull away, and now he's always so angry at me.'

'I don't know what's up with him,' Bernard said. 'You've done everything right – more than right. You even said you'd like to adopt him.'

'I would, but . . .'

She trailed off as their next course arrived: brisket of beef and coriander in a steamed bun. Agneta thanked the waiter and sat quietly as Bernard was served a dish of langoustines in a dill broth.

'I'll do anything to make you stay,' he said, his face solemn.

'If I felt like you were doing that, or even something close, it would be different,' she said. 'But I just feel so alone in this relationship, and I have for a while now.'

'And that's because of Hugo?'

'Yes, or . . . because of the way you are with him.'

'It's just that . . . You know what he's like. If I give him even the slightest criticism, he puts that face on, immediately . . . And if I don't stop, he gets up and walks away, and then I don't see him for days.'

'But that's all just a fucking power play,' she said, as quietly as she could.

'I'll be a better man from now on,' Bernard promised.

'Was that you or the langoustines talking?' she attempted to joke.

'I'm being serious. I'm going to try.'

'You're already a good man,' she said, holding his gaze.

Agneta looked down and realised that her big mistake had been to tell Hugo that she wanted to adopt him at the stroke of midnight on New Year's Eve. Bernard had been thrilled and hugged her, but Hugo's face had hardened and he had turned and stormed off to his room without another word.

Deep down, she knows that it was more to do with her own vanity than anything, to her trying to be a better mother than Claire.

Agneta doesn't know how she could have been so stupid.

She suspects that one of the reasons she blurted out what she did at New Year was because her own adopted mother had provided her with so much love and comfort. Her birth mother died of breast cancer in a shanty town outside of Dakar, Senegal, when she was just three.

'Bernard . . . what I said about going to stay with Mum feels a bit hasty now, considering all this madness with Hugo,' she said with a sigh. 'It's not all your fault; I've made plenty of mistakes too . . .'

'So does that mean you'll stay?'

'We need to stick together and be there for each other. That's all that matters right now.'

'Thank you, that's a huge relief,' he said, his eyes welling up.

After a main course of crispy kale, roast venison with celeriac cream and a quick glass of grappa to finish off, they went back up to their room.

Agneta pours herself more coffee, grabs a Danish pastry and gets back into bed.

The tip of her tongue has just touched the vanilla cream when Bernard calls.

'Good morning,' she says.

'Did I wake you?'

'No, I'm just eating breakfast. What's happening with Hugo?'

'The whole thing seems so bloody bureaucratic. I spoke to his lawyer, or whatever he's called. He has a meeting with the prosecutor this afternoon,' Bernard tells her. 'I understand that they have to take this seriously, but throwing a teenager in a cell? That's just not right . . . not unless there's a very good reason.'

'Are you going to be there for the meeting?' she asks.

'We'll see. I said I'd like to be, but I honestly don't know. I just want to get Hugo home, run him a nice hot bath and cook him a juicy Salisbury steak.'

'How are they getting on with the search?'

'They've just this minute finished . . . They were mostly focused on his room, took all of his gadgets and seemed pretty interested in your underwear drawer, but they didn't touch my little jar.'

'God, that never even crossed my mind . . . Lucky you're a white man.'

'Pale, stale and male.'

On his desk, Bernard has a glass jar labelled DAGENS NYHETER CULTURE that is jam-packed with cannabis. Every now and again, after a long day at work, he likes to roll a joint and smoke it with Agneta on the veranda overlooking the lake.

7

It has already been dark for hours when Agneta turns off onto the steep driveway and parks in the snow-dusted space outside the house, gets out of the car and plugs in the charging cable.

She can sense that something is wrong the minute she opens the front door. Bernard's briefcase is lying on the tiled floor, and the hallway is full of loose sheets of paper covered in footprints. His winter coat is in a heap beside the sideboard, his brown shoes kicked off just outside the kitchen.

Agneta hangs up his coat and puts his shoes on the doormat, gathers up the sheets of paper and grabs his briefcase.

She finds Bernard drinking water by the kitchen sink. The tap is running, and he keeps refilling his glass and gulping it down.

'Bernard?'

He flinches and turns around, staring at her with a strange expression on his face, as though he can't quite remember who she is.

'Are you OK?' she asks, setting his briefcase down on the counter.

'They're remanding him in custody, under full restrictions,' he mumbles.

'But you said—'

'I know. I'm trying to find out what rights I have, how it all works . . .'

'You need to talk to the solicitor.'

'I have. He's the one who called.'

Bernard trails off and lifts the glass to his mouth again. His hand is shaking so much that the water spills down his chin.

'I know you must be upset,' Agneta says, rubbing his back. 'But we need to find out what this means . . . what we can do to get Hugo home and what we need to do if it goes to trial.'

'I know, I know, it's just . . . This is all just so damn wrong, that's how I feel . . . I don't know how he is, whether he's OK, whether they've been good to him.'

'Take a deep breath, Bernard,' she says softly. 'You'll give yourself a panic attack.'

He turns around and stares at her in despair.

'I'm not allowed to see him,' he says, eyes welling up.

'Surely you have a right to see your own son?'

'Not while he's under full restrictions. No visitors, no phone calls. The only person he's allowed to see is the solicitor.'

'I might not get it, but I hear what you're saying.'

'It's madness,' Bernard groans, clapping a hand to his mouth.

Agneta swallows hard and forces back the tears. She doesn't feel she has the right to start crying.

'Come on, let's sit down,' she whispers after a moment.

'What?' he mumbles, too lost in thought to process what she just said.

'Come with me.'

'Sorry, it's just so . . .'

He follows her over to the kitchen table, where she pulls out two chairs. They sit down.

'I really did think they would straighten this all out right away,' she says. 'That it was all just a big misunderstanding.'

'I know, but clearly it isn't. The prosecutor genuinely seems to believe that he's a murderer,' says Bernard.

'And what do you think?' Agneta puts her hand on his.

'About what?'

'The caravan.'

'Do you think Hugo killed someone?' he replies, trying to keep his agitation in check.

'That's not what I'm saying, but—'

'They showed us photographs from the crime scene during the remand hearing . . . What happened there, it was completely horrific . . .'

'Bernard, you know that murders happen. That even murderers have parents.'

'Sorry, of course,' he says, rubbing his forehead. 'But I have to believe Hugo. He says he woke up in the caravan when the police arrived . . . He had no idea what was happening, initially thought he was still here.'

'We believe him, of course we do. That's our role in all of this. But we can't be naive either.'

'But when it comes to Hugo I probably *am* naive,' says Bernard. 'I don't know where he sleeps, who his friends are . . . Sometimes he's black and blue when he comes home, sometimes he has a new tattoo. Sometimes he's clearly high as a kite.'

'Seventeen is a difficult age . . .'

They both sit quietly for a moment. Bernard's hands are trembling in his lap. Agneta has just opened her mouth to ask what the prosecutor seems to think happened when he starts talking again.

'I had a quick chat with Lars,' he says, looking down at his phone. 'He was in a meeting, but he said he'd call me back.'

'You're going to tell him what happened?'

Yes, because . . . As you said, this really could go to trial, and if that happens then we'll need Lars on our side . . . He's a respected figure, and he knows more about Hugo's problems than anyone.'

Hugo was only six when they first took him to the sleep clinic, and Bernard spent hours driving him to and from Uppsala over the months that followed. But when they found out that Lars Grind lived in a villa only a kilometre away, in Mälarhöjden, Hugo started getting a lift with the doctor instead.

Bernard and Claire soon began to see Lars and his then-wife, Malva, socially. They became firm friends, going on holiday together and celebrating each others' birthdays. Following his separation from Claire, Lars was a source of great support to Bernard, and their friendship has continued since Agneta entered the picture.

'I like him, you know that, but he is a bit . . . weird,' she says. 'He looks at everyone like they're one of his research subjects, even when he's just here for dinner.'

'Mmm, he did ask a few too many questions last time.'

'Yeah, like what I wear to sleep.' Agneta smiles.

'Lars is just passionate about what he does. He struggles with boundaries and—'

Bernard stops talking when his phone starts ringing.

'It's Lars,' he says, getting to his feet to answer the call.

'Always nice to hear from my favourite author,' Dr Lars Grind says in his husky voice.

'Are you coming over for dinner on the twenty-sixth?'

'Oysters?'

'Eight o'clock,' says Bernard.

'I'll be there at seven.'

'I know.'

'Have you been out to the house lately, by the way?' asks Grind.

'Not in years.'

'Good, forget I mentioned it. Let it sink back into your sub-conscious . . . glug, glug, glug.'

One summer evening, while they were drinking beer and grilling meat on the jetty, Lars Grind had jokingly mentioned his nose for business. Before he began his medical training, he had obliterated his savings buying a plot of industrial land with a disused silo not far from Enköping. He had then launched and shut down a whole host of different businesses there: minigolf, ostrich breeding, a climbing wall, a flea market and long-stay parking.

Following a ruling in the environmental court, however, the use of industrial land for commercial operations was banned unless the area had been properly decontaminated – a financial impossibility for Lars.

Just like that, he discovered that he couldn't even *give* the land away.

Six months later, Bernard had asked whether he could borrow the house on the property. He and Claire had been fighting a lot, and he wanted to go out there to write in order to meet a deadline.

'So, tell me, what's going on? What's this about Hugo?' asks Lars.

Bernard turns his back to Agneta and clears his throat.

'He's in a spot of bother . . . He was sleepwalking, and the police found him at the site of a murder.'

'Good God,' Lars whispers.

'He's being held in custody. They think he killed someone,' Bernard continues, his voice wavering.

'You should have talked to me.'

'It all happened so quickly. But I was wondering . . . if it goes to trial . . .'

'Of course.'

'OK, great. Thank you for being such a wonderful friend.'

8

Nils Nordlund turns off the shower, grabs a fresh towel from the shelf and dries himself off in front of the foggy mirror.

In the past, people occasionally told him that with his pale-blue eyes, muscular biceps and blond stubble, he looked like one of the cops from *Miami Vice*.

These days, both the resemblance and the TV show are a thing of the past.

His feet are weary after a long day at the Retail Technology Show. He has a headache, and his ears are still ringing after countless conversations with exhibitors and colleagues.

Nils has just opened his toiletry bag to look for his deodorant when he hears his phone ringing and heads back through to his cramped hotel room.

The black headboard of the double bed is pushed up against a feature wall of cork tiles. His phone is on the pillow. Nils unplugs it from the charger and sees that Tina is video calling him, and he sits down on the edge of the bed to answer.

'Where are you?' she asks in her bright voice.

'In my room.'

'But I've called you ten times, and your last seminar ended at six,' Tina says, taking a seat at their kitchen table.

He studies her face, taking in her pretty, sharp eyes; the eczema around her mouth, and her short, spiky hair.

'I was in the shower,' he mumbles.

'Why?'

'Why do you think?'

He adjusts the towel around his hips. The air in his room is cold on his damp skin, and he shivers.

'Why are you sitting like that?' she asks, leaning in to the camera.

'What do you mean?'

'Up against that dark wall. Show me the whole room.'

'Tina . . .'

'Come on, before she has time to sneak out.'

'I'm on my own, Tina. I just took a shower,' he explains, turning the phone around. 'There's the door, there are my clothes, there's the window, the desk . . . the bathroom, the shower.'

'Show me under the bed.'

He stares at her, at her odd smile, and realises that all of the cupboards in the kitchen behind her are open.

'Here's under the bed,' he says, dropping onto one knee.

'Now behind the curtains.'

Nils braces himself against the mattress, gets up and moves over to the window.

'OK. There . . . and there.'

The sky outside has grown dark, and the streetlamps have come on. On the other side of the road, he can see a red-brick office building.

'I want to know who you've been flirting with today.'

'No one,' he replies, turning his attention to Tina again.

'Don't lie. That's all men do at trade fairs.'

'Not me.'

'Is that because you don't want to, or because you know I'll be able to tell?'

'Because I don't want to,' he says with a sense of exhaustion, slumping back down onto the bed.

'You look sexy,' she says.

'Right? I'm completely wiped out. The air in the conference hall is so dry, and the place is so loud. You don't realise it at the time, but it's hard work.'

'No propping up the bar tonight, then?'

'Not for me,' he says. 'I'm going to get another couple of hours' work done, have dinner with the gang and then get an early night so—'

'Emilia is shouting for me,' she cuts him off. 'I love you. Don't do anything stupid. Speak later.'

Nils Nordlund is a civil engineer by training, but he works as a product designer for Top Solutions, a consulting and competence partner with a focus on IT, management and technology. He spends almost all of his time working on client analyses, aiming to develop a deeper understanding of customers' needs, desires, behaviours and emotions.

He left his home in Örebro early that morning, to drive to the trade fare in Kista, just north of Stockholm, despite Tina screaming that she would be gone by the time he got back. Her jealousy began spiralling out of control when she was pregnant for the first time, claiming that all men cheat on their wives as their bellies get bigger. Nils had hoped it was just a phase, but if anything, things have only got worse. Tina scours his phone for proof of his infidelity, calls him constantly, follows him, interrogates him, argues and screams at him.

Once, two years ago, he came home late after seeing some old school friends. He was a little drunk, but he quietly unlocked the door, tiptoed inside and came round on the hallway floor a few seconds later. She had cracked him over the head with the heavy pestle from the kitchen, and he had to go to hospital for six stitches above his right ear.

They spent two months in couples' therapy after that, and he repeatedly told the truth: that he had never cheated on her.

Tina's jealousy has become unsustainable, but Nils has always felt that he needs to stay with her – for the kids' sakes, if nothing else.

But now he is no longer sure.

Around two months ago, Tina confessed that she had cheated on him in order to get revenge, so that he would know how she feels.

He hadn't wanted to hear any of the details, but she insisted on telling him about the Friday night when she went out with two of her best friends from Axfood. They had gone to Chilango, and she had spotted a man at the far side of the bar.

Tina said that she had smiled every time he met her eye, and that she had held his gaze for a little too long. Just before one in the morning, she and her friends had left the bar, but she had pretended she needed to go back inside to use the toilet right as their bus arrived. She went in alone, sat down on the empty stool beside the man and ordered a glass of wine.

'Aren't you going to ask if he was handsome?' she wondered, pausing for a moment. 'I'd say so. Tall, with brown eyes. Probably only twenty-three or twenty-four . . . I can't remember his name right now, but it was something foreign . . . Anyway, after chatting for a while I told him that I wanted him – right there and then. He followed me into the ladies' . . . Stop blubbing, I want you to hear this. He pushed me up against the wall, kissed my throat and my tits. I pulled my knickers down, tossed them into the sink and hoicked my skirt up . . . His hands were shaking as he put the condom on, and he got me up against the wall again and pushed inside. He was fucking me like a bull, but he slipped out. I pulled the condom off and whispered that I wanted him to come inside me, just like you do with your whores. Then I turned around and braced myself against the toilet, and he did me from behind with his massive dick. My God . . . He *roared* when he came. Probably made everyone in the bar choke on their drinks.'

She stopped talking and stared at him with glassy eyes, her face revealing some sort of frightened arousal.

After that, it was as though something had snapped inside Nils.

Last week, he created an account on Victoria Lace, a dating site for people in committed relationships. The homepage was black and gold, with a large picture of a beautiful woman with dazzling blue eyes, red lipstick and a black lace mask. The copy was full of lines like 'find your secret affair' and 'make life worth living' alongside guarantees of discretion and confidentiality.

Nils spent hours on the site, and eventually got in touch with a woman called Mikaela from Norrviken, close to Kista. She is thirty-two and married to an older man she loves. She wrote that she has no intention of leaving her husband, but that she misses the thrill and raw horniness of casual sex.

Mikaela was clear when they talked that she wanted to do it in the car, that she had often fantasised about it, and they have arranged a first meeting outside Edsviken Tennis Club. As Nils makes his way through the hotel lobby, he takes out his phone and switches it to silent to avoid being disturbed by Tina.

9

A light snow has started to fall as Nils Nordlund drives away from the conference centre and leaves the huge glass tower block behind.

Despite the anxious knot in his gut, he knows that this is something he needs to do – at least once – if he wants to save his marriage to Tina.

He drives slowly through a residential area, past large, brightly lit homes, but after just a few minutes, he reaches the last property. A hazy pool of light spills through the hedge, then the darkness takes over.

Nils slows down and switches his headlights to full beam.

In their bright glow, the narrow road looks like a dark red carpet stretching out in front of the car.

The pools of water in the potholes are covered in shimmering ice.

At the edges of the tunnel of light, he can see frosty grass and bare branches.

Nils passes a playground, and then the high fences surrounding the tennis courts come into view.

He slowly approaches a small, cream-coloured building with a deserted outdoor seating area and a shuttered ice cream kiosk. On the gable end, there is a sign that reads: WELCOME TO EDSVIKEN TENNIS CLUB.

The gravel crunches beneath his tyres as he turns off into the empty parking area and comes to a halt.

Nils checks the time. Five minutes to ten.

His heart starts pounding as a new wave of anxiety hits him, and he feels himself break out in a sweat.

He leans back, closes his eyes and tries to compose himself. To bring his breathing under control. Maybe this isn't for him after all, he thinks. He could just admit that, say, 'Sorry, Mikaela, but this isn't going to work,' and go on his way. Then again, he's here now. He might as well give it a chance. It could be the start of something new, a turning point for him.

He peers out through the side window.

The only working streetlamp is behind the little building, half obscured by trees.

Beyond it, he can make out the tall reeds down by the shore and the empty marina.

In her last message, Mikaela gave him clear instructions: to park his car here, turn off the headlights, move over to the passenger side and tilt the seat back as far as it will go, then put on Roy Orbison's *Lonely and Blue* and wait for her.

OK, he thinks as he gets out of the car.

It is bitterly cold outside, his breath forming clouds in the air. The only sound he can hear is the soft rustling of the wind in the reeds.

As Nils makes his way around the bonnet, he notices another car parked over by the fence surrounding the tennis courts.

He gets into the passenger seat and closes the door, tilts it back so far it is practically horizontal and then connects his phone to the car's Bluetooth speaker. After finding the right album, he presses play.

Music fills the car, Roy Orbison's distinctive voice singing about how only the lonely know how he feels tonight.

The screen of Nils's phone goes to sleep, and he glances over to the other car by the tennis courts. He can't see anyone through the dark windows, and has just started to wonder whether it might simply be parked there long-term when the flare of a match lights up the interior.

In the glow of the flame, he catches a glimpse of blonde hair, a pale hand and a fur collar.

A moment later, all he can see is the reddish tip of the cigarette, widening to an orb every time she draws smoke into her lungs.

Nils thinks about Mikaela's profile picture. She had blurred out her face, but her body was beautiful. Spellbinding.

It is ten minutes past ten.

She's probably just as nervous as he is, he thinks. Or maybe she simply wants to finish her cigarette first.

He turns towards the water and sees the wind rippling through the reeds down by the shore.

Roy Orbison is now singing about his baby going off with someone new.

Nils squints over to Mikaela's car again, leaning closer to the window, but he can't tell whether she is still inside.

The tennis net sways softly in the breeze.

From the corner of one eye, he notices a movement, and he turns his head. Something just passed through the edge of the circle of light on the other side of the kiosk.

Maybe it was a bird, he thinks. Or a deer.

He turns down the volume slightly, his eyes on the empty seating area and the swaying reeds.

Just as he is about to turn back to her car, there is a knock on the window. The shock makes him flinch. Nils hopes she didn't notice and attempts to smile as he fumbles with the handle. The door swings open, and he gazes up at the dark figure outside.

She takes a step back from his car and half-turns towards the tennis courts.

'It's cold out,' he says, shuffling over to make room for her when there is a sudden bang.

Steel on sheet metal and plastic.

The jolt reverberates through the car.

A sharp, heavy blade has appeared where his face was a second earlier.

Nils has no idea what is happening, but he scrambles away in panic.

Her axe swings through the air again, at a different angle this time. It hits the seat, causing the stuffing to spill out as she yanks it back.

His mobile phone clatters into the footwell.

Nils clambers over the gearstick into the driver's seat.

The entire car shakes when the windscreen shatters.

Cubes of glass rain down on him as he pushes the door open and tumbles to the ground outside. He crawls away across the gravel and sees the woman coming around the car. He manages to get to his feet, but loses his balance and hits his head on the drainpipe on the side of the building.

Nils raises his left hand in an attempt to defend himself and ward her off. She swings the axe, and he ducks, but he feels a sharp blow to his knuckles and sees the heavy blade dig deep into the wall behind him.

He trips over a terracotta pot holding a dead plant, but manages to stay upright. His heart is pounding, and he can still hear Roy Orbison singing in the distance.

Nils tries to run down to the water, but his legs are so weak that he has to stop. A warm liquid hits his hip and ankle, followed by a searing pain in his arm, and he looks down and whimpers when he sees that half his hand is missing.

The blood is pumping out in agitated spurts.

He passes the only working streetlamp, moving as fast as he can, conscious of her footsteps behind him. After a moment or two, he breaks into a brief run, gasping in pain, and makes his way in among the tall, dense reeds.

It's Tina, he thinks. She must have lured him into a trap, put on a disguise and come out here to mutilate him. To kill him.

Legs shaking, he keeps moving. The dry reeds give way, crunching as they snap beneath his feet.

Nils tries to protect his bleeding hand in his armpit, but even the slightest touch hurts so much that he groans loudly.

A dark bird flaps into the air in front of him.

He changes direction and sees the reeds slowly covering up his trail.

Crouching as low as he can, Nils keeps moving away from his car. Any minute now, he thinks, he'll sit down and wait quietly until she gives up and goes away.

He keeps his hand raised, but he can feel the hot blood running down his forearm. Each jolt of pain is so bad that he almost passes out.

His heart is beating far too fast.

Nils changes direction again and steps on a thin layer of ice, which cracks loudly beneath his feet. He turns around and sees the woman coming towards him through the reeds. She is much closer than he had realised, and he panics and rushes out towards the water. The ice breaks under his weight, and his feet get wet. He'll wade out to the rowing boat by the jetty instead, he thinks.

The freezing water envelops his shins.

The woman trudges after him with the axe resting on her shoulder.

He reaches the edge of the reeds and sees the light from the buildings on the other side of the water shimmering on the black ice.

Nils stops, panting for air. The water is above his knees now, the cold air clawing at his lungs. He tries to steady himself against the ice with his right hand, but it is as thin as a single pane of glass.

He can hear the woman's heavy footsteps behind him and knows he needs to keep going, but all his strength has deserted him. The waves from her movements wash bloody water up onto the ice in front of him, and he just has time to start a prayer before she reaches him.

10

The photograph shows a man frozen solid in a lake. He is on his knees with the water up to his waist, and his severed head is lying on the ice in front of him.

There is little doubt that this latest murder was carried out by the same perpetrator, turning the prosecutor's theory completely on its head.

Seventeen-year-old Hugo Sand will be released without charge.

Joona enlarges the image and studies the wound on the man's throat.

A single stroke.

The axe had a wider blade this time, and was swung horizontally.

The bright lighting in the office is reflected in the dark sections of the images on the screen, in the blood that has flowed down the victim's back.

Early that morning, Joona sat down to read the printouts from Hugo's phone.

The teenager has three close friends and occasionally exchanges brief messages with his father, but it is the texts to and from his girlfriend, Olga Wójcik, that are most interesting.

On a couple of occasions, the pair touch upon their plans to take a trip to Canada next summer, and it is clear that they have been trying to save enough money for the flights.

In one message, Hugo writes that he feels low and exhausted after school, and Olga replies that she will give him medicine and take care of him.

The reference to medicine may well just be part of some private game, but Joona instinctively associated her words with the traces of benzodiazepine found in Hugo's blood and had just decided to bring her in for questioning when the call came in from Edsviken Tennis Club.

A group of children from a preschool class had found the body, and one of their teachers had called 112 as they ushered them away from the jetty and the shore.

Joona immediately got in touch with Kronoberg Remand Prison to make sure Hugo hadn't escaped, and learned that he had fallen out of bed during the night and was currently in the medical wing.

The crime scene had been cordoned off into an inner and outer perimeter by the time Joona arrived. He spoke to Erixon and his team of forensic technicians, and didn't leave until he had a clear under-standing of what had happened there.

Sitting at his desk now, he remembers the divers in their dry suits, gathering chunks of ice in the hope of securing biological matter or fibres, taking samples and examining the lake bed. They photographed those parts of the victim that were beneath the surface of the water and then transferred him onto dry land. Once that was done, they turned their attention to his severed head and removed large sections of the thin ice, preserving them in various cool bags.

Joona leans in to his computer screen and studies the close-up shots of the victim's broken windscreen. It has bowed inwards in a fine web of cracks, and the driver's seat is covered in tiny chunks of glass beneath the oval-shaped hole left by the axe.

There is a knock at the door, and Magda Brons, the secretary to the head of the National Crime Unit, comes into the room, jewellery jingling. She tells him that the doors of the large meeting room are now open.

'He'd like you to come right away.'

'OK,' says Joona.

The new head of the NCU is a man by the name of Noah Hellman. He is just thirty-eight, and has never worked as a police officer in any real sense. Instead, he has a doctorate in political science and spent several years as the Security Service's representative on the Police Authority's national management committee. The other bosses like him, and he is already popular with the rest of the department, a skilled media communicator with his own professional Instagram account.

Joona makes his way down the corridor, past the curtained windows and over to the open door. In addition to a number of bar stools and a drinks trolley, Noah has had a pool table installed in the meeting room, and he is busy chalking his cue when Joona comes in. He looks up and gives him a boyish smile.

'My man,' he says.

'Magda said you wanted to see me?'

Noah is wearing a pair of red trainers, jeans and a pale-blue overshirt. He is clean-shaven, but his dirty blond hair is getting in his eyes.

'The murder at the tennis club . . . What similarities are there with the previous one?' he asks.

'The victim is male, around the same age, and he was killed with an axe . . . His wallet and phone are both missing, too,' Joona replies.

'Was the first man robbed?'

'Hard to say. There wasn't any money in his wallet, and he wasn't wearing a wedding ring.'

'What about differences?'

'I haven't examined the body,' Joona begins. 'But the first victim was completely dismembered, while this—'

There is a loud crack as Noah knocks the cue ball into the pack, and Joona's mind drifts back to the two divers transferring the victim into a body bag. His blood hadn't yet coagulated, and it seeped through the frozen surface of his neck wound. The shirt he was wearing had ridden up, and he had a long, vertical gash across his chest, likely from the edge of the ice when he slumped to his knees.

Aside from his severed head, the only other sign of injury was the fact that he was missing half a hand.

The divers zipped up the bag and dragged it ashore, causing the yellowed reeds around them to bend and break, and a dusting of snow to dance in the air.

'What were you going to say?' Noah asks as he moves around the table.

'That the killer left this victim immediately after the fatal blow.'

'I've seen the pictures, of course, but I'm having a little trouble making sense of what happened where.'

'The victim was in the passenger seat in his car, with the backrest fully reclined, when he was first attacked,' Joona explains.

'That much I got.'

'The axe missed him; there was no blood in the car.'

'So he ran down to the water?'

'He climbed over the centre console when the windscreen broke and escaped through the driver's side door while the perpetrator moved around the bonnet. They swung the axe again, severing the fingers on his left hand and striking the wall of a building nearby. The victim then ran and tried to hide in the reeds – bleeding heavily and in shock – but he was followed. He entered the water, possibly in an attempt to swim away, and that's where the perpetrator caught up with him.'

Noah studies Joona with a sceptical smile.

'You sound pretty damn confident.'

'We haven't been able to lift any footprints from the gravel in the parking area, but it's still possible to read the different stages – the damage to the car, the blood spatters on the ground . . .'

'I believe you, I believe you, it all sounds plausible enough. I'm listening. It's just that I'm not a proper police officer.' Noah smiles. 'I'm a careerist, a fucking careerist. I'll be totally open about that. Today, I'm head of the NCU, and tomorrow, I'll probably be the district police chief . . . I'm sociable, I like going for after-work drinks, but I also make sure that things get done.'

'That's all that matters,' says Joona.

'Liking after-work drinks? No, but seriously, I'm all for a bit of fun around here, but I also want to keep the press on a tight leash, if you catch my drift.'

'I can take care of myself.'

'You know, I was warned about you, Joona, but I wanted to make up my own mind . . . and so far, I like what I see. The prosecutor tells me she doesn't think we have any chance of a conviction with the teenager, so she's dropping the preliminary investigation. The case is back in our lap now, and plenty of people are desperate to take over, but I want you to do it.'

'Thanks.'

'We're in the process of recruiting a new partner for you – and don't just tell me you want to work with Saga Bauer again.'

'I want to work with Saga.'

'Who doesn't?' Noah jokes. 'I mean, she's one of the best. Truly. But it's too soon.'

'Then I'd rather work alone.'

'Ha. I knew you'd say that. The trouble is I need team players.'

'You need all sorts.'

'Maybe so, but—'

'If I solve this case, I want you to bring Saga back into the group.'

'It's your job to solve cases. You can't start negotiating—'

'I do more than just my job.'

'So I hear,' Noah says wearily.

'Which means I can negotiate.'

'No, it—'

'Yes.'

Noah sighs and rests the pool cue on his shoulder.

Joona knows how Saga seems, and he also knows that she has a long way to go before she finds inner peace.

In an act of self-loathing following the death of her half-sister, Saga sought out one of the surgeons who had been present in the operating theatre. She began a relationship with him in order to be humiliated and punished, to brand herself with shame.

The last time Joona visited her apartment on Tavastgatan, the place was a physical manifestation of her state of mind. On the kitchen table, there was a mouldy loaf of bread beside an open jam jar with a spoon inside. Saga was sleeping in a narrow bed without any sheets, and she spent most of her time reading scientific articles and medical textbooks on child surgery and the treatment of palpitations.

The only thing she knew for sure was that she never wanted to become emotionally attached to anyone again.

Joona knows that Saga comes into the office every day and that she does everything that is asked of her in her part-time job with the Intelligence Unit, but her true potential is woefully underused.

She needs to feel needed, otherwise she will go under.

Noah chalks his cue and moves around the table again.

'Hugo Sand has been released,' he says. 'Though he's not quite off the hook for the first murder yet – assuming they're definitely connected.'

'They are.'

'Personally, I don't think it's possible for someone to chop people to pieces with an axe in their sleep,' Noah says as he hits the cue ball, which slams into the yellow with a loud crack.

'No, but who knows?'

'It seems more likely that Hugo killed the man and then fell asleep. Maybe he's got narcolepsy or something . . . and now he's using an old sleepwalking diagnosis to explain what he was doing at the scene.'

'The thought did cross my mind.'

'And then you dismissed it?'

'No.'

'So you genuinely think he was sleepwalking?' Noah asks, in a different tone of voice.

'I've been reading up on it, and it really could be that simple,' says Joona. 'He used to go to the campsite a lot when he was younger, and something made him go back there in his sleep.'

'What, and by coincidence it just happened to be at the same time a murder took place?'

'One coincidence is nothing. Almost all witnesses are coincidental,' says Joona. 'It's only when we've got several links that we can start talking about connections.'

'What, and we've only got one coincidence so far?'

'Exactly.'

'So he could be either a witness or a perpetrator?'

'Or neither.'

'But you don't think so?'

'No.'

'So what's the next step?'

'I'm going to pay Hugo a visit, apologise on behalf of the justice system and interview him as a potential witness.'

'Even though you think he could be guilty?'

11

Bernard had been waiting in Agneta's freshly washed Lexus for almost an hour when Hugo finally emerged from Kronoberg Remand Prison.

The teenager was carrying his possessions in a plastic bag, and he paused on the pavement with his shoulders hunched. Bernard got out of the car, waved to his son and then walked around to the passenger side to open the door like some sort of chauffeur.

Two hours have now passed, and Agneta is busy frying three thick pieces of sirloin steak while Bernard sets the table and prepares a salad.

The beta blocker she took earlier has her heart wrapped in its calming embrace.

It could be hormonal, but over the past year everyday situations have started to make her feel anxious and uncomfortable, and open conflicts have become downright unbearable.

Hugo comes into the kitchen and saunters over to the stove. He is barefoot, wearing jeans and a shiny black shirt, with a black beret on his head. He smells like Bernard's shower gel.

On the white sideboard, there is a box full of books, the Portuguese translation of the latest novel in Bernard's series.

'So, how does it feel to be home?' Agneta asks as she grinds pepper onto the meat.

'One prison gives way to another,' Hugo replies without looking at her.

'Is that so?'

He shrugs and tucks his necklace inside his shirt, then checks his phone.

'What do you mean?' Bernard asks as he puts the steak knives down beside their plates.

'I've got a chemistry test tomorrow, a biology test next week . . .'

Agneta lifts the melted butter from the stove and slowly pours it into the vinegar and egg yolks.

'Are you hungry?' she asks with a smile as she mixes the béarnaise.

'Yeah,' he replies without any enthusiasm.

'That reminds me,' says Bernard, glancing down at a scrap of paper. 'A detective called while you were in the shower, the one who interviewed you in custody . . . Joona Linna. He said he wanted to talk to you. Sounded very friendly, and—'

'OK.' Hugo sits down at the table.

'Here's his number.'

'Just share the contact with me.'

The others take their usual seats.

'Hat off, please,' says Bernard.

Hugo doesn't seem to register his request, just sips his water and starts eating.

'Hugo?'

With a sigh, the teenager takes off his beret and drops it to the floor beside his chair. He has a bandage on his forehead, crusted with dried blood.

'What happened?' Bernard asks in a raised voice, getting to his feet.

'Man, chill out,' Hugo mumbles.

'Can I see?'

'Stop it,' he says wearily, tilting his head away.

'What happened, Hugo?'

'Nothing, I just fell out of bed in my cell.'

'You were sleepwalking, you mean?'

Hugo shrugs, and Bernard takes his seat again.

'Because you're going through a serious episode at the moment, aren't you?'

'I dunno.'

Bernard runs a hand across the table. 'I spoke to Lars, and he said that he—'

'What the hell did you do that for?' Hugo snaps. 'You don't need to talk to him. I can handle this myself, I told you.'

'I just asked if he could help if this went to trial.'

'Ugh, please.'

'He knows what he's talking about, Hugo. He's been a great help to you, and—'

'Yeah, *such* impressive results,' Hugo cuts him off, gesturing to his own head. 'I'm just as fucked up as I was when I first went to see him.'

'You know, I remember what things were like when you were little,' Agneta says, speaking up for the first time. 'We had to take turns sitting by your bed, night after night . . .'

'Thanks a bunch.'

'And it wasn't until you were admitted for the second time that things got a little better,' she continues.

Hugo sighs and turns his attention to his phone.

'No sighing, please,' says Bernard.

'OK.'

'And no phones at the dinner table.'

'God, what is *up* with you?' Hugo mutters.

'We need to talk, about your behaviour and your tone here,' he says. 'Towards us – towards Agneta, who I love, and who has only ever been kind and loving towards you.'

'Whatever.'

'No, I mean it . . . I'm serious, Hugo. You can't keep living here if you're going to behave like this.'

'Fine,' Hugo says, getting up and grabbing his laptop from the counter.

'I'm talking to you. I really need—'

Hugo leaves the kitchen.

'Please don't walk away while I'm . . .'

Bernard hurries after him into the hallway.

Still sitting at the kitchen table, Agneta hears a hanger screech against the rail and the repressed anxiety in Bernard's voice as he tries to reassure his son.

'We can work this out, Hugo,' he says.

She doesn't catch the boy's response, because the shoe horn clatters to the tiled floor, and the front door opens and slams back against the wall.

'You'll always be welcome here, you know that. I didn't mean—'

Bernard follows Hugo outside in his stockinged feet, and Agneta hears him shout 'sorry' with heart-breaking anguish.

* * *

Hugo passes the tall maple, whose red leaves have always reminded him that his mother moved back to Canada. He strides up the driveway, hears his father shouting behind him, and continues along Pettersbergsvägen. When he reaches Bellman's Well, he turns right and stops. He lowers the bag containing his laptop and chemistry book to the ground and does up his black leather jacket before setting off again.

In his pocket, his phone starts vibrating, but he ignores it.

Hugo doesn't know what the problem is, or why he feels so trapped, suffocated. Agneta's presence always makes him ashamed at having lost touch with his real mother.

He knows that he is unfair towards her, but his life is none of her business. That's just the way it is. She exists, and he does, too. But he has just been released from prison, and his dad is going to throw him out, and it's all her fault.

Hugo never asked for a new mother, he never chose her. It was his dad who brought her into their lives, who let her move in and wanted to share a bed with her.

He knows he was an anxious child, but he had no choice; he was afraid of going to sleep, didn't want to sleepwalk, and she was the only one who was there for him. He couldn't help but turn to her for comfort, to cling to her even though all he wanted was his own mum.

Once, after Hugo woke up in the patch of nettles behind Dr Grind's garage, she sponged him down with cold water and applied a menthol-scented ointment to soothe the stinging.

He can still remember the feeling of cold, invisible leopard spots all over his body.

Hugo went out to pick wild strawberries afterwards, threading them onto a long blade of grass and giving them to Agneta to say thank you. He had never seen her look happier than she did then, and an icy chill gripped his heart and he ran away and sat down on a bench in Krausparken.

Before Hugo met Olga, Agneta had almost made him forget his real mum.

12

The roar of the traffic on Södertäljevägen fades slightly as Hugo rounds the corner of the grubby nougat-coloured apartment complex, enters the code and makes his way inside.

He stands quietly for a moment in the dim stairwell outside Olga's door, undoes his coat and pushes his long hair back from his face.

The cold air has left his cheeks rosy and his nose red.

Hugo raises a hand and presses the tip of his index finger to the worn buzzer. He hears the shrill sound through the letterbox, followed by her shuffling footsteps on the linoleum floor.

The lock clicks, and the handle turns.

'Hugo?' she says, her face tense. 'You can't just show up here like this. You have to ring before you—'

'I know, I'm sorry, but I was about to lose my shit at home. I had to get out . . . and then I got scared you'd say no if I called.'

She smiles at him, but the tension from a moment ago is still lingering in her eyes.

'I never say no to you, do I? But I have a life, a job, things that need doing.'

'Do you want me to go?'

'I'm not saying I'm not happy to see you, because I am,' she says, her tone a little warmer now, leaning in to hug him.

Hugo takes off his boots and puts them on the shoe rack, then hangs up his coat and turns to look at her. Olga will be thirty-six in January, but she is only five foot one, with defined muscles and a slender neck. She has wavy, dyed blonde hair and an unusually symmetrical face. Her makeup is always flawless, and she wears silver studs in her brow, nose and both ears.

She is barefoot in her slippers, and is wearing a pair of black leather trousers and a white, unbuttoned blouse. Her tattooed arms and bare breasts almost seem to be glowing through the thin fabric.

'So, how was jail?' she asks.

'Pretty OK.'

She leans back and studies him with a wry smile. 'You're a tough guy now, huh?'

'Is it that obvious?'

'No.' She laughs.

Hugo follows her through to the kitchen.

She has a heraldic tattoo of an eagle wearing a golden crown between her shoulder blades, garlands of flowering vines on both arms.

On the kitchen table, there is an empty wineglass beside her laptop. The air is heavy with the scent of garlic, cumin and fennel from the cast-iron pot on the stove.

'Have you eaten?' she asks.

'No, but don't worry.'

'It's still hot.'

Olga sits down at the table, closes her laptop and puts it on the windowsill, beside a potted fern. Hugo carries the pan over to the table, then takes out a plate and some cutlery. He grabs himself a wineglass, pulls a napkin from the holder and sets it down beside his plate.

'On the left,' she says.

He moves the napkin to the other side, takes the bottle of wine out of the fridge, pops the cork and refills her glass.

'Thanks.'

Hugo pours himself a drink, then sits down and dishes some of the dal onto his plate.

'So, what's going on at home?' she asks.

'I can't even . . . It's like Dad is always trying to correct me when Agneta is around, and it's so fucking annoying, I . . . God . . .'

She watches him as he starts eating.

'You might end up being kicked out if you're not careful.'

'Legally, Dad has to support me while I'm still studying.'

'And are you?'

'You want to know if I'm keeping up with my studies?' he asks with a smirk.

'It's important.'

'Man, I've got so many mums these days!'

Olga laughs and leans back in her chair, making her blouse fall open. The fabric catches on the silver rings in her nipples.

'Which one do you like best?' she asks.

'Seriously, though ... just talking to Agneta makes me feel like I'm betraying my actual mum.'

'It was your mum who betrayed you, not the other way around ... She chose the drugs, and—'

'It's an illness.'

'I know that, but still ... You're both going to feel this betrayal when you meet, at least at first.'

Their plan is to fly to Montréal, rent a car and drive to Claire's family home in the small community of Le Grand-Village. If she no longer lives there, they figure they will probably be able to find someone who knows where she is. Olga has explained that they will have to approach Claire slowly, that it is important for Hugo to show he hasn't come to ask anything of her, nor to accuse or blame her; simply that he wants to start over and get to know her again, reconnect as an adult.

'You should demand compensation from the police for locking you up for no reason,' she says, swirling the wine in her glass.

'Nah, I don't care.'

'It could help pay for the trip, though.'

'I saw that you'd added more money,' Hugo says, putting down his cutlery.

'Yeah, a bit.'

It bothers him that she no longer treats herself to anything, that she saves all the money she can spare for his sake.

'We have to live in the now, too,' he says.

'We do. I think we do. It's just . . . at this rate, we're not going to have enough.'

'I know, and I'll sort it. I'll get hold of my share.'

'I have a few other things on the go, too. At the club. They might bring in a bit more.'

Hugo fiddles with the silver coin he wears around his neck and thinks about the fact that he hasn't told his father about his plans. He knows that Bernard will probably be upset on Agneta's behalf, but that he will also tell him he is doing the right thing. In truth, he would probably offer to help fund the trip, maybe even ask to tag along, but Hugo feels strongly that this is something he needs to do on his own, that it is all about him and his mum.

'Tell me about the caravan again . . . it was kind of hard to keep up over the phone,' Olga says, taking a sip of her wine.

'What do you want to know?'

'You woke up there and . . .?'

Hugo shakes his head.

'It all happened so fucking fast. I was dreaming about the skeleton man again, and then there was this loud bang. The cop had shot the floor right in front of me, and then they dragged me out. Cuffed me, frisked me, all that crap. I didn't really see everything, but there was so much blood, a chopped-off arm. It was crazy . . . And then they took me to jail and someone from forensics showed up for my clothes and a load of other stuff . . . You know, scraping under my nails, a pee sample, blood, hair.'

'Because they thought you were the one who'd done it?'

'Guess that's not so weird, really. I mean, it was kind of hard to explain what I was doing there. I'd been sleepwalking, but why *there*? I dunno. I used to hang out at the campsite all the time, but I don't really know what they were thinking.'

'Does this mean you're having one of those episodes you told me about?'

'Seems like it. I talked to my doctor.'

'Dr Grind?'

'He wants me to go to the lab for a few nights, as soon as I can, so he can check whether there's anything new going on in this sweet brain of mine, but I don't feel like I've got time right now.'

'Imagine if he's been programming a bunch of sleepwalkers to kill people,' Olga says, topping up their glasses.

'Crazy good plan.'

'I think so,' she replies, trying to hold back a smile.

'It would explain everything.'

'He could be doing it for the military or the Security Service . . . I don't know if I'm brave enough to let you sleep over now. I mean . . . what if you slice me open in your sleep?' she says.

'Don't say that.'

When Hugo finishes eating, Olga opens her laptop while he clears and wipes the table and does the washing up. Once he is done, he leans back against the counter and watches her until she looks up.

'What?'

'You're so beautiful,' he says.

'Maybe you'd like to show Olga everything you've learned so far?' she says, getting up.

'Now?'

'Unless you've got other plans?'

She kicks off her slippers and stands on tiptoe as he kisses her and caresses her breasts beneath her blouse.

Seven months ago, Olga started commenting on Hugo's posts on social media, and they met at a bar and began a no-strings relationship.

She immediately took it upon herself to give him an education in sex, teaching him that he needs to shave before he goes down on a woman and that the clitoris isn't just the little nub visible on the outside, but a large area in and around the vagina.

He remembers her matter-of-factly explaining that everything men have, women have too, and vice versa, but that a woman's glans is five times more sensitive and shouldn't be touched right away.

'When the time is right, when you can see that she's ready . . . lightly kiss that whole area. Lick it gently,' she said. 'Take it easy, pay attention and let her guide you, and it'll be great.'

Olga kisses his throat and whispers that they should take things through to the bedroom, unbuttoning her trousers and tugging them down along with her knickers.

The thin fabric of her blouse flutters around her as she walks. She has the name Jacek tattooed on her right buttock, a tribute to her first boyfriend, but she has promised to have it removed as soon as she has the time and money.

Hugo follows her out into the living room, where the long burgundy curtains are drawn over the window and the balcony door. Beside the sofa, there is a small brass drinks trolley – something she found in a dumpster and restored herself – cluttered with bottles of Polish vodka and cherry liqueur.

They make their way down the hall, past the bathroom and into the bedroom.

There is a pillar candle burning on the shabby chest of drawers, and the wax is glowing, the flame flickering anxiously.

Olga tosses her blouse onto a stool, pulls back the covers and lies down, naked, in the bed. She has her ankles crossed, her hands folded beneath her head.

The candlelight dances slowly over her body.

Hugo quickly gets undressed, crawls on top of her and parts her thighs. He kisses the smooth skin between her legs and looks up. Olga smiles at him and adjusts the pillow beneath her head.

'You found your way, my sweet prince . . .'

He caresses her with his tongue until she pushes his head away, rolls onto her stomach and gets up onto all fours.

Hugo enters her from behind, thrusting slowly as she strokes herself with one hand.

'Don't stop,' she whispers.

Looking down, Hugo sees the name Jacek trembling with every pump. He speeds up, causing the coin on the chain around his neck to thud against his chest. He hears her quickening breaths and notices the sweat glistening on her back.

The flame in the candle tilts, and its glow flickers up the wall behind the bed.

Olga lets out a long, low moan and slumps onto her stomach. Hugo tries to keep going, but she rolls over onto her side. Her thighs are trembling, and she is panting, both hands cupped between her legs. After a moment or two, she turns onto her back, her body relaxed. She looks up at him.

'*Êtes-vous fatigué?*' she asks with a smile.

She parts her thighs again, and Hugo gets on top of her and pushes inside. He feels a kind of youthful despair as he nears climax, and as ever, she lets him come inside her.

13

Olga and Hugo are in bed, their limbs entwined. Her eyes follow the shifting circle of light on the ceiling, and before long she hears him fall asleep. She should get up and take a shower, she thinks, but instead she lets her eyelids droop.

When she wakes, the bed is empty. The room is cold, and Olga wonders whether Hugo has gone home. It is one in the morning, and the candle on the chest of drawers has almost burned out.

The flame flares upwards every now and again, then quickly shrinks back.

The floor creaks underfoot as she gets up and squints out into the hallway.

The bathroom is dark.

She hears a series of soft bangs through the walls.

Olga shudders and moves over to the hook on the wall. She takes down her thin robe, pulls it on and ties the belt around her waist.

The flame surges again, as though in one last show of strength. The warm glow pulses over the ceiling and walls.

Olga walks out into the hall and sees her own shadow on the floor in front of her before the light from the bedroom fades.

'Hugo?'

The bathroom door is ajar.

She can hear a faint clinking, scraping sound from somewhere, and she stops to listen, searching for movement in the dark gap between the bathroom door and its frame.

There are another couple of thuds, possibly from the kitchen this time.

Olga keeps moving, eyes darting between the bathroom and the greyish gloom up ahead.

She passes the doorway and feels herself tense now that she can no longer keep one eye on the darkness.

The metallic scraping sound starts up again, seemingly from the living room.

She glances back and sees the shifting glow of the candle in the bedroom, then makes her way through the open glass door.

The sofa, coffee table, bar cart, bookshelf and TV are all wrapped in a nocturnal dusk.

Olga gasps when she notices the shape behind the curtains over the balcony door.

'Hugo?' she whispers.

The figure slowly turns around and stares at her through the thin fabric.

It is Hugo.

His arms are hanging limply by his sides, and a large kitchen knife catches the light in his right hand. The fabric over his face ripples with every breath.

'What are you doing?' she asks, though it dawns on her that he must be sleepwalking the minute the question leaves her mouth.

Hugo takes a lingering step forward from behind the curtain. He is wearing his black jeans and an inside-out T-shirt. His glazed eyes are locked on her face, and his lips are moving softly, as though he is trying to speak but can't find the right words.

'Put the knife down,' she says, swallowing hard. 'I want you to—'

Olga stops talking as he starts moving straight towards her, striding across the floor. She stumbles back into the bar cart, causing the bottles to clink and a carafe to fall to the floor. It breaks with a loud crash, and shards of glass scatter across the carpet. Olga turns around and runs out into the hall with her robe fluttering behind her, but she slips and crashes into the wall.

She can hear his heavy footsteps as she hurries back to the bedroom and slams the door so hard that the key jumps out of the lock.

A faint flame is still flickering in the base of the candle.

The belt of Olga's robe is caught in the door.

Her heart is racing.

She grips the handle with both hands and sees, in the fading light, that the key has landed over a metre away from her.

The flame shrinks, taking on a bluish hue.

There is a soft crackling sound, and the room is plunged into darkness. The powerful scent of wax fills the air.

Olga can hear that Hugo has stopped just outside. He tries the handle, but she manages to hold it steady. His hands move across the door, the tip of the knife scraping against the frame. With her foot, she searches blindly for the key.

Right then, Hugo tugs on the belt of her robe. She sways, still gripping the handle, and feels the heat from the friction as he pulls the belt clean out of the loops holding it in place.

She tries to breathe as quietly as she can, but her hands are clammy and her legs have started to shake.

In the dim city light filtering in through the curtains, she can make out the shapes of her furniture and the dark sheen of the key.

Olga manages to nudge it towards her with her foot, and she takes one hand off the handle and bends down. Just as she reaches the key, Hugo makes another attempt to open the door. She loses her grip and quickly straightens up. Olga throws her weight against the door, pushes the key into the lock and turns it with trembling hands.

Hugo starts muttering to himself, then wanders off down the hallway.

Olga waits for a moment with her ear pressed against the wood. She hears the same scraping sound as earlier, followed by a single thud. After that, nothing.

She grabs her phone from the bedside table and turns on the torch. She then unlocks the door and uses it to illuminate the hallway in front of her as she leaves the bedroom. Following the bloody footprints, she makes her way past the bathroom and through the door into the living room. Hugo is back behind the curtain, and has just managed to open the balcony door. Olga watches as he drops the knife, steps outside and swings one leg over the railing.

* * *

Bernard and Agneta are in their sunroom, drinking tea and eating crispbread with cheese. It is quarter past one in the morning, and the only source of light in the room is a frosted tealight holder on the table.

Agneta is wearing a cardigan over her nightgown, and has removed her makeup and applied night cream to her face, neck and hands. Bernard is in a pair of blue tracksuit bottoms and a faded T-shirt from the Edinburgh International Book Festival.

'You don't have to stay up for my sake, you know,' he tells her for the third time.

'It's OK, I want to . . . Let's just drink our tea and try to work out whether there's anything else we can do.'

'Thank you.'

'You've called all of his friends?'

'Yes.' Bernard sighs.

'How can it be that none of them know anything?'

'I think they were telling the truth. That's how it felt, anyway . . . They said that Hugo has a girlfriend but they've never met her, didn't even know her name.'

'Maybe he really is in love.'

'Almost sounds that way.'

Bernard's hand shakes as he breaks off a piece of crispbread, spreads a thin layer of butter and adds two slices of cheese.

'I tried to find Olga online,' says Agneta. 'But there are too many of them. Thousands. What I said might—'

'We don't even know if Olga is her real name.'

Agneta turns towards the water. The houses on Björnholmen, in the middle of the narrow inlet, are all dark.

'Your anxiety is infectious,' she says. 'But the fact is . . . I know he has school in the morning, but he's a seventeen-year-old with a girlfriend, and it's only one a.m. Maybe it's not *so* unusual?'

'Except he's in the middle of a serious episode at the moment, which means he isn't sleeping well and could nod off anywhere – on the metro, in a bar . . .'

Bernard finishes his crispbread and sweeps the crumbs into a small heap on the table in front of him.

'I appreciate that you tried to talk to him, anyway. I know it isn't easy,' Agneta says softly.

'No, it . . .' He trails off and takes a sip of tea.

'What?' she asks.

'He'll be eighteen soon, and I'm just so scared of driving him away. I desperately want him to be a part of my life.'

'Of course.'

'And I think he needs me, too, even if he can't see that himself right now,' Bernard says, checking once again that he hasn't switched his phone to silent. 'I'm just afraid he'll do something stupid, in desperation . . .'

'I know.'

'I'd never forgive myself.'

'For what?'

Bernard gestures dejectedly before getting up to pour more tea.

'You know it isn't right to let him be so rude to me,' Agneta says calmly. 'It isn't helping him, nor is it showing him love . . .'

'No, but—'

'And it'll end up wrecking our relationship.'

'We can't let that happen,' he says, looking her in the eye.

'No.'

'You know, I've been thinking about when we first met . . . We were so in love, head over heels, but Hugo never had a say in any of this. It feels as though it was my fault things moved so quickly. I needed to forget Claire, and Hugo needed a mum.'

'Especially since she doesn't make any effort to contact him.'

'She does, just not often enough.'

'Hugo misses her.'

'This might not be the right word, but it's as though she left a void inside him,' says Bernard.

He turns to the window, watching a light out in the dark strait.

'I've been in his life for as long as Claire was,' says Agneta.

'I know that,' he replies, meeting her sad eyes. 'But it isn't about you; you've done everything right.'

Agneta loathes herself whenever she turns her frustrations on Claire and allows resentment to cloud her thoughts.

It's just that Claire had everything, a perfect young son, and she still chose the drugs over him. She never even manages to reach out to him on his birthday, doesn't have the energy to call at Christmas.

Agneta sips her tea, then lowers her cup and makes an effort to change the subject.

'How are you getting on with your new book?'

'Let's throw a veil over that, to paraphrase Henning Mankell,' he replies.

'Come on, tell me. Is it going well?'

'Yes, though I've been thinking that I should probably try something new soon.'

'I know there are so many demands on you, so much expectation. I do. But at the same time . . . you can't just plagiarise yourself because that's what everyone wants. You need to find the magic in your writing, as you always say,' she tells him, pressing a hand to her heart.

'I love romance.'

'I know, but your mind could be slightly tainted from all the years of—'

'Tainted?' he asks with a smile.

'Sorry,' she says, holding her tongue.

'So what should I do? Write a crime novel or—?'

'No, but I did actually have an idea.'

'OK.'

'I hope you'll take this the right way,' she says. 'But I think you should write an honest and deeply human true crime book about all of this. You, me, Hugo . . . the police and two murders.'

He puts his cup down and studies her. 'I'd have to talk to Hugo first.'

'Of course.'

'But it's not a bad idea.'

'I could help with the research,' she says. 'I have contacts on the force, and—'

'We could write it together,' he says, getting to his feet excitedly. 'I'd love that.'

Bernard runs a hand through his hair and looks down at her.

'On an equal footing, you and me,' he says, pacing about the room.

'My name first.' She grins. 'Just kidding.'

'No, I agree, your name first,' he says, with a newfound intensity that makes her laugh. 'This is such an exciting idea. I really do think this could be something, I—'

Bernard stops abruptly when his phone starts ringing. The name Hugo, followed by three red hearts, flashes up on the screen.

'Hugo?'

'Is that Bernard?' asks a woman's voice.

'Yes, who is this?'

'It's Olga.'

'What's going—'

'Hugo was sleepwalking,' she interrupts him. 'He was trying to climb over the railing on my balcony when I found him.'

'Is he hurt?'

'No, he's fine, just a few scratches. But he's really shaken . . .'

Agneta moves over to Bernard so that she can hear what Olga is saying.

'When he woke up and realised how bad it could've been, he flipped,' she says. 'He started pacing about, telling me all this weird stuff from the caravan . . .'

'He can be quite groggy if he's woken from an episode of sleep-walking,' says Bernard.

'I didn't know what to do.'

'Can I talk to him?'

'He's in the shower.'

'Do you know whether he has his pills with him?'

'Yeah, he took some Atarax.'

'Good.'

'But I still think it would probably be best if he went home. I didn't want to put him in a taxi without checking you were there first.'

'We're here, but I'll come and get him myself,' says Bernard, turning towards the hallway. 'Where do you live?'

'Jenny Linds gata . . . Number eight.'

'I'll be there in fifteen minutes.'

'OK, I'll bring him out.'

'Thank you for ringing,' Bernard tells her before ending the call.

14

The press conference at the Police Authority building has been underway for forty-five minutes when the spokesperson finally opens the floor to questions.

The air in the room is stale, heavy with the scent of coffee, gingerbread and damp coats.

Microphones from the various television and radio stations have been set up on the table at the front of the room where Detective Superintendent Joona Linna is sitting between Noah Hellman and a tall woman in a pair of red glasses.

Noah gets up and jogs over to the podium. He runs a hand through his hair and gazes out at the assembled media with a slight smile. The head of the NCU isn't in uniform. Instead, he is dressed casually, in trainers, jeans and a grey T-shirt over a red long-sleeved top.

As ever, Agneta was taken to one side to be searched when she arrived, and while she was waiting in the lobby, a journalist from TV4 came over and told her not to stand around doing nothing after someone spilled coffee on one of the tables. Agneta didn't say a word, just went through to the ladies' toilet and grabbed some paper towels to mop up the mess.

She is now sitting towards the front of the room, on the right-hand side. She has attended two police conferences previously, for the true crime pod she does work for, but she feels different this time. Slightly nervous.

On the whole, many of the grand ideas cooked up late at night – fuelled by a glass of wine or two – never survive to see the pale light of day, but when Agneta went down to the kitchen that morning, she found the table covered in sticky notes. The first row summarised the press coverage of the case, the second all of the information the Police Authority had released so far, and the third focused on their exclusive knowledge of Hugo.

'I haven't lost my marbles,' Bernard had said, beaming at her. 'But I really do think we could be on to something here!'

'Writing a book together, you mean?'

'Yes, it's perfect,' he said as he loaded a tray of scones into the oven. 'Because of Hugo, first and foremost. Because we're able to tell his story from the inside . . . But there's also the fact that you're an accomplished crime journalist – even if you haven't been given credit for it – and my experience as an author, that I can actually write pretty well when I put my mind to it.'

Bernard had tentatively broached the topic with Hugo in the car home from Olga's apartment the night before. Hugo had been drowsy from his medication, but when Bernard promised to give him a veto over anything that might one day be published, he had given his father the green light.

An *Aftonbladet* journalist with a bloated face and white stubble gets up from his chair and sniffs loudly.

'From what you've said, it sounds like the two murders are connected,' he says.

'You know what I'm going to say,' Noah replies with a smile. 'That's something we're looking into.'

'Still, it seems pretty likely that two axe murders in the space of four days . . .'

'As I say, that's something we're looking into,' Noah repeats, pointing to a woman from the TT News Agency, who raises her hand.

'Is this part of the escalating violence we've seen between the various criminal networks over the past year?' the man from *Aftonbladet* continues.

'As things stand, there's nothing to suggest that, but we're exploring every angle,' says Noah.

'What other possible motive could there be?' the journalist asks, sniffing loudly again.

'I'm afraid I can't speculate on an ongoing investigation – that's your job,' Noah says with disarming bluntness.

Before the laughter has completely died down, Agneta raises her hand. She manages to catch Noah's eye just as the man from *Aftonbladet* claims that he has a source who says the victims were sexually abused.

'I can't comment on the investigation in question,' says Noah, pointing to the woman from TT again.

'You had a suspect in custody,' she begins, breathing heavily through her half-open mouth.

'According to the tabloids.'

'According to our sources, he has since been released. Has he been cleared, or does he remain a suspect?'

'He was in custody at the time of the second murder,' Noah replies.

'But he was arrested at the scene of the first. Does that mean he is actually a witness?'

'I see you're still pretending not to understand that the principle of secrecy applies to preliminary investigations,' Noah says with a smile.

'Just doing my job,' she retorts.

'And mine is to round off and thank you all for coming today.'

'One last question,' Agneta speaks up, getting to her feet.

'OK.'

The beta blocker she took half an hour ago is keeping her heart rate calm and her breathing even, but Agneta still feels butterflies in her stomach.

'Isn't it true that the witness you just mentioned was a minor, and was remanded in custody on fairly shaky grounds?' she asks in a steady voice. 'That a search was carried out at his home and that he sustained injuries while in custody, because you didn't take his diagnosis seriously, and—'

'If he sustained injuries while in custody, that is unfortunate. That sort of thing should not happen . . . And if it did, there'll be an internal investigation,' Noah explains, with warmth in his voice. 'But as far as the legal process is concerned, we follow established protocol – as we must – even if that does occasionally mean that innocent people spend a few days in custody.'

'There has already been another murder,' Agneta presses him. 'And I'm assuming you plan to question the witness about what he saw, but—'

'He's already been questioned.'

'Only as a suspect,' she says. 'My question is how you aim to protect him if he helps you.'

'Given that he's over fifteen, he has a legal obligation to testify.'

'But in reality, surely it's a matter of mutual trust?'

'I hope we all trust in the police's ability to do their job,' Noah says with a wave as he leaves the podium.

The press spokeswoman takes over to wrap up the session, and Agneta sits down.

Before she left home that morning, Bernard had encouraged her to record the entire press conference and then stay behind to jot down her immediate thoughts. As the chattering journalists file out of the room, she writes a few words about feeling slightly offended when the others talked about Hugo, about the sweat she saw dripping from the tip of Noah's nose and landing with a soft crackle on the microphone beneath him, and the fact that Joona Linna didn't say an entire word, despite the fact that his boss seemed to be desperate for him to speak up several times.

She quickly turns to a clean page in her notepad when she notices the detective approaching between the chairs.

'You're Agneta Nkomo, aren't you?' asks Joona.

'Is it true that the victims were sexually abused?'

'No, there was no indication of that.'

'OK, thank you.'

'I actually have a meeting scheduled with Hugo tomorrow,' says Joona, turning a chair around and sitting down.

'You could have mentioned that during the press conference.'

'I didn't want to draw attention to him.'

'Shouldn't he be given witness protection?'

'We can look into it, but I'm afraid it's a pretty convoluted process – just so you know. The key thing right now is that you're careful. No posting on social media about what he's doing, where he is, and so on.'

'Should I be worried? Is he under threat?'

'We're not aware of anything concrete, but he is our only witness and as you say, we haven't interviewed him yet.'

'So you think he might be able to help you?'

'You never know, but I just can't drop the thought that Hugo should be able to remember the things he saw while he was sleep-walking – given that he's capable of opening doors, following roads, getting through gates, and so on,' says Joona.

'I see what you mean . . . but it's not always clear-cut,' she replies. 'All I know is that when he sleepwalked when was younger, we used to try just to steer him back into bed, but sometimes he resisted. There were times when he almost started to panic, when he was convinced he needed to escape . . . And if we accidentally woke him up, he would remember things in that moment. But if you asked him about them later, they were gone.'

'So the memories are there, but he loses contact with them?'

'The same thing happened last night. He started sleepwalking at his girlfriend's place,' Agneta explains. 'She woke him up as he was trying to climb over the balcony railing, and apparently he was talking about the caravan.'

'What did he say?'

'I don't know. Hugo can't remember, and we don't really know her . . . We don't know her at all, in fact.'

15

Jack is waiting, as usual, by the concrete steps beneath the low skyway. He glances over towards the square and the strange red church building.

The sky is dark and heavy.

The cold air helps to alleviate the stench of old urine from the corner nearby.

Used condoms, latex gloves, sooty scraps of foil, pouches of snus and cigarette butts litter the ground around the rusty drain cover.

This might not be the most picturesque spot in Stockholm, but it is secluded. No CCTV cameras and five possible escape routes, two involving stairs.

Jack is shivering, despite the fact that he is wearing two pairs of sweatpants, a fleece and a black hoodie. He has a beanie on beneath his hood, mittens and red trainers with thick soles.

An old regular from the Bengali restaurant nearby comes down the steps, takes a seat on the concrete and shakes out a cigarette.

"Sup?' says Jack.

'Not much. Shitty vibes in the kitchen today.'

Jack moves over to the wall beside him. He already has a wrapper of twenty fentanyl pills in his hand, and he puts it into the dead bush beside the steps. The man takes the pills, shoves them in his pocket and leaves a small plastic chutney jar in the same place. He then takes one last drag, drops his half-smoked cigarette to the ground and gets up and leaves without another word.

Jack puts the jar straight into his rucksack. He knows he doesn't need to count the money inside, but he will probably do so all the same.

Leaning back against the grubby brown metal door, he checks the time on his phone. His first shift will be over in forty minutes.

That morning, Jack took his little brother to school as always. He talked about how important it is that he studies hard if he wants to be an archaeologist, that he needs to get top grades.

'I know, I can do it,' his brother had replied.

'You should look a bit happier, then.'

Jack himself left school without any qualifications. He has ADHD, but because he was caught with THC in his urine, he was never given any help. Instead, he wound up in this alleyway, self-medicating with amphetamine and racking up debt.

A cute girl with plaits and a skateboard under one arm pauses a few metres away and peers back towards the square.

'What you looking for?' he asks.

'I heard you sold GHB,' she says, nervously eyeing him up.

'Just ran out,' he lies, in an attempt to protect her.

'OK.'

'But I've got some E if you want it.'

She nods and happily pays triple the street price for two hits before hurrying away.

A gust of wind blows dust and rubbish over the cracked tarmac.

Jack can't stop thinking about what he saw yesterday, when he went to drop off the money.

The set-up is always the same: Jack hands over the cash to Ibra, who is waiting by the playground in his black van, then he goes to collect the new stash from the tyre swing.

Yesterday, after Ibra drove off, Jack climbed the low fence and grabbed the vacuum pack from the swing. As he straightened up, he noticed a white Volvo parked over by the tennis club, and realised there was music coming from it.

A weird, old-fashioned song, carried on the wind.

Jack shoved the package in his rucksack and left the playground through the gate. The hinges creaked, chirping like a nest full of baby birds.

He got on his e-scooter and started riding along Neptunusvägen in the dark. The only streetlamp wasn't working properly, the bulb flickering on and off.

He remembers thinking that people must still try to knock them out with a single kick, like they did when he was a kid.

There was an old car parked at the end of the road, and for a split second, the streetlamp illuminated its windscreen.

With a sudden sense of watchfulness taking over him, he cruised alongside the rocks marking the edge of the grass.

Snatches of the strange music reached him on the breeze.

Jack could see the tall fence around the red clay tennis courts, but beyond that everything was dark.

The streetlamp light continued to flicker on and off, and in its sudden glow he saw a bloody figure clutching an axe in one hand.

The brief bursts of light made it look like they were staggering towards the old car across the yellowed grass.

Jack sped up, swinging around the car and away from the lake. His legs felt like jelly all the way back to Kista.

He can't get what he saw out of his head, and knows he should call the cops to leave an anonymous tip-off.

Jack caught a glimpse of a face. He has been thinking about it all day and knows he would be able to give a good description – both of the bloody figure and of the car, which had a cluster of air fresheners hanging from the rear-view mirror.

'I'll do it,' he mutters to himself. 'I'll call it in.'

He looks down at his phone. It would be good to head into one of the nearby shops to warm up for a bit, but he doesn't have time.

He needs to get over to the playground.

Jack walks down the alleyway towards the square, unlocks one of the e-scooters and sets off for Edsviken.

When he reaches Neptunusvägen, he slows down and lets the scooter fall into the grass by the side of the road. He takes off his rucksack and shoves his mittens inside, then pushes back his hood and makes his way over to the black van.

As ever, one of the tinted side windows is slightly open. He knows Ibra will be sitting on the other side, in a bulletproof vest and with a Glock in his hand.

Jack pushes the black bag of money through the gap, and the van pulls away.

He opens the gate to the dark playground and hears the hinges creak. The frozen sand is hard underfoot, crunching beneath his shoes.

He cuts between the miniature climbing wall and a pale-blue slide, and walks over to the swings by the back wall and the dark trees.

Jack looks around, thinking about the bloody figure he saw in the blinking light. About the axe in their hand, and the way they were moving over the dead grass like some sort of demon.

Glancing over to the tennis club, he notices that the police have cordoned off the area around the courts with blue and white tape.

A knot of anxiety settles in his gut.

There are two deer in the middle of the grass, and they both raise their heads, suddenly on high alert.

The wind blows a plastic ball along the edge of the wood.

Jack reaches into the tyre swing and finds the stash, but when he tries to take it out he realises that it is stuck.

The deer bolt away, and he hears a branch break among the trees.

He doesn't want to rip the bag and risk losing any of the drugs.

He takes out his phone, turns on the torch and has just got onto his knees to get a better look when he hears something rustle behind him.

Jack turns his head and sees a person striding towards him, but he doesn't have time to get up before something slams into his head.

His teeth smash together, and his phone drops to the sand. His head feels heavy and unsteady.

Jack is still on his knees, and he knows that he should pull his knife to defend himself, but he feels oddly weak.

Blood trickles down his face and neck, dripping onto his phone and turning the beam of light from his torch pink.

Somehow, as his field of vision starts to shrink, he understands that the blade of an axe has just sliced through his hat and skull, burying itself deep in his brain.

Jack just has time to think about his little brother's sulky face, his fair eyebrows and the dinosaur plaster on his forehead, and then he loses consciousness.

16

The sunlight filtering in through the dirty windows at the National Crime Unit makes the flecks of dust shimmer in the air.

Joona is at his desk in the investigation room.

Through the closed door, he can hear the monotonous whirr of the printer in the copy room, spitting out sheet after sheet of paper at high speed.

The autopsy has yet to take place, but everyone on the team is convinced that the young drug pusher found dead in the playground by Edsviken Tennis Club was killed because he saw something when Nils Nordlund was beheaded.

The bosses have decided not to make this information public so as not to scare any other potential witnesses from coming forward.

A team at the NCU has been tasked with searching for any old cases with similarities to the two primary murders, but so far they have drawn a blank.

Joona has attempted to reach Hugo's girlfriend, Olga Wójcik, a number of times, and she has now been summoned for a formal interview.

In just a short period of time, the investigation has become incredibly complex.

Every member of the team has been compiling information in a chronological order in a shared Excel file, but it feels as though the more good, old-fashioned detective work Joona and his colleagues carry out, the more locked doors they find.

They have no CCTV footage and no neighbours to question, and their interviews with the victims' friends and relatives have so far proved fruitless.

The IT technicians have been scouring the dead men's online activities, but have yet to find a single detail that could point to any sort of motive. No blackmail, no black market loans or drug use, no gambling addictions or interactions with the criminal underworld.

There is a knock at the door, and Noah Hellman comes into the investigation room, followed by his secretary. He pauses in front of Joona's desk, runs a hand through his hair and frowns.

'I could have done with your help at the press conference earlier,' he says.

'It's not my job to help you in press conferences,' Joona replies.

'You really are stubborn, aren't you?'

'Give Saga a chance. We need her.'

'We've already discussed this.'

'Joona . . .' the secretary says calmly.

'I'll let you win at pool,' Joona continues.

'Wow . . . You think you're that good, do you?'

'OK, then let's try this: if I beat you, you have to bring Saga back.'

'Nice try, but she's not ready to—'

'She is,' Joona cuts him off, getting up from his chair.

He leaves the office and takes the lift down to the garage level, walks through the tunnel beneath Kronobergsparken and gets into his car. He then drives up the long ramp and comes out into the bustling Fridhemsplan.

On the pavements around him, people hurry by with their shoulders hunched, heads lowered in the frigid air.

The Christmas tree seller has candles burning by their stall.

A man drags a black plastic bag out of a fast food kiosk and uses his knee to swing it up into a dumpster.

In less than twenty minutes' time, Joona is due to hold his second interview with Hugo Sand.

As things stand, Hugo is their only witness. Their only way into the empty room in which two men have been singled out and murdered in an extremely violent manner.

The teenager claims not to remember anything, but given what Agneta said about him having some access to his memories when he first wakes from sleepwalking, the things he saw must be in there somewhere.

The traffic becomes backed up in the approach to the Essingeleden, slowing to a crawl. A yellow air ambulance hovers over the rooftops and trees in Gröndal.

If the usual interrogation technique doesn't work today, if Hugo refuses to give in to the human urge to confess, then Joona has a plan.

The boy seems to have a complicated relationship with his father, testing his boundaries in an attempt to assert his independence and possibly even make Bernard prove his love.

The traffic starts flowing normally again once it passes the barriers that have been put up around a large hole in the tarmac.

Joona is working on the theory that Hugo is relieved the prosecutor dropped the case against him and released him from custody. He plans to reinforce that feeling and – without lying – get the boy to believe that he no longer needs to stick to every detail of his initial statement.

He drives slowly down the narrow road in Mälarhöjden. To his right, there are a number of exclusive lakefront properties. To the left, behind the high supporting wall, the steep gardens belonging to the houses further up the slope loom above the road.

Joona slows down, passing the iron gates flanking the driveway and pulling up in a small parking area.

The mailbox is full of damp flyers.

As he gets out of the car, Joona finds himself thinking about the second prong of his strategy: encouraging Hugo to ignore Bernard's attempts to stop him from talking.

That will require him to plant a seed of doubt in Bernard's mind, making him think that his son hasn't quite been fully cleared and, at the opportune moment, causing him to worry about Hugo saying too much.

The idea is that if Bernard tries to stop his son from talking, it will have the opposite effect, for the simple reason that people don't like to be told what to do.

Joona makes his way in through the gates and down the driveway towards a grand yellow home with a black gable roof.

Beyond the house, the large lawn slopes down to a small cabin by the water.

Joona walks straight over to the door, taking his phone out of his inner pocket, starting the recorder and putting it back into his jacket.

He rings the bell and hears a digital tune echo inside, followed a moment later by footsteps on the tiled floor.

Bernard Sand opens the door.

His greying hair is standing on end, and he has dark bags beneath both eyes, but he is clean-shaven and wearing a brown corduroy suit with leather patches on the elbows.

'Joona Linna,' says Joona, shaking his hand. 'We met while Hugo was in custody.'

'Of course. Come in, come in. You can leave your coat here,' says Bernard. 'I'm sorry if I seemed a little guarded last time we met; this whole business has been terribly hard. Particularly for my son, of course, but also for me. Do you have children?'

'An adult daughter,' Joona replies as he hangs up his coat.

'Ah, then you know what it's like . . . Come in.' Bernard leads him down the hallway. 'I thought we might sit in the kitchen. Or perhaps you'd rather I didn't stay? I'm not quite sure how these things work.'

'It'd be fine for you or Agneta to join us.'

'Agneta is at the office all day.' Bernard pauses outside the closed kitchen door, turns to Joona and attempts a relaxed smile. 'Hugo isn't a suspect anymore, is he? I mean . . . It's awful to admit, but when the solicitor called to tell us about the second victim . . . That was the first time I've ever thought that there might be an upside to murder.'

'The investigation hasn't been closed, it has just entered a new stage where the prosecutor no longer suspects Hugo of any crime,' Joona explains.

'And you?'

'So long as something isn't impossible, it's still possible.'

'Even murdering someone in Sollentuna while locked up in Stockholm?'

'You're an author,' Joona points out.

'He could have been working with someone else . . . if that's what you mean?'

'All I'm saying is that it isn't impossible . . . Though I see Hugo as a witness at present.'

'So you don't think we need a solicitor anymore?' Bernard asks with a frown.

'I don't think so, but if you'd feel more comfortable having one then that's fine. Hugo is a minor, and this is a formal interview.'

Bernard knocks softly and opens the door to the kitchen, where there is a brass Advent star hanging in the window. Hugo is sitting at the table with a can of Red Bull and a dog-eared chemistry book in front of him. He is wearing glasses, and has his hair tied up in a bun.

The teenager is pale and beautiful, if a little rough around the edges, with his tattooed arms, the dark gash on his forehead, the yellowing bruise on his cheek and bandages on three fingers.

'Hi,' says Joona.

'Hi.'

'We met while you were in custody. My name is Joona Linna, and I'm a detective with the National Crime Agency,' he says as he shakes Hugo's hand. 'I've taken over the investigation, and I want to start by apologising for the time you spent in Kronoberg. The prosecutor made a mistake and . . . I know it's been hard on you.'

'I'm home now,' Hugo replies, lowering his yellow highlighter to the table.

'But not completely cleared, just so you know,' Bernard speaks up.

'No possible scenarios will be ruled out until I've solved the case,' Joona explains.

'You seem pretty sure you'll be able to,' Hugo says, looking up at him with a flicker of interest.

'Yes,' Joona replies as he takes a seat opposite him.

17

Bernard glances over to Joona and pulls out a chair for himself, then hesitates with his hand on the backrest and asks whether he would like a coffee.

'Please.'

'Strong and black, I'm guessing?'

'Sounds good,' Joona replies with a smile. He takes out his phone and sets it down on the table, then turns back to Hugo. 'I'll be recording our conversation today, just so you know.'

'Look, I don't want to be rude or anything,' Hugo tells him, 'but I really need to study for . . .'

He pauses when the coffee grinder starts whirring and leans back in his chair, scratching his stomach through his faded *Actes Sud* T-shirt.

'I won't take up too much of your time,' says Joona.

'It's just that I've got a test today.'

The hissing and bubbling from the coffee machine fades, and Bernard sets a cup and saucer down in front of Joona.

'Thanks.'

'I guess I'm also not really sure why you're here,' Hugo continues, though he closes his chemistry book.

'We consider you a witness, even though you've said you don't remember anything.'

'I don't.'

'I'm assuming your solicitor took you through what to say before the first interrogation?' Joona begins.

'We talked, yeah.'

'But things changed following the second murder?'

'Yeah.'

'That must have come as quite a relief?'

'I mean, I already knew I was innocent, so . . .' says Hugo.

'Of course.' Joona smiles. 'But ultimately it comes down to you convincing everyone else . . . And in order to do that, it's not unusual for people to fine-tune their story a bit.'

'What are you trying to say?'

'That I've come here so that you – now that you're a witness rather than a suspect – can tell me anything you might have been advised not to share before. Anything that might have made you look suspicious even if you were innocent.'

'I just told the truth,' Hugo says, fiddling with the ring in his lower lip.

'You said that you sleepwalked to the campsite and woke up in the caravan when one of the police officers fired his weapon. That, for you, it was like you jumped from being awake in your bed at home to lying on the bloody floor. In your first interview, you said that you didn't remember anything between those two points, but I think you do.'

'Nope.'

'But sleepwalkers see their surroundings, even though they're not awake. They don't crash into furniture, they're capable of unlocking doors, and so on,' Joona points out.

'That doesn't mean they remember it, though.'

'But you do, don't you?'

'You don't have to answer that,' says Bernard.

'What do you remember?'

'Don't answer that,' Bernard repeats. 'You don't have to—'

'It's fine, Dad,' Hugo snaps. 'I want to help, but I really don't remember. I never do. I think the dreams are too powerful.'

'What dreams?'

'Intense nightmares . . . They're the reason I sometimes wake up in weird places.'

'Do you remember the dreams afterwards?' Joona asks as he takes a sip of his coffee.

'Bits and pieces,' Hugo replies with a shrug.

'So do you remember any bits and pieces from the night you woke up in the caravan?'

'No idea, but it's always the same thing: I have to get away. None of it means anything.'

'But what did you see when you woke up?'

'I was fucking terrified. They were screaming at me, and there was blood everywhere.'

'That's your immediate impression, but what did you really *see*?' Joona presses him.

'What do you mean?'

'There was a lot of blood in that room, but it wasn't *everywhere*.'

'No, OK,' Hugo says wearily.

'I'm looking for specific observations. Details.'

'I've told you what I remember.'

'We often register more than we realise.'

'Do we?' Hugo sighs.

He gets up, takes a glass from the cabinet above the counter and stands with his back to the room as he runs the cold tap.

'You're wearing a silver ring in one nostril, another in your lower lip, and six earrings. The one in your left lobe is a garnet heart. Your dad doesn't like it when you bite your nails, but you do it anyway, whenever you're stressed. You broke your collarbone as a child, and you're wearing a washed-out T-shirt from *Actes Sud*, which is a French publisher, but—'

'I didn't know that,' Hugo says, turning off the tap once his glass is full.

'You also wear designer clothes, like your Tom Ford cardigan, but you don't take care of them. There's a thread hanging from the left cuff, by the way. You should cut it off and—'

'Bravo,' Hugo interjects, turning to face Joona. 'Except I've never broken a bone.'

'Sometimes I'm wrong ... but not about the fact that you have bandages on three fingers and a fresh bruise on your cheek,' Joona continues, looking up at him.

'No,' Hugo says as he sits down.

'What happened?'

'I sleepwalked again last night. Tried to open a door using a knife and ended up cutting myself.'

'Here?' Joona asks, though he already knows the answer.

'No, at my girlfriend's place,' Hugo replies as he takes a sip of water.

'Go on.'

'So . . .' He sighs. 'I dreamed I was being chased and was about to jump off her balcony when she caught me.'

'You dreamed that you had to escape from her apartment?'

'No, I'm always at home in my nightmares. It doesn't matter where I actually am. Someone is trying to kill my family, and sometimes I manage to get Mum and Dad out, but I usually fail.'

'You remember trying to jump off your girlfriend's balcony?' says Joona.

'No, that's just what she told me once I'd calmed down.'

'But before you calmed down, you remembered details from the campsite?'

'Who told you that?' Hugo takes his hand from the glass and presses his cool fingertips to his eyelids.

'What did you remember?'

'I've forgotten,' the teenager mumbles.

'Do your nightmares always take place in the same location here?' asks Joona.

'No. Sometimes they start in my room, or in my old bedroom upstairs. Sometimes I'm running down the stairs, sometimes down the hall. Sometimes I'm in the basement. I think they're more connected to Mum and Dad than the place itself.'

'Could you show me your old room?'

'There's nothing to see . . .'

'It'll be quick.'

'Fine.' Hugo sighs and gets up.

Joona's real reason for wanting to see the old bedroom is that it gives him a natural excuse to ask to see the teenager's current room.

They leave the kitchen and walk through a handsome library filled with tall bookcases, armchairs and a large fireplace.

'I've been asking about your nightmares because I think they're obscuring your real memories from the caravan,' Joona explains as they climb the creaking staircase.

'I don't have any memories.'

When they reach the landing, they turn left, through a door with a window in it and into a small room. The walls are pale blue, and the navy blind is dotted with stars. There is a narrow bed and a set of shelves full of children's books and plastic trophies. The floor is cluttered with moving boxes and games like Monopoly and Scrabble. A folded chessboard has been shoved into a bag, and there are cables, games consoles, Lego sets and a Super Mario Bros skateboard.

'So you sometimes dream about this room?' Joona asks as he looks around.

'Yup,' Hugo replies, scratching his tattooed forearms.

'And does it look like this, or how it was when you were younger?'

'Like when I was younger.'

'Could you describe it for me?'

'Listen . . . I really don't feel like we're getting anywhere here,' says Hugo. 'And I seriously need to study.'

'I know,' Joona replies, holding his gaze. 'But I'd like to remind you that we've got a sadistic killer on the loose, and that's no small thing.'

When he turns back out into the hallway, Joona gets a glimpse of another bedroom straight ahead. He can see a large bed with a grey quilted throw, a floor lamp with a grey snakeskin shade and a grey lambskin armchair.

Joona and Hugo make their way down the stairs, turning right and passing the narrow entrance to reach another hallway with white panelling.

On the wall to the left, there is an old Chinese abacus.

Joona gets a brief look at the lounge at the end of the hall before Hugo shows him into his current bedroom.

'You're in a nightmare when you sleepwalk,' he says. 'That's what drives you, but you're also seeing reality – furniture, people . . . Yet when you wake up in the morning, you don't remember anything you really saw.'

'Pretty much, yeah.'

'But if you're woken while you're sleepwalking, you're still in contact with the part of your brain responsible for storing real visual impressions.'

'Maybe. I dunno. How would I know?'

The large bed is unmade, and there are books and pieces of clothing strewn across the floor. The round lampshade sways softly in the draught.

An armchair has been pushed up against a door that doesn't seem to be in use.

On the wall above the desk, there is a framed page from the manuscript of Cormac McCarthy's *Blood Meridian*, complete with clear imprints from the typewriter.

In the half-open desk drawer, there is a pack of condoms, a paleblue handkerchief and a black plastic vape. On a spiral-bound notepad, Joona notices the words, 'I can never catch up with her in my dreams, but in reality, I'm getting close.'

18

A cluster of bare trees races by on the right-hand side of the road, followed almost immediately by a small, frostbitten churchyard.

After leaving school for the day, Hugo caught the commuter train to Uppsala, where he changed to the number eight bus.

He is listening to music and gazing out of the window as the road winds its way past dark fields, barns and corrugated steel buildings, but when the bus approaches Ultuna, he presses the stop button, gets up and moves towards the middle doors.

He gets off outside the old specialist rehabilitation unit.

The air is raw and damp on his face.

With his rucksack slung over one shoulder, he starts walking along Dag Hammarskjölds väg.

Hugo remembers his father driving him out here when he was younger, explaining that Ultuna had once been a cult site for the Old Norse god Ull.

As ever, he turns off onto the narrow road past the pumping station.

For the past fifteen years, the psychologist and neurologist Lars Grind has been running a sleep research project here in collaboration with the university hospital, treating and studying various parasomnias with a particular focus on somnambulism.

Hugo was admitted to the specialist rehabilitation unit when he was six, and was later moved over to the newly established Sleep Science Lab.

He remembers next to nothing from his first meeting with Lars Grind, nor any of the nights of careful monitoring while the doctors tried out various medications.

Lars started giving Hugo a lift to and from the clinic, and eventually became good friends with his parents, coming over for dinner at their house and buying him Christmas presents.

The modern industrial building housing the most advanced sleep research facility in the country is on the other side of a high fence. Signs warning passersby about alarms, security firms and video surveillance shake in the wind.

The metal roof is currently the same shade of white as the overcast sky.

Hugo pauses in front of the gates, reports his arrival over the video intercom and waits to be buzzed in.

He makes his way into the building through the main entrance, saying hello to the woman behind reception before continuing down the hallway to Lars Grind's office.

The pink WILLKOMMEN sign is already illuminated, but Hugo still knocks before opening the door and stepping inside.

'*Bienvenue*, welcome,' the doctor says with a smile as he looks up from his computer.

'Thanks.'

Lars Grind is a short man with a wiry frame and a bald head. He has a thin face, with delicate features and pronounced cheekbones.

He gets up from his desk, and the skin around his eyes creases as he shakes Hugo's hand.

'Sit, sit,' he says.

Lars doesn't really seem to have aged since he first met him, Hugo thinks. His eyes might be a little wearier and the shiny patch on his shaved head a little bigger, but he still dresses the same and still wears aftershave that smells like wet goat.

'You might not have had a confirmation, but you'll graduate this spring,' Lars says with a smile.

'That's the plan,' Hugo replies as he sits down.

'Good.'

Lars knew Claire, and for a time Hugo occasionally tried to ask about her. In the end, however, he stopped because the doctor always looked so pained as he tried to think of something positive to say.

That might also be why Hugo avoids having dinner with him as much as he can without seeming rude.

'Shouldn't you have uncovered all the mysteries of sleep by now?' he asks.

'Ah, ha ha. Yes, you might think so, but we've probably a way to go yet,' says Lars, holding up his thumb and index finger. 'In all seriousness, though, we've just started trialling a few alternative medicines alongside melatonin and clonazepam.'

'Like what?'

'Microdoses of tramadol.'

'Unexpected.'

'Not really, but it took a little while to get it approved,' Lars explains, fiddling with a small carved monkey wearing a Santa hat.

'I was actually going to ask if we could just up my melatonin a bit and see how it goes at home,' says Hugo.

Lars puts the monkey to one side.

'I know where you're coming from, but you're already on a fairly high dose,' he replies, straightening the signet ring on his little finger. 'I'd like to do a thorough assessment of you today, including neurological status, before we start trying to get the right medications at the right level.'

'So I'm stuck here?' Hugo jokes, though a real sense of unease has crept up on him.

'You'll be home in time for Christmas,' Lars assures him with a wry smile.

'If only in my dreams,' Hugo mumbles, running his fingers through his long hair.

'No, really . . . You'll be home by then, because I'm coming over for oysters on the twenty-sixth,' Lars says, opening a document on his computer.

'Right.'

'So, tell me. I hear you've had a few incidents lately?'

'You could say that.'

Lars gives him a long, searching look.

'This murder business was rather horrible,' he says with a dark undertone in his voice.

'Insane.'

'How have you been? Are you sleepwalking every night at the moment?'

'Pretty much, yeah.'

'And each time is advanced?' Lars asks, clasping his thin hands on the desk in front of him.

'I've managed to get out – except when I was locked up.'

'OK, we'll start with the usual questionnaire,' says Lars. 'And tomorrow we can get going with the in-depth interviews and self-assessment.'

The printer starts to whirr, and when it stops, thirty seconds later, Lars gets up, reaches for the sheets of paper and staples them together. The doctor has a dark bruise on his throat, Hugo notices. Almost as though someone has tried to choke him with one hand.

* * *

With Lars Grind's printed questionnaire in his hand, Hugo strolls through to the spacious dayroom with its knotted pine tables and chairs. A heavyset man with a shaved head is sitting with his back to him, reading a book in the glow of a pink table lamp.

Hugo tiptoes over to him.

The man's orange fleece is snug over his broad shoulders, and he has a roll of fat at the top of his neck.

Hugo pauses beside him, taking in his shaved head, bushy black beard, thick forearms and short, stubby fingers.

'Boo!' he says.

The man's chair creaks as he slowly turns around and looks up with a frown.

'Hugo? What the hell are you doing in Uppsala?'

'No idea, I woke up here.'

The man laughs and gets up to embrace Hugo, but he is so tall that his arms hug the air above the teenager's head.

'Where the fuck did he go?' Bo mumbles, as he always does, before bending down to give him a proper hug.

Bo Balderson is from Kiruna, in the far north of Sweden. He works in the forestry industry and, like Hugo, is both a sleepwalker and one of Lars Grind's longstanding patients.

He has a white plaster on the bridge of his nose and a bandage around one wrist. On the table beside his coursebook in constitutional law, there is an empty coffee cup.

When they last met at the Sleep Lab, Bo had made the journey south after being handed a suspended sentence for assault. He had left the construction site barracks in his sleep one night and seriously injured the foreman.

Bo's solicitor lodged an appeal on the grounds of lack of intent, citing a 2016 Prosecution Authority report on somnambulism that determined that a person could commit both violent and sexual acts while sleepwalking.

'How long have you been here?' Hugo asks.

'Almost two weeks.'

'Is Rakia still around?'

Bo squints at Hugo. 'You've got a thing for her, huh?'

'Bien sûr,' Hugo replies disarmingly.

'Don't you?'

'Yeah.' He grins.

Bo laughs. 'She's still here. It's the same as ever. New PhD students, new administrators, but otherwise it's like time stood still . . .'

Hugo takes a seat opposite Bo and turns his attention to the questionnaire. He flicks past the information section and the rules of conduct, enters the wi-fi password on his phone and starts answering the questions. He crosses box after box, lying about his drug use and alcohol intake but otherwise sticking to the truth.

'We the only ones here?' he asks after a few minutes.

'Nah, man, the place is packed. There's a cute girl who screams so loud I nearly shat myself, and a little ghost kid too . . . A nerdy guy in a sailor suit.'

19

Three hours later, Hugo has given all the required samples, undergone the usual examinations and eaten dinner in the dining hall.

He is messing about on his phone in the dayroom when Lars Grind comes in and asks him to follow him.

'I thought we'd put you in the suite,' Lars says as they walk down the corridor. 'You've stayed there before, haven't you?'

'Yeah, once. Who am I shar—'

'No, no, it's all yours this time.'

'Phew, thanks.' Hugo smiles.

'But I do need to ask you one small favour. Don't go into the other bedroom, please. It's important. Don't even open the door. It's to do with an independent research project.'

'OK.'

The doctor pauses once they reach the suite. 'I'm heading home now, but if you need anything you can always call me.'

'Night,' says Hugo.

He opens the door and steps into the dark hallway, accidentally knocking the lock button on the wall before managing to find the light switch. There is a click as the door locks. Hugo heads straight through to the bedroom, dumps his rucksack on the bed and then pops his head into the lounge area. The pale-grey curtains are drawn, and there is a burgundy blanket folded neatly on the sofa. On the low coffee table, the staff have left a bowl of red apples. A TV has been mounted on one wall, and there is also a bookshelf with soft lighting and glass doors.

A dull anxiety stirs in the pit of Hugo's stomach. He really doesn't want to be here. Sleepwalking has already taken up far too much of his life. He wants to move in with Olga, travel to Canada with her and reconnect with his mother.

He knows that if he opens the curtains in his suite, all he will see is a photograph of the Swedish countryside. The artificial light behind it is on a timer, programmed to change in line with the real shifts of night and day.

Hugo goes through to the kitchenette, where there is a small drop-leaf table and two chairs, a toaster and a set of blunt knives.

When he was younger, Hugo found Lars Grind's interest in him flattering – funny, even – but since the doctor moved to Uppsala, he feels more like an eager relative who is much too keen to stay in touch.

Hugo continues down the hallway, past the bathroom, and stops in front of the closed door to the second bedroom.

He isn't sure what he is doing.

Lars asked him not to open the door, but he feels like he needs to see what is on the other side.

Someone has carved a downward arrow into the varnished wood.

Hugo reaches out and turns the handle. It isn't locked.

He opens the door and peers into the darkness on the other side.

Cool air floods towards him, carrying the scent of fabric and dust.

He blinks and waits for his eyes to adjust, and little by little the room starts to emerge.

It looks exactly how he remembers it: identical to his.

Around three metres beyond the threshold, however, there is something on the floor. It looks like a long line of pebbles.

Steadying himself against the doorframe, Hugo leans forward and realises that they are pistachio shells.

Someone has laid out perhaps two hundred pistachio shells in a straight line between the wardrobe and the wall.

Hugo takes a step back and shudders. Maybe he should call Lars, he thinks. Admit to accidentally opening the door.

He glances over to the wardrobe, convinced that he has just seen a movement inside the slatted door, when he hears a loud knock behind him.

Hugo's hand is shaking as he carefully closes the door.

Whoever is outside knocks again.

He hurries back into the hallway, presses the lock button, opens the door and feels a rush of warmth and relief when he sees Rakia standing outside. The Tunisian research nurse is in her fifties, with tinted glasses, shoulder-length hair, heavy eyeliner and red lipstick.

'Rakia,' he says with a smile. 'Come in, come in.'

'I need to hook you up to some sensors,' she says neutrally, pushing a trolley of wireless polysomnography equipment into the room.

'I was starting to wonder when you'd drop by to say hi.'

She doesn't reply, just follows him through to the bedroom, parks the trolley beside the bed and stamps on the wheel lock.

'I've checked your stats, and everything looks normal,' she says without meeting his eyes.

'OK, great.' Hugo takes a seat on the edge of the bed.

'Your P-ASAT level is a bit high, which we'll look into, but it shouldn't affect anything else.'

'How're things?'

'Fine . . . thanks for asking.'

Rakia works quickly to attach a number of sensors: ten to measure brain activity and six his heart rate, two to track his eye movements and four to detect any muscle tension or leg twitches.

Once she has gone, and the electric lock has clicked behind her, Hugo gets out of bed. The sensor pads tug at his skin with every movement.

He doesn't feel particularly tired, but he grabs his toiletry bag and goes through to the bathroom to wash his face and brush his teeth. He then fills a glass with water in the kitchen and returns to the bedroom. After putting the glass down on the nightstand, he gets into bed and writes a text message in the warm glow of the reading lamp.

Maybe I could sleepwalk all the way to Canada, save having to pay for my plane ticket.

Olga replies immediately, with a 'haha'. Hugo sees that his father has sent several messages, but he doesn't have time to reply before Olga calls.

'I'll help you if you can't save enough,' she says.

'If my grades are OK this term then I'm going to get a weekend job at Starbucks . . . earn me some dough, yo.'

Olga laughs. 'Really, Hugo? *Dough?*'

'What?'

'You're just so Swedish,' she says cheerfully. 'You're rich, live in a great house, go to a good school.'

'Busted.'

'Yup.'

'Guess I might as well admit that I'm thinking of swallowing my pride and asking Dad—'

'You're breaking up a little.'

'He has some money saved in case I ever want to study abroad. No idea how much,' Hugo continues. 'The man's clueless when it comes to that sort of stuff. Sometimes he buys shares, sometimes he opens investment accounts . . . He's got gold in his office, dollars and euros. Just last week, he was talking about buying a bit of forest outside of Gävle.'

'Are you planning to tell him . . . th y ar goi . . . try to find your mum?'

'Might as well tell him the truth, yeah.'

'What?'

The line crackles.

'How lon . . . yo goi . . . to be there? I miss you already,' she says.

'Lars wants me to stay for a week, but I'm going to try to get out sooner.'

'I . . . I thi . . .'

The call drops.

Hugo notices the low hum of the ventilation system, followed by what sounds like a dog barking through the walls.

Olga rings him back after a few minutes.

'The line's really bad,' he says.

'Can you hear me now?'

'Yeah. I've been thinking about what you said about Canada. That . . . that even if we don't find Mum, at least I tried . . . I really believe that. I can't just sit around, waiting forever.'

'I got a bonus, so I paid it into the account.'

'You shouldn't do that until I've caught up,' he says.

'Stop, it doesn't matter. Let me do it my way. You've got your dad, but I have to work.'

The line crackles, and when Olga next speaks her voice sounds much closer.

'Are you allowed visitors there?' she asks in a flirty tone.

'All these electrodes *are* pretty sexy.'

'I'm . . . s . . . re the . . . are,' she stutters before the call drops again.

A few seconds later, a text message arrives. *Night night, I love you, dream about me,* followed by three red hearts.

Hugo puts his phone down beside the water glass and realises that his eyelids are heavy. Maybe he is tired after all, he thinks, reaching up to turn out the lamp.

The soft glow from the amber nightlights emerges in the darkness, accompanied by the small LEDs on the cameras.

The first couple of nights at the lab always feel a bit strange, trying to sleep while covered in sensors, knowing that he is constantly being monitored.

Hugo closes his eyes and thinks about the fact that he hasn't seen any of the other patients yet. He did hear a soft, monotone voice in the corridor while he was eating dinner, and guesses it must have been the boy Bo mentioned.

His thoughts turn to Rakia's chilly, almost hostile attitude earlier, and he wonders whether he just imagined the special bond they had when he was younger, desperate for a mother figure. He lies still, listening to the quiet clicking sounds. He knows they are coming from

117

the cameras and motion sensors, but in his mind's eye he sees someone dropping pistachio shells in a neat line on the floor. Hugo is just about to drift off to sleep when something jolts him wide awake. At first, he isn't sure what it was. His heart is beating so hard that he can hear his blood pounding.

It was a scream.

A terrible howl from a woman cut through the walls, almost as though she were standing by the foot of his bed in the darkness.

20

The island of Laxön in the middle of the powerful Dal River is connected to both shores by four narrow bridges. At one point in time, the Svea Engineer Corps was garrisoned there, and a number of the former military buildings now form part of Älvkarleby Youth Hostel.

In order to guarantee a bit of privacy, Pontus Bandling has booked the entire Officers' Villa for the night, despite the fact that he and Kimberly will likely only use the bathroom and main bedroom.

The warm glow of the fire in the tiled stove flickers over the double bed, and the sweet aroma of burning birch drifts through the air.

The hostel staff have gone home for the evening, leaving Pontus with instructions to drop the key into the letterbox if he checks out before they return tomorrow morning.

He knows he isn't the only guest; someone else is staying in the next building over. He caught a glimpse of a slim figure in one of the windows when he went out to the car to grab his bag earlier.

Delicate snowflakes had settled like a veil over his windscreen.

Pontus shoves a red Christmas tablecloth and two cushions he knows Kimberly will hate into the empty wardrobe, pours himself a glass of the whisky he brought with him and sits down in the armchair to wait.

His phone pings with a message from Kimberly. She writes that she will be with him in ten minutes, and he replies to say that he has left the door unlocked.

The fire crackles, and the wind whistles in the chimney.

Above the brass hatch on the stove, the white tiles are sooty.

Pontus lifts his glass to his lips. From the corner of one eye, he notices a movement, and he turns towards the window.

It is almost pitch black outside, but he can make out the frosty white branches of a bush beyond his reflection.

He sips from his glass, taking in the scuffed furniture, the rag rug on the worn floorboards and the strange floral wallpaper.

Through the open doorway, he can see into the bathroom, with its exposed pipework, gold-framed mirror, discoloured grout and folding shower screen.

He hears what sounds like someone opening the cabinets in the kitchen, but assumes it is just the heat causing the old studs in the walls to expand.

Outside, a car approaches and comes to a halt. The doors open, and a low male voice asks if she would like him to wait. Pontus doesn't catch Kimberly's reply, but he hears the man say that he can be back within fifteen minutes if she calls.

The flames surge as the front door opens, followed by the confident click of heels on the floorboards.

Kimberly pauses in the bedroom doorway, shakes her white sheep-skin coat back from her shoulders and lets it drop to the floor.

Her hair is glossy and voluminous, and she is wearing red lipstick and a short silver sequin dress. Her legs are bare.

'Did you start the party without me?' she asks.

'No, I've been waiting for you,' he replies with a smile. 'I lit a fire and took—'

'I can see that,' she cuts him off, moving forward.

Kimberly takes in the room, turning around and letting her arms swing. 'What a shithole,' she mumbles before meeting his eye, a contemptuous look on her face.

'Always so beautiful,' he says.

'Hmm,' she mutters as she moves over to the window.

'Do you want anything?'

'What kind of fucking question is that?'

'I brought some great red wine, malt whisky . . .'

'You're kidding, right? I've got four hours before I have to go,' she says, kicking off her silver pumps.

'I'm just trying to be polite.'

'You're just a prude,' she says, turning to him again.

'That's not true. I'm not – not with you.'

'With your sweet little wife, though. With her jewellery that's so expensive it looks fake, and all the botox, spandex and Wolford tights.'

'OK,' he says with a calm smile, setting the glass down on the table.

'I don't know why you don't just fuck some life into her.'

'We have sex. You know that.'

'You make love.'

'We—'

'You make love,' she cuts him off. 'It's not the same thing.'

'You seem to know everything.'

'I just think it's funny to hear you defend her before you tear my knickers off.'

'You know I'm addicted to you,' he says, getting up.

'Say that again.'

'You're like a drug, Kimberly.'

She laughs contentedly and pulls the zipper of her dress down from her armpit to her hip. One of the silver sequins drops to the floor.

'Like coke?' she asks.

'Better.'

'Crystal meth?'

'I don't know.'

'Crystal meth,' she repeats with a smile.

'Now?'

She raises an eyebrow, and he goes to fetch a brown leather case from his bag. He puts it on the table, sits down and takes out an old shaving mirror with a slim metal frame.

Out of nowhere, the feeling that someone is watching him makes him glance over to the window again. The glass is dark, but there could easily be someone standing just outside, looking in at them.

He should draw the curtains, he thinks as the image of someone drawing a sad face in the frost on the window takes over his thoughts.

'The clock's ticking,' she mutters impatiently.

Pontus breaks the seal on a small glass tube, takes out the cork and taps the contents onto the mirror.

A crystalline powder the colour of wax.

He halves the pile using a tarot card, shapes it into two long lines, then gets up and hands a narrow silver tube to Kimberly.

Holding her hair back with one hand, she bends down, snorts her line and wipes her nose. Breathing heavily, she lets out a loud groan, staggers back, slumps onto the bed and curls up in the foetal position.

'You OK?'

'Fuck, fuck,' she pants.

'Kimberly?'

'What?'

'Are you OK?'

'Good,' she says with a smile.

Pontus takes the tube from her hand and moves back over to the mirror on the table. He bends down over the powdered methamphetamine and inhales.

As he straightens up, he feels a burning sensation in his nose and sinuses. The powder leaves a bitter taste at the back of his throat, and his eyes have just started to water when the drug kicks in with frightening force.

'Christ,' he hears himself mutter.

The hairs on the back of his neck are standing on end, and a lust-filled electricity floods through his veins as a veil of crushed ice passes over him.

Pontus gropes for something to steady himself against, slumps onto the bed and falls to the floor. His heart is racing, and he is breathing rapidly through his half-open mouth.

The first wave of euphoria is overwhelming, all-encompassing.

'Yeah? You OK?' she asks.

'Almost, just give me a second,' he says, trying to blink away the blindness.

From the almost unbearable peak, he slowly sinks to a plateau where he knows he might stay for hours.

Kimberly throws her dress to the floor and stands in front of him, legs apart, in her sheer black underwear.

Pontus gets up on trembling legs, his mind crystal clear and flash-lit from the inside. He unbuttons his shirt as he circles her with his eyes fixed on her crotch.

'Come on, then,' she says, backing up towards the bed. 'Come on, for God's sake.'

He pushes her onto the covers, pinning her down with one hand between her breasts as he yanks off her knickers with the other.

They have been married for twenty years, and have a twenty-two-year-old daughter.

Pontus is the vice chancellor of Dalarna University, and spends four days a week in Falun before returning home to Uppsala, where they have a grand apartment on the top floor of a late nineteenth-century building.

Her real name is Caroline Bandling, and she is the managing director of BC Group, a financial advisory and management company. Kimberly is simply her persona when she meets her husband at basic motels and hostels somewhere between Falun and Uppsala.

21

Under influence of the methamphetamine, the couple have been having sex non-stop for four hours when Kimberly's phone pings for the second time with a reminder about a video call with a major investor in California at 03.45.

The fire has died down in the stove.

They haven't had anything to eat or drink, and have barely exchanged a single word, but she has had more than twenty orgasms, Pontus five or six.

Kimberly turns on the light and takes a quick shower before getting dressed – not bothering with her underwear – and calling her driver.

Pontus hears that her voice is huskier than usual.

Her eyes are bloodshot, and she is busy touching up her lipstick in front of the mirror when he moves over to her, pulls up her dress and enters her from behind.

They return to the bedroom and continue to have sex for another forty minutes before a third alert on her phone makes them stop.

Kimberly gets out of bed, sits down on the floor and pulls on her pumps. She then stands up on unsteady legs and leaves the room without even glancing back at him.

Pontus remains where he is, heart pounding. He hears the front door slam, followed by the sound of her footsteps and the chauffeur's polite voice. The car doors open and close, and the gravel crunches beneath its tyres as it pulls away.

He should take two milligrams of Xanax and ten of zopiclone, he thinks, so that he can try to get a bit of sleep. His alarm is set to go off at seven, and then he will have to eat a quick breakfast, drive back to Falun and head straight to work.

He hears the same rattling sound from the kitchen again, as though someone has just opened the cutlery drawer.

It is quarter past two in the morning, and he is wide awake. He could easily have continued having sex; his erection is still rock hard, his muscles quivering.

Pontus raises his right hand and tentatively examines his forehead. The skin feels tender, and he suspects he will end up with a bruise. He had been doing Kimberly from behind when she cried out in orgasm and slumped forward. He collapsed with her and cracked his head against the headboard.

Four crazy hours.

The drug turbocharges the limbic system, causing the heart to race, endorphins to pump, and an intense longing to throb in his loins.

The increased blood flow made Kimberly's skin hot to the touch and turned her lips a deeper shade of pink.

Pontus closes his eyes as fragmented memories from the past few hours wash over him.

The goosebumps on the waxed skin of her mons Venus when she parted her thighs.

The bedside lamp that toppled over and hit the floor with a strange metallic clang.

The faded tattoo on his bulging stomach, glistening with sweat.

Her sucking on his fingers, pushing them inside herself, swollen and wet.

Him crawling between her legs and licking her. Seeing her tense her thighs and buttocks before groaning loudly.

'Keep going . . .'

Her straddling him, a bead of sweat dripping from the tip of her chin. Him squeezing her breasts with both hands, pushing them together and seeing the fine lines on her chest stretch up to her throat.

She was completely electric.

Some five or six times, he had flipped her over onto her back, pumping harder as she bucked her hips towards him.

'Don't stop, don't stop . . .'

Those are the words she repeats most frequently on nights like this, but he would never stop; he is always utterly fixated on his own pleasure. An urge beyond all reason. A chemical rutting period, as she likes to call it.

He pulled out and ejaculated onto her stomach. His seed trickled along the scar from her caesarean section when she reached over to turn off the first alarm, then she rolled onto her front and raised her backside towards him.

Pontus is lying quietly in bed, but he is still high and can't stop thinking about sex. He also knows that Kimberly has probably started masturbating in their Mercedes-Maybach.

He pictures her with her legs spread in the backseat, caressing herself, pushing three fingers inside and failing to hide her orgasm from the driver.

Deep down, however, he knows that probably isn't the case. He knows that Kimberly will have already begun to morph back into his wife in the car. To Caroline, who – with a self-deprecating laugh – would say that a crystal-clear mind and a throbbing clitoris are the ultimate combination when doing business.

Pontus gets out of bed and checks his phone. He writes a quick text to Kimberly, asking her to come back, but she replies with nothing but a heart.

He notices that the veins on his arms are protruding as he picks up his clothes, turns them right side out and gets dressed with trembling hands.

His coat is hanging in the wardrobe, and he pulls it on, goes through to the porch, pushes his feet into his boots and opens the yellow double doors to the veranda.

The air outside is wonderfully cold.

He makes his way down the steps to the frosty lawn.

Tiny snowflakes swirl through the air.

The light from his room spills out onto the green garden furniture, and he takes a step back and turns around. From where he is standing, he has a clear view of the bed, the pillows, the messy sheets and the damp mattress. The minute the drugs took effect, he forgot all about drawing the curtains.

Pontus pulls his coat tighter, ties the belt around his waist and starts walking north along the narrow road.

The darkness between the trees is impenetrable.

Clouds of white breath hang in the air around his mouth.

He feels invigorated and full of energy, as though he could walk the eighty or so kilometres back to Uppsala and continue having sex with his wife once her meeting is over.

Pontus makes his way out onto a narrow wooden bridge and sees the full river surging around the bend with silent intensity.

The snowflakes dancing in the wind vanish as they hit the dark surface.

He becomes conscious of his own heavy footsteps, and his mind drifts back to the story of the Three Billy Goats Gruff his father used to read to him.

'I've got two big spears, and I'll poke your eyeballs out!'

He reaches the other side and continues towards a large, dark wooden building.

Pontus realises that he forgot to check whether anyone had actually drawn a sad face in the frost on their window.

Pausing beneath a streetlamp, he notices that his fingertips have turned grey in the cold air. He shoves his hands into his pockets and decides that it probably isn't the best idea to walk to Uppsala after all.

The snow has started coming down more heavily now, and he has to blink frequently to clear the flakes from his eyes.

Pontus turns right onto Brobacken, and the roar from the main channel of the river grows louder the closer he gets.

As he makes his way out across Karl XIII's bridge, the water is almost deafening.

The streetlamps in front of him look like snowy orbs of light, hovering silently in the darkness.

On the other bank, the old power station looms so tall that it merges with the black sky and the falling snow.

The river is unusually high, frothing as it hits the breakwater. The inky backwater swirls in anxious circles below the turbines.

Pontus can no longer hear his own footsteps, and he flinches as a car passes close by.

As the glow of the rear-view lights disappears between the trees, he thinks he catches a glimpse of someone standing at the far end of the bridge.

At first, he decides it is probably just the swirling snow thrown up by the car, but it really is a person.

I must still be dreaming, Pontus thinks, pausing in the middle of the river. He uses his hand to shield his eyes, but the figure is now nowhere to be seen.

Perhaps he was mistaken.

He lowers his eyes and sees the snowflakes settling on the yellow lichen growing on the wooden railing. He sees his dirty black boots and the gaps between the planks, the water surging down below.

Going out in this state was a bad idea, he thinks. He should head back to the villa and wait for the comedown.

Snow blows across the bridge at a right angle to the churning water, as though he is standing at the centre of a swirling white cross

Pontus squints over to the far side again.

This time, there is no doubt about it: there really is a slim figure standing right by the bridgehead.

What are they waiting for?

It is impossible to see their face in the haze.

Pontus decides he should keep walking, possibly even say hello, but that he would rather not stop to chat.

He reminds himself to act normally if they do exchange a few words, that he can't forget that he is likely radiating a kind of manic energy, his pupils dilated.

Despite that, something makes him hold back, and he can't bring himself to start walking. Instead, his eyes start compulsively scanning the driving snow again.

The figure is a little closer now, even though they seem to be standing perfectly still.

Pontus feels a childish fear of the dark take hold of him, and he lifts his hand to shield his eyes again.

As he does so, the figure starts walking towards him, stooped over with a hood or shawl covering their head. They are getting closer to the next lamppost, causing the snow on the ground to swirl up behind them like some sort of train.

Pontus sees something gleam in their hand, and wonders if they are using some sort of walking stick.

Their movements do seem disjointed, halting.

The object in their hand catches the light again, giving Pontus time to catch the flash of an axe blade.

He feels a sting of anxiety in the pit of his stomach.

This is surreal, he thinks. The urge to turn and run takes hold of him, but he decides against it, knows that the drugs can cause rash behaviour.

It's probably just a forest ranger out clearing fallen branches from the road.

And yet ... There is something off about the person up ahead, something that just doesn't feel right.

The snow and the shifting light from the streetlamps make it look as though they are approaching at a speed that seems out of sync with their movements.

Pontus realises that he can't simply stand still, waiting for them to reach him, and he hears a rattling sound, like small pebbles in a bag.

He turns around, his mouth suddenly bone dry, and decides to walk away as fast as he can without breaking into a run.

He takes a step forward, but something immediately yanks him back. Glancing down, he realises that the belt of his coat is caught on the railing.

The slender figure has almost reached him now, their heavy footsteps thudding against the boards.

Pontus tugs at the belt, but it is well and truly stuck, and he has just started to struggle out of his coat when the broadside of the axe hits him square on the cheek.

His head snaps to the side, and his left knee gives way.

His vision goes dark and he falls blindly, somehow managing to break his fall with his hands. He scrambles up onto all fours and spits out his broken teeth.

A string of bloody saliva dangles from his mouth.

There must be some sort of misunderstanding, he thinks. He just needs to get to his feet and run.

Right then, for some reason, he remembers the tiny, tame bees from his childhood.

'God,' he pants, straightening up.

The roar of the river comes surging back to him, as loud as a freight train. It is dark and it is snowing, and he feels confused, can't immediately remember where he is.

Pontus reaches up and touches his face, taking in his sticky hair and the bump on his cheek. He feels a searing pain, and he gasps.

'I've got money,' he slurs, taking out his phone. 'I can make a transfer. Just give me your account number and . . .'

Swallowing blood, he dials 112 and puts his phone down on the railing. He is just about to explain that there is a limit of two million on his account when the figure twists towards him again.

Their shoulders move jerkily, with a dry, rattling sound.

The blow knocks Pontus to one side. The blade of the axe has struck his upper arm, and the pain is immediate and unbearable.

'What the hell, you hit me!' he cries out in shock.

He reaches for the wound with his other hand, groaning in pain. He can feel hot blood and soft flesh, smooth edges and broken bone. This can't be happening. He is about to pass out, needs to lie down. His arm has been completely severed, and the only thing holding it in place is a scrap of fabric from the inside of his shirt and coat sleeves.

'Listen,' he says between shallow breaths. 'Listen, I don't know what—'

The next stroke hits him in almost exactly the same place, knocking the wind out of him and causing him to stagger to the side and crash against the railing.

His arm drops lower, now hanging by his thigh.

The pain is explosive, like hugging a red-hot poker. Impossible to let go, no matter how much it hurts.

Pontus is pulled along with the blade as the person yanks it back, but he remains on his feet.

He splutters and sees the axe swinging through the air again. The sharp blade is getting closer to his face, but for some reason he finds himself thinking about the bees gathering nectar from the heather.

They were early bumblebees. A tiny species, no bigger than a pea.

As his head is severed from his body, he remembers the way he used to tame the little bees by cupping his hands around them. The shockwave meant they were unable to fly for a few minutes, and they would crawl over his skin as though they felt some sort of affection for him. As though they actually wanted to stay.

22

Joona and his team from the NCU met with the Prosecution Authority this morning, to take them through the current state of the investigation.

They have spoken to the family of the second victim, to his friends, colleagues, fellow conference delegates and hotel staff.

Test results, autopsy reports and forensic analyses continue to flood in, but as yet they haven't made any breakthroughs.

Two targeted victims and one dead witness.

There are no obvious links between the three, which led Joona to say what no one wanted to hear:

'We'll have a new victim on our hands soon.'

He is now alone in the investigation room, studying the photographs on the wall and thinking about the similarities and differences between the two primary murders.

Both were married middle-class men with children.

Josef Lindgren's body parts were scattered between different rooms in the caravan, while Nils Nordlund was found on his knees in the water with his head on the ice in front of him.

The first victim had repeatedly visited free porn sites online, and had on three occasions posted in a thread about buying sex on Flashback, where someone had recommended that he turn to the Darknet. He had downloaded and installed a Tor browser in the spring, but there is no way of knowing whether he ever actually used it to procure sex.

No trace of pornography was found on either of the second victim's computers, nor did he use any encryption software. Nils Nordlund's phone is still missing, however, which means that they do not yet have the full picture of his activities. It has likely been destroyed or deactivated, because it no longer seems to be in use.

The door opens and Saga comes into the room. She sits down opposite Joona, leans back and meets his eye.

'I shouldn't be here,' she says quietly.

'But I really need your help.'

'You usually get by just fine without me.'

Joona knows that if he manages to solve this case, it will open up an opportunity to talk about recruitment. Noah will be relieved, hold a press conference, and then they can sit down and talk about the future.

Everyone knows that Saga is the only suitable partner for Joona, and it really would do her good to return to operative duty.

Her beautiful face is so open and troubled. Her eyes have a darkness to them, and there is an air of desperation about her. Her hair, which once came down to her waist and was plaited with colourful ribbon, is now tied back in a severe ponytail.

Saga currently works part-time behind a desk in the Intelligence Unit, but she wants to be a detective with the NCU and has already spoken to an HR manager.

He listened to what she had to say, took notes and then asked whether she was ready for it, whether she thought she would be able to cope.

'Yes,' she replied with a smile.

'I'm afraid I don't agree.'

She very nearly managed to thank him for his time, get up, tuck her chair back beneath the table and calmly leave the room. But instead, four framed diplomas ended up shattering on the floor, and she was left with eight stitches in her knuckles and a disciplinary pay deduction.

'I don't want to get you in trouble,' Joona tells her. 'But it's hardly your fault if you happen to hear someone thinking aloud.'

As she gets up and studies the images, he takes her through everything they know so far.

133

'Makes me think of medieval punishments,' she says once he has finished. 'You know, like being hung, drawn and quartered, disembowelment and . . . what else, breaking on the wheel, mutilation.'

'Punishment,' Joona nods.

'Aggravated capital punishment, I think it was called.'

'If that's the case, what's the crime?'

Joona's work phone starts ringing, and when he sees that the call is from Agneta Nkomo, he tells Saga he needs to take it.

'It was nice being involved, even for a bit,' she says with a smile as she leaves the room.

Joona moves over to the window to answer the call, looking out across the bare trees in the park. He sees a bearded man standing beside one of the rubbish bins with a half-empty bag in his hand, trying to shake frozen Coca-Cola out of a can.

'I just wanted to let you know that Bernard and I have decided to document this period in our lives, with the intention of possibly writing a book about the murders and Hugo's part in the investigation,' Agneta tells him.

'I suspected as much when I saw you at the press conference.'

'We feel that Hugo gives us a unique perspective.'

'Tell him that Hugo agrees, too,' Bernard speaks up in the background.

'I don't know whether you heard that,' she continues. 'But Hugo is on board with the idea, and he's promised to help as much as he can . . . We think we might be able to get him to remember more details.'

'If he does, if he remembers anything else, I'd like you to let me know.'

'Absolutely. I mean, the book is one thing, but we're not going to feel safe until this is all over.'

'I can understand that,' Joona replies, turning back to look at the photographs on the wall.

'Hugo told us that the victim in the caravan had a pale band of skin on his ring finger,' Agneta goes on.

'That's a good first step.'

'But not from when he was sleepwalking,' she points out.

'No, but I wanted to ask—'

'I'm just wondering . . . Sorry to interrupt,' she says. 'I'm wondering if the victim was robbed?'

'The principle of secrecy is pretty strict when it comes to preliminary investigations.'

'I know, but we're not going to publish anything until the case is over.'

'I'm trusting you not to leak any of this to the press,' says Joona. 'But both of the victims seem to have been robbed of their valuables.'

'But that can't be the motive, can it?'

'Who knows?'

Joona returns to his desk, sits down and leans back in the creaky chair.

'I have an idea I'd like to run by you,' he continues. 'You don't have to give me an answer right now, but hear me out at the very least.'

'OK . . .'

'My department often works with a doctor specialising in PTSD and other psychological traumas, and he sometimes uses hypnosis to help victims and witnesses heal and remember.'

'Seriously?'

'Yes.'

'But what if Hugo admitted to something . . . I don't know . . . something illegal while he was under hypnosis?' Bernard asks in the background.

'I understand your concerns, but we wouldn't be able to use any of it against him in a court of law. It has no evidentiary value, but it could lead to a breakthrough in the case.'

'We'll think it over and talk to Hugo,' says Bernard.

'Thank you.'

23

The dark brick villa with the steeply sloping roof is in one of the oldest areas of Gamla Enskede, just south of the Avicii Arena.

The garden is bare and wintry, with a layer of frost on the patio furniture and a rusty hammock tugging on its supports.

Erik Maria Bark is standing in one of the large windows, looking out towards the gravel driveway and the open gates on to the road.

He can feel the heat of the radiator against his thighs and the chill of the cold glass on his face. In the living room, Miles Davis' spellbinding 1960 concert in Stockholm is playing softly over the speakers.

Erik's heart rate quickens as a car pulls up on the street, slowing again as it turns off onto his neighbour's driveway.

He is conscious that he must look like some sort of lonely old grandfather in the window, so he turns around and makes his way through to the kitchen, the varnished oak floor creaking underfoot. Glancing over to the table, he worries that folding the napkins into Christmas trees might have been a step too far.

Erik tries to tell himself that he still looks pretty good for his age, despite the fact that his hair is greying, the bags beneath his eyes are bigger than ever and the laughter lines more prominent.

He is middle-aged now, and has started leaving a trail of reading glasses wherever he goes.

Today, he is wearing a blue shirt made from such thick denim that it is practically a jacket. That's a good thing, he thinks, because it acts a bit like a girdle and helps to hold in his stomach. He has spent the afternoon cleaning, putting out fresh towels and changing the bedsheets.

He goes back through to the living room and has to fight the urge to text her as he checks his phone.

Without really paying any attention to what he is doing, he moves over to the window and peers out just as she walks through the gates. She spots him, and he gives her a silly little wave as the car on the road behind her pulls away.

Erik met Moa on a dating app, and they spent a long time messaging back and forth before eventually getting together for coffee at Stockholm Central. On their second date, they went to an exhibition of modern art at an auction house, and pretended to be interested in bidding on an erotic work before going for a drink at a bar nearby.

The last time they met, they ate Chinese food at Surfers and split the bill.

Today, for the first time, she is coming over to Erik's house for dinner. She sent him a recipe in advance, and has promised to show him how to make the perfect truffle pasta.

Moa Nygaard is a trained chef who worked in some of Stockholm's most popular restaurants before moving to Växjö and becoming a sous chef at PM & vänner.

Her last relationship was with a man called Bruno, an administrator at Linné University, and she has a daughter with him.

Moa inherited her parents' house to the north of Stockholm when they died, and after Bruno got a new position at Södertörn University, they moved in. She took a year's paid maternity leave, then found a job in Bobergs matsal in central Stockholm.

Moa has been honest with Erik that Bruno can be difficult, and that he still hasn't found a place of his own to live despite the fact that they have been separated for over a year.

She lets him stay in her guesthouse and says, 'Bruno thinks we're still together, but we're not. He knows that, but he's an idiot. I just don't want to make a big deal out of it, for Matilda's sake.'

Erik has already made his way through to the hall when he hears the doorbell ring. He waits for a moment, then starts to worry that she might be able to see him through the patterned glass, and hurries over to open the door.

Moa is wearing a brown aviator jacket with a sheepskin collar, and her short blonde hair is gelled up in a slightly punky style.

'You made it,' he says.

'I took an Uber,' she replies, pressing her lips together to stop herself from grinning.

'Of course. I saw the car.'

He takes her heavy jacket and hangs it up, then moves back into the hallway with an over-the-top 'come in' and manages to knock a straw Christmas goat from the sideboard as he waves his hand behind him.

Moa has on a pair of low-cut leather trousers and a loose gold top that leaves her shoulders and stomach bare.

She follows him through to the kitchen – which smells of truffle, garlic, Parmesan and fresh basil – and over to the table.

'Nice,' she says, reaching for one of the folded napkins.

'It is almost Christmas,' he says, taking a bottle out of the wine cooler and holding it up for her to see. 'How about a ripassa?'

'Perfect.'

He opens the wine and pours two glasses, then hands one to Moa and looks deep into her pretty green eyes.

'Cheers.'

'Cheers,' she replies with a smile, her pointed teeth poking out from beneath her lip.

They both take a sip, and Erik tries to joke about how nervous he is for her to try his pasta sauce, telling her that it feels like he is on a cookery show and the judge is about to come in.

'But everything went OK, didn't it?' she asks, glancing over to the sauté pan on the hob.

'I think so . . . I don't know.'

'A lot of it really just comes down to having confidence in yourself.'

One of her tattoos is visible above the waistband of her trousers, a delicate lacy pattern in black ink.

Erik moves the greasy can of sardines and the jar containing the black truffle to one side and wipes the counter with a piece of kitchen roll. He then rinses a few chives and cuts them into the sauce before offering her a spoonful.

'Nice,' she says, giving him an appreciative nod. 'Really.'

'But?'

'Personally, I think pasta needs a bit of acidity to really make it sing,' she says after a moment.

'But I added the red wine vinegar.'

'I know.'

He takes out a clean spoon and tries the sauce himself.

'I forgot the lemon,' he says, reaching for one from the net and grating a little zest into the pan.

Moa playfully guides him through the finishing touches, showing him how to balance the seasoning and thicken the sauce. Erik then mixes it with some rigatoni in a warm serving dish and scatters a few basil leaves over the top.

* * *

They are now sitting across from each other at the table, eating the pasta. Erik pours more wine, and she praises his cooking again.

He uses the corner of his napkin to wipe a creamy lip mark from his glass before helping himself to more food.

'You have beautiful hands,' she says, reaching over to stroke the back of one of them, resting on the table beside his glass.

'Do you think so?' He looks down at it, as though he has never noticed it before.

'How was your day?' she asks.

'Oh, nothing special. I tried to write a little . . . an article about the dual nature of the voice in my field. Attentive and reassuring, yet also authoritarian.'

'Interesting.'

'What else . . . I finished reading a German thesis about hypnosis and hallucinogens, which was pretty cool. And I saw two clients, too.'

'Women?' she asks, lowering her fork.

'Yes.'

'Do they . . . I've been wondering, don't they fall in love with you?'

'No.'

'What?' she asks, astounded.

'If they do, they manage to hide it very well.'

'Or maybe you're just not so attuned to signals of that kind,' she says with a smirk.

'I think I'd notice.'

'You haven't noticed that I want to kiss you. A lot.'

'Ah, you've got me blushing now . . . But the truth is that I've probably become more cautious about . . . interpreting certain things . . . Sorry, I don't know what I'm trying to say here.'

'You're trying to change the subject,' she says with a smile.

'I'd really like to kiss you, too.'

'But?'

'I don't want to rush it, to force anything . . . I'm so glad you're here, that you wanted to see me again. You're so attractive, vibrant and interesting . . . and you have incredibly sweet ears.'

'But . . .?'

'I'm not like all the exciting people you must meet through your work, with their cool clothes, tattoos and muscles.'

'You've been working out, you said.'

'That's true . . . Does it show?'

'No.' She laughs.

'Well, my muscles have definitely been aching,' he says, massaging his shoulder.

'I can help with that,' she says, getting to her feet.

Erik sees her breasts sway beneath the gold fabric of her top, and he quickly looks away. She moves around the table, and he feels a shiver pass down his spine as she pauses behind him.

Embarrassingly enough, what he said is true. He has started working out since he met Moa. He goes down to his son's old gym in the basement almost every day, and his muscles really have been aching.

She massages the back of his neck, pressing down on his shoulders and squeezing the muscles.

'Oof,' he sighs.

'Did that hurt?'

'It's OK, just—'

'Are you scared of me?'

'No.'

She kisses his cheek from behind, then steps to one side and looks down at him.

'No?'

'I'm pretty tough,' he says.

'You don't *look* tough.'

'Do so.'

'We can have a safe word,' she says, her face solemn.

'What?'

Moa roars with laughter.

'Sorry, I'm only kidding. God, I just wanted to startle you,' she says, covering her mouth to hide her smile.

'OK.'

'Erik? I was only kidding.'

He catches her hand and presses it softly to his lips. She gently caresses his neck, running her fingers slowly through his hair.

Erik's phone is lying on the table in front of them. It is set to silent, but the screen lights up with a message from Joona.

I need your help.

Moa picks up the phone and hands it to Erik. She apologises for accidentally reading the message, but says it could be important.

'Thanks.'

'A patient?'

'No, a friend . . . A detective.'

'You should call him.'

'I'll do it tomorrow.'

'I should probably get going anyway. I have to be up early in the morning,' she says.

Dr Erik Maria Bark is a specialist in psycho-traumatology and disaster psychiatry, and spent four years leading a ground-breaking research project into deep hypnotic group therapy at the Karolinska Institute. He is a member of the European Society of Hypnosis, has written a major standard work on the subject, and is now considered one of the foremost authorities on clinical hypnosis in the world.

24

The three northbound lanes of the motorway are clogged with dirty cars, buses and lorries, a steady stream of traffic flowing past industrial units selling cut-price sports gear, furniture and building materials.

As Joona and Erik drive to Uppsala in Joona's car, he tells his friend that Valeria's father has passed away. She didn't make it in time for the funeral, but she is currently in Brazil to support her mother.

Joona thinks about the small box of dark chocolate coins Valeria gave him before she left. She knows all too well that he loves chocolate, but also that he doesn't think he deserves anything sweet.

'Would you do me a favour and just eat them?' she said with a smile. 'Eat the chocolate and think of me.'

'I'll be thinking of you anyway.'

'So stubborn,' she sighed.

Joona has decided that he will allow himself one of the coins once he makes a concrete step forward in the case.

Erik starts talking about how beautiful he thought their summer wedding was, laughing at the fact that his son Benjamin got drunk and tried to flirt with Lumi.

'He didn't stand a chance,' the doctor continues with a smile.

Joona pictures Valeria in her thin, pearl-white wedding dress, a crown of lingonberry leaves in her hair.

Their guests' voices echoed through the church they had decorated with foliage, between the limewashed walls and the vaulted ceiling, the runestones and the medieval altarpiece.

Tears had started spilling down his cheeks when he felt how much Valeria's hand was shaking as he pushed the ring onto her finger.

Their friends and family stood up as the newlyweds left the church to Bytt-Lasse's melancholy bridal march.

Lumi's smiling face. Valeria's boys and their families.

And then the scent of light summer rain on the steps outside, veils of mist rising from the fields and meadows.

Joona realises he is driving a little too fast.

To the left of the motorway, the ground slopes up towards the top of the esker and the old gravel pit.

A place that is etched deep inside him.

It was here, many years ago, that he made one of the decisions that would darken his soul. He knew he had changed forever as he watched the body roll down the slope, tumbling like a corpse into a mass grave.

Joona doesn't feel any instinct to kill, but he is capable of killing on instinct if that is what the situation demands of him – as he was taught by Lieutenant Rinus Advocaat. Assessment, decision and action have to take place simultaneously.

He maintains his tight grip on the wheel until they have passed Rosersberg Palace, and he runs a hand through his hair, glances over to Erik and then resumes their earlier conversation about their visit to the Sleep Science Lab.

When Joona called Erik, he told him all about the preliminary investigation, the brutal murders and Hugo Sand's remarkable role in what had happened.

'Sleepwalking – and sleepwalking during REM sleep, in particular – is a complex thing ... And as I say, it's not really my specialism,' Erik explains now.

'I think I'm starting to understand how it works from Hugo's point of view,' says Joona. 'He seems to remember fragments of some kind of panicked dream that takes place in his parents' house, but never anything he actually experiences, despite having his eyes open.'

'Because the dream overpowers everything else going on in his brain,' Erik says with a nod.

'At least in retrospect ... But Agneta told me that Hugo often remembers things if he's woken suddenly while sleepwalking.'

'Interesting.'

'He had an episode at his girlfriend's flat and was about to climb over the balcony railing when she woke him. Apparently he started talking about things he'd seen at the campsite, but by the next morning it was all gone.'

'What does the girlfriend have to say?' asks Erik, looking down at his phone.

'We can't get hold of her.'

A pebble hits the windscreen, leaving a small glittering star on the glass.

Erik sends a red heart emoji to someone.

'The whole team is getting frustrated,' Joona says as they pass a long line of taxis queuing for the turn-off to the airport. 'I need a breakthrough ... We're stuck.'

'But I just heard that the powers-that-be have brought in an internal ban on you lot having wooden soles on your shoes, because—'

'Stop,' Joona says with a smile.

'Because they always have time to put down roots otherwise.'

'Please. That joke is so old, it's not OK.'

Erik laughs and tips his head back against the rest with a satisfied smile as Joona admits that it really does feel as though they are rooted to the spot. They have opened the box and started turning over the jigsaw pieces, but have yet to find two that fit together.

'There don't seem to be any old cases involving axe murders that fit the pattern,' he continues. 'We've reached out via Europol and Interpol, but who knows ... Maybe it's just these murders. Maybe there won't be any more. They might not even be connected.'

'But you think they are.'

'We're keeping an open mind, looking into the victims, comparing shoeprints, tyre treads and that sort of thing ... We've been trying to establish whether the same car turns up in the vicinity of both murders, but we're talking about large areas with multiple CCTV cameras.'

'So what happens next?'

Joona sighs. 'Our profilers think we're probably looking for a loner, likely someone with antisocial traits, possible addiction issues ... Someone who lives alone, given how bloody they must have been – especially after the first murder.'

'Mmm.'

'We're checking everyone who was released from prison or psychiatric care recently, scouring our databases, looking into forensic records, you know ... the usual. It just feels so frustrating.'

'Because you're working against the clock,' Erik suggests.

'No,' Joona replies, his voice barely audible.

'No?'

'No.'

'And here I was thinking that you were starting to suspect a serial killer.'

'It's unlikely,' says Joona, turning down the heater.

'But you've got a gut feeling?'

'Maybe.'

They pull up by the fence outside the Sleep Science Lab, and Joona gets out of the car, buzzes the intercom and then gets back behind the wheel to wait as the gate slowly swings open.

Erik has been engaged by the Swedish Police Authority on a handful of occasions over the years. Around the world, law enforcement agencies turn to hypnotists to support witnesses who, for one reason or another, have trouble with their memory.

Joona's great hope is that by putting Hugo Sand under hypnosis, the teenager will be able to provide them with a description of the killer.

25

A research assistant in a pair of tinted glasses comes out to meet Joona and Erik in reception. Speaking softly, she leads them past a small pantry, down a corridor with shiny plastic flooring and through to the unit.

'Office, office, day room, bedroom, cupboard, bedroom . . . And this is the suite,' she says, opening a blue door. 'You can go straight in. They're waiting for you in the lounge.'

'Thank you.'

Joona and Erik make their way down a hall to a brightly lit room where the TV screen is dark and the curtains are drawn.

Hugo has his long hair loose, and he is sitting in an armchair opposite a slim man with a bald head and a thin face. On the low coffee table between them, there are two glasses of water, a bowl of clementines and a pot of snus.

The man gets to his feet with a smile. He welcomes them and introduces himself as Lars, failing to mention that he is the senior doctor and lead researcher. His feet are pushed into a pair of loafers, and he is wearing a blue crewneck sweatshirt that brings out the pale colour of his eyes.

'An honour,' Lars says as he shakes Erik's hand. 'I've been following your work for many years. Very impressive.'

'Thank you,' Erik replies with warmth in his voice.

'Our fields are very much siblings,' Lars Grind continues, turning to Joona. 'The word hypnosis actually stems from the ancient Greek for sleep.'

'He used to be a lecturer,' Hugo mumbles, scratching his tattooed forearm.

'Hello again,' says Joona.

They sit down, and Lars explains that the suite is designed to resemble a regular apartment, but that it has been specially adapted for sleepwalkers and fitted with motion detectors and cameras.

'Everyone wants to know what's going on up here,' Hugo says, pointing to his own head. 'I just wish you could crack a little hole with a spoon and have a look inside.'

'Erik Maria Bark is probably the closest we can get to that,' Lars Grind replies with a smile.

'Sorry, I know you've driven all the way up here from Stockholm,' says Hugo. 'But I feel like I should say that I'm not sure I even *believe* in hypnosis.'

'I hear that rather often,' Erik says calmly. 'But in truth, there isn't much *to* believe in; this isn't magic or spirituality. Hypnosis is simply a tried and tested method of reaching a state of physical relaxation and mental focus. Imagine going to the cinema and being so engrossed in the film that you forget you're sitting in a dark room with a projector ... Hypnosis is a bit like that, but rather than getting caught up in a film, you're using your new-found concentration to dig deep in your memory.'

* * *

Hugo leans back in his chair and decides that both Joona and Erik seem nice. They clearly have a lot riding on this, and he thinks he will be able to help them, but they definitely aren't on his side. He can't afford to forget that.

He knows that Joona hasn't fully ruled him out as a suspect yet, and Erik almost seems to be quivering with anticipation at the prospect of hypnotising him. The man is practically salivating.

'Where do you think will work best?' asks Lars.

'This will be just fine, if we can lower the lights a little,' says Erik.

'Don't I need to lie down?' asks Hugo.

'Only if you want to, but anywhere where you're sitting comfortably will do.'

'OK . . . just don't be too disappointed if it doesn't work.'

Joona gets up and turns off the ceiling lights, then moves back over to the seating area and dims the floor lamp.

'I want to emphasise that resistance is possible – this isn't like anaesthesia,' Erik begins. 'Hypnosis requires a certain level of participation on your part, and it's important that you're participating willingly, that you know you can break the hypnosis at any moment.'

'Let's give it a try,' Hugo says with a smile, pulling his long hair back in a ponytail.

'I'll be here the whole time, guiding you through the relaxation and deep focus.'

'OK.'

'Just sit comfortably, with both feet on the floor and your hands on the armrests,' Erik continues in a warm voice. 'Close your eyes and breathe calmly – in through your nose and out through your mouth . . . Steady, even . . . Feel the weight of your feet, completely relaxed, with your thighs resting on the cushion beneath you and your back against the chair . . .'

Hugo remembers having done something similar during PE class once, and he finds it interesting that he can shift his focus so easily between different parts of his body, really relaxing in the process.

He smirks slightly at the thought of how serious the three men around him are, how much faith they seem to place in hypnosis.

'Feel your eyelids growing heavier with each breath you take.'

There is no escaping how funny the situation is, the fact that he is sitting in an armchair with his eyes closed, trying to do exactly as Erik tells him.

Erik calmly works his way through Hugo's body and gets him to relax his face. No smile, no gritted teeth or furrowed brow.

'Just listen to my voice,' he says softly. 'You don't need to worry about anything else right now . . . You are in a state of deep relaxation, and if you hear anything other than my voice then just let it pass you by. Become even more relaxed and focused on what I say.'

Hugo realises that Erik's warm, low voice feels like an embrace, and he enjoys the slight dryness to it. Maybe he was a smoker, he thinks. Or maybe it's just his age.

'I'm going to count backwards from one hundred now, and all you need to do is listen carefully to every number. With each one you hear, I want you to breathe out and sink deeper into relaxation ... Ninety-nine, ninety-eight ...'

At first, Hugo thinks he might be doing it all wrong, but he decides he doesn't care. He finds his own pace and notices that his breathing quickly falls into sync with the doctor's countdown.

'You're comfortable now,' Erik continues. 'You're focused on my voice, on the descending numbers, and I'd like you to imagine that you're making your way down a long staircase ... With every number you hear, you take another step, becoming increasingly relaxed and calm. Seventy-seven, seventy-six, seventy-five ...'

Hugo tries to follow the instructions as best he can, imagining the stairs at home, various grand hotel staircases with red carpets, but before long he realises he has started to picture a spiral staircase he has never seen before.

It is made from pale-grey metal, and it leads straight down into the earth.

Moving in time with his breathing and the doctor's words, he makes his way down. He takes cautious steps, but the entire structure shakes softly each time.

'You're continuing down the stairs, step by step. Sixty-four, sixty-three ...'

Hugo puts a hand on the banister, trying to focus on the voice as he walks. He imagines that the spiral staircase has begun to turn, like some sort of drill to the underworld.

'Fifty-eight, fifty-seven ...'

He sees a dirty handprint on the rail and starts moving more quickly, though his breathing is getting calmer. It feels as though he is being sucked downwards. The metal steps clang with each step, reverberating into the deep.

'You're still going down, and with each step you take you'll become a little more relaxed, a little more focused on my voice . . . Forty-three, forty-two . . .'

Hugo has started running, clinging onto the banister, and can feel the centrifugal force from the centre column. The brackets have begun to shake, and he can see sand trickling down the shaft, like the steady flow in an hourglass.

Erik's counting has slowed, but Hugo is now hurtling downwards, and it feels as though the countdown will never end.

'Fourteen . . . thirteen,' the doctor's monotone voice continues. 'When I get to zero, you will be at home in your bed on the twenty-sixth of November . . . You're relaxed and able to calmly observe everything you see. Nothing here is dangerous. Twelve, eleven . . .'

Hugo focuses on Erik's voice and loses contact with his body as he throws himself down the stairs four at a time.

'Three, two . . . one . . . zero. You are now lying in your bed on the twenty-sixth of November.'

Hugo stops dead on the spiral staircase and closes his eyes.

'It's around one in the morning, and you are asleep, but something makes you open your eyes.'

He does as he is told and stares out into the darkness in his pale-blue room. The blind is closed, revealing its familiar pattern of a starry sky.

His heart is pounding.

Hugo has been lying perfectly still in bed with his hands clamped over his mouth, trying to remain hidden. But the gunfire has now stopped, and the screams have faded.

The platoon has left the house.

With their rattling automatic rifles and barked commands, they stomped down the stairs and headed back out to their black SUVs.

Only the leader is still here, and Hugo knows that they need to escape.

Mum and Dad have emptied their bank accounts and transferred all of their savings.

Hugo quietly gets out of bed, tiptoes over to the doorway on trembling legs and peers out into the hall. He sees his father on his knees, tearfully trying to explain that he has given them everything he has, but the skeleton man isn't listening; he wants more.

'There's some money and a bit of gold in the cupboard in the attic,' says Mum. 'Not much, but—'

The skeleton man hits his father in the head with a spade. His mother screams and her voice breaks. The blows continue, gradually becoming sluggish, the sound wetter.

'He's hitting him over and over,' says Hugo, his voice barely audible. 'There's so much blood.'

'Who is?' asks Erik.

'The ske-le-ton . . .'

Hugo pulls back when the skeleton man leaves his parents' room, dragging the spade behind him as he starts climbing the stairs to the attic.

The blade clanks dully against each step.

Hugo hurries out of his room and down the hallway, meeting his mother's eye through the window in the middle door.

There is a loud crack as the skeleton man uses the spade to force open the old wooden cabinet in the attic.

His mother waves for him to come towards her.

'Where are you?' Erik asks softly.

'I . . . I don't want to,' Hugo replies, licking his lips.

His mother is confused, with flecks of blood all over her face. He grips her hand and pulls her towards the stairs down to the library.

'Are you still at home?' asks Erik.

'Mum can't get the front door open,' Hugo whispers. 'I don't want to die, we need to get out . . . We need to run, to hide and—'

'Hugo, listen to me now. Listen to my voice,' says Erik. 'This is just a dream – a dream you can control . . . You are standing in the hallway and you want to run outside, but instead you stay where you are. Find your way back to that steady breathing again. In through your nose, out through your mouth . . . None of this is really dangerous. You're perfectly safe, and you can turn around without needing to be scared.'

'I can hear the spade hitting the tiles behind me.'

'Turn around.'

'Mum opens the door and runs . . .'

26

Joona can hear the fear in Hugo's voice, and he follows the movements of his eyes beneath his closed lids, sees his slack mouth and the cold sweat running down his cheeks.

It is as though the teenager doesn't realise that he is taking them through the nightmare that drove him out of the house on the night of the murder.

The rings in his lip and nose reflect the soft glow of the floor lamp, shimmering like droplets of water.

Erik has a focused look on his face, breathing in and out in time with the boy, and he gives him a few seconds before he tries again.

'You're breathing calmly, and you're concentrating on my voice,' he says. 'None of this is dangerous. You are perfectly relaxed . . .'

Joona has asked Erik to encourage Hugo to describe everyone he sees, regardless of whether they belong in his dream or reality, because the brain doesn't distinguish between the two when it comes to memories.

'You're looking straight at the man who is walking towards you, and you aren't afraid,' Erik tells him. 'And as soon as you feel ready, I'd like you to describe him for me.'

Joona notices the hidden imperative, the direct orders Erik uses whenever he wants to guide a particularly powerful memory.

But Hugo remains quiet, his breathing quickening, and one of his feet lifts up off the floor.

Joona glances over to Lars Grind and sees that he is attempting to maintain some sense of professional calm, despite the unsettling dream Hugo is gradually revealing to them.

'Hugo, listen to my voice,' Erik tries again. 'I'm telling you that you're safe here, that you can . . . Tell me what you see!'

'The barrier across the road. Damp leaves, butterflies,' he mumbles.

'You're already out.'

'I'm taking the shortcut through the woods, walking as fast as I can. I can see Mum over by the old open-air theatre.'

'You've escaped the house and—'

'I'm running, but he still catches up with me,' Hugo says with rising intensity. 'I don't know how. He's so slow, but he still manages to catch up with me, and—'

'Wait, Hugo. You can stop and—'

'He's killing me,' Hugo cuts him off, his voice raised.

Joona watches as the boy's chest strains. His thin silver chain pulls tight around his neck, and dark patches of sweat have begun to appear beneath his arms.

One of his hands starts to shake, almost spasmodically, and Erik puts his own hand on top of it until it calms down, then he continues in a soothing voice.

'Listen to me, Hugo. This is just a dream; nothing bad is going to happen to you. You've stopped, and you're now standing still. You can hear his footsteps behind you, and you turn around.'

'It's dark. I don't understand, it's—'

'Look at the man.'

'I don't know if it is a man. It's just a pile of skulls. Bits of bone moving like a person.'

'It's good that you're looking at him, because we know now that he's part of your nightmare and that you don't need to worry about him anymore . . . You can keep going to the campsite, and—'

'He's dragging the spade behind him, I can hear the blade on the gravel,' Hugo continues in a panicked voice. 'He's getting closer. I don't understand . . . His back is weird, like a porcupine . . . The bones sticking out of him are rattling, a load of broken ribs that—'

'Hugo, listen to my voice. You can trust me. He isn't real . . . Relax your body and focus on the weight of your eyelids.'

'I need to find Mum,' he whispers.

'Your breathing is calm and steady, and you are relaxed. I want you to keep walking now, just like you did that night. You're passing the sports field . . . Three, two, one, and you've reached the entrance to Bredäng Campsite.'

* * *

The flags of the Scandinavian countries are flapping on the poles by the gates, and there are people dressed for hot weather milling around the reception building and on the patio outside the restaurant.

Hugo tries to mask the fear on his face. He can't afford to start running, can't stop to talk to anyone, can't call the police; he just needs to find his mum and hide with her.

He keeps walking down the road, past the crowded tent pitches.

A young girl in a sunhat is fast asleep in a pushchair. Her orange water pistol has leaked, leaving a dark patch on her flowery dress.

Hugo's heart is racing.

No one realises the skeleton man is getting closer to the campsite.

'Are you there now?'

'Yeah, it . . . it's full of people, all over the place.'

'That's just part of the dream,' says Erik.

'What?'

Hugo looks out across the muddle of tents and caravans, at the seagulls, folding chairs, cool bags, women in swimsuits, men in shorts and sunglasses, children kicking footballs, and empty bags of crisps.

'You know that it's the middle of the night,' Erik continues. 'It's dark, and it has started snowing. It's cold. The campsite is closed for the winter.'

A boy is sitting inside a small goal, eating an ice lolly. A dog snaps at the water flowing from a hosepipe, and a bare-chested man takes a picture of himself on his phone.

'I don't want to die,' Hugo whispers. 'I need to find Mum and hide . . .'

'Just pause for a moment. Look at the campsite and try to see it as it really is,' Erik tells him. 'It's quiet, it's dark, and it has started to snow.'

White flakes slowly drift down onto an elderly couple sunning themselves in front of a caravan. They have a pale-blue thermos and a pack of biscuits in the basket between them.

'No,' he replies, his voice wavering.

'What do you see?'

'I don't know,' Hugo replies, continuing along the path. 'There's a woman in a red bikini . . . Her shoulders are sunburned, and she's got a tattoo of a spider at the base of her spine . . . I have to step onto the grass to get past this huge guy who—'

'Feel free to stop and look at anyone you like,' says Erik. 'Look at the man on the path, describe him to me.'

'He's standing with his back to me, in a pair of white shorts and a stripy short-sleeved shirt . . . He's balancing a massive inflatable flamingo on his head, holding it with both hands . . .'

'Really look at him now, take your time. You'll notice that he's transparent, that you can see reality through him.'

The sunlight filtering through the flamingo has cast a pinkish shadow onto the man's forearms. His hair looks like it has recently been cut, and he has a pale tan line at the top of his neck.

Hugo studies the man's shirt, straining over his back, and realises he can see the empty tent pitches between the dark-blue stripes.

Snow has started falling on the deserted campsite, settling on the litter on the yellowed grass, on the electricity poles, the bare trees, the dark branches and the rows of static caravans in the distance.

'It's dark . . . and deserted,' says Hugo.

27

Hugo's foot knocks the floor lamp, and the parrot-print shade wobbles, causing the light to bounce around the room for a moment.

During hypnosis, a person typically looks as though they are asleep, despite the fact that their brain is more active than it is while they are awake. But Hugo's body is tense, twitching as he works through his memories.

Joona is thinking about something Erik said as they got out of the car and walked across the parking area towards the lab: that he thought the real test would be their patience and ability to navigate through Hugo's double-exposed world.

The teenager has been caught up in his nightmare since the hypnosis began, but he finally seems to have taken a cautious step out into reality.

The campsite is dark and deserted, he said.

Hugo really does remember what he saw while he was sleepwalking. This is it; they are approaching the hypocentre of the night.

Joona double-checks that his phone is still recording.

Lars Grind rubs his bald head. He seems uncomfortable, his eyes dark and oddly wide.

Hugo is slumped back on the sofa. His slack mouth is still half-open, but the fear on his face is plain to see.

'Tell me what you're doing,' says Erik.

'I'm walking towards the old caravans, the ones closest to the lake.'

'You're looking for your mum in the dream, but she isn't there; the campsite is deserted.'

'I don't know . . .' Hugo shakes his head, saliva coating his lower lip.

'What do you see?'

'At first I thought it was just the headlights from a car on the main road, but it's a torch . . .'

'Where?'

Hugo lets out a soft whimper. It only lasts a few seconds, but it almost makes it seem as though they have an abandoned child in front of them.

Lars Grind looks troubled, and he raises a hand to catch Erik's attention. The hypnotist briefly meets his eye before turning back to Hugo.

'Is there someone there? At the campsite?' he asks.

'Yeah . . . I'm following them . . .'

Hugo's breathing becomes anxious, and he starts scratching at the armrest with his right hand.

'You can see someone with a torch?' Erik says softly.

'It's a woman . . . with a shiny coat and blonde hair. She turns left, across the playground.'

'Describe her. Take your time. Breathe deeply and speak slowly.'

'The light . . . from her torch . . . It sweeps over the rough sand.'

'What does she look like?' Erik's voice is low but intense, his eyes focused and alert, the veins on his head beginning to protrude.

'I don't know, she's too far away, walking between the rows of dark caravans.'

'But you're following her?'

'Yeah.'

'What do you see now?' Erik asks.

'She stops and turns the torch off . . . but I can see another light, further back . . . In one of the caravans.'

'Can you see anyone else?'

'No, but the lights are on . . . I can see it through the curtains.'

'Do you know who is inside?'

'Mum?' he whispers.

'Your mum is part of the dream,' Erik explains.

'No, she—'

'I want you to focus on the woman with the blonde hair now.'

'She's standing outside the caravan.'

'Move a little closer.'

'The light from the window is shining on her hair.'

'Can you see her face?'

'No, because . . . she's got her back turned to me.'

'Stay there and study her more closely, focus on the details.'

'The sports bag in her hand looks heavy. She's dirty, and . . . her fingers are the colour of bone . . . too many, really thin . . .'

'What is she doing?' asks Erik.

'She puts the bag down, opens it and takes something out, then she walks over to the door and goes inside,' Hugo replies.

'What did she take out?'

'I don't know.'

'Let's just rewind a little . . . You see the blonde woman put her bag down on the grass?' says Erik.

'Yes.'

'Look at her face.'

'I can't see it,' he mumbles.

'Reflections,' Joona says quietly.

'Are any of the windows on the caravan dark?' asks Erik.

'The one on the door.'

'Focus on that as she moves forward to go inside.'

'It's too quick, she's already gone in and closed it behind her,' he says, tears streaming down his cheeks.

Lars Grind gets up and taps his watch, as though to tell Erik that it is time to stop.

'Go back in your memory,' Erik continues. 'It's cold, and there are snowflakes swirling through the air. The woman puts the bag down. You can see her hands, but they're normal hands – she isn't a skeleton, just a regular woman . . .'

Hugo's muscles tense, as though he is trying to get up from the armchair.

'What does she take out of the bag?' asks Erik.

'I can't see,' he whispers.

'There's no need to be afraid, Hugo, it's all going to be OK. You have plenty of time to take in every detail. The woman slowly moves towards the door. The light from the window hits her face from one side, and just as she is about to open the door, you see her reflection in the dark glass.'

'I can see her reflection,' says Hugo. 'But she has her head lowered, like she knows I'm looking at her.'

'Hold on to that image. Can you see anything?'

'Just a bit of her skull, with cracks from her eye sockets going up over her forehead . . . She opens the door with her left hand and hides the axe in her right hand behind her back . . .'

28

Joona thanks Erik as he drops him off on the street outside his house in Gamla Enskede, then drives back to Stockholm, parks his car in the garage beneath his building, takes the lift to his floor and calls Valeria.

'Sweetie?' she answers.

'It's good to hear your voice. How are you doing?'

'I'm OK. Mum spends most of her time staring out of the window, so I've been dealing with all the relatives coming over with food and flowers.'

'How are you feeling?'

'Dad was an old man.'

'I know, but still . . . It doesn't matter how old we are, or whether we know it's coming, losing a parent is still hard.'

'It is. I've been thinking a lot, crying a bit,' she says.

'I miss you.'

'You haven't eaten your chocolate coins, have you?'

'I've started *looking* at them.'

'You could come over here,' she says. 'Can't you do that?'

'I wish I could.'

'Come and get your honey,' she whispers.

They talk for a while, until there is a knock at the door and Valeria says she has to go and see who it is.

Joona is still smiling as he goes through to the kitchen and puts his phone on the counter. He makes himself a simple pasta dish with Italian salami, then sets the little table by the window, sits down and gazes out of the window.

Beneath the dark night sky, the city looks like a bed of glowing embers.

As he eats, his thoughts turn to the investigation and the fact that they have finally made a breakthrough. It was as though one of the many locked doors suddenly clicked and creaked open.

Hugo proved to be incredibly susceptible to hypnosis, entering into a deep trance almost immediately. Erik carved a furrow in the sand, and the boy followed it like he was water.

When they lifted him out of hypnosis at the end of the session, his face was pale and sweaty. He stared straight ahead for a moment or two, then mumbled 'never again' over and over.

Erik hadn't been prepared for the power that was unleashed, and said later that such intense hypnosis was extremely uncommon. Despite years in the field, he had only ever come across a couple of people who had even come close to anything like what Hugo experienced.

During the session, he had repeatedly encouraged Hugo to try to see through his nightmare, and in the end the teenager had managed to give them their first description of the killer.

A blonde woman in a shiny coat had gone into the caravan with an axe hidden behind her back.

Joona lowers his cutlery and thinks about how hard he and his team have been working, how their unorthodox methods have finally produced a description.

'Not too shabby, Joona,' he says to himself.

He takes one of the chocolate coins out of the box and pops it into his mouth, closing his eyes for a moment.

When he came round, Hugo had been shaking so much that Lars Grind had had to give him fifty milligrams of Atarax to quickly dull his anxiety.

As the doctors attempted to calm the teenager, Joona went out into the corridor to call Erixon. Among the thousands of biological traces recovered from the caravan, the technicians had found a long blonde hair without a root.

'And I'm guessing you need answers yesterday,' Erixon replied.

'Unless you can do it any quicker.'

'I'll try, but you know how things are.'

The National Forensic Centre processes around thirteen thousand DNA samples a year, and simply doesn't have the resources for a quick turnaround. Thanks to Joona, Erixon has already used up a lifetime's quota of priority cases.

Joona's thoughts turn to the two premeditated murders and the niggling sense that, once again, he is chasing a serial killer.

Serial killers are rare, no doubt about it, but there are also far more of them than are ever brought to justice.

Sweden is a small country with a functional social security net, and of the twenty-five thousand or so people reported missing every year, the majority are eventually found safe and well.

Statistically speaking, however, around three thousand of them turn up dead. And thirty are never found.

Many are not victims of any crime, but there is definitely scope for some to have fallen prey to unknown serial killers.

On top of that, there are all the unreported cases, missed leads and opportunities no one is willing or able to talk about.

Across the world, the majority of all serial killers operate under the cover of armed conflict. They are soldiers, willing to do whatever is asked of them in battle, but their psychological driving force is pathological.

Many serial killers fall under the umbrella of organised crime networks, while other faceless perpetrators stalk the corridors of neonatal wards or palliative care facilities like angels of death. Some are protected by religious organisations.

And those serial killers whose victims come from the most margin-alised groups of society – street children, the homeless, drug addicts, sex workers and refugees – tend not to be caught.

It is only when the victims belong to a certain social class, when the circumstances cannot be explained away, that the perpetrator attracts attention – and is labelled a serial killer.

With the bittersweet taste of chocolate still lingering in his mouth, Joona wonders whether he isn't some kind of serial killer too.

On the basis of certain criteria, the answer would be yes, but not the most important of all: the drive.

He has a trail of dead bodies behind him, and he can almost always hear the sound behind his back: the rustling of feathers and the pecking and cawing of crows.

But that isn't his goal; it's the price he pays.

He has to believe that.

Joona has often thought that regardless of a serial killer's choice of victim, the setting in which they are active and their individual justifications for killing, they are all actually incredibly alike.

No one can singlehandedly create life, but a serial killer fills the emptiness inside themselves with others' deaths. Their motives may vary – some believe they are punishing sinners or cleansing society, some that they are sparing their victims from suffering; others still reduce murder to a pragmatic consequence in order to satisfy their need for money or sex – but all lack empathy for their victims.

Joona would guess that the person they are currently trying to stop sees their own driving force as economical, killing the best way to do away with any witnesses, but in actual fact it is the other way around.

The murder itself is always the focus.

The economical explanation is, in essence, a fictitious motive dreamed up to prevent the killer from becoming incomprehensible to themselves, to keep the looming madness at bay.

29

Joona clears the table, starts the half-empty dishwasher and then moves over to the window in the living room and looks down at the church tower outside.

Not for the first time, he tells himself that he needs to stop this killer. That the responsibility lies with him.

If he manages it, and Noah Hellman is happy . . . well, then he might just be able to get the boss to listen to him about wanting to work with Saga again.

Joona thinks back to his initial encounter with her, to the colourful ribbons in her hair, her temperament and her self-confidence, and he smiles when he remembers that her first words to him were, 'I don't want you here, this is my investigation.'

His eyes drift over the rooftops to the pale green towers of Police Headquarters, and he mumbles, 'The hunt starts now' and dials Erixon's number.

'How's it going?' Joona asks. 'What does the lab say?'

Erixon takes a deep breath. 'I feel like lying down and dying like a beached whale,' he replies.

'How long?'

'Given the hair is broken and doesn't have a root, we're talking about mitochondrial DNA . . .'

'I know,' says Joona.

'There's a three-week wait. We—'

'Ask them to prioritise it. We need answers. We'll have another victim soon.'

'I've already told them that,' Erixon replies with a sigh.

'Tell them again.'

Joona rests his head against the cool glass for a moment before sitting down in his armchair and checking to see if he has any messages. He sent out a request over the national communication system used by the various emergency services earlier, asking for information about any cases that bear even the slightest resemblance to his.

Don't wait, get in touch right away. This is urgent.
Incredibly urgent.

He has tried to secure additional resources, but it is the same old story as ever. Thanks to chronic understaffing, following the recommendations laid out in the Police Authority's framework for tackling serious crime is simply not possible.

Despite that, every member of his team understands the gravity of the situation and has been working flat out to comb through cold cases, knock on doors in the area around the tennis club and trawl through the CCTV.

Joona's work phone starts ringing, and he takes it out of his jacket pocket, looks down at the display and answers the call.

'Hi. I'm sorry to ring outside of working hours,' says a woman's voice.

'What are *those*?' he asks.

'Sorry?'

'Working hours.'

'Ah, I'm not sure,' she says with a laugh. 'My name is Anna Gilbert, from the prostitution unit here in Stockholm.'

'You've been doing great work.'

'I saw your request,' she continues. 'And this might not have anything to do with your case, but I felt like I should reach out all the same, so at least I can say I passed it on.'

'Good.'

'Because you'll never find a link in any of the databases. It's really nothing but a persistent rumour.'

'Go on.'

'For the past few years, there's been talk among the sex workers we come into contact with of a blonde woman who robs johns – and she's been doing it with increasing levels of violence,' she says.

'I'm listening.'

'This is outside of my purview, and like I say . . . we don't even know whether it's just an urban myth. But at the same time, you know . . . for obvious reasons, johns aren't usually keen to talk to the police, even if they're the victim of some sort of crime.'

'No.'

'I reached out to the Mika Clinic, which helps people selling sex . . . Two of them had heard about this blonde woman, and one of them actually had a counselling session with a girl who mentioned her just last week.'

* * *

Anna Gilbert helped Joona to arrange a meeting with the sex worker in question that same evening. Her name is Tiffany Eklund, and she operates out of a studio flat close to Frihamnen.

Joona is now on his way over there, driving past the University of the Arts and the brutalist concrete building housing the Swedish Film Institute beneath a dark winter sky.

It doesn't take him long to reach the huge warehouses and storage tanks on the outskirts of the port, and he turns off onto Sandhamnsgatan and pulls up outside Tiffany's building.

Her apartment is on the ground floor, with bars over the windows.

The stairwell is shabby but clean.

Joona rings the buzzer on a door with a label for TOP SOLUTIONS on the letterbox, then waits as she studies him through the peephole. The lights in the stairwell go out, but he presses the button on the wall and they immediately come back on.

He hears the security chain rattle, and the door opens.

'I've got an appointment at nine,' he says.

Tiffany Eklund is a slim woman in her thirties. Her dyed blue hair is growing out, and she has chapped lips, a swollen eye and dark bruises on her cheek and throat. Her pink fluffy dressing gown is untied, and beneath it she is wearing nothing but a pair of silver hotpants and a see-through bra.

The air in her hallway smells like sweat, chewing gum and old clothes.

Tiffany sniffs loudly and turns around on unsteady legs, leading him past a small kitchen nook where there are two packs of quick-cook macaroni on a shelf.

Joona takes off his coat, drapes it over his arm and follows her into a cramped room. The sheets on the bed are crumpled, and the floral curtain is drawn over the only window. On the little dining table, there is a plastic bag full of makeup and medication. He notices a box of condoms on the nightstand, beside a pump bottle of lube, a pack of gummy dummies and a roll of kitchen paper.

As Tiffany sits down on the edge of the bed with a sigh, her robe opens wider. She has a number of tattoos, piercings in her bellybutton and nipples, and a pale scar down one side of her torso.

Joona pulls the only chair across the scratched linoleum floor and drapes his coat over the backrest, then sits down opposite her and holds up his ID.

'Right, so you're a cop who thinks he's getting freebies, huh?' she says impatiently.

'I just need to ask you a few questions.'

'Yeah, sure, everyone needs something . . . Not my problem,' she says, staring at him with an open mouth.

Her makeup looks several days old, like she has just touched it up rather than washing her face and starting afresh.

'I'd like—'

'You're so fucking ugly,' she cuts him off. 'If I had a knife, I'd slice your face right off, and I'd be doing you a fucking favour.'

One of her legs has started bouncing up and down, and she mumbles 'God' and glances towards the hallway.

On the floor beneath the table, there is a pink perfume bottle with the words SHEER LOVE on the gold label.

'I'll go once you've answered m—'

169

'Go fuck yourself! You hear that? If people see me with a pig . . . who's gonna pay for that, huh? You'll scare 'em all off.'

She reaches up to scratch her head, and Joona notices that she has needle marks on her wrist and the back of her hand.

'I can pay you to talk,' he explains.

'It'll cost you double.'

'OK.'

She agitatedly rubs the corner of her mouth and stares at him.

'C'mon, then. Didn't you want to talk? What the fuck is this?' she asks.

'I was wondering if—'

'Talk!' she snaps, waving impatiently.

'I will.'

'The clock's ticking, pig.'

She has goosebumps on her legs, small beads of sweat glistening on her forehead.

'There's a woman who has been robbing johns,' he says.

'You're in the wrong place, 'cause I've never robbed anyone. I'm a good girl. I love my guys and they love me.'

'I wasn't talking about you . . .'

'Are you thick in the head, or did you have a stroke or something? You're so fucking slow,' she says with a hoarse laugh.

'Can I go on?'

'Jesus Christ.'

'Are you listening?'

'This whole cop thing . . . is it like rehab or something?'

'Tiffany, I'm not going to pay you if you don't—'

'Man, it's war,' she shouts, pointing at him. 'I'll ring Sorab, I swear. And you definitely don't want him showing up.'

Her nose has started running, and she licks the mucus from her top lip.

'I can see that you're antsy because you're going into withdrawal, and—'

'You can't see shit. What the hell do you know? Go fuck yourself.'

'I just wanted to say that there's help if you need it. The methadone programme, for exa—'

'Give me money. Give me a bunch of fucking money,' she snaps. 'That's all the help I need.'

'Can I ask my questions now?'

'Why, you need to get back to the care home or something?' she asks, her leg bouncing again.

'Last chance, Tiffany,' Joona says, leaning forward. 'There's a blonde woman who has been robbing johns across Stockholm.'

'It's easier just to spread your legs.'

'She assaults the men. Have you heard of her?'

'Yeah.'

'Really?'

'Yeah, what the hell, I just told you. I had a guy who got fucked up, but it was a while back now. Last year, maybe.'

'Do you have his name?'

'Do you have his name?' she parrots in a mocking voice.

'Come on, Tiffany.'

'You really are thick,' she says, baring her yellow teeth in a grin.

Joona gets up and buttons his jacket.

'Fine,' she blurts out. 'He was all jumpy when he came over here, so I asked what his fucking deal was and he said he'd been unlucky with some girl, that she'd robbed him, snapped his dick and knocked three teeth out.'

'Did he say anything else about her?'

'Nah, just that she was an ugly fucking whore.'

'I really need to talk to him, Tiffany.'

'Not my problem, darling.'

'I'm just thinking . . . it can't be good for you if the johns are scared, can it?'

She stares at him, pouting unhappily.

'When are you seeing him next?' he asks.

'Time's up.'

'Call Sorab and I'll talk to him instead.'

171

'I'll kill you,' she shouts. 'You're not talking to him. He'll break your fucking neck and throw you out the window.'

'Call him.'

'No way!'

'When is the john next coming to see you?'

'You're a pain in the goddamn ass, man,' she says, scratching her neck. 'Look, he's not coming again . . . we didn't click. I heard he's a regular with a girl called Lena O now.'

Joona reaches for his coat, pays and leaves two cards on the table, one for the Blenda women's refuge and the other for Talita, a non-profit that helps women find a way out of prostitution.

'Call them. They're on your side. Truly,' he says as he leaves.

30

Joona pulls on his coat in the stairwell, then makes his way out into the cold night.

A cat is sniffing around a heap of rubbish bags and discarded beer cans.

He can hear the whirr of a helicopter in the distance, and he notices an empty pack of Tramadol on top of a telecoms cabinet.

Joona turns the corner and sees two men standing beside his car.

Someone has walked the same route as him with a can of red spray paint, leaving a wavy line on the facade of the building, over the bricks, windows and doors.

As Joona gets closer his car, he sees that the two men are trying to jimmy the driver's side door with a thin piece of metal.

He reaches into his coat pocket and finds his key fob.

'You need any help, lads?' he asks.

'Huh?' mutters the older of the two.

Joona holds his other hand up in the air and clicks his fingers. The headlights on his car flash, and the wing mirrors fold out.

'What the fuck . . .' mumbles the younger man.

'*Juoskaa kuin kanit,*' Joona says with a smile, flashing them his police ID.

The would-be robbers drop their tools, turn and run, cutting across the dark patch of grass beside the convenience shop and jumping the low fence.

Joona moves around the car and sees that they have damaged the paintwork on the door. He opens it and gets in behind the wheel, then calls Anna Gilbert to tell her about his meeting with Tiffany and ask about Lena O.

'Yeah, I know who she is . . . Olena Veronina. She's from Ukraine, wound up becoming an escort girl after the Russian invasion. We've actually been in touch with her recently.'

'Do you think she might be willing to talk to me?'

'You'd need an interpreter, but she's pretty sharp, studied civil engineering back home.'

'Anything else I need to know?'

'No . . . well, other than that she doesn't want to talk about the people she left behind. She sends everything she earns to her family, but she doesn't have any contact with them.'

'Can you arrange a meeting with her? The sooner the better.'

* * *

It is five to nine in the morning when Joona gets to Café Elektra in the Västberga industrial estate. He buys a cup of coffee and a sandwich, then sits down at one of the tables to wait.

The paper tablecloth in front of him is decorated with a festive cross-stitch pattern, wishing him a Merry Christmas.

Last night, he woke from a nightmare with a racing heart and teary eyes. He got up and washed his face, took twenty milligrams of morphine, then crawled back into bed and felt himself sink into a warm, artificial calm.

His head now feels heavy, and he is slightly queasy.

Through the window, he notices the interpreter smoking on the other side of the road. Their paths have crossed a few times over the years, but he doesn't remember her name. She is in her sixties, with oversized glasses, a hard face and short grey hair.

He watches her take one last drag on her cigarette before stamping on the butt, reaching into the pocket of her denim jacket for a pack of gum, waving at someone and crossing the street.

The interpreter comes into the café with another woman, who looks to be around forty. The second woman is bare-faced, with pale-blue eyes and thick blonde hair. She is wearing a navy sweater, black trousers and leather boots.

They make their way over to his table, and Joona gets up to say hello and ask what he can get them. The women sit down as he goes over to the counter to pay for their coffees and sandwiches, and the interpreter moves the basket of ketchup and mustard over to the next table and takes out a notepad and pen.

'Thank you for agreeing to meet me,' Joona tells Olena once he gets back.

The interpreter scribbles something in her notepad, then translates his words. A moment later, she does the same for Olena's reply.

'I'm happy to help if I can.'

They start eating, and after a few minutes Joona puts what is left of his sandwich to one side, takes a sip of coffee, lowers his cup to the saucer and looks up at Olena. She takes another bite, then wipes her mouth with the napkin and meets his gaze.

'I've been wondering . . . how do you find your clients?' he asks.

The interpreter repeats his question in Ukrainian, listens to Olena's answer and mimics her tone of voice as she translates it back into Swedish.

'They make a request, and if it's a new name I look them up on various forums before I start communicating with them,' she says, turning the page in her notepad.

'What do you talk about?'

'What he's looking for, the price, the rules . . . Mostly so I can get a sense of who he is, see whether any alarm bells start ringing,' Olena replies softly.

'Do you save the messages?'

'No. I promise discretion. That's important, for all of them.'

'But isn't it useful to save at least some kind of information about your clients?'

'No. Like what?'

'Names, phone numbers, preferences. I don't know.'

Olena shakes her head. 'I don't.'

'So you don't have any details saved on your computer, or on your phone? No cashbook or any physical records like that?'

'No, I'm sorry,' she replies, running a hand over the blue fabric cushion on her chair.

Joona nods, finishes off his sandwich and wipes his mouth.

'OK, Olena, I'm going to get straight to the point . . . I was told that you have a regular who was robbed by another sex worker.'

Olena starts talking, and the interpreter begins scribbling again. The older woman asks a question, listens to the answer, nods and then turns to Joona.

'I saw him maybe eight times in total, but he had some kind of breakdown. The last time we met, about six months ago, it was impossible to have any sort of conversation with him. He was convinced a criminal network had put a price on his head, and he thought I was working with them.'

'Did he ever talk about the robbery, when he was beaten up?' asks Joona.

'Only once, the first time.'

'What did he say?'

'Not much. He wanted to search my place to make sure there was no one hiding,' she says. 'I asked him why, and he told me about the assault, that a prostitute had lured him into a trap . . . and that she hadn't looked anything like her pictures.'

'What did she look like?'

'He didn't say, just that she was ugly and crazy and that she started hitting him with a metal bar – in the face, on his back and between his legs.'

'Do you know her name?'

'She seems to be one of the women who changes her alias and the forum she uses pretty often, but he called her Miss Liza . . . followed by a string of expletives.'

'Miss Liza?'

'Yes.'

'Do you know anything else about her?'

'No, I'm sorry.'

'OK, I won't take up any more of your time, but is there anything I can do for you? Anything at all?'

'I don't think so, thank you. I know what you're getting at, but if I stop doing this then I'll be letting my family down and I can't do that. It would all have been for nothing then,' she replies, eyes welling up as she holds his gaze.

31

Joona hangs up his coat and jacket by the door to the investigation room and turns on the electric Advent candles in the window. His curly blond hair is getting long, and is still as messy as it was when he first woke that morning. If Valeria had been there, she would have told him to run his fingers through it, if nothing else.

He sits down at the meeting table with his colleagues Rikard Roslund and Stina Linton.

Rikard is a detective inspector, and has had to fight to keep his position since the new boss arrived. He has sharp features, thin lips and hazel eyes. His short hair is reddish brown, and almost shimmers like bronze beneath the harsh lighting in the office.

Stina is an experienced detective superintendent who joined the NCU from Malmö a few years back. She has pale skin, a small, plump mouth and furrowed cheeks. Her short black bob is flecked with grey, and she wears black-rimmed glasses and a self-imposed uniform of a brown or grey sweater with trousers and flat shoes.

Their chairs creak as they return to their desks to search for any mention of Miss Liza online. Working methodically, they trawl through the various sites used to sell and procure sex – Real Escort, Happy Escort, Escort 46 – with no real idea whether the ads are real or scams.

Joona finds a Flashback thread in which someone describes the current situation with the robber as being like Russian roulette for johns. He reads the jokey, mocking, aggressive conversation from start to finish, but none of the posts mention a specific location, name or alias.

With a sigh, he turns to the window. He can see the reflection of the small, pointed bulbs from the Advent candles in each of the three layers of glass, and notices that delicate snowflakes have started to fall over the dark park outside.

'I've got her,' says Stina, turning her screen towards the others.

The ad for Miss Liza is at the very bottom of the page, meaning she isn't one of the site's verified users. The first picture is of a pretty, wide-eyed blonde with dimples. She looks to be somewhere around twenty, and is perched on the edge of a gilded armchair in her underwear. In the second picture, she is naked, shot from behind in a lavish hotel room.

Alongside the images, there is a list detailing her height, weight, hair, eye and skin colour, her waist and hip measurements, bra size, pubic hair preference, piercings, and so on.

Beneath that, the services she offers are provided: vaginal, anal and oral sex, oral sex without a condom, CIM, CIF, COB, strap-on, cunnilingus, rimming and domination.

Her phone number and payment details are also given, as are her prices – which vary depending on the time and location of any meeting.

'OK, so who's going to call her?' Stina asks as she takes off her glasses.

'I can do it,' Rikard volunteers. 'So long as I know what to say.'

'Make up a name,' Joona tells him. 'And book a session with her today.'

'Today? It's just that I have to go home and take the dog out,' he explains, leaning back in his ergonomic chair.

'Would seven thirty work?' asks Joona.

'Sure, I guess so.'

'We need to pick somewhere quiet, but still close to town,' Joona continues.

'I don't know why, but the Dialog Hotell in Lidingö immediately sprang to mind,' says Stina.

'Good,' says Joona.

'Seven thirty, Dialog Hotell,' Rikard repeats. 'What service should I ask about?'

'Sex without a condom,' Stina suggests.

'That's not listed on her page.'

'Exactly. Say you'll make do with oral otherwise.'

'OK,' he sighs. 'Should I try to negotiate on the price?'

'Maybe . . .'

'No, tell her you'd be willing to pay more if she does what you've asked for. That way she'll know you've got money,' says Joona.

Rikard signs the log, and Stina opens a plastic pouch and hands him a clean, untraceable phone.

Joona plugs in an external microphone, starts the recording and puts on a pair of headphones. Rikard takes a deep breath, runs through what he is going to say and hits dial, but the number is no longer in use.

'Shall we keep looking?' asks Stina, lowering her headphones to the desk.

'Yes – both for Miss Liza and the picture of her linked to different names,' Joona replies, rolling up his shirt sleeves.

He has a large pink scar on his forearm, from a training exercise in urban warfare in the Netherlands. A red-hot round from an M240 Bravo grazed his arm, melting his jacket onto his skin.

Stina prints out two A3 copies of the photographs of Miss Liza and pins them up on the wall. The three detectives then go through to the pantry for coffee and gingerbread before returning to the investigation room, sitting down at their computers and divvying up the remaining websites between themselves.

A sluggish fly buzzes through the office and lands between the blue and red folders in an open filing cabinet.

It doesn't take long for Rikard to find another two ads featuring the same name, picture and telephone number on different sites.

Joona scrolls through ladys.one, and sees the images flicker by: young women in bikinis, bare breasts, underwear, smiling faces, genitals and backsides. He loads the next page and has just started skimming over the near-identical ads from another sixty sex workers when he stops dead.

This time, the blonde girl with the dimples is calling herself Cherry Pop. The services she offers are the same, but the phone number is different.

'I'll call her,' says Rikard, reaching for the burner phone.

They start the recording, and Rikard composes himself and dials the number, but yet again it is no longer in use.

The team continue their search, sipping their increasingly cold coffee. After half an hour, Rikard gets up to go to the toilet. Stina puts in some eyedrops, opens a new website called Escort Heaven and, as ever, clicks to confirm that she is over eighteen. Just ten ads in, she spots the familiar photograph of the young blonde woman. On this page, her name is Jezebel.

'I've got a new number,' she says as Rikard comes back into the room.

'New number,' he mutters, taking a seat at his desk.

'For Jezebel this time.'

They repeat the same process as earlier, putting their headphones on and starting the recording. Rikard enters the new number and hits dial. It rings twice before going to voicemail.

'You've reached Jezebel,' says a sensual female voice. 'Leave your name and how you'd like to be contacted, plus the service you're looking for, and I'll get back to you.'

'Hi, my name is Roger,' says Rikard. 'You can reach me on this number. I'm interested in meeting at a hotel tonight. Regular sex, maybe a two-hour session . . . I'll tip well if it's really good. Give me a call if you're interested.'

He hangs up.

'Nice,' says Joona.

'You should be an actor,' Stina says with a grin.

'Right? I've got it,' he jokes. 'Rich guy, confident on the outside, but with serious mummy issues.'

The team have just started closing the tabs for various websites when the untraceable phone rings, and they quickly put on their headphones and start the recording again. Rikard takes a few seconds to compose himself before he answers.

'Roger speaking.'

'You called me a few minutes ago,' a woman replies. 'Are you free to talk?'

'Hold on a sec ... let me just close the door,' Rikard tells her, pausing briefly. 'OK. Hello.'

'How do you want to pay?'

'However you like. American Express, cash, crypto.'

'Cash is best.'

'No problem.'

Stina has started picking the bobbles from her dark-grey sweater and piling them up beside her keyboard.

'You mentioned regular sex. What did you have in mind?'

'Nothing weird, we just do the deed. No stress. Normal.'

'OK.'

'Ideally without a condom,' he says, lowering his voice a little.

'No.'

'Plenty of people do.'

'Not me.'

'I'll pay extra,' he says.

'How much?'

'I don't know ... Double if you let me come inside you.'

'Double double,' she says.

'OK.'

'Where should we meet?'

'There's a place in Lidingö, the Dialog Hotell ... It's perfect, because the reception closes at six.'

'I'll find it.'

'Tonight, seven thirty.'

'Eight would be better for me.'

'OK. I'll text you the room number once I'm there.'

'See you later, then,' she says, ending the call before he has time to say another word.

They take off their headphones, stop the recording and look up at each other.

'She sounded nice,' says Stina.

'She actually did,' Rikard says with a smirk.

'But if she's the person we're hoping she is, she's extremely dangerous and violent. Don't forget that ... She's probably unwrapping a brand-new axe as we speak,' Stina reminds him.

'Nah, I trust her,' Rikard jokes. 'I think she really liked me.'

'I'm going to go and see Noah about backup,' Joona says, getting up and leaving the room.

32

Rikard Roslund stops to let Velour sniff a telecoms cabinet as they turn back towards the house. He waves when he notices one of the neighbours in their kitchen window, then makes his way in through the garden gate. The dog sits patiently on the doormat, waiting for him to dry her feet before she lumbers through to the kitchen.

Kennet's shift at Danderyd Hospital doesn't end until seven. The chronic lack of nursing staff means he works far too much, which is great for their finances but not much else.

They have been together for six years and like to tell friends that they live the perfect middle-class life, but that is no longer true for either of them. Kennet struggles with depression during the winter months, and one February evening almost a year ago, he overdosed on sleeping pills.

Rikard found him on the floor by their bed when he got home from work, with froth clinging to the corners of his mouth, and grey skin.

Thank God for activated charcoal, Kennet sometimes jokes.

He now takes antidepressants, and they have put it all behind them, but Rikard still feels betrayed – deeply.

Rikard gets changed, grabs the envelope full of cash he signed out earlier, shoves the notes in his wallet and takes his Glock 45 out of the gun cabinet.

He used to dream about retiring early and moving to Palma with Kennet, sitting on the balcony with a crime novel and a glass of cold rosé, but nowadays the thought just makes him sad.

It isn't Kennet's fault; he can't help his struggles. Rikard himself had a serious eating disorder when he was younger, but was fortunate enough to get help from a specialist clinic. Just three years later, he had recovered. He started working out, and eventually applied to the police academy.

After checking the time, Rikard eats a quick sandwich in the kitchen. He is just feeding Velour when Joona calls to tell him that the backup team is ready and in position.

He leaves the house, locks the door and gets in the car to drive south to Lidingö. The plan is to stop somewhere along the way to put on his body armour, rather than doing it when he gets to the hotel. Jezebel could very well be staking out the entrance, waiting for him to arrive, after all.

The tactical unit and sharp shooters are all in place, poised to make a swift intervention and block off all exits.

Rikard will head inside, pay for a room and then text Jezebel to let her know the number.

He will keep the door locked while he waits, and once she knocks, he will give the green light over the radio. Two tactical teams will then move in with weapons and stun grenades and carry out the arrest.

If she tries to break through the door with the axe before his colleagues arrive, Rikard will fire as many rounds as it takes to stop her.

He asks himself what it says that he has chosen to act as bait for a serial killer – like a worm on a hook – over an evening at home with his partner.

This is part of the job, of course, but the truth is that it feels like something has stagnated between him and Kennet lately. They have both been too tired for sex.

Rikard had been planning a romantic evening in. He was going to set the table, light some candles and make Kennet's favourite meal. But instead, he is alone in the car with a gun on the passenger seat and a gnawing anxiety in the pit of his stomach.

He is approaching Lahäll on the motorway when the phone he has been using to communicate with Jezebel pings with a message. Rikard gets into the outside lane, takes the next exit and pulls over to the side of the road by a Max burger restaurant to read the text:

Hi. Need to meet somewhere else. Hope you haven't gone out to Lidingö already, because I've booked room 111 at Hotell Norrort in Vallentuna. Afraid I'll have to cancel if that doesn't work for you.

Works for me.

Come as soon as you can. The door code is 1939.

Rikard turns around and starts driving north again, calling Joona from his usual phone to tell him about the change of plan.

'We're calling it off,' says Joona. 'Head home.'

'I'm almost there. This is our only shot. I'll arrest her and wait for you. Just get there as quick as you can.'

'OK, but listen to me: we're coming. Wait outside. Do not go in. You're only there to observe.'

* * *

After turning off from the 264, Rikard Roslund stops at the side of the road, gets out of the car, pulls his stab vest over his head and adjusts his shoulder holster. He then puts on his black windbreaker, does up the zip, gets back in the car and sets off again.

The hotel looks like an enormous lump of metal in the middle of the drab industrial estate.

Beyond the high fences on both sides of the road, Rikard can see workshops, plumbing wholesalers and sheet metal firms.

Yellow light spills across the tarmac from the petrol station nearby, and the flags in the forecourt flutter limply in the gentle breeze.

There isn't another soul in sight.

Rikard turns off into the hotel parking area and pulls into a space, watching as a skinny fox drags a dead crow from the road to the ditch.

He is currently thirty kilometres from the hotel in Lidingö, and has just calculated that the first members of the tactical unit should be with him in twenty-five minutes when he gets another message from Jezebel:

I need to know if you're coming.

Wait. I'm almost there.

He switches his comms unit to silent and gets out of the car. The temperature has dropped, but he doesn't think it will snow; the dark sky is almost clear.

His breath forms a pale cloud in the air around his face.

Rikard doesn't know whether he is being watched or not, and he tries to be discreet as he takes a picture of the two other cars parked nearby.

On the main road, a lorry thunders by. The ground shakes, and its headlights sweep over the hotel.

The stab vest makes Rikard's movements feel heavy and awkward as he walks over to the door, enters the code and heads inside.

The unmanned reception is spacious, with large windows out onto the parking area and a spiral staircase leading up to the first floor. A heap of Christmas decorations has been dumped on the floor by the desk: electric Advent candles, tinsel, fairy lights, fake trees and boxes of red baubles and elves.

The only sound he can hear is the low hum of the air conditioning.

There is no sign of any other guests.

Rikard follows the signs past a simple dining room. The tables are bare, the cushions missing from the chairs. On a counter to one side, there are a number of shiny canteens, a coffee machine and a microwave. A patio door leads out to a seating area with a view of the main road and a plastics manufacturer.

He continues down a gloomy corridor.

The lighting is so dim that the floor seems to vanish beneath his feet unless he is standing directly beneath one of the weak bulbs.

The plastic numbers on the grey doors sweep by almost hypnotically. 131, 130, 129.

As he walks, he realises that the strange, dreamlike feeling that has taken over him is partly down to the brown carpet muffling his footsteps.

Someone could be walking right behind him, and he wouldn't have a clue.

Rikard feels a rush of fear, and he stops and looks back over his shoulder before continuing.

A cleaning cart is blocking the hallway up ahead, and he has to push it out of the way to get past, causing a stack of fresh towels to tumble to the floor.

Rikard peers back again, thinking about the picture of the cute girl with the dimples in the ad.

Jezebel.

He knows that the person he is about to meet is probably someone else entirely, but she is most likely a woman, and – given that no one has mentioned either a man or an accomplice – likely working alone.

An ugly fucking whore, one of the victims said.

In Rikard's mind's eye, another image has taken hold. The cute girl is no longer smiling. Her face has hardened, and her chin is jutting out. She is almost two metres tall, gripping the axe in her hand so tightly that her knuckles have turned white.

Her forehead is flecked with hundreds of tiny red droplets, as though she has just walked through a light rain of blood.

33

Rikard pauses and tries to calm his breathing. He inhales deeply through his nose, then exhales through his mouth, forcing back the images by reminding himself why he is here.

He simply can't allow Jezebel to get away. This might be their only chance before she kills again. Possibly their only chance ever.

Rikard knows that he is here to arrest a suspected serial killer, but Jezebel thinks she is here to rob and possibly even kill a john.

He continues down the murky corridor and notices that one of the doors has been left open.

It isn't her room, but it could be a trap.

Rikard tugs down the zip on his windbreaker and reaches inside. Gripping his gun, he slowly makes his way forward.

He glances back over his shoulder before nudging the door open and peering into the room.

In the strange yellow light from the petrol station, he can make out a narrow bed with a crumpled terry throw.

A vision of Jezebel flickers through his head, cutting the cable ties securing her new axe to the glossy cardboard packaging and then loosening the plastic cover from the blade.

His heart rate picks up.

Rikard's hand is clammy, and he lets go of his pistol, wipes his palm on his thigh and moves over to the corner, where the corridor turns sharply to the left.

He stops and listens.

Through the walls, he hears a dull clatter.

He slowly edges forward.

Behind him, something clicks.

She could be waiting just around the corner. She could be standing less than a metre away.

In the window, Rikard can make out the faint reflection of the hallway to the left. He presses up against the wall in an attempt to get a better look, then hesitantly moves another step closer.

A car drives by outside.

Rikard studies the row of reflected doors in the glass.

The sparse lighting resembles some sort of illuminated garland.

At the far end of the corridor, he can see a grey blob. A dark shadow, quivering slightly.

He takes a deep breath, swings around the corner and feels his heart pounding in his chest.

Rikard blinks firmly.

It looks as though there is a small, broad-shouldered man standing at the other end of the corridor, and Rikard has already reached for his gun before his brain manages to process what he is seeing.

It is just a chair with a hoodie draped over the backrest and a pair of trainers on the floor.

'God,' he whispers as he starts moving again. 'It's OK, I can do this . . .'

He passes an alcove containing a small pantry with a fridge, an oven and a small stovetop. On the stainless-steel counter, there is a white plastic chopping board.

His body armour is heavy and uncomfortable.

He continues along the row of closed doors.

Jezebel is a woman, he reminds himself. He is an armed police officer who has carried out hundreds of arrests over the years.

Despite that, he can hear the blood thundering in his ears as he reaches her room.

The door is ajar.

He moves to one side so that he can see in through the narrow crack.

The scratched laminate flooring is bathed in yellow light.

He can hear a low, monotonous roar.

Rikard knocks and takes a step back to wait. Staring in through the crack, he remembers the photographs from the crime scenes: the head on the ice, the body parts in the caravan, the blood on the walls and floor.

Reaching beneath his jacket again, he grips the handle of his gun and opens the door.

His heart rate rises even higher as he walks down the cramped hallway.

The bowing floor creaks softly underfoot.

The door to the bathroom is closed, the shower running.

The unnatural golden light from the petrol station fills the room.

Rikard keeps going, taking in the dark TV mounted on the wall to the right, a little of the window, more of the floor and the foot of the bed.

He steps forward out of the hallway and scans the main room. His eyes dart over to the corner, sweeping across the small desk, the chair and the wardrobe.

There is a red bra on the neatly made bed.

He moves over to the desk and waits for Jezebel with his back to the wall.

The shower is still running.

The yellow light from outside highlights the dirt on the windows.

Rikard adjusts his vest beneath his jacket and studies himself in the dark TV screen beside the bed.

He looks like a tin soldier, as grey as a field mouse. Trapped in a corner.

His eyes drift over to the hallway.

Jezebel is still in the bathroom.

The bra catches his attention again, and he realises he didn't look beneath the bed.

She could be hiding under there.

He gets down on all fours to check.

The floor under the bed is dusty, strands of hair caught around the legs.

A strange image pops into Rikard's head, of a buzzard perched on top of a dead tree, staring down at him with a pair of beady yellow eyes.

He hears another thud through the walls, and he quickly straightens up, dries his clammy palm and grabs his gun from the holster.

Rikard coughs to muffle the sound as he grips the grooved slide, pulls it back and feeds a cartridge into the chamber.

Outside, a car swings around the roundabout.

Its white headlights sweep across the room and are gone.

Gripping his pistol by his side, Rikard moves back towards the hall.

The corridor outside is dark.

He knocks on the bathroom door, waits twenty seconds and then tries again, a little harder this time.

'Hello? Jezebel? I just wanted to say that I'm here,' he shouts.

The shower is too loud for him to hear whether she has replied or not, so he knocks again, then opens the door. Hot steam floods out towards him. The water in the shower is hitting the curtain, making it pulse in time with the rhythmic roar.

'Jezebel?'

On the floor by the toilet, there is a pair of red knickers. The mirror above the sink is fogged up, and the condensation is dripping from the ceiling.

Rikard steps forward into the damp heat and raises his pistol. He has just reached out to push the curtain to one side when something hits the back of his head.

The power of the blow makes him stumble, and he grabs the shower curtain in an attempt to break his fall, tearing it from the rail as he drops to his knees.

The shower is empty. It was a trap.

Groaning, he half-turns, bracing himself against the toilet as he tries to get up, but something hits him again before he has a chance.

His head snaps forward, and his mouth smashes into the plastic toilet lid.

The light is snatched away from him, and a black sail flaps across his vision.

A moment later, he regains consciousness.

The bathroom is spinning, and he struggles to make his eyes focus.

Rikard can taste blood, and his head is pounding.

With a groan, he pushes himself up and manages to get onto his feet. He turns around with his weapon raised.

This time, the metal bar hits him square in the wrist, and his gun clatters to the floor beneath the sink.

Jezebel is breathing heavily through her nose, and she lashes out at him again, following his movements with wide eyes.

She is in her fifties, with a wrinkled face and pursed lips. The muscles in her neck are taut, and the pink dress she is wearing is damp beneath both arms.

Rikard spits blood and staggers forward.

She backs up and takes another swing at him, but he uses his forearm to deflect the blow and tries to hold her back. The scent of perfume from her warm body fills his nose as they crash into the hallway wall.

She gasps, and her metal bar thuds to the floor with a hollow clang.

Rikard can feel the blood running down the back of his head, trickling inside his collar and over his spine.

The floor seems to tilt beneath him, and he feels like his legs might buckle at any moment.

Moving as fast as he can, he staggers out into the corridor, using his right hand to support himself against the wall.

In the confusion, he finds himself thinking that he should have stayed home and eaten a romantic dinner with Kennet after all.

Right then, he hears a gunshot behind him. Jezebel has his Glock.

He tries to run, but crashes straight into the wall.

'Die, you bastard!' she shouts, her voice faltering.

His footsteps sound like soft thuds beneath him, and to his right, the doors race by. He passes the little pantry and slows down, gasping for air. Spitting blood, he turns around and thrusts an arm out in order to remain upright.

A framed print of a pine forest falls to the floor.

Jezebel is now nowhere to be seen.

His ears are ringing, and his headache is so bad that he feels physically sick.

As Rikard starts moving again, he catches sight of himself in the window. He hurries around the corner and walks straight into an old man in a white bathrobe and slippers.

Rikard keeps going, wiping the blood from his lips. Jezebel must have chosen a different route, he thinks. She will probably be waiting for him in the lobby, behind the pile of Christmas decorations.

34

Rikard lumbers along the corridor on unsteady feet. He glances down at his bloodied hand with a strange, dreamlike feeling as he passes the cleaning cart, then pauses outside the dining room, straining to see whether he can hear anything from the lobby between ragged breaths.

The pain radiating from the back of his head is almost unbearable.

His legs are like jelly.

Rikard turns into the dining room, crosses the bowing laminate floor and tries to open the patio doors.

He feels a searing pain in his injured wrist as he tugs at the handle.

The door is locked.

Panting heavily, he takes a step back and kicks it as hard as he can. His foot makes a dull thud as it hits the glass, but the door doesn't budge.

He has just turned around and started scanning the room for somewhere to hide when he sees Jezebel coming towards the dining room from reception. She pauses outside, uses his pistol to tap on the window in the door, and waves.

Rikard grabs the microwave oven, yanking out the plug in the process, and carries it back over to the patio doors. Lifting it above his head, he hurls it through the glass.

Jezebel opens the door and fires his gun. The bullet slams into the wall two metres away from him.

Rikard kicks out the shards of glass and crawls through the hole to the patio. The broken window crunches beneath him. He steps over the low hedge and starts running towards the petrol station.

He can hear a large vehicle approaching, and the cold air claws at his lungs.

Jezebel is right behind him.

Up ahead, on the other side of the fence around a HVAC firm, Rikard spots a security guard with a torch.

'Help!' he shouts.

The guard glances in his direction and then starts walking towards his car. He turns off the torch, gets in behind the wheel and takes out his phone.

Rikard runs out into the road just as a lorry appears from the right.

The driver slams on the brakes, and the tyres screech against the tarmac. The man turns the wheel, and the heavy vehicle thunders past Rikard with only inches to spare.

It crosses the hard shoulder, careens into the ditch and slams into a lamppost. The light goes out, and the post topples like a felled trunk, bringing down a banner for Christmas trees with it.

The lorry crashes through a couple of bushes and a low fence before making it up the embankment to the road on the other side. Soil and debris spray across the tarmac. The trailer sways as the driver accelerates, and a moment later it vanishes out of sight.

'God . . .'

Heart racing, Rikard is hurrying towards the roundabout in the yellow light from the petrol station when he notices Jezebel approaching from the side. He stops, turns to face her and holds up both hands.

'I'm a police officer, I—'

She pulls the trigger, and the bullet slams into his vest. Rikard feels a burning sensation on the left-hand side of his torso, and he staggers back, grabs a branch in an attempt to stay upright, and hears the gunshot echo between the buildings.

* * *

Joona is driving at 210 kilometres an hour when he brakes and turns sharply to leave the motorway. His tyres scrape against the edge of the island in the middle of the road, and he accelerates along the 264 in the darkness.

He turned on his hidden blue lights and left the rest of the tactical unit behind on the E18. The connection with Rikard had dropped just before he left Lidingö through the Northern Link tunnel, and Joona realised that his colleague had decided to go in, that something unforeseen had drawn him into a situation, despite the direct order to hold back.

Industrial buildings race by outside, fleets of machinery and high fences.

He is approaching the hotel at high speed when he passes an articulated lorry with two broken headlights.

To one side of the road, a lamppost is lying in the ditch.

There are dark skid marks across the carriageway, with earth and clumps of grass dragged across the tarmac.

From the petrol station nearby, yellow light floods out across the road.

Joona is planning to drive straight over the roundabout to get to the hotel when he spots Rikard on the grass in the middle.

His colleague's face is bloody.

Joona lifts his foot from the accelerator and stamps on the right-hand pedal. He feels the brakes shudder through the car.

Somewhere nearby, a gun goes off.

The sharp crack reverberates between the buildings.

Rikard is hit in the abdomen, and he grabs a branch, tearing off the dead leaves as he staggers back before managing to regain his balance.

A blonde woman wearing a black coat over a pink dress is standing a few metres away from him with a Glock 45 in her hand.

She is breathing heavily.

The magazine is clearly empty, but she pulls the trigger repeatedly before tossing the gun to the ground.

Joona's car shakes as it mounts the kerb at the side of the road and comes to a halt on the yellowed grass. He opens the door and pulls his own weapon from his shoulder holster as he runs towards the roundabout.

The woman takes a utility knife from her coat pocket, drops the black sheath and starts walking towards Rikard.

Joona pauses when he reaches the cobbles by the edge of the roundabout and takes aim at the woman.

'Police! Stop and drop your weapon!'

She half-turns to look at him, gripping the red handle tight.

'Police!' Joona repeats as he moves closer. 'Throw the knife towards me!'

The woman looks distraught, mascara running down both cheeks. She turns away from Joona and looks down at the knife in her hand.

'I just want to talk to you,' Joona says calmly. 'But first I need you to drop the knife.'

He can hear the tactical unit's sirens approaching through the industrial estate.

The woman shakes her head and turns away from him, hunching over to slash at her wrist. She groans in pain.

Joona starts running.

'Get down on the ground!'

She sways unsteadily on her high heels.

Joona takes aim at her again, and has just held out a hand to help her when she lashes out unexpectedly.

A lightning-fast jab of the knife, like a snakebite.

The blade slams into his protective vest.

The woman yanks the knife back and swings it up towards his throat.

Joona blocks her arm, locking it and jerking it upwards, breaking her shoulder. She screams, and the knife drops to the grass.

He kicks out her feet from beneath her, and she lands heavily on her back. Her pearl necklace hits her in the face.

As Joona uses his foot to knock the knife away from her, he notices that there is no blood on her wrist.

She only pretended to cut herself.

He rolls her onto her front and feels the heat radiating from her body as he cuffs her arms behind her back.

Her right heel has snapped, and is hanging loosely from the red leather.

Rikard stumbles back and slumps to the grass as the tactical units finally arrive. He lies down, staring up at the night sky.

Joona is the only one still on his feet.

His colleagues' headlights illuminate him from all four sides, building a cross of light in the otherwise deserted industrial estate.

From above, the roundabout resembles an old drawing of the solar system, with rings of cobbles, gravel and more cobbles around a central circle of grass.

35

It is eight o'clock in the morning when Joona enters the interview room, where the woman who called herself Jezebel is waiting with a guard. She has now been identified as Jenny Gyllenkrans, a fifty-two-year-old, single, childless resident of Norrköping who sits on the city council for the Liberal Party.

Joona says a quick hello to the guard and takes a seat across the table from Jenny.

Her face is bare, emphasising the deep furrows around her mouth, and her blonde hair loose. Instead of a pink dress, she is now wearing loose prison-issue clothing, and has been given a sling for her broken shoulder.

Before coming into the interview room, Joona spoke to Erixon. The forensic technician told him that Jenny's car, a five-year-old Lexus, is a match for the tyre tracks found at the campsite, meaning that analysis of the strand of hair has now been given priority.

'How is your shoulder?' he asks.

'A bit sore,' she replies without looking at him.

'Have you been given anything for the pain?'

'It's fine.'

'Do you want to see a nurse?'

'No need.'

'Just say if you change your mind.'

'Thank you,' Jenny whispers, straightening the sleeve of her sweatshirt.

Stina Linton comes into the room, says hello and sits down beside Joona.

'Shall we get started?' he asks.

Stina quickly takes Jenny through the formalities, explaining the process and informing her of her rights and obligations before telling her that the interview will be recorded.

'You're being held on suspicion of attempted murder, aggravated robbery, assault and guns charges,' Joona begins. 'But that's not what I want to talk to you about.'

'OK . . .' Jenny replies, a crease between her brows.

'Do you know what I want to ask you about?'

She shakes her head, still avoiding his eye.

'We have reason to believe that you were at Edsviken Tennis Club at around ten p.m. on the night of 27 November. Is that correct?'

'No.'

'We also have reason to believe you were at Bredäng Campsite at around two a.m. on 26 November. Is that correct?'

'Don't know.'

'In your own words, could you tell us what you were planning to do at Hotell Norrort in Vallentuna yesterday evening?'

'You lured me into a trap,' Jenny says, staring down at the table.

'But what were you planning to do there?' Joona presses her.

'Nothing. Meet a guy.'

'Are you a sex worker?'

'No.'

'But you pose as one?'

'That's not against the law.'

'But robbery and assault are.'

'Buying sex is illegal,' she says, meeting his eye for the first time.

'You frequently change your alias,' Joona continues. 'But always use the same picture, of a young woman – yourself, when you were around twenty.'

'Twenty-one,' she replies, unable to hide her surprise.

'What happened to you then?'

Jenny looks down again. She takes a deep breath, as though she is about to start talking, but doesn't manage a single word. Tears roll down her cheeks and drip to her lap. She dries her eyes, lifts her head and tries again.

'When I was seventeen, I met a man through a classified ad,' she begins. 'He was Swedish, but he lived in Brooklyn. He'd just started an economics degree there, and he was smart and funny and loving . . . He sent a few sexy pictures, so I sent some back. It was all so exciting – it felt like things were *finally* happening for me – but when I started planning a trip to New York to see him, something changed. I remember wondering whether he was already married or something . . . Anyway, by the time I realised he'd been grooming me, it was too late. I was embarrassed, scared, and I tried to break things off with him, but he threatened to share the pictures I'd sent with my school, said he'd send them to my family if I didn't give him more. That went on and on, and he kept asking for more – and worse. I started thinking about killing myself, but I couldn't do it because I wanted to live. Not that I would've felt that way if I'd known what was going to happen next . . .'

She pauses for a moment and dries her cheeks.

Stina passes her a tissue, and she mumbles a thank you, blows her nose and continues.

'He forced me to go over to his place, and it turned out he wasn't in New York after all. He lived half an hour away, in Nacka . . . And he was a disgusting old man, ugly and aggressive. He made me have sex with him, and he filmed it . . . and this went on until I was almost nineteen . . . That's when he forced me into prostitution. I would've topped myself right there and then, just to get out of it, but he showed me the messages he'd been sending my little sister and said he'd do the same to her if I refused . . . so I met a bunch of other men in a small flat by Gullmarsplan. They were literally queuing to get in, and he said they could do whatever they wanted with me as long as he got paid . . . After three years of that, he got caught up in a police raid. They found out he'd been grooming a whole load of girls, that he'd forced four of us to become prostitutes, and he was sent down – for two measly months. I wanted ten million in compensation, but I only got eleven thousand . . . so now I'm clawing the rest of it back myself.'

As she stops talking, she starts picking at a scratch on the table.

'So it's all about money?' Joona asks.

'Yes.'

'And a hatred of men buying sex?'

'What do you think?'

'I think your hatred overwhelms you from time to time, and you use an axe rather than an iron rod and a knife.'

'An axe?' she repeats, fixing her absent eyes on him.

'You're suspected of murder, and you're going to be remanded in custody,' Stina Linton explains.

'Murder?' Jenny smiles uncomfortably.

'Your tyres match tracks found at Bredäng Campsite on 26 November . . . and we also have a blonde hair from the scene of the murder.'

'But I haven't murdered anyone, as far as I know.'

'We'll be handing the case over to the prosecutor now, and your custody hearing will start tomorrow at the latest.'

Joona's phone buzzes, and he sees that he has a text from Erixon. He apologises and opens the message:

Results in from the lab: the blonde hair from the caravan is NOT from Jenny Gyllenkrans.

He puts the phone screen-down on the table and studies Jenny for a moment before continuing the interview. She is sitting quietly with a sad look on her face, picking at a hangnail on her thumb.

'What were you doing at Bredäng Campsite on 26 November?' he asks.

Jenny lets out a deep sigh and looks up at him.

'I know why you think it was me,' she says, briefly meeting his eye. 'Because I'd arranged to meet a john in caravan fourteen . . . The place was closed for the season, which suited me just fine.'

'OK, so you drove over there, parked by the gates, grabbed your metal bar and your knife and walked over to the caravan?'

'Yes.'

'What time was this?'

'Five to one.'

'Go on,' says Joona.

'I saw that the light was on in the caravan, so I thought the john must already be in there,' she says, getting lost in thought.

'What happened next?' asks Stina.

'What happened? I stopped dead,' she mumbles.

'Why?'

'Because I saw a guy go round the back of the caravan.'

'Could you describe him?'

'Long, dark hair . . . I can't really remember. Jeans and a green sweater.'

'And what did you do then?'

'What did I do? I heard some loud noises from inside . . . thuds, things breaking. And then a load of blood sprayed across the window, so I turned around and left as quick as I could. I got in the car and drove home.'

'Did you hear any voices inside the caravan?' asks Joona.

'No, don't think so . . . No.'

'For the record, I need to ask if you ever set foot inside the caravan.'

'I didn't.'

'And you're sure?'

'Yeah.'

'What was the closest you got to the caravan?'

'Maybe twenty metres,' she replies.

'You were on your way towards it, but you stopped because you saw a man outside the caravan?'

'Yes.'

'And then you heard noises inside?'

'Yes.'

'What were you thinking then?'

'At first, I thought the john must be the aggressive type, that he'd flipped for some reason and started trashing the place.'

'But you didn't immediately leave?' says Joona.

'We're only talking about a few seconds. But when I saw the blood . . . there was so much of it, all over the window. I mean, there wasn't anything I could do. He wasn't alone in there, he was in a fight or something, and I started thinking about gangs . . . I just wanted to get away.'

'Did the man with the long hair go inside the caravan?'

'Not that I saw.'

'And did you see anyone else at the campsite?' asks Joona.

'No.'

'Did you notice anything else?'

'Don't think so.'

'Were there any other cars in the parking area?'

'Yeah . . . The john's was there, plus another one. An old banger, parked a bit further back.'

'What kind of car did the john have?' Joona asks, though he already knows the answer.

'A Mercedes.'

'Colour?'

'Silver.'

'And the other car?'

'It was a rusty old Opel . . . a Kadett. With one of those screw-on roof rack things.'

'What colour?'

'Pale blue . . .'

'Do you remember the registration number?'

'No.'

'None of it?'

'Sorry.'

'Was it Swedish?'

'I don't know.'

'Anything else? Was there any damage to the body? Any stickers, a tow bar?'

'No idea, I just wanted to get away.'

Joona leans across the table.

'You were parked beside the john's Mercedes, which was over by the gates. When you reversed out of the bay, you would have pulled towards the Opel. You must have seen it in the rear-view mirror.'

'Yeah, it . . .'

She trails off and starts picking at the scratch on the table again.

'Did you see anything in the rear lights?'

'There were some of those little tree things that smell like pine in the windscreen,' she says, licking her lips.

'Air fresheners?'

'Yeah, but that was the weird thing,' she says, meeting his eye. 'There were probably fifteen of them hanging off the mirror, in a big bunch.'

36

Amina Abdallah feels the chill through her wetsuit as she wades out into the freezing river with her lemon-yellow kayak.

Half an hour ago, she pulled into a parking bay by the end of the bridge and loosened the straps on the roof rack. The sun was high in the sky, but a stubborn band of last night's snow was still lingering in the shade up against the wall.

Amina carried the kayak and the rest of her gear down to the pebbly shore just below the Älvkarleby Power Station.

She is now getting ready to set off, and can feel the current pushing her kayak to the right over and over again.

Strictly speaking, she should be in the kitchen at home right now, but she needed to get out, to clear her head.

The roar from the turbines and the surging water is almost deafening.

Her older brother Ali has just come back from Wadi Halfa, and though he is crashing at her place in Skutskär, he seems to expect to be treated like some sort of king. In his view, she should be serving him sugary tea between meals, waiting on him hand and foot and addressing him as 'Your Excellency'.

Ali spent three years working on the railway in Sudan, but after injuring his knee he flew back to Sweden, leaving his wife and three kids behind. Now, he spends his days slumped on Amina's sofa, watching Arabic-language TV with the Koran in one hand.

He goes on and on about how unfair life is, pushing conspiracy theories, talking about moral decay and repeating disinformation – claiming the Swedish authorities steal Muslim children and that it's against the law to burn the Torah but not the Koran.

Ali doesn't have a job, but Amina works in a nursery and does extra shifts cleaning offices at the weekend. She supports her mother and little sister, does all of the shopping and cooking, and looks after her uncle's kids every Friday.

'I'll find you a good Nubian husband,' Ali told her, not for the first time, as she set down a plate of booza in front of him.

'I don't want a husband,' she replied.

'I'm ashamed of you. Everyone is.'

'Well, don't be,' she mumbled as she left the room.

She balances her paddle across the kayak, adjusts her helmet and straightens the tow line around her waist, then looks out at the river and the writhing current.

Amina has signed up for the Swedish kayak cross and white water kayaking championships, and has been told that she has a good chance of getting onto the national team if she wins.

The competition will be held in Åmsele next summer.

She has no idea whether she is good enough, and knows she should really join a club of some kind, but she doesn't have time to socialise. All she wants is to get out onto the water.

Amina first started kayaking in high school, but she has only ever been out on her own since then, for fun, and doesn't know how she might get on at the championships.

Despite that, she dreams of winning.

A spruce branch floats by, and she waits for it to pass before gripping both sides of the cockpit and lifting herself up. She swings both feet inside and lowers herself onto the seat.

Amina's kayak is a narrow rocker with a relatively short stern and a V-shaped hull, making it extremely manoeuvrable and easy to tilt when dealing with waves.

She isn't planning to go far today, just wants to feel the power of a couple of rapids, practise some peel outs and eddy turns and work on her speed down to Kullens badplats. After that, she'll get changed and catch the bus back up to the bridge to get her car.

She fits her spraydeck and pushes off, paddling gently.

The surging water from the power station gives the kayak real momentum, causing it to shoot forward like an arrow. Amina quickly works up to a fast stroke rate, twisting her torso and keeping her hips loose, driving herself downriver.

She wants to pick up as much speed as possible before hitting the Klockarharen rapids.

Her body is desperate for the adrenaline rush.

The kayak catches the wind blowing in from the flat landscape to the right, and she has to take a few extra strokes to adjust her course.

The water glitters brightly.

Amina picks up the pace to the right-hand side of the island and can see the low suspension bridge across the river up ahead.

Someone has attached a metal ladder rope to the bridge, and it is trailing in the water in the middle of the channel, pulsing unnaturally like a fishing line with a salmon on the end.

She decides to paddle beneath the bridge, to the right of the ladder.

As she drifts past the little island known as Korallen, she comes too close to the shore. She doesn't notice the large rock lurking just beneath the surface until her bow hits it, and the kayak immediately flips, plunging her into the icy water.

Amina is upside down, surging forward in the powerful current.

From beneath, the surface of the water looks like aluminium foil.

She gets ready to roll before she runs out of air, leaning forward and pressing the paddle to the side of the kayak.

Above her head, green rocks and swaying seagrass race by.

The sunlight ripples through the water.

She knows she needs to make use of the current as she rights the kayak.

The river is roaring in her ears.

Amina realises she must be getting close to the bridge, and she twists around and tries to look downstream in an attempt to avoid hitting the ladder.

The cold water makes her eyes ache.

Green eddies swirl past her, carrying fragments of plants and sediment.

She speeds past a dark log on the riverbed, eyes still scanning all around.

Just then, she hears herself scream underwater.

A grey body without a head is hanging from the ladder.

It is caught between two rungs, spinning slowly like some sort of propellor. The severed vertebrae in its neck seem to glow white amid the pale-pink tissue.

Amina passes the rotating body, then tenses her stomach, swings the paddle out in a quarter-circle, breaks the surface with the blade, jerks her hip and pulls back. The kayak rolls, and she swings up out of the water, head last.

The light is blinding.

Amina takes a deep breath and then leans as far back as she can, spluttering for air. Once she has regained her balance, she quickly starts paddling towards a calmer patch of water, fumbling for the bilge pump with shaking hands.

* * *

Joona leaves the Police Authority building and walks down one of the paths in Kronobergsparken in the afternoon darkness.

The news is reporting that Storm Eyolf is approaching from the Barents Sea, in a wide front covering the Kola Peninsula, the White Sea and the Baltic, but there is almost no breeze in Stockholm.

On one of the park benches, a man with a beard is huddled in a sleeping bag, surrounded by plastic bags, cans and grubby possessions.

'We've gotta be patient with AI,' he mutters with a wheezy laugh.

Joona walks past him and turns off onto another path. Between the trees, he can see the lights of the buildings on Parkgatan glittering warmly.

A weary-looking man in workout gear and a winter coat is standing beneath one of the streetlamps with a pit-bull terrier on a lead. Without warning, the dog starts barking at something in the darkness. It pulls on its lead with such force that the man has to take a couple of steps forward before he manages to restrain it, but the dog rears up on its hind legs and continues to bark.

Joona left the interview with Jenny Gyllenkrans with what is likely a description of the killer's car: a rusty, pale-blue Opel Kadett with a roof rack and around fifteen air fresheners hanging from the rear-view mirror.

Probably to dull the stench of rancid blood, he thinks as he climbs the steep slope.

Once he had asked everything he wanted to know, Stina Linton showed Jenny a sketch of the parking area at the campsite with a mark indicating the location of the victim's Mercedes, and asked Jenny to point out where both her own car and the old Opel had been parked.

With a bit of luck, they might be able to pinpoint the killer's tyre tracks, and possibly even shoeprints.

It is definitely a step forward, though the message from Erixon revealing that the blonde hair in the caravan was not Jenny's also came as a disappointment.

The minute Joona left the interview room, he paused in the corridor to read Erixon's brief report in full.

The special thing about mitochondrial DNA is that it comes from the mother's egg cell, meaning a child's mtDNA is a direct clone of their mother's.

The only changes in this particular type of DNA – passed down since the very first mother – are a long line of mutations, and it just so happens that mutations are precisely what scientists focus on when attempting to match DNA.

The lab results for the mtDNA from the strand of hair showed that it was not a match for Jenny Gyllenkrans, nor anyone else in the usual registers or databases.

Despite his powerful internal drive, Joona doesn't usually allow himself to feel frustrated. He knows that preliminary investigations can take time, and that the trail sometimes goes cold before new leads rise to the surface.

This time, however, he feels acutely impatient, because he is convinced they are chasing an active serial killer.

There will be another murder, and soon.

It is like a grass fire approaching the edge of a forest.

They are close, and they need to extinguish the blaze before it spreads any further.

Thanks to Hugo Sand's testimony, they have a first description of the killer: a woman with long blonde hair.

They have a strand of her hair from the caravan, and because the lab prioritised their case, they also have her mitochondrial DNA.

Using commercially available genealogical databases, they could probably identify – and possibly even arrest – her today.

But following a pilot case in which the police used ancestral DNA to solve a double murder in Linköping, the Authority for Privacy Protection ruled that the use of such databases runs counter to Swedish law.

Without realising it, Joona has walked to the far side of the park and through the gate to the old Jewish cemetery. He leaves a small white pebble among the others on his friend Samuel Mendel's grave.

He no longer knows what to say to him, but he stands quietly for a moment, looking down at the headstone, as the first soft white flakes begin to fall from the dark sky.

The snow soon grows heavier, lingering on the ground for a few seconds before melting away.

Joona leaves the cemetery and makes his way up towards the play area, watching the teenagers playing basketball behind the tall fence. He takes out his personal phone and calls Agneta Nkomo.

'Hello?'

'Hi, it's Joona Linna again,' he says. 'I wanted to ask if you could help me with something.'

'Of course, if I can.'

'As a police officer, I'm not allowed to use commercial databases to match DNA, but that rule doesn't apply to journalists.'

The basketball hits the fence in front of Joona and bounces down to the tarmac.

'Do you have the killer's DNA?' Agneta asks in disbelief.

'In all likelihood, yes. A blonde hair from the caravan.'

'OK, wow . . . Yes, I can help,' she says.

'There's only one database that handles this particular type of DNA.'

'No problem, I'll do it . . . and I assume it's urgent?' she says.

'It is.'

'Have you made any other progress?'

'We're in the process of tracking down a suspected escape car, an old Opel.'

'So you still think robbery is the motive?'

'It's not the primary motive, in my opinion . . . That wouldn't explain the degree of violence. But robbery is probably part of the explicit drive.'

Once Joona has shared everything he can and they have ended the call, he sends an encrypted message containing the DNA profile from the blonde hair to Agneta. He then sighs and turns back towards the station in the snow. His work phone starts ringing before he gets there.

'Linna,' he answers.

'This is Jaromir Prospal, detective superintendent with Northern Uppland,' says a man with a glum voice. 'I think we might have something for you.'

37

Joona is standing in the middle of the suspension bridge, looking down at the surging water below. The maritime police have travelled upriver from the Bothnian Sea in a boat with a crane, and a diver has attached a harness to the dead body and cut through the rope ladder with a pair of bolt cutters.

The winch starts to turn with a low whirr.

Water pours off the body as it breaks the surface and the team work to bring it onboard into an open cadaver bag.

The deceased is an adult male, and he seems to have been in the water for around three days.

Swollen and grey.

His right arm and head are both missing, likely making him the serial killer's third targeted victim.

He has a boot on one foot, but the other is bare, and his toenails are blue against his pale skin. He is wearing a coat, black trousers and a wrongly buttoned shirt.

According to detective superintendent Jaromir Prospal, he is likely Pontus Bandling, who was reported missing by his wife a couple of days ago.

The local police have found traces of blood further upstream, on Karl XII's Bridge, right by the power station. The body must have drifted downriver on the current before becoming caught on one of the ladders used by recreational fishermen in the area.

* * *

The melancholy detective superintendent is waiting for Joona at the end of the bridge in an unzipped floor-length down jacket. He has puffy bags beneath his weary eyes, a goatee, a tattooed neck and a mullet.

'I'm thinking about dropping the investigation into Pontus Bandling for petty drugs offences,' Jaromir jokes half-heartedly.

'What kind of drugs?' Joona asks.

'We found half a vial of meth in his hotel room, maybe three grams, plus some coke and a bit of weed.'

'For personal use, I presume?'

'We'll have to see what the autopsy shows,' Jaromir mumbles.

The maritime police back up against the current, turn their boat and disappear into the distance.

Tiny snowflakes swirl over the dark water.

Jaromir turns back to the suspension bridge, where the remains of the rope are swaying in the current.

'Hard to believe he could've lost both his head and his arm in the rapids,' he says.

'It was an axe,' Joona replies.

'You could see that from the bridge?'

'Yes.'

'Then I'm guessing you probably want to take a look at his room?' says Jaromir, heading back towards the cars.

* * *

After a short drive to the Officers' Villa on Laxön, the two detectives park on both sides of the dead man's Bentley, get out of their cars and pause around twenty metres from the cordoned-off building. Jaromir explains that forensics have already photographed everything, but that the technicians won't touch anything until Joona gives them the green light.

The blue-and-white tape flutters and strains in the wind.

Jaromir shoves his hands in his pockets and pulls his coat tight as he explains that Pontus' wife Caroline called the police at seven a.m. on 2 December to say that she was worried because she couldn't get hold of her husband. The call handler tried to reassure her, to say that he had probably just slept in, that his phone had run out of charge.

An hour later, Caroline phoned again, having spoken to the university in Falun where he works; he had never been late for the morning meeting before.

'We sent a car over here and found the door unlocked,' Jaromir continues as they move towards the building. 'He hadn't checked out, and all his things were still here. The place was a bit of a mess, but we couldn't see any blood, no sign of violence. It was only when my colleagues found the vial of white powder that they cordoned off the room to wait for forensics.'

Jaromir hands Joona a pair of shoe covers and tells him that the dead man's wife has already been in touch with Missing People to request a search party. Her lawyer has also called the regional police chief to demand a dog patrol, and added that they would be hiring a private investigator from Stockholm.

The detective stamps the snow from his combat boots before he and Joona pull on their shoe covers and head inside, sticking to the step plates that have been laid out.

The air in the bedroom smells like perfume and smoke, and the sheets are messy, the duvet heaped on the floor.

A pair of navy-blue boxer shorts have been draped over the valet stand, and there is a dark-brown leather briefcase leaning against the radiator beneath the window, a single man's sock on top of a Burberry cabin bag.

On the floor by the stove, there is a near-full bottle of Highland Park whisky.

Over by the bed, on the nightstand, a small mirror flecked with powder has been left beside a metal straw and a tarot card. It is the Hanged Man, featuring a picture of a youngster in a pale-blue shirt, hanging upside down from a wooden post with a snare around his foot.

A reproduction Carl Larsson painting has been taken down and propped up, facing the wall, and a pair of black lace knickers have been hung from the nail in its place.

* * *

216

Joona is driving back towards Stockholm on the E4 when Jaromir calls to tell him that the deceased's identity has now been confirmed as Pontus Bandling. Breaking the news of a death is one of the toughest jobs a police officer can face, but Joona offers to stop off in Uppsala to let Bandling's widow know.

They are looking at three premeditated murders now, he thinks, which makes it a definite series. This will undoubtedly be the biggest investigation of the year. There is nothing wrong with Noah Hellman – he's a good boss – but he refuses to admit that their chances of stopping the killer would be much higher if he would just allow Saga to join the team.

* * *

Joona opens the door to a handsome building from the late-nineteenth century and gets into the lift. He presses the button for the top floor, and the mechanism creaks as it carries him upwards.

He can't bring himself to look in the mirror.

Telling a person that someone they love is dead is probably the most fraught type of communication there is.

A few words marking the point of no return.

So final, almost an insult to the concept of free will.

Our utter impotence in the face of destiny is never clearer than in that moment.

The brain frantically searches for a way out, a mistake, but eventually has no choice but to give up. And a moment later, the heavy wave of grief hits the bereaved with full force.

The lift reaches the top floor, and Joona opens the gate and steps out onto the landing. He takes a deep breath, then moves forward and presses a finger to the bell. It doesn't make a sound, but Caroline Bandling quickly opens the door.

She is a striking woman in her fifties, wearing a pair of wide-legged beige trousers and a matching cardigan with a fitted waist.

Behind her, Joona can see a spacious oval hallway with milky marble flooring, an enormous chandelier and a pale-grey silk ottoman.

217

Caroline is wearing barely any makeup, and is enveloped in the scent of expensive soap. She tries her best to maintain her composure, but it is clear from her eyes that she is petrified.

'My name is Joona Linna, and I'm a detective superintendent with the National Crime Unit in Stockholm,' he begins, holding up his ID.

'No . . .' she whispers, clasping her shaking hands.

'Could I come in?'

It is as though he can feel the power of her frightened heartbeats pulsing through the air. The colour drains from her cheeks, her chin begins to tremble, and she swallows firmly.

'Is it Pontus?'

'I'm afraid to have to tell you that—'

'No,' she cuts him off, shaking her head.

'He has been found dead.'

'Don't say that.'

'I'm so sorry for your loss.'

'No, no, no . . .'

Her face crumples and becomes a picture of unbearable loss, and she slumps to the floor. Joona rushes forward and helps her back to her feet. She falls into his arms, clutching him to her. Her body feels red-hot, trembling against his.

'God, I don't want . . .'

'I know,' he says softly.

Her breathing is ragged, but after a moment or two she pulls back and attempts to compose herself. She looks up at him, tears running down her cheeks, and tries to dry her eyes with shaking hands.

'Sorry,' she says between sobs. 'Please, come in.'

'I really am sorry for your loss.'

'Thank you,' she says, pressing a hand to her mouth for a few seconds. 'I have a private detective here. She'd just turned down the job.'

'I can come back later.'

'No, she's about to leave . . . If you'll excuse me, I just need to . . . Give me a few seconds,' Caroline says, turning away.

38

Joona watches as Caroline hurries away on unsteady legs, hunched over slightly.

He waits a moment, then walks through to a parlour with a large Isaac Grünewald painting hanging on the wall, gold leaf joinery, stucco work and an enormous crystal chandelier.

He continues through the heavy double doors into a corner room with windows looking out onto the Fyris River, taking in the oak panelling, floor-to-ceiling bookshelves and three different seating areas.

A blonde woman in her thirties returns a volume of Descartes' letters to the shelf and half-turns towards him. She is leaning on a cane in her left hand, but she moves it over to her right as he approaches, possibly to avoid having to shake his hand.

'I overheard what you just said to Caroline. Incredibly sad news, but I'm glad for her sake that it's you leading the investigation,' she says. 'I'm actually a little starstruck to meet you.'

She has a scar on her face, stretching from the edge of one eyebrow to her chin.

'Your work on the porcelain children case was impressive,' Joona replies, pausing a few metres away from her.

'Don't forget to ask Caroline about her sister-in-law. That's where I would've started, anyway.'

'OK,' says Joona.

The woman starts making her way towards the hall, the tip of her cane thudding softly against the Persian carpet. Joona holds open the heavy salon doors for her.

'You know, I just pretend to be helpless for the advantages it brings,' she jokes.

'Same here.'

Joona follows her over the creaking parquet floor and out into the hall, where she drapes her coat over her arm, opens the front door and turns to him.

'Leave some cases for me, Joona,' she says as she leaves.

He moves back through the parlour to the large living room and hears Caroline wailing through the walls.

Joona sits down in an armchair, takes out his phone and skims through his messages. On the coffee table, there is a book of Mikael Jansson's photographs from various Formula One races.

After a few minutes, Caroline Bandling comes in and sits down opposite him, crossing her legs and apologising for making him wait. Her eyes are puffy and red, but she is just about holding it together, like the first delicate ice in winter.

'Julia has gone,' he says.

She nods, clasps her trembling hands on her right thigh and meets his eye.

'Are you *sure* it's Pontus?' she asks.

'I'm afraid so.'

Her face crumples again, and she turns away and presses a hand to her mouth. Swallows hard and looks at him.

'Sorry, I'll pull myself together,' she says, clearing her throat.

'Take however long you need.'

'You've got a job to do,' she says, drying her cheeks. 'It's just that I'm struggling to take it all in . . . You'll have to forgive me.'

'Caroline, you've just received the worst news possible, and it's no problem at all if you want to wait a few days . . . But I'm going to need to ask you some questions.'

'It's OK,' she says, clasping her nervous hands again. 'Just start, and we'll see . . . How it goes, I mean.'

'Thank you,' Joona replies. He starts the voice recorder function on his phone and sets it down on the table in front of her.

'You've got a hole in your jacket,' she says.

'I do.'

'I can mend it, if you like.'

'Thanks, but I'll do it this evening.'

'I'd like to, it'll help calm my hands.'

Caroline gets up and leaves the room, returning a few minutes later with a sewing basket. Joona takes off his jacket and hands it to her.

'It's very kind, but you really don't have to.'

She reaches for her reading glasses and then takes out a few different threads, holding them against the material before eventually settling on the right colour.

'Don't tell me you were shot,' she mumbles.

'Stabbed, actually.'

She looks up and gives him a soft smile, as though he were an unruly child. Joona sits down opposite her – still wearing his shoulder holster on top of his grey shirt – and watches as she deftly sews up the hole from the inside so that it is no longer visible.

'I was happy with Pontus,' she says as she ties and cuts the thread. 'We used to say that we were always young together, if you see what I mean . . . And we planned to keep it that way, until we were really old.'

She switches to a finer needle and thread and mends the glossy lining before turning the jacket the right way out and handing it back to him.

'That was so kind of you, thanks,' he says as he pulls it on.

'No problem.'

'The two of you have a daughter together, and Pontus has a sister . . . Do they know he was missing?'

'Only my sister-in-law . . . She told me she thought he was having an affair,' Caroline says with a sudden smile.

'And you're sure he wasn't?'

'Yes, I . . . I think I can be pretty confident about that.'

'But she thought he was?'

'OK,' she sighs. 'What I'm about to say is extremely personal . . . but when Pontus first vanished, I called her and she told me that she'd been keeping a secret for a while, that she felt so guilty about it and hadn't known what to do . . . At some point over the summer, she'd seen a rather saucy text Pontus had written, arranging to meet a woman called Kimberly at a hotel in Gävle.'

'What did you say to that?'

'God,' she mumbles, picking a loose thread from her trousers. 'I had to explain that *I'm* Kimberly, that it's a game of ours, a sort of roleplay . . .'

'We found drugs in his hotel room.'

'Do I need a lawyer?' she asks calmly.

'I wouldn't say so. I don't care about the drugs, in any case. All I need to know is where you got them from, the dealers you're in contact with and whether you have any debts.'

'Our finances are stable . . . and Pontus always gets whatever he wants from a member of staff at the university.'

'Did he have any enemies?'

'Hold on a minute, I just need to . . . You said you were with the NCU in Stockholm. Why do Uppsala police need help from the NCU?'

'As the investigation is still ongoing, I'm afraid I can't say.'

'Was he murdered? Is that it?'

'How long did you stay in Älvkarleby?'

'Kimberly got there at nine p.m. and left at two the next morning,' she replies. 'My driver can confirm that.'

'Is there anything else I should know?'

'I don't even know what happened to him.'

'Still.'

'I'm not sure, this is all a bit much. You could leave your card.'

Joona reaches for his phone and shares his contact details with her before getting up from his chair.

'One piece of advice . . . talk to your family before they hear what happened from elsewhere,' he says.

'I'm going to go and see our daughter now,' she says, standing up too.

'Yes, it would probably be good for you to be together now.'

'Amanda is going through a bit of a difficult period at the moment,' she explains. 'She suffers from schizophrenia and is currently on the psychosis ward at the University Hospital, which is reassuring, but it's not going to be easy to break the news to her.'

39

For the team at the NCU, Friday began before the sun had even risen with a festive Saint Lucy's day procession. It meant that Joona had glitter in his hair during the morning meeting, where he found out that it would be two weeks before the National Forensic Centre would have time to process their samples.

Three frustrating days followed, involving nothing but interviews with the victims' friends and relatives, more fruitless rounds of door knocking and attempts to locate the Opel. They trawled through vast amounts of material from the CCTV cameras around the campsite, tennis club and Älvkarleby, but failed to find even a single sighting of the Kadett.

* * *

Joona's apartment is dark when he gets home. He turns on the light in the kitchen, puts a pot of potatoes on to boil, fries the meat patties he made that morning and whips up a quick cream and cognac sauce. Earlier that day, he sent a message to Saga asking if she would like to join him for dinner, but she replied the way she always does: 'Thanks, but I can't make it tonight.'

In silence, Joona sets the table for one, opens a bottle of non-alcoholic beer and sits down to eat, adding lingonberry jam and pickled cucumber to his plate.

He misses Valeria so much that he finds it nearly impossible to avoid thinking about Leila's glowing needles and twisting columns of smoke.

His soul has sustained a number of deep wounds over the years, and in his darkest moments he has occasionally turned to opium. The drug enables him to sink to the very bottom, almost on the brink of death, before returning to the surface.

He doesn't want to go back there now, to feel the opium's cold embrace, largely because he wouldn't be able to bear seeing the disappointment in Valeria's eyes once she realised what he has done.

I'm weaker than I am strong, he thinks. But my greatest weakness is that I have to keep pushing myself forward, that I'm incapable of giving up.

Joona does the dishes, wipes the table and is just putting the leftover food into the fridge when his phone rings. He moves back over to the table, sees that Agneta is calling, and immediately picks up.

'Are you free to talk?' she asks.

'Of course.'

'I've got the results already,' she says. 'Paid slightly more for the express service. As I understand it, we've got a good match considering it was mitochondrial DNA.'

'How good?'

In the background, he catches Bernard saying something in an excitable voice.

'There's only one mutation separating them,' Agneta continues. 'Which means the match could only be the child, mother or sister of the killer.'

'Could you—'

Joona stops talking when he hears his phone ping, and he sees that Agneta has shared a contact with him:

Elisabeth Olsson
4416 18th St., San Francisco, CA 94114, USA
Phone: +14 158311200

Joona thanks her and ends the call, then immediately dials the number she gave him. He hears it ring, the sound travelling through a fuzzy, pulsing abyss for a moment before there is a click and the connection becomes crystal clear and oddly intimate.

'Elisabeth,' a woman says, as though she were standing right in front of him.

'Hello. My name is Joona Linna, and I'm a detective superintendent with—'

'What's happened?' she asks, sounding panicked.

'I'm in the process of investigating a serious crime here in Sweden, and I need to ask you a few questions.'

'What sort of crime?'

He can hear shrieking, laughter and whistles in the background, and realises she must be in a playground or a school yard.

'Our investigation has thrown up a close match for your DNA, and I was wondering if you have any children . . . or a mother or sister who might have been in Sweden over the past few weeks.'

'I have a sister in Sweden,' she replies, swallowing hard.

'No children?'

'Yes, but they're five and eight.'

'Can you corroborate their alibis?' Joona jokes.

'I'm not so sure about the little one,' she replies, a smile in her voice.

'Noted.'

'I have almost no contact with my sister, but I'm guessing she still lives on the family farm,' she continues.

'Where is this farm?'

'I call it a farm, but it's really just a load of junk in a hole called Rickeby . . . I grew up there.'

'Rickeby . . . in Vallentuna?'

'That's the one.'

'Could you tell me your sister's name?'

'Lotta . . . Ann-Charlotte Olsson.'

'Have you spoken to her recently?'

'What's this about?'

'I'm afraid I can't discuss an ongoing investigation.'

'But I'm guessing it must be worse than benefit fraud or moonshine?'

'Yes.'

Joona thanks Elisabeth Olsson for her help and sits down at the dining table with his laptop in front of him. He searches Ann-Charlotte Olsson's name and looks up the address. There are five small buildings visible in the satellite images, tucked away at the end of a gravel track between woodland and fields.

'Stay right where you are,' he tells them.

Joona gets up and moves over to the window, gazing northwards over the city. He then calls Noah, who brings his pool cue down on the edge of the table in frustration.

No one knows for sure how the killer came to be known as the Widow in the department, but everyone has warned Joona against using the name – or the term 'serial killer' – around the boss.

'We've had a breakthrough . . . a DNA match for the hair. A woman in Vallentuna.'

'Seriously?'

'Yes, but I had to go via the commercial genealogy route,' Joona confesses.

'Don't tell me that,' Noah groans. 'I'll have to fire you. You know that, don't you? If I know about this, I have to take immediate action.'

'You can just report me to the Special Prosecutor's Office.'

'Do you *want* to be reported?'

'I know I went against the Authority for Privacy Protection ruling, but that's because we'll have a fourth and fifth murder on our hands otherwise.'

'God, I'm going to have to put Petter in charge now, aren't I?' Noah sighs. 'Not that there's anything wrong with him, but we'll lose focus and—'

'Start by asking the union for advice.'

'Maybe I should, but the union . . . they could take weeks.'

'That would be a shame,' Joona replies with a smile.

For a few seconds, neither man speaks. A pool ball thuds softly against the cushion before knocking into another ball with a low crack.

'OK, what the hell, I hear you,' the boss says with another sigh. 'Let's do this: I'll ask the union for advice, and you can keep investigating in the meantime.'

'I need a tactical team and a drone unit within the hour,' says Joona.

'To bring in a woman for questioning?'

'A suspected serial killer.'

'Let's not use that label.'

'Serial killer?'

'Christ . . .'

'Just give me a tactical unit.'

'It was your choice to go it alone,' Noah replies.

'Are you serious?'

'You'll have to do this without me . . . Ask the local station in Täby for help. Ask Norrtälje.'

'Can I take Saga Bauer?'

'You already know the answer to that.'

Joona ends the call as he makes his way out into the hall, puts on his shoes and leaves his apartment. He locks the door behind him and runs over to the lifts.

* * *

Joona heads north, passing the university before joining the E18.

With Noah refusing his request for backup, he calls the regional command centre to ask about any patrol cars in the area. The duty officer contacts four vehicles, of which two immediately respond to his call.

Ann-Charlotte Olsson, the suspected killer, is registered as living with a man called Åke Berg and their two children, one of junior school age and the other younger. Both parents have criminal records, with convictions for fraud, tax evasion, threatening behaviour, assault and handling stolen goods. They are long-term unemployed and, following a number of reports of concern for their children, have been under investigation by social services over the past five years.

The traffic on the six-lane motorway flows forward through the wide bends with a fluid elasticity.

To one side of the road, three enormous silos covered in blood-red graffiti loom like the remnants of an old border fortification, and then the countryside becomes increasingly rural: forests, fields and dark lakes filling the ancient fissures in the land.

Joona leaves the motorway at the exit for the 280 and makes his way to the meeting point on increasingly narrow roads.

On the far side of a three-way junction, he spots a police car blocking the road, preventing any traffic from driving past Rickeby.

Joona pulls up to it and comes to a halt.

Two plainclothes officers are waiting for him, shoulders hunched against the cold. Their breath forms hazy clouds in the air in front of them.

Joona gets out of the car and walks over to greet them.

'Gregory,' says the elder of the two.

'Peck,' says the other. 'It's Peter, really, but you get it?'

Gregory is a stocky man in his forties. His eyes look watery behind his steel-rimmed glasses, and he is wearing black jeans and a brown leather jacket. Peck can't be much older than thirty, with acne scars on his cheeks and prominent front teeth. He is wearing a green hoodie beneath a blue windbreaker, plus a pair of navy outdoor trousers with pockets on the legs.

Joona explains the situation to them, neglecting to mention that he would have preferred backup from the National Tactical Unit and a drone team.

'We're here to bring Ann-Charlotte Olsson in for questioning, in other words,' he continues. 'She's been linked to four murders so far, and there's a real risk she won't come willingly . . .'

'We'll have to ask nicely then,' says Gregory.

'Her husband, Åke Berg, could also be there, and they have two young children who—'

'We know the family,' Gregory cuts him off. 'Her lot have always lived round here. They bicker with the neighbours, get up to all sorts. Petty fraud, troll accounts, benefit fraud, renovating stolen cars . . . they've got a contact over at the industrial paint place. They're trouble-makers, no question, but they're not dangerous.'

'Any weapons?' asks Joona.

'Not registered, no. But I'm pretty sure there'll be a shotgun or two knocking about.'

'Will they recognise either of you?'

'Doubt it,' Gregory replies.

'We'll go over there and ask Ann-Charlotte to come with us to Norrtälje for questioning, that's all,' says Joona. 'Keep things low-key and try to avoid making an arrest, but if we have to take more of a hard line then so be it.'

'OK,' Peck mumbles.

'And if it comes down to it, your safety takes priority,' Joona continues. 'Retreat and wait for backup . . . No guns unless absolutely necessary.'

'We're pretty far from the Stockholm slums here,' Gregory says with a grin, pushing his glasses back onto the bridge of his nose.

'What sort of service weapons do you have? Sig Sauer?' asks Joona.

'Yeah.'

'P239s,' says Peck.

The two men show Joona their pistols.

'When did you last fire them?'

'God . . .' Gregory says with a sigh. 'I was at the range . . . when was it? Might've been last year, or the one before that.'

'But you carry out your function checks regularly . . .?'

'Yeah, of course,' he replies.

'Peck?'

'Not always,' the younger man admits, eyes on the ground.

'Do you carry backup weapons?'

Gregory shakes his head.

'But I've always got one of these on me,' says Peck, holding up a distress flare.

'He got lost as a trainee,' Gregory explains with a laugh.

'It's funny, I know,' Peck tells Joona, 'but seriously . . . it gets super dark out here in the country . . . Everything looks the same – all the fields, forests, barns. Mile after mile after mile.'

40

Without a word, Gregory and Peck open the boot of their car and put on their body armour. They pull on their coats over the top, then follow Joona down the narrow road towards the turnoff to Rickeby.

'These politicians, they always promise lower petrol prices . . . We fell for it last time, and we'll fall for it next time, too,' says Gregory. 'Because the truth is that unrealistic promises sound better than realistic ones . . . It's like a self-playing piano.'

'You could always vote for one of the left-wing parties instead . . .' Peck suggests hesitantly.

'What was that?'

'I said—'

'I can't hear a fucking word you say,' Gregory cuts him off. 'You talk like a little bitch.'

'Easy,' Joona warns him.

The road meanders through a dark field, snow lingering in the furrows in the earth, a hunting stand over by the edge of the woods.

'Tougher sentences, the politicians say . . . and the journalists, they lick their arses like dogs,' Gregory continues. 'But tougher sentences won't make a fucking bit of difference. We don't have the bloody capacity; the courts can't keep up as it is, and the prisons are already full.'

'What we need is preventative work,' says Peck. 'And a social—'

'What?'

They pause behind a red barn right by the turnoff. The ground around them is littered with fallen roof tiles. It is hard to tell whether or not this building is also part of the Olssons' farm.

'Nice and quiet now,' Joona says softly. 'No visible weapons, no raised voices.'

They make their way down the narrow gravel track, Joona taking the lead and the two local officers bringing up the rear.

Their footsteps and breathing are the only sounds they can hear.

In the ditch, something flashes.

There is a white plastic motion detector mounted to a gatepost at one side of the road, and they have just triggered the alarm.

'Well, they know we're coming now,' says Joona.

It feels as though the temperature drops as they continue.

The air smells like snow.

Through one of the windows in the main house, Joona notices the pale glow of a television. The light flickers sombrely over the low branches of the spruce trees outside.

Someone is chopping logs nearby, heavy blows followed by the thud of wood on wood.

The three officers slowly approach the dilapidated farm buildings.

In the yard, there is an old caravan with a green tarpaulin draped over one side, a white pickup and eight cars that have been largely stripped out.

The track swings off behind a barn before leading them in between the buildings, and on turning the corner they see a slim, bare-chested boy chopping wood over by a hydraulic splitter.

A brood of hens moves uneasily between broken buckets, car seats, blackened exhaust pipes and mufflers.

The three police officers pause in the middle of the yard.

Peck blows on his frozen fingers.

Beside the front door, a small Swedish flag hangs limply from a rusty pole.

There is a brown refrigerator up against one wall, beside a tap and a metal washbasin.

Four folding plastic chairs have been arranged around a metal table.

A man emerges from the open garage. He has slim shoulders and grubby hands, and is wearing rubber boots and a green raincoat buttoned over his rounded belly. It is Åke Berg, Ann-Charlotte's partner. His greying hair is pulled back in a ponytail, and he has a paisley scarf tied around his head.

'Everyone's seen that goddamn ad, huh?' he says, tightening the belt on his coat. 'We've only got ten sacks of seed potato and three sacks of chicken shit left.'

'But we—' Gregory begins.

'No one wants chemicals in their food, but there's chemicals in all the fucking food,' Åke continues. 'That's why we're self-sufficient. We've got hens, sheep . . . fields, greenhouses.'

'We're here to speak to Ann-Charlotte,' Gregory tries again.

'Yeah, her raspberry jam . . . Fuck me, it's good. But we only sell produce in the summer.'

The low sound of the TV in the main house is audible, and Joona tries to peer in through the window. The boy is still chopping wood, but he glances over to them every time he positions a new piece on the block.

'Could we come in?' asks Joona.

Åke uses his thumb to wipe his nose.

'No can do, Lotta's snoozing.'

'Then maybe you could do us a favour and wake her up,' Gregory says, pushing his glasses back onto the bridge of his nose.

'Soon enough, yeah . . . But talk to me first. Doesn't sound like you want to buy jam,' says Åke, pulling out one of the chairs by the table. 'Sit down, tell me . . . What d'you actually want?'

'This only concerns Lotta,' says Joona.

'Right-o. Sit yourselves down and I'll go and get her,' Åke replies, nodding to the chairs.

He studies them as they sit down around the metal table. The ground is strewn with cigarette butts and empty beer bottles, and their breath forms clouds in the cold air.

Åke half-turns away from them and reaches into his raincoat. He pulls out a length of fishing line and winds the loose end around his index finger.

Using his left hand, he sets down four tin mugs on the table, followed by a bottle of murky liquid.

'We were at the Christmas market over in Karby last year,' he says. 'Y'know, selling sweet pretzels and hotdogs at jacked-up prices . . .'

Åke moves over to the fridge and returns with a jam jar without a label. He then fetches a plate of small grey balls, possibly some type of dumpling.

'You've gotta try some of our snacks and must.'

'Thanks,' says Gregory, popping one of the balls into his mouth. It crunches between his teeth as he chews.

'Knut! Come and open the bottle,' says Åke.

The boy brings the axe down on the chopping block and shuffles over to the table with his head bowed. His face is grubby, his thin body covered in bruises.

He takes the bottle from his father and holds it out to the police officers like a waiter in a restaurant.

'Who wants a sup, then?' Åke asks as he takes a seat.

'Go and get Lotta,' Joona tells him.

'He'll have some,' says Åke, ignoring him and pointing at Peck.

The boy unscrews the lid, fills the mug in front of Peck and takes a step back. Joona opens his windbreaker slightly in case he needs to access his gun.

'Try the must,' says Åke.

Peck pretends to take a sip.

'Very nice.'

The boy fills the remaining mugs with the murky liquid and leaves the bottle on the table. The pungent aroma of alcohol and raw onion hangs over them for a moment before dissipating in the wind.

'Give it a proper go,' says Åke.

Peck does as he is told and immediately grimaces.

'It's quite bitter, but . . .'

'You should ask for a Baileys next time,' Gregory tells him, taking a drink from his own mug.

'What d'you reckon, then?' asks Åke, turning to Gregory with a strange glimmer in his eye.

'Nice and strong.'

A grubby-faced girl in a pink nightie appears from the side of the garage. She is holding a struggling rabbit by the ears in one hand, its long back feet practically dragging on the ground.

'Might as well sit here and enjoy ourselves for a bit,' says Åke. 'The chicken balls and drinks are on me, and you can to tell me exactly why you want to talk to Lotta.'

He smiles, revealing that he has no molars.

'We can come back next week,' says Joona.

'Like hell.'

The boy scratches his arm. His lips have taken on a bluish tinge.

Small snowflakes swirl through the air above the gravel.

Gregory pops another chicken ball into his mouth and chews noisily.

The young girl is staring at them. The rabbit in her hand has stopped struggling, but its nose is still moving in time with its rapid breathing.

'Doesn't seem like you're going to tell me why you're here, huh?' Åke mutters.

'We're here to talk to Ann-Charlotte,' Peck tells him.

'You lot are really fucking repetitive, you know that?'

'That's not our intention,' says Joona. 'We'll come back another day.'

'Drink your damn must,' Åke replies, looking him straight in the eye.

'No.' Joona slowly gets to his feet.

'The boy's freezing. You should let him go inside,' says Gregory.

'Mind your own fucking business,' Åke snarls, a menacing tone to his voice.

'I'm just saying that—'

'Shut your mouth. Knut, get over here.'

The boy takes a step forward, and Åke slaps him. He staggers to one side, but doesn't raise his head.

'God . . .' Peck whispers to himself.

The boy stands still for a moment, then quietly moves back over to the chopping block and gets to work.

The hens peck at the ground around him in the darkness.

'We're going,' says Joona.

Åke leans back, breathing heavily. He loosens the belt of his raincoat, giving Joona's colleagues a glimpse at what he already suspected might be underneath: several large packs of explosive strapped around his torso.

'Sit down, the lot of you. Sit down and put your hands where I can see 'em,' Åke tells them.

The detonator has been pushed into one of the bales, right through the protective paper. The safety catch is off, and the fishing line around his finger is tied to the fuse.

'For your own sakes,' he explains, studying them with a glazed look in his eyes. 'If you want to avoid an accident, that is . . . Me, I don't care either way.'

41

Time seems to grind to a halt – as it does in the cold glare of a camera flash – as Gregory and Peck realise that Åke could detonate the belt before either of them has time to react.

If he yanks the fishing line, the small charge inside the detonator will set off an explosion, a blast large enough to kill them both and destroy most of the buildings around them.

Joona takes his seat, and Gregory and Peck slowly put their hands on the table. The colour has drained from both of their faces, and their eyes are wide and panicked.

'People like me spend their whole lives preparing for a visit from people like you,' Åke mutters. 'But you think you can just waltz in here, wave a few papers and take our kids away.'

'No, we—'

'Yeah, yeah, you just want to talk to Lotta,' he says with a smile.

'We do.' Peck nods.

'Everyone knows the politicians are corrupted by the power elite, moving taxpayers' money to their own accounts . . . It's no secret . . . But what does that make social services, the courts, the police? Mercenaries and traitors, that's what . . . Snatching our kids and selling 'em to the Jews.'

The boy approaches the table with an elk rifle.

'Tell your son to put that gun down and go inside,' says Joona.

'Dad?' the boy asks, pausing a few metres away.

'You can start by shooting this Jew if he doesn't drink up, Knut,' says Åke, pointing at Peck.

The boy raises the rifle, rests the butt on his shoulder and takes aim. Peck quickly picks up his mug, takes a sip and presses his lips together.

'More,' Åke barks, pulling the fishing line taut.

'I'm OK, thanks.'

'Is this really the hill you want to die on?'

The boy's finger is now on the trigger.

Peck drains the rest of his mug in two big gulps and wipes his mouth with the back of his hand. Åke refills the mug and then leans back and studies the three officers.

'Social workers . . . Who do you think you are, eh?' he says. 'Coming to my farm, asking your questions . . . We've said we don't want anything to do with you, but you just keep on coming back.'

'I hear what you're saying, but I think there's been a misunderstanding,' Gregory tries to explain.

'We don't need no supported accommodation for—'

'We're not from social services.'

'No?'

'No, we're police,' says Gregory.

Åke stares at him and slowly grinds his teeth. The rifle is too heavy for the boy, and the barrel has begun to tremble in his hands.

'We understand that you want to be left alone, and we respect that,' says Peck, anxiously licking his lips.

'Oh, I like this. This is perfect,' Åke says with a grin. 'Police officers, drinking methanol and eating human flesh, talking about respect.'

'We'll come back another day,' says Joona.

'Or not. What d'you reckon?' Åke asks, tentatively pulling on the line. 'I swear, I don't give a damn. I'm not going to rot away in some fucking Guantánamo.'

'I feel weird,' Peck tells his colleague.

'Just take it easy,' Gregory whispers.

'Sorry, but I think I need to lie down.'

'You'll stay right there!' Åke snarls.

Peck gets up on unsteady legs, knocking his chair over behind him and clapping a hand to his mouth.

'Shoot the Jew!' Åke shouts. 'Shoot him before—'

A sharp crack cuts through the air, reverberating between the buildings. The recoil causes the boy to stumble back. Peck is hit, and he sways to one side. The full metal jacket bullet has gone straight through his throat, and blood has begun to spurt out of the exit wound and down his back.

The boy's eyes are wide, his lips pressed tightly together. He knocked over a bucket of hen feed when he lost his balance, and he casts an anxious glance in his father's direction.

'Sorry,' he whispers.

Dark blood is now pouring down Peck's torso, and he gropes for something to lean against, reeling back.

'Shoot the rest of 'em now.'

Gregory breathes heavily through his nose as he attempts to pull his gun from his holster with shaking hands.

The boy turns the rifle on him, lifts the butt to his shoulder and closes his left eye.

'Don't do anything stupid now,' Gregory tells him, holding up both hands. 'Listen to me . . .'

Joona notices the fishing line slacken when Åke leans forward, and he leaps up and pulls the man towards him like a shield.

The boy turns towards them with the rifle.

As Joona pulls Åke back with him, he uses his free hand to reach beneath his coat and examine the damp blocks of explosive.

'Run!' Åke tells the boy.

Joona finds the detonator and pulls it out just as the father tries to break free. Åke swings around, jolts his arm upwards and hits Joona on the cheek. The two men lose their balance and crash into the table.

Joona drops the detonator.

The mugs tip over, and the bottle shatters on the ground.

'Dad,' the boy gasps, following their movements in an attempt to get a clear shot.

Joona grips the barrel of the rifle and yanks it to one side just as it goes off. The bullet whizzes past his face, making his ears ring, and the hot metal burns his palm.

He tears the gun out of the boy's hands, and the child loses his balance and falls hard onto his knees, but he doesn't seem to react to the pain.

The detonator is now swinging around Åke on the fishing line, and Joona swings the gun around and rams the butt into his nose.

Åke's head snaps back, and he slumps to the ground with a look of confusion on his face.

His mouth and chin are bloody.

Joona strides over to him and stamps on the detonator, pressing it down into the gravel as Åke yanks on the fishing line.

The small charge goes off beneath Joona's boot. He feels a jolt in his knee joint, and dust and small pebbles spray out to both sides of his foot.

The girl drops the rabbit, which hits the ground, scrambles to its feet and bolts away.

Peck's eyes are closed, and he is breathing wheezily.

The boy gets up with an absent look on his face, blood seeping through the knees of his trousers.

'Get the air ambulance out here!' Joona shouts.

He grips the elk rifle with both hands and sees Gregory pointing his Sig Sauer at the ground, loading a round into the chamber.

'Sorry,' the boy whispers.

'Get down!' Gregory snaps, taking aim at his chest.

'Lower your weapon,' Joona warns him.

The boy turns away and sways unsteadily.

'Stop, or I'll shoot!' Gregory yells as the boy starts walking.

'Secure and holster your weapon,' Joona shouts.

'He shot Peck, for fu—'

'That's an order!'

Gregory steadies the pistol with his free hand and curls his finger around the trigger.

'Look away if you don't—'

The butt of Joona's gun hits him square on the temple, causing his head to jerk to the side. Gregory slumps over and manages to catch his glasses just before they hit the ground.

Joona steps forward and kicks his colleague's pistol beneath the house.

Åke has managed to get to his feet and is hurrying away across the gravel, his ponytail thudding between his shoulder blades with each step he takes.

Peck is still sprawled on the ground, spluttering blood onto his own shoulder.

The boy is standing over by the frozen field with a glazed look on his face.

Joona calls regional command and requests backup and an ambulance as he sets off after Åke, who is running towards a rusty pickup over by the tool shed.

The girl watches him go without a single flicker of emotion.

'Helicopter!' Joona repeats, right as he hears a loud whooshing sound.

Peck has fired his distress flare. It races past him, low to the ground, and hits Åke on the back as he opens the car door.

The bright magnesium light briefly illuminates the vehicle before the explosives detonate in a large, deafening fireball.

The shockwave is like a powerful kick to the ribs, and rocks and splintered wood fly through the air.

Joona lands on his back, his head slamming into the ground. The pickup rolls twice and then comes to a rest on its side. Burning wreckage from the shed is thrown into the field, and gravel rains down on the courtyard.

Joona gets to his feet.

Through the dust and smoke, he can see a crater in the ground where Åke was standing just a moment ago.

The young girl is bleeding from a gash on her forehead.

On the ground in front of her, there is a sooty severed thigh.

'Fuck,' Gregory whimpers.

A large chunk of the main building is gone, and every window is broken.

A dead pine is in flames.

The hens that flapped up into the air come back down to land.

A piece of shrapnel from the explosion has penetrated the rain drum, and a thin, white cascade of water has begun to spurt out through the hole.

42

It is seven thirty in the morning, and Joona is walking down a corridor in the women's wing of Kronoberg Remand Prison with the duty officer.

During the day, the inmates' cell doors are all left unlocked, and there is nothing but a red line marking the staff area.

They pass the day room, where a grey-haired counsellor from a visiting addiction team is talking to a thin woman who is clawing at her forearms.

Ann-Charlotte Olsson is being held on suspicion of drugs offences, handling stolen goods, weapons offences and violations of the law governing flammable and explosive substances.

The forensic investigation is ongoing amid the wreckage of the farm in Rickeby.

Joona's ears are still ringing after the explosion, as though the sound of the wind blowing through the trees in a forest follows him wherever he goes.

Peck was conscious when he was airlifted to hospital, and remains in a serious but stable condition. Gregory has been suspended from duty, and a case has been opened by the Special Prosecutor's Office.

The first three police cars arrived at the scene ten minutes after the explosion, and just twenty minutes later the yard and road up to the farm were packed with emergency vehicles. Their blue lights swept over the fields and the bare trees, illuminating the increasingly heavy snowfall.

The fire was put out, and the children were looked after by two female officers while they waited for social services to arrive.

As they walk down the corridor, the prison officer tells Joona that they are trying to create a humane atmosphere in this particular wing.

'I'm not saying the women here are angels, but just about all of them have been forced into crime or addiction by men . . . threatened, abused and raped.'

Someone has been baking, and the sweet aroma of cinnamon and caramelised sugar fills the air.

After forcing the front door, Joona entered what was left of the farmhouse and found Ann-Charlotte dozing on the sofa in front of the TV.

She is a tall woman with large breasts, glasses and short blonde hair, and is wearing pink velour trousers and a Taylor Swift T-shirt.

There was a pack of oxycodone on the table in front of her, alongside an empty ice cream tub with a spoon in it.

'He actually did it, huh?' she slurred, unable to fully open her eyes. 'I was starting to think it was all just talk . . .'

The officer pauses outside a door and gives it a firm rap.

'Lotta? You've got a visitor,' he says, opening the door slightly. 'Can we come in?'

Through the narrow gap, Joona gets a first glimpse of her sitting on the narrow bed in a green prison-issue tracksuit and a pair of slippers.

Lotta has an angry-looking rash around her mouth, and her glasses are dirty, her eyebrows plucked to thin lines.

The small room smells of stale coffee and hand cream.

'I'm sorry to be the bearer of bad news,' Joona tells her, taking a step forward, 'but forensics have confirmed that Åke Berg died in the explosion at your farm . . . My condolences.'

'Boom,' she says flatly.

She picks up a pot from the table, opens the gold plastic lid and pushes a pouch of snus beneath her top lip.

'I'm going to be recording our conversation from now on,' Joona continues, taking out his phone.

'Åke was a conspiracy theorist,' she says, her eyes on the wall. 'Which is pretty bloody convenient, especially for blokes . . . you know?

Means it's not your fault that life turned out the way it did. You're a winner, you're smart, you really see what's going on in the world, but since everything's rigged against you, there's no point even trying.'

'Ann-Charlotte, you're being held here on suspicion of a number of different crimes,' Joona begins. 'But I'm here to talk about—'

'I don't know where he got the idea that social services were trying to take the kids and sell them, but he was obsessed with it,' she goes on. 'Really put his foot down and decided he'd be willing to die for the sprogs, even though he'd barely paid them any notice for years.'

'I know this is a lot, but—'

'But the truth is it's really bloody hard for social services to take your kids away, even if you wish they would,' she says, burping quietly. 'We had hundreds of reports, concerned chats, and they did millions of investigations . . . But, like, I already know I'm not mum of the year. I've got a bad back, I pop all sorts of pills and the kids don't go to school. Even the bailiffs had given up. There was nothing left to take wh—'

'Listen,' Joona interrupts her. 'A witness saw you at Bredäng Campsite early in the morning on 26 November.'

Her eyelids flutter. 'Me?'

'Yes.'

Lotta's thin lips curl into a crooked smile.

'OK, except . . . I've never been there, didn't even know it existed . . . Why the hell d'you think I'd be running about some shitty campsite when I've got a yard full of crap at home?'

'We found your DNA.'

'At the campsite?'

'Yes . . . A strand of hair.'

'One of mine?' She massages the back of her neck.

'When did you cut your hair?'

'Last spring.'

'This short?'

'Shorter,' she says, running a hand over her scalp. 'I've sold it a few times, to a wigmaker on Storgatan.'

'You sold your hair?'

'Never thought of that, did you?' she replies with a grin.

'No.'

'So you killed my man and blew the farm to pieces for a fucking wig?'

'A prosecutor will be taking over the preliminary investigation into the drugs offences, weapon offences and—'

'That was all Åke.'

'OK.'

'You'll be needing tighter bars if you're planning to lock him up,' she says, leaning back.

Joona leaves the room and walks back down the corridor. The sweet scent of buns is gone, and this time all he can smell are the drains.

From behind one of the steel doors, a woman screams.

Joona knows that they will have to track down the person who bought the wig, but above all he needs to head back over to the Sleep Lab with Erik Maria Bark and beg Hugo Sand to agree to another hypnosis session. The teenager must have seen something other than the blonde hair and the shiny coat.

As Joona leaves the prison, there is just one thought going through his mind. He thinks he can see a pattern among the victims, at long last. They are all men who have taken sexual risks.

43

It is almost midnight, and the sky is a murky shade of black, flickering orbs of snow pulsating around the streetlamps.

Hugo pushes his hands beneath his armpits in an attempt to warm them up as he approaches the doorway on Jenny Linds gata. He heads straight inside, so cold that he is shaking, and brushes the wet snow from his head. He then climbs the stairs and presses a finger to the worn buzzer.

On hearing it ring, he takes a step back, runs a hand through his damp hair and unbuttons his coat.

Olga slowly opens the door and stares out at him from the dim hallway in her leopard print bra and black leather skirt.

'Sorry for just turning up like this,' he says, 'but I didn't have anywhere else to go.'

Her kohl-lined eyes are heavy, her expression oddly indifferent and her pink lips parted slightly.

'Hugo?' she mumbles.

'I don't want to cause any trouble . . .' he explains as her heady perfume fills his nose.

'What're you doing here? Shouldn't you be in Uppsala?' she asks in a flat tone of voice.

'I bailed. Couldn't just sit there like some fucking lab rat.'

'Man, what the hell . . .'

Her blonde hair is loose, the soft waves resting on her shoulders.

'I wanted to ask if I could sleep over,' he says with a rising sense of unease.

'Sleep over? God, just go back to the clinic,' she slurs, trying to close the door.

'I can't.' Hugo flashes her an involuntary smile as he reaches for the handle.

'It's not going to work this time, though,' she mumbles.

'Just one night.'

She sighs and turns away from him, reaching behind her back to scratch between her shoulder blades as she walks through to her bedroom. She has goosebumps on her slim legs, he notices, and her muscular arms are dotted with dark bruises.

Hugo closes the door and follows her in.

The pink lampshade on the ceiling casts a circle of light onto the smooth bedspread.

On the floor by the mirror, a thin young man in loose black clothing is doing his makeup. He has a shaved head and an old scar stretching from his left temple to beneath his ear.

'We were just heading out,' Olga says, pulling on a purple blouse with a fitted waist.

'Hi,' says Hugo.

The young man glances up with a pair of big, dark eyes, then turns to Olga with a blank look on his face. His rose gold signet ring flashes as he rubs his pale lips.

'Hachim is from Morocco. He doesn't speak much Swedish,' she explains before saying something to him in French.

'I could wait here,' Hugo offers.

'No, it . . . You can't. It'd be better if you just came with us, but . . . God, I said I'd help him with a job and—'

'I get it.'

'Do you? Because I don't think you do.'

'Are you high?'

Her thin bracelets clink softly as she buttons her blouse.

'*On y va*, Hachim. The car'll be here in three minutes,' she says as she hurries out of the bedroom.

Hugo dumps his bag on the floor by the bed and follows them out into the hall. Olga laces up her shabby boots and reaches for her black leather jacket from the hanger. Hachim pulls on a thin white jacket and a pair of trainers.

They leave the apartment and make their way down the stairs.

A small, dirty Uber is waiting outside the pizzeria. Snowflakes swirl through the air in the light from the streetlamps.

'It'd be better if you just went home,' says Olga.

'I can't,' Hugo replies, fiddling with the silver coin around his neck.

They squeeze into the backseat with Olga in the middle, and as they leave Hägersten, Hugo tries to find his belt in the sandy cracks between the seats.

'Where are we going?' he asks.

'Just some place.'

Olga leans her head against Hachim's shoulder and whispers to him in French, trying to get him to relax, to smile.

The car takes them along Södertäljevägen, heading towards central Stockholm. There is still a lot of traffic on the roads, and the streetlamps and headlights illuminate the car at regular intervals.

'Man, you have no idea what I've been through these past few days,' Hugo begins.

'I guess I would've asked if I cared . . . No, sorry. I do,' she says. 'But I don't have time to play mum right now . . . I've got something important to do, and you can't ruin this for me, that's all.'

'Ruin what?'

'I mean, just the fact that the police want to talk to me all of a sudden isn't exactly what I need right now.'

'Sorry, but . . .'

Hugo trails off and stares out through the side window with burning cheeks.

After twenty minutes, the Uber drops them off in an area of old factory buildings in Hjorthagen.

The air is freezing, and Hugo can hear music coming from several directions.

Above the road, a pair of trainers are hanging from a cable, swinging in the breeze.

The windows of one of the buildings in front of them have all been boarded up, and there are construction fences and concrete pillars blocking it off from the road. The saw-tooth roof and tall chimneys almost seem to be straining up towards the low sky.

The people queuing outside are penned in between riot barriers. A woman flicks a cigarette in Hugo's direction, and sparks fly from the glowing tip as it hits the ground by his feet.

Olga waves to one of the doormen and they bypass the line, joining a throng of people in the dark entranceway. Hachim blows on his fingers in an attempt to warm them up.

They pass the cloakroom and head through to a club with black walls and loud music.

Red lights flash above the half-empty dancefloor.

On the stage, a heavily made-up woman in a blue wig and silver bikini is laughing and vogue-dancing.

A new track begins, and Hugo feels the bass pulsing through his chest as he watches the woman drop into the splits and roll over onto her stomach to writhe around in some sort of stylised mock intercourse.

'Hugo, hang back,' Olga snaps.

A stocky man in a black vest barges through a group of people and comes over to them. He has hairy shoulders and enormous biceps. He grips Olga's face with one hand, squeezing her cheeks so hard that he forces her mouth open, then stares aggressively at her, shouts something into her ear, shoves her back and walks away.

'What was all that about?' asks Hugo.

'Nothing I can't handle.'

They push their way over to a black rubber door and walk along a row of toilet cubicles, eventually coming out in a gloomy courtyard. Despite the snow, three men in dark coats are smoking beside a couple of old industrial ovens.

The ground is littered with rubbish, old plastic drums, car tyres, a broken umbrella and empty egg cartons.

On an oil drum, a man with scarred cheeks and a silver sequin shirt is busy shooting up.

By the door of the building opposite, a huge man in black combat gear is holding an automatic rifle.

'Olga,' he says joylessly as they approach.

'VIP guests,' she replies with a smile.

He doesn't reciprocate the gesture, just stares at her with a neutral expression. Hachim seems uncomfortable and says something in French. Hugo pulls his coat tighter and notices a piece of silver tape with the word REDRUM written in red ink on the top of the doorframe.

The burly bouncer allows them to pass without another word.

Olga opens the door, and the others follow her into a narrow corridor lit by the pale-green glow of an emergency exit sign.

Agitated voices reach them through the walls.

They walk past a number of closed doors, and in a red plastic bucket on the floor, Hugo notices three mobile phones.

Olga opens a metal door to a room containing a blue denim sofa, a low coffee table with a grubby glass top and a couple of yellow plastic folding chairs.

'You can wait here, Hugo,' she says, shooting him a quick glance.

'But I don't understand what—'

'You don't need to understand.'

'Great,' he says, moving into the room.

The door swings shut behind him, and he hears their footsteps fade down the corridor. The room smells like dust and old fabric. Beside an empty Coca-Cola fridge, he notices, there is a dented suitcase.

Hugo slumps onto the sofa, unbuttons his coat and leans back. He fiddles with the ring in his lower lip, checks his phone and sees that he has ten missed calls from his dad.

Coming to the club was a mistake, he thinks. Olga is stressed, and she is taking that out on him. He should have just gone home, eaten dinner and studied for his exam.

Muffled voices and music drift through the walls.

In the corner, there is a floor lamp without a shade, the bare bulb casting a circle of light onto the rough wall.

After around twenty minutes, the door opens and Olga comes into the room and hands him a plastic glass of beer.

'Thanks. I just wanted—'

'I need you to stay here till I come to get you,' she says.

'OK, but how long are—'

'Did you hear what I just said?'

'I heard you.'

Her thin bracelets are caught on her hands, and she lifts both arms into the air to shake them back.

'Take this,' she says, putting a small white pill on the arm of the sofa.

'What is it?'

'Just trust Olga.'

She looks down at her phone, then turns around and leaves the room.

Hugo sips his beer, wipes the head from his top lip and lowers the cup to the table. His eyes drift over to the little white pill.

He pops it into his mouth and washes it down with a mouthful of beer. It leaves a bitter taste on his tongue, and he takes another swig of beer to rinse it away.

Hugo is messing about on his phone when he starts to feel a pleasant prickling sensation in his knees and toes. It slowly spreads upwards, making his lips tingle.

He looks around the windowless room, at the closed door, the dented metal and the worn handle.

There is a soft whirr from the vent up by the ceiling, dust swirling in the glow of the lamp.

Hugo reaches for his phone again, but his mind starts to drift, and he struggles to focus.

A quiet euphoria takes hold of him.

The beat of the music rises, and he hears voices and footsteps in the corridor outside.

Smiling, he pushes his phone back in his pocket. He hears the rushing sound of water in a pipe and tips his head back against the cushion.

Hugo closes his eyes and wakes an instant later when someone's palm strikes his cheek.

Anxiety surges through his veins, and his heart starts racing.

He is standing in the middle of a room full of monitors and desks, and a burly man with a tattooed face grips his throat with one hand and hits him again with the other.

'Answer me!' he shouts. 'Or I'll tear your fucking arms off!'

'Sorry, I—'

'Who the fuck are you?'

Hugo realises that he must have been sleepwalking. Through a pane of glass, he can see a number of brightly lit booths containing webcams.

'I'm Hugo. I came here with Olga.'

In one of the booths, a young man with a wet towel over his face is strapped to a tilted table and a broad-shouldered man wearing a latex hood seems to be raping him. The young man's body is tense, his back arched in a long, drawn-out convulsion.

'Did she say you should be here?' the tattooed man asks, his grip tightening on Hugo's throat.

'No, I—'

'This isn't a goddamn playground,' the man snarls as he lets go of him.

'I got lost and—'

'Get the fuck out of here!'

In the next booth, a slim man with a thick chain around his neck is on his knees. He has an apathetic look on his bloody face, an older man's penis in his mouth.

In the third booth, a boy is curled up on the floor in his underpants, catatonically shaking his head.

44

It is just after eight in the morning, but the sky outside is stubbornly dark. Bernard is at the computer in his office, still in his navy-blue dressing gown, with a mug of coffee beside the keyboard in front of him.

Against the back wall of the room, he has a seventeenth-century Järvsö cabinet painted in egg tempera to look like a summer sky dotted with white clouds.

In the window, a candle is burning in a bronze chamberstick. The warm yellow flame is reflected in the glass, and beyond it, he can see himself sitting beneath the beams in the cold glare of his computer screen. The unruly grey hair on his head looks like a tuft of frosty grass.

Bernard has just typed up Agneta's notes from the police press conference and her conversations with Joona. She has done a great job, her observations full of nuance and vivid details.

The day before yesterday, he managed to get hold of Hugo at the lab and he asked how the hypnosis session had been.

'You don't get it,' his son had said. 'It was like I was right back there in the nightmare. I was fucking traumatised afterwards, had to take some Atarax just to keep it together.'

'But did you manage to help the police?' Bernard asked.

'Don't think so, it was pretty much all nightmares, but they were right that I remembered some stuff from the campsite. I saw the caravans and the snow . . . and maybe the killer, too. A woman with an axe.'

'A woman? Was it a woman?'

'I don't know, Dad. That could've just been part of the dream, too. I'm so confused right now.'

'Sorry, I'm just curious,' Bernard had explained. 'I don't mean to put any pressure on you, because there's absolutely no rush as far as the book is concerned. You share what you want to share, at your own pace. You know that. It's what we agreed.'

When Bernard is focused on his writing, he tries not to worry about Hugo. He blocks out anything that makes him feel stressed or anxious and attempts to avoid all thoughts of email interviews with Spanish newspapers or readers' letters to his column in *Expressen*.

He has been in his office since five thirty this morning, and has finally managed to find his creative flow, writing well.

The rattle of his fingers on the keys slows, and he looks up as though he has just come round to reality.

The candle seems to have paled since the sun came up, with the sky brightening and the choppy waters of Lake Mälaren taking on the same colour as raw steel.

Bernard glances down at his phone and sees that it is now quarter past nine.

He checks his emails, and quickly skims through a message from his agent, telling him that he has been nominated for a German literary prize and encouraging him to share the news on social media.

There is an email from a French film producer, confirming their plans for dinner this evening, and his American publisher has forwarded a starred review from *Publishers Weekly*, along with a message to say that they are still keen to organise a tour for him next autumn.

Bernard has just signed a digital renewal agreement for his first three books with an Italian publisher when Agneta sends a personalised bitmoji of herself waking up happy on a heart-shaped pillow. Bernard replies with his own bitmoji in which he has huge hearts for eyes, then gets up and heads down to the kitchen to make her a coffee.

On Saturdays, he likes to make various pasta dishes for brunch, taking them upstairs with two small glasses of red wine and crawling back into bed with Agneta to eat.

Today, the plan is to fry off some garlic in butter and olive oil before adding red pepper and ginger, sugar snap peas, fresh prawns and penne.

But first, she needs to drink her coffee and read the news.

Bernard climbs the stairs to their bedroom with a mug of coffee and some dark chocolate. Agneta has already opened the curtains, and is sitting in her bed with her iPad. She gives him a strange look as he comes into the room.

'What is it?' he asks.

'Hugo has given an interview to *Aftonbladet*,' she says.

'What?'

His hand shakes as he sets the cup down on her bedside table and takes the iPad. The headline of the piece is AXE MURDERS – SLEEP-WALKER POLICE'S ONLY WITNESS.

'What on earth . . . Did they go to the lab?'

'Read it and you'll see.'

He skims through the piece, staring in disbelief at the photographs of Hugo leaning back against a damp concrete wall.

A sense of unease rises up in Bernard as he sits down on the edge of the bed and rereads the entire text.

'God,' he whispers.

'I know,' Agneta mumbles, reaching for his hand.

'Why is he doing this?'

* * *

After getting dressed, Agneta heads down to the kitchen. She reads a press release from the Swedish Publicists' Association on her phone and sends a quick message to turn down an assignment reviewing a performance at the Modern Dance Theatre.

Through the walls, she hears Bernard shuffle down the hall to open the door for Hugo.

'Could you take your earbuds out?' he asks.

'I'm not listening to anything.'

'Do it anyway.'

Agneta is still at the table when they come into the kitchen. She realises she hasn't taken her beta blocker yet, and her heart rate immediately picks up.

Hugo's clothes are crumpled, and his messy shoulder-length hair is tied back in a low ponytail.

She has given up in her attempts to hug him, but she smiles and says hello, holding his gaze for as long as she can before asking if he would like a coffee.

The teenager shrugs, says something she doesn't catch and drops his earbuds into his shirt pocket.

'Shall I make you a latte?' Agneta asks.

'He can make one himself if he wants one,' Bernard replies.

'What a warm welcome,' Hugo mutters, slumping down onto a chair at the table.

He hasn't shaved, Agneta notices, and he has bloodshot eyes and dirt beneath his nails.

'We need to talk,' Bernard says, taking a seat opposite him.

'Yeah, you said on the phone.'

'Could you tell us why you ran away from the lab?'

'I didn't *run away*, I just grabbed my stuff and left.'

Agneta sees Bernard nod slowly and run a hand over the table.

'I'm going to have to call Lars to apologise,' he says, more to himself than anything.

'What, why? It's not like I *have* to be there,' Hugo replies, his eyes on his phone.

'That's why we need to apologise. It's a matter of trust, of common courtesy.'

'Fine, whatever,' he sighs.

'Could you put your phone down?'

'God, chill out,' Hugo says with an irritated smile.

He is still looking at his phone, scrolling between posts, clearly aware that they are both watching him, that Bernard is waiting.

'Where did you sleep last night?'

'Crashed at a friend's place,' he says, lowering his phone to the table.

'Not at Olga's?'

'Nah.' Hugo tugs gently on the ring in his lower lip.

'Why not?' asks Bernard.

'She was working.'

'Where?'

'Does it matter?'

'Is it a secret?'

'God, can we stop talking about this now?'

'I'm just trying to understand what's going on in your life, Hugo,' Bernard explains, placing one hand on top of the other in an attempt to stop them from trembling.

'You can't.'

'Not if you won't tell me anything, no.'

Hugo gets up and walks over to the fridge. He takes out a can of Red Bull, cracks it open and takes a sip, then burps and drinks some more.

'You've been sleepwalking a lot lately, and you seem to be having one of your worst episodes yet,' Bernard continues.

'Yup,' Hugo says with a sigh, shaking the last few drops into his mouth.

'Don't you think that's something you should consider?' Agneta asks, conscious that her breathing is quick and shallow.

'I don't care.'

'That's rather immature.'

Hugo tosses the empty can into the sink and looks straight at her.

'I'm talking to my dad.'

'I know that, and I—'

'So maybe you should go and do something else while—'

'Hugo,' Bernard snaps. 'This attitude of yours is not OK. Agneta is as much a part of this family as you or I.'

'More, seems like.'

'More?' Agneta repeats.

'Come on, Dad. You've got to agree that I have the least say round here.'

'Oh, stop.' Agneta smiles, but her heart is racing.

'I wasn't talking to you!'

'But maybe you should—'

'Everything in this house, it's all on your terms. *Everything*,' Hugo shouts. 'I have to tiptoe around just so I don't end up being kicked out of my own home.'

Agneta attempts to laugh, but she quickly stops when she realises there is a risk he might take it the wrong way.

'OK,' says Bernard, holding up both hands. 'Can't we just try to act like normal people and talk about the things we need to talk about?'

'Gotta do what you gotta do,' Hugo mutters, biting his thumbnail.

'We saw your interview in *Aftonbladet*,' Bernard begins.

'Yeah, sorry if I spoiled your book,' Hugo says as he takes a seat at the table again.

'Is that what you think this is about?'

'Yeah, I do, because the books always come first.'

'Oh, you're being *too* childish right now,' Bernard tells him, raising his voice.

'I'm leaving if you're just going to shout at me,' says Hugo.

'Hugo, please listen to your dad,' says Agneta. She feels like she is finally starting to regain control of herself. 'This has nothing to do with our book. You know he's upset because he's worried. This could be dangerous. You've just been outed as the sole witness to a murder.'

The teenager stares at her with a blank look on his face.

'But I don't remember anything.'

'*We* know that, but no one else does,' says Bernard. 'To anyone reading your interview, it sounds like you're a real eye witness. Don't you see that?'

'But I said . . . I just said I was there, that I'm trying to work through my memories . . . The journalist twisted everything.'

'Because they don't care. They don't care that you're a target now.'

'Stop it . . .' Hugo says, a flicker of fear passing over his young face.

'I don't want to frighten you, but this killer, she's not just going to give up. She doesn't want to stop, and she won't allow anyone to stop her,' says Bernard. 'And if she believes what she reads in the paper then there's a real risk she might try to find you and stop you from talking.'

'You should be given witness protection,' says Agneta.

'Probably . . .' Hugo nods, holding her gaze for a moment.

'OK, good. I'll speak to the detective, but I think the bar for that sort of thing is usually quite high,' says Bernard. 'Otherwise, I think the lab is probably the best place for you right now. Certainly better than here. I mean, the staff are there around-the-clock, and they have high security. Alarms, cameras.'

Hugo picks up his phone to check whether he has any new messages, and Agneta finds herself wondering whether he might have had a fight with Olga. She noticed a darkness to his expression when her name came up earlier.

'Is that plan OK with you?' she asks. 'Going back to the lab unless we can get you police protection?'

'Guess so.'

'But?'

'The hypnosis . . . I don't know, it was really horrible.'

'Wasn't Lars there?' asks Bernard.

'Yeah, but what was he meant to do?'

'He's meant to look out for your best interests,' says Bernard. 'That's his job.'

'I want to help the police, though.'

'And that's great.'

'But I can't hack being hypnotised again. I'm not going back if I have to.'

'I can bring it up with Lars, if you like.'

'Yeah.'

'You started to remember things you saw that night, though, didn't you?' asks Agneta.

'I dunno, it was crazy. They seem to think I saw the killer, and maybe even the murder, too.'

'Hugo, it would be an incredible help if you could write everything down,' says Bernard. 'Anything to do with the hypnosis. How it felt, what the hypnotist said, what you said, et cetera, et cetera.'

'I'll try.'

'Have they told you they want to try again?' Agneta asks.

'No. I don't know. But I've been thinking about it and don't think I can take it.'

'You absolutely don't have to, just so you know,' Bernard tells him. 'I mean . . . they've already had you in custody and accused you of all sorts of terrible things.'

'OK, I know that wasn't right,' Agneta speaks up. 'But at the same time, we're talking about a murderer here. Someone who has killed at least two people with an axe. *Slaughtered* them . . . Imagine if you could help stop this madwoman.'

'I know,' Hugo replies, his voice little more than a whisper.

45

Linus has been following Ida's car all the way from central Stockholm, and he pulls up behind her on the driveway of a 1970s slope house in Stocksund.

The cool lighting in the garden makes the white brick facade, the window frames and woodwork look like the icing on a gingerbread house.

Towards the bottom of the slope, a sailboat with a rusty keel is chocked up beneath a tarpaulin.

Linus watches Ida reach for her bag on the passenger seat and close the door. Her leather coat is unbuttoned over her burgundy dress.

The air is crisp and cold as he gets out of the car, locks up and follows her over to the house, the neighbourhood so quiet that he can hear the frigid wind blowing through the bare branches of the trees in the distance.

Ida drops her keys, and they jingle as they hit the cracked paving stones.

'Nice place,' he says, pausing behind her.

She bends down to retrieve the keys, then opens the door and turns off the alarm. After dumping her bag on the sideboard, she turns on the light and hangs up her coat.

'Remind me where Sven Erik is,' says Linus.

'In Tenerife, on a golf trip,' she replies without looking at him.

'Right, right.'

As Linus takes off his shoes and puts his jacket down on the floor by the wall, Ida makes her way through to a large lounge with a scratched floor.

* * *

Ida Forsgren-Fisher is a twenty-six-year-old graphic designer at an ad agency, with wavy blonde hair and pale-blue eyes.

She flicks the switch on the floor lamp, casting a warm glow over the coffee table, then turns around and studies Linus in the hallway.

He has a hole in one of his socks, and she watches him twist the fabric so that it is hidden beneath his foot.

She turns on the patio lights.

The reflections in the glass always create the illusion of inside and out switching places, and it looks as though Linus is walking across the yellowed grass towards the house, when in actual fact he is making his way down the hall to the lounge.

They are both members of the Engelbrekt Church chamber choir, Ida a high soprano and Linus a baritone.

They were rehearsing a work by Hildegard av Bingen earlier this evening, and the music and lyrics from the twelfth century had risen towards the vaulted ceiling in the chancel.

'Can you see the lake . . . or the sea, or whatever it is, when it's light?' he asks, gesturing vaguely towards the floor-to-ceiling glass.

'Yeah, from every window. Feels like this place was built for the views,' she replies.

Linus is four years older than Ida, with a master's degree in literary studies, but he shares her passion for the Pitch Perfect films. His parents are from Estonia, and he is incredibly blond, with pale brows. He often radiates a nervous, slightly jittery energy, though he really opens up once you get to know him.

Ida can feel the music from choir practice lingering in her as if some sort of wistful anxiety, but that could just be down to what they are about to do.

'I need wine,' she says.

They head upstairs, and she realises that her legs feel slightly shaky. Through the gaps between the worn treads, she notices her son's missing soft toy on the floor by the door to the boiler room.

When they reach the landing, she turns on the cabinet lights in the open-plan kitchen and leads Linus over to Sven Erik's new wine fridge.

'You're the expert, you pick,' she says as she takes out two glasses.

'Expert is a bit . . . Uff, my voice sounded weird there,' he says nervously. 'Expert is a bit much, but I'll happily take a look . . .'

'Red,' she says.

He opens the tall door and takes out a couple of bottles to study the labels.

'Great wines . . . What do you fancy? A Pomerol?'

'Don't mind. You pick.'

'A 2016 Château Lagrange,' he says.

Ida catches sight of herself in the large mirror on the wall, and is taken aback by the intensity on her face.

Her eyes are bright, her cheeks flushed and her lips parted.

She hears Linus pull out the cork and pour the wine. He runs an antiquarian bookshop-cum-wine bar, and often says that it is easier to sell old wine than old books.

Ida turns to him with a smile and whispers a soft thanks as she takes the glass he holds out to her. They toast and both take a sip.

'Very nice,' he says quietly, holding the wine up to the light. 'But it'll be even better once it's had time to breathe.'

She strokes his arm. 'I read the book you gave me. It was . . .'

'What did you think?'

'I liked it, a lot.'

'I'm pleased to hear that . . . God, I sound like someone out of a Bergman film again,' he says, laughing a little too loudly.

He gave her a copy of *This is How You Lose Her*, a collection of short stories by Junot Díaz, last week, and she devoured it over the course of two evenings.

Ida reaches for his free hand and presses it to her cheek. She holds his gaze and hopes that they both start to feel a little more relaxed soon.

'What are you thinking about?' he asks, leaning back awkwardly against the island, where the wood veneer has started to bubble.

'This. Us . . .'

Linus looks down and swirls the wine in his glass, high up the curved sides. He lifts it to his nose and inhales, then takes a small sip with a frown.

'Incredibly good Merlot,' he says.

'You really do like wine, don't you?'

'Does the hat wear a funny Pope?' he replies, glancing up with a thoughtful look on his face. 'Did I just say what I think I did?'

'I thought it was a joke.'

'Good . . . let's pretend it was.'

'Does the hat wear a funny Pope?' she repeats with a smile.

'Stop.' Linus laughs.

Ida pours herself another glass. He has barely touched his, she notices, and she puts the bottle back down on the moisture-damaged counter and checks her phone to see if she has any messages.

'I'm just going to nip to the loo,' she says.

She goes through to the main bathroom, locks the door behind her, lifts the toilet lid and looks down at her phone as she pees.

Ida met her husband, Sven Erik Fisher, through work. He was the managing director of a large payment services company that hired the ad agency where she was a graphic designer, and once the campaign was over, he invited her out to dinner. She felt flattered by the attention, ended up drinking far too much, went home with him and wound up pregnant.

Their son Oliver turned five this summer.

Ida is twenty-six, and Sven Erik is sixty-eight and retired.

It often feels as though she is just pretending to be an adult – playing families in this strange house – when what she really wants is to catch the train back to her parents' place in Katrineholm, put on some comfy clothes and let them fuss over her while she watches TV.

Sven Erik has been married three times, and has four adult children. He has lived in South Africa and California, and once drove across Australia on a motorcycle.

Ida was only twenty when they met, and he was the third man she had ever slept with.

She doesn't want to hurt him, but nor is she prepared to be old before she even turns thirty.

She has spent a lot of time thinking about this, and is convinced he would rather she cheat on him than lose her entirely – though of course she can't know for sure.

Ida has tried to ask for advice from various places, but she hasn't managed to get any answers.

She fills the toothbrush mug with lukewarm water, rinses between her legs and dries herself off with a hand towel. She then wipes the toilet seat with paper, flushes and washes her hands.

She first started flirting with Linus towards the end of August, and so far they have held hands in secret, gone out for a drink after choir practice three times, and kissed twice.

But tonight is the night it finally happens. Sven Erik is away, and Oliver is sleeping over at his best friend's house. The thought gives her butterflies.

46

Ida quickly brushes her teeth and dabs a few drops of perfume onto her throat before leaving the bathroom. She finds Linus right where she left him in the kitchen, still nursing his glass of wine.

'Would you like to see the bedroom?' she asks.

'OK.'

'You all right?' She smiles, but her brow is knotted.

'Yeah, I think so.'

'Come on.'

He finishes the last of his wine and puts the glass down.

'You know . . . I've joined the Civil Rights Defenders,' he tells her. 'Or their network, anyway. To try to protect democracy.'

'That's great. I'd like to do something like that too,' she says, glancing towards the bedroom.

'It's free, so it wasn't a big deal in that sense . . . But I think we could really make a difference if we—'

'Absolutely.'

'Right now, I'm thinking that I . . . that maybe I should try to focus on Swedish democracy.'

'I feel safer already,' she says with a grin.

Ida looks down at her phone again. Her son Oliver has type one diabetes, and she can't help but feel anxious. She tells herself that she should relax, that his friend's mum is a nurse and that she knows what she is doing, that she will check his blood sugar levels and that he has a spare insulin pen with him, just in case.

'Could I use your bathroom?' asks Linus.

'Nope, sorry,' she replies with a laugh. 'Just kidding. It's through here.'

He smiles as he follows her out into the hall, where the walls are clad in dark green paper.

'Sweden is actually ranked first globally in terms of freedom,' he tells her as they walk. 'But at the same time, the safeguards we have for democracy are incredibly weak.'

'Oh?' she says, pausing outside the bathroom.

'It's hard to believe, but there's basically nothing protecting the constitution. The independence of the judiciary isn't guaranteed either . . . I mean, the system is working at the moment, but it might not be in five years' time, and that should probably worry us more than it does.'

'I'll be in the bedroom, which is just there . . .' she says, pointing to another doorway.

He locks the bathroom door behind him, and Ida heads back into the kitchen. She pours herself another glass of wine and carries it through to the bedroom. After taking a sip, she lowers it to the nightstand, then checks her phone and switches it to silent. She dims the lights, and has just started to fold back the bobbled bedspread when Linus comes into the room.

Ida moves over to him, standing on her tiptoes to give him a quick peck on the lips.

'Shall we take our clothes off?' she whispers.

'Now?' he asks, swallowing hard.

'We can get under the covers.'

They undress, half turned away from each other. Ida tosses her dress onto the armchair, and Linus neatly folds his shirt and balls up his socks. Her bra straps have left deep grooves in her skin, and he keeps his underpants on as they get into bed.

They lie face to face, gazing into each other's eyes, and quickly warm up.

Oddly enough, Ida doesn't feel any guilt. What they are doing feels natural. Right.

The mattress creaks as she wriggles towards him, and they kiss, calling each other Bumper and Amy, Perfect Amy. Ida laughs softly, her lips against his throat, then kisses him. She strokes his cheek and kisses him again.

'Come here,' she whispers, trying to pull him on top of her.

'I don't have any condoms.'

'It's OK, I'm on the pill,' she lies.

His hands are like ice, and she shivers as he strokes her breasts.

'Come on.'

Linus pulls down his boxers and climbs on top of her. His entire body seems to be shaking, and he doesn't have much of an erection, but still manages to enter her when she parts her thighs and closes her eyes.

'No stress,' she whispers.

He lies still for a moment, then starts moving a little, to avoid slipping out.

Ida groans quietly. She is incredibly wet, but she doesn't know whether he is getting any harder; she can barely feel him. She has been looking forward to this moment for so long.

Linus begins thrusting a little harder, and she sighs and grips his buttocks, pulling him towards her and trying to get him to pause deep inside her. She wants him to keep going, to get harder and fill her, flip her over and do her from behind.

'Don't stop,' she whispers, right as he lets out a loud groan and slumps down on top of her.

His back is sweaty, his heart pounding and his breath hot on her throat. He pulls out and rolls over onto his back.

'Sorry,' he says, looking away.

'Come on, don't say sorry. That felt great.'

'I don't usually . . . you know . . .'

'We can do it again, a hundred times,' Ida tells him as she gets out of bed.

She opens the connecting door to the nursery, where the passageway has been reconfigured as a linen closet, and takes two clean towels from the shelf. The doorway at the other side is blocked by the large cupboard containing all of Oliver's toys.

Sven Erik doesn't want their son to get into the habit of climbing into bed with them, which means that Oliver just lies there screaming for his mum until she goes through to see him.

Ida and Linus take a shower together. She hands him one of the towels when they step out of the cubicle, but she notices that his back is still beaded with water as he gets dressed in the bedroom.

His hands seem to be shaking as he buttons his shirt.

'You can stay over, if you like,' she says, pulling on a purple robe. 'I could make lemon pasta.'

'Thanks, but I have to get back and do some work . . .'

'Sure.'

She follows him down to the front door, and they kiss three times before he leaves. Ida locks the door behind him and turns out the light in the hallway.

The endorphins are still making her body tingle as she wanders through to the lounge. She doesn't want to stand in the window and watch him drive away, but she does it anyway.

Linus walks over to his car and uses the fob to unlock the doors.

As the lights flash, Ida thinks she catches a glimpse of a blonde woman standing by the gateposts.

Up in the bedroom, her phone starts ringing.

Ida climbs the stairs, automatically peering down at the cuddly toy she spotted earlier by the door to the boiler room and the garage.

As she reaches the kitchen, she decides that the woman by the driveway could be the Russian's new wife. Last spring, the old one got bored of taking the Dachshund out for walks in her fancy Gucci clothes and moved back to St Petersburg.

Her phone has stopped ringing by the time Ida reaches the bedroom, but she sees that she has a missed call from Sven Erik.

Oliver also sent her a message saying goodnight an hour ago, but she was too busy having sex with Linus to notice, and it is now too late to reply.

She tightens the belt of her robe and peers out at the lights from Linus's car through the hedge. He drives slowly down the road and turns right, and then it looks as though he stops on the hill and turns off the headlights.

Logically, she knows that his car just pulled out of view, behind the neighbours' extension or something similar, but it really does feel as though he has come to a halt.

The wind howls around the house, and she hears the loose drainpipe out back creaking.

Ida goes through to the kitchen and opens another bottle of red wine. It is the same type as earlier, only older, from long before she was born.

Probably really expensive, she thinks as she fills her glass, swirls the wine and takes a sip.

'Great Merlot,' she says, imitating Linus.

The wine leaves a dry, lingering taste of wood in her mouth.

In the windows, the darkness beyond the reflected kitchen looks impenetrable.

Out of nowhere, Ida feels a rush of fear that Linus has hit a child on the hill. She knows it is nothing but a dark fantasy, but he *did* have a glass of wine.

With a smouldering sense of anxiety, she picks up her phone and sends him a red heart. He doesn't reply, and she gazes out into the darkness, thinking about the *Aftonbladet* interview with the boy who witnessed a bloody axe murder while he was sleepwalking.

Ida puts her phone down and realises that she can't remember whether she locked the door after he left. She goes to the top of the stairs and pauses, listening for sounds like a child left home alone. Other than the usual creaking of the wooden floors, the house is quiet.

With one hand on the banister, she starts making her way down the stairs.

'Fuck!'

A deer bolts across the floor in the lounge, past the sofa and towards the hall.

She will never get used to these reflections in the glass, she thinks. Sven Erik's enormous barbecue always looks like some sort of covered grand piano in the lounge.

The reflections create the illusion that it is snowing inside, that there are great tits swooping over the table and rabbits hopping over the rug.

A few clumps of dust blow out from beneath the sofa and roll towards Ida's feet, and she turns around and sees the curtains rippling in the sudden draught.

The door to the guest room swings shut with a click.

Ida moves out into the dark hallway.

The only source of light is the little green LED on the alarm unit.

As she grips the handle, she remembers that she locked the door when Linus left.

Outside, the drainpipe shakes again.

Ida turns around and starts making her way back towards the lounge, but stops dead when she sees that the Russian woman is now standing on the deck.

Her dog must have escaped, she thinks, and is just about to go out and ask if the woman needs any help when she realises with a shudder that the windows have tricked her again.

The woman is in the house.

Adrenaline floods through her veins.

Ida turns back around. She thinks she can see the figure reflected in the reeded glass in the front door, and she slowly sinks to the floor.

47

Ida is on her knees among the shoes and boots in the hallway, hands pressed to her mouth to muffle the sound of her breathing.

This can't be happening, she thinks. This can't be happening. The woman is in the house.

Ida watched as she bumped into the floor lamp, causing the orb of light to sway.

She needs to call 112, but her phone is on the bench in the kitchen upstairs.

Her breathing is much too quick.

She slowly turns around and squints back towards the lounge, taking in the sofa, the candles on the coffee table, the reflections in the glass.

Her panicked brain desperately tries to come up with a logical explanation, and she asks herself whether Sven Erik might have been calling to tell her that the woman was coming over. Maybe he said she could swing by to borrow something.

If that is the case, she might already have left through the patio doors.

Ida crawls forward over the vinyl floor as quietly as she can, feeling stray bits of gravel and damp pools of melted snow beneath her palms.

She can see a little more of the lounge now.

There is no one there.

She slowly gets up, legs shaking, and hears the parquet floor creaking beneath the weight of someone slowly moving across it.

Ida takes another step forward, glances to the left and sees the woman in the angled window. Her reflection is cautiously picking its way across the patio, past the barbecue and towards the rusty fence.

That means she is actually heading towards the door to the boiler room beneath the stairs.

Ida only has a few seconds.

She needs to get to her phone.

The door to the boiler room opens and closes.

Ida tiptoes out from the hall and sees herself on the lawn in front of the apple tree. She then hurries over to the stairs and starts climbing them as quietly as she can.

She looks down, between the steps, and gasps.

The woman isn't in the boiler room at all. She is standing just outside, hidden in a dark corner.

Ida meets her eye.

The woman lunges forward and swings an axe, and Ida just has time to lift her foot before the sharp blade slices through the tread and hits the side panel.

She screams and starts running, reaching the kitchen counter and managing to knock over her wineglass as she grabs her phone.

It falls to the floor and shatters on the tiles, causing wine to spray across the cupboards and kick plates.

Ida can hear the woman's heavy footsteps on the stairs as she hurries through to the bedroom, locks the door behind her and backs away.

Her hands are shaking so much that it takes her three attempts to unlock her phone.

The woman is now tugging on the door handle.

Ida dials 112.

The call handler answers just as the intruder starts pounding on the door.

'You have to help me,' Ida whispers.

'What's the nature of the emergency?'

'There's a madwoman in my house,' she says between shaky breaths.

'What do you mean by a madwoman?' the call handler asks in a patient voice.

'A woman with an axe, she's broken in.'

'Is anyone hurt?'

Ida screams as the axe slams into the solid wood door.

'What's happening? Do you need help?' asks the call handler.

'You have to come, as soon as you—'

There is a cracking sound as the blade hits the door for a second time.

'Where are you?'

'I've locked myself in the bedroom.'

'What's your address?'

Ida reels it off and hears the call handler's fingers rattling over the keys.

'A patrol car is heading to you now,' he says.

'Oh God,' Ida gasps as the axe hits the door again. 'Please, tell them to hurry.'

'Could you give me your number in case the line drops?'

'There's no time, she's using the axe—'

There is another loud thud and a splintering sound as the blade breaks through the panel.

'Talk to me. Are you alone?'

'Yes, I'm alone!'

'Do you know who the woman is?'

'Please, just send help, I don't know what's going on.'

The next blow causes pieces of broken wood to fall to the floor.

Ida realises she is out of time, and she ends the call, opens the door to the linen cupboard and shoves a pile of towels to the floor. She then climbs up onto the shelf, pulls the door shut behind her and crawls forward. Using her shoulder, she tries to move Oliver's big wooden cupboard, but it is too heavy.

From the bedroom, she can hear more loud bangs and cracking.

'Please, God. Please, God,' she whispers between quick breaths.

She manages to find a foothold, and she pushes back using her legs. The cupboard budges slightly, no more than around ten centimetres.

The woman kicks the door to the bedroom open.

Ida whimpers as she tries again, pushing as hard as she can. This time, the heavy cupboard slides across the floor. She can taste blood as she squeezes through the gap onto the carpet on the other side.

Oliver's roller blind swings in the draught from her movements.

Ida gets up on shaking legs, straightens her robe and tightens the belt, then tiptoes as fast as she can over to the door.

She steps on one of her son's toys, making it squeak loudly.

Back in the main bedroom, a window breaks.

Ida opens the door.

Her feet barely make a sound as she runs through to the kitchen and down the stairs, but the woman comes after her, stomping loudly.

Ida swings around the corner at the bottom of the stairs and reaches the door to the boiler room. Between the steps, she can see the woman's legs, and she quietly opens the door, hurries through and pulls it shut behind her.

The ground source heat pump, underfloor heating manifold and boiler make the cramped space hot.

Ida blinks in the darkness, breathing heavily through her nose.

She can't see a thing as she fumbles her way over to the narrow door to the garage.

Something clicks, and there is a hissing sound.

She has almost reached the door when the hem of her robe catches on a pipe.

Her heart is beating so hard that she can hear her blood roaring in her ears.

The fabric strains as she tugs on it, and she has to take a step back and unhook it from the pipe before she can keep going.

The nightlight on the ceiling casts a pale bluish glow over the plastic boxes of Christmas decorations, bikes, roof racks, summer tyres, lawnmowers and bags of compost.

The rough concrete floor is cold beneath her feet as she runs over to the button for the automatic garage door and presses it.

There is a loud whirr as the mechanism starts to turn, but after just a few seconds the door shudders to a halt and starts closing.

Ida glances back at the door to the boiler room, presses the button again and reties the belt around her robe. As before, the garage door starts to open, grinds to a halt and closes again.

Something must be blocking the mechanism.

In the boiler room, the light comes on.

A thin chink of it spills into the garage like a crack in the floor.

Ida presses the button and runs over to the door. She gets onto her back and starts crawling through the gap as soon as it is wide enough for her head. The door shudders as it stops rising and begins lowering for the third time. Ida desperately tries to get out, but the door is too quick and pins her down by the waist.

The cold night air claws at her lungs.

Panting heavily, she tries to drag herself through, grazing the skin on her hips.

The mechanism starts turning again, and the door begins to lift. The pressure on her eases, and she scrambles to get out with a whimper.

Right then, she spots her neighbour, the former Chancellor of Justice. He is standing with his back to her as his old Labrador sniffs a lamppost a little further down the street.

'Help!' she shouts as she feels the woman grip her ankle and drag her back inside.

Ida's head thuds against the concrete floor, and her robe rides up beneath her.

Yet again, the garage door closes with a whirr.

Ida is sobbing, and she lashes out with both feet, rolls over onto her stomach and scrambles onto her knees.

She has just started to get up when something hits her hard on the back, and her legs give way beneath her.

She attempts to break her fall as she crashes to the floor, but her forehead hits the rough concrete.

Ida tries to get up again, but she can no longer feel the lower half of her body.

As it dawns on her that her spine has been severed, she screams, and an excruciating wave of pain surges up through her torso.

The muscles in her upper body tense convulsively. Her heart is racing, and her breathing is laboured.

Ida hears herself roar in terror, breaking her nails as she frantically claws at the concrete.

She knows she needs to get out, but that isn't a conscious thought; it is an animal urge to survive.

The woman is breathing heavily, and she kicks a stool angrily out of the way. Growling, she paces around Ida and nudges her twice on the cheek with her axe.

'Please,' Ida begs her.

Panicking, she tries to drag herself back towards the boiler room, but the woman lashes out with the axe and chops off half of her right hand.

Sparks fly as the sharp steel blade hits the concrete.

Ida is drifting in and out of consciousness, but she can see one of the sparks hovering in front of her like a small fairy with fluttering silver wings.

A pool of blood has begun to form beneath her.

She allows herself to relax, resting her cheek against the cold floor.

Ida registers the woman's axe beginning to sever her limbs as nothing but a series of soft jolts, like the points on the railway taking her back to her mum and dad.

48

Hugo is sprawled on his bed, sucking on a CBD vape and scrolling on his phone. The light is off, and the rice paper shade hangs above him like a pale winter moon.

He is wearing a pair of striped pyjama bottoms and a flowery T-shirt, and the dense network of tattoos on his arms make his skin look bruised.

Outside, the sky is dark.

Hugo is daydreaming about his trip to Canada, about getting to know his mother again when he takes her out to a restaurant full of colourful lights and gives her his lucky coin. His silver dinar.

He hears Agneta laugh upstairs, and he closes his eyes.

An hour ago, they ordered pizzas and ate a late dinner in the kitchen. His dad said he was happy that the family was back together again, and opened a bottle of American wine called Opus One that his editor at Knopf had given him in New York.

Hugo's thoughts turn to the hypnotist and the fact that when Erik Maria Bark tried to get him to describe the reflection of the blonde woman's face, he had seen the skeleton man from his nightmare, his skull and cracked eye sockets.

Could it be another case of double exposure? Maybe the woman was wearing some kind of weird makeup, or maybe she had heavy eyebrows that cast shadows onto her forehead.

Hugo puffs on his vape and decides that this is probably something he should share with his dad, that he and Agneta might be able to use in their book.

He stares up at the lampshade and tells himself to write it down before he forgets it, but changes his mind when he realises his notepad is out of reach on the armchair blocking the disused door into the living room.

Hugo lowers his phone to his chest and slumps back against the pillow.

Every time he inhales on his vape, a small light comes on at the end of the device, casting a soft glow onto the ceiling.

He closes his eyes for a moment to compose himself before he puts the vape down on the nightstand, picks up his phone and calls Olga.

'Hi, babe.'

'Are you alone?' he asks.

'Very.'

'Who was that guy at your place?'

'Which guy? Oh, you mean Hachim? I helped him with a job,' she replies, sipping something.

Hugo sits up and pushes a pillow behind his back.

'Olga, we need to talk . . . What was going on there? Redrum is . . . I mean, that's not a normal club.'

'Normal club? I hate normal clubs. They're all so fucking lame and—'

'But that place . . .' he cuts her off. 'Do you even, like, know what was going on—'

'Enough of the fucking moralising. What the hell's wrong with you?' she says with a laugh.

'I just want to know what you're mixed up in.'

'Relax. I know a bunch of people. What can I say? I told you not to come. Hachim likes posing, and he earns a fucking fortune. It means he can send a bunch of money home,' she says, a new defensiveness to her voice.

'I saw someone being raped,' says Hugo.

'It's all fake, don't you get it?' she replies, softer this time. 'These guys, they make so much every day. People aren't allowed to actually hurt them. It wouldn't work if they did.'

'I dunno . . . I know what I saw.'

'Everyone sets their own rules.'

279

'OK, great . . . so everyone's happy?'

'Come on, Hugo. There are broken people everywhere . . . You know I'm not all sweetness and light, but I'm nice to you.'

'Are you?'

'If you're nice to me, yeah.'

Hugo hears her light up and take a deep, bubbling drag on a pipe. He lies still, looking out of the window. The blinking light of a plane cuts across the night sky.

'Did you have time to check whether my mum is registered in Le Grand-Village?' he asks once the bubbling stops.

'Huh?'

'We talked about it, her family home was there . . . You said you'd check with the Canadian authorities.'

Désolé, mais je n'ai pas eu le temps.

She takes another hit on the pipe and holds the phone away from her as she coughs.

'This is important to me,' he explains.

'It's important to you, you want us to go there, but clearly I don't earn money the right way,' she snaps.

'Come on, I just don't want you getting mixed up in anything bad.'

'Olga's a big girl.'

'OK.'

Through the phone, Hugo can hear subdued dance music.

'I added more money to the account, anyway,' she says after a moment.

'Me too.'

'I saw. That's great . . . though we still have a long way to go,' she says, clearing her throat. 'I know you don't really want to ask your dad for a loan, but we could pay him back together, come up with some sort of repayment plan and—'

'It's just that he already thinks I'm a failure,' Hugo speaks up.

'You're not a failure.'

'Yeah, I am.'

'In that case, anyone who hasn't written an international bestseller is a failure.'

'Nah, it just applies to me,' he says with a sigh.

'And that's why you can't borrow money from him?'

'I would rather not.'

'Would he notice if you just took some from his safe?' she asks after a moment.

'No, but I would never do that.'

'OK, but as a loan?'

'I've already embarrassed myself enough with that *Aftonbladet* interview.'

'It's your life. You're allowed to do whatever you want. You don't have to sit there and take his shit,' says Olga.

'He was just worried . . .'

'Worried,' she repeats, taking another drag. 'Do you want to come over?'

'I can't, I'm heading back to the lab in the morning. Thinking about helping the police again.'

'Why?' She laughs.

'Because that's, like, the basic requirement of moral courage: trying to help if you can,' Hugo replies, feeling his eyelids grow heavy.

They have just ended the call when Hugo hears quick footsteps on the stairs from the floor above, followed by a hesitant knock on his door. He sighs and closes the drawer in the nightstand, then gets up, steadies himself against the wall with one hand and unlocks the door.

'Come with me,' Bernard whispers.

'What's going on?'

His father is wearing his navy-blue dressing gown, and his hair is standing on end, his eyes anxious.

'There's someone outside, in the garden,' Bernard explains.

'What? Who?'

'Just come with me.'

As Hugo follows his father down the dark hallway, he thinks about how similar the situation is to his nightmares.

The floorboards creak underfoot, and the crystals on the baroque wall sconce clink softly as they pass.

They make their way into the large library, where there is a staircase up to the next floor. The door to the kitchen is wide open, and the window out onto the drive shimmers darkly. It feels like a beady eye, following them up the stairs.

On the first floor, the lights are out and the curtains drawn. The only source of illumination is coming from the main bedroom, where Agneta is standing beside the bed with a tablet in her hand. In the pale glow from the screen, her hair looks grey. She has her glasses on, and is wearing a pink cardigan over her nightie. Her cheeks are glossy with night cream.

'Is he still there?' Bernard asks quietly.

'Yes.'

'Does someone want to tell me what's going on?' says Hugo.

'Keep your voice down,' Bernard tells him, taking the tablet from Agneta and putting it down on the bed. 'We don't know what's happening, but there's someone sneaking around in the garden.'

They huddle together so that they can study the feed from the six security cameras outside.

'I can't see him,' says Bernard.

Agneta reaches out and touches one of the six frames, making it fill the screen.

The cameras have switched to night-vision mode.

A figure dressed in black passes through a dark spot and moves around the east wing of the house before disappearing from view.

'Jeez . . .' Hugo whispers.

The bushes in the garden look like black cracks against the light dusting of snow, but towards the top edge of the screen, the soft glow from the Christmas lights on the driveway is visible.

Agneta switches back to the main feed.

The intruder is now on the third camera, crossing the grass by the sunroom where there was once a small play area.

They pause in a dark corner.

'Is he taking a piss?' Bernard asks, enlarging the image.

The camera is mounted almost four metres above the ground, and the wide-angle lens makes the facade of the building bend like a bow.

'What's he doing?' Hugo whispers.

The man is standing with his back to the camera, holding something in his right hand. It almost looks like a short magic wand, shiny and black at one end. He raises his arm and makes a few exaggerated movements towards the wall before setting off again.

Agneta switches to the next camera, covering the other side of the sunroom.

'Where the hell did he go?' asks Bernard.

They switch back to the overview feed, but the figure in black has vanished.

The lamps lining the footpath resemble small balls of light. The wooden bench by the lilacs is just about visible, but other than that the screen is dark.

The intruder is still nowhere to be seen.

'The door's locked, isn't it?' Agneta asks. 'You locked it earlier?'

'I don't know,' Bernard replies. 'I think so.'

'After taking the rubbish out?'

'I think I locked it,' he says, gritting his teeth.

Hugo thinks he spots movement on the fourth camera, and he enlarges the feed covering the west wing of the house. The intruder is now visible from above and to one side as he moves forward, takes off his rucksack and stops outside Hugo's bedroom window.

'Call the police,' says Agneta.

'Hugo, call them now,' Bernard blurts out.

'What should I say?' Hugo asks, unlocking his phone just as the alarm starts blaring.

A loud, pulsing siren fills the house, and the lights in the garden come on.

Bernard's phone starts ringing, and he fishes it out of the pocket in his robe.

'It's the alarm compa—'

'Answer it!' Agneta tells him.

Hugo looks down at the tablet again, but the intruder is gone. He switches to the six-camera view and hears his father giving the operator the security code and quickly explaining what is happening before ending the call.

'What did they say?' asks Agneta.

'They're on their way,' Bernard replies. 'Said they'll be here in fifteen minutes and that—'

He stops talking at the sound of a loud thud on the floor below.

'They said we should lock ourselves in the bathroom and get in the tub.'

In the hallway downstairs, the crystals on the wall sconce jingle softly. Agneta hurries over to the door and turns the lock. Bernard's hand is shaking as he dials 112, and Hugo reaches for the cast-iron poker from the stand beside the stove.

49

Shortly after the sun dips below the horizon, the blue glow of the atmosphere begins to emerge. The ultramarine light is reflected in the thin layer of snow among the houses, almost as though the ground itself were illuminated.

Joona pulls up to the police cordon and is quickly waved through. He drives along the row of stationary patrol cars and parks behind the command unit. After getting out, he makes his way over to the inner cordon, holds up his ID and, once he is allowed to pass, continues down the drive.

An ambulance is parked outside a tired-looking 1970s house with large windows facing out onto the water. Behind the wheel, the driver is sitting with his face in his hands.

A large white forensic tent has been erected on the driveway, lit up from the inside like a marquee at a crayfish party.

Joona watches as an officer in uniform vomits to one side of the garage while his partner rubs his back.

Forensic technicians wearing protective suits over their thick winter coats are busy photographing the ground, and their flashes light up the snow with an aggressive brightness.

Joona says hello to an officer with a red nose standing guard outside the tent, and asks for Erixon.

'Knock, knock,' the officer says as he pushes back the rustling material.

'Who's there?' a woman's voice replies.

'Police.'

'Police who?' she asks without looking up.

'Police, open the door,' he says with a grin.

Joona ducks down and steps into the tent. He greets the woman from the National Forensic Centre and sees her blush.

There is a whirring space heater on the ground, and the hot air is making the roof of the tent bulge upwards.

The biggest of the two tables is cluttered with BioPack bags, storage envelopes, boxes, OH film, transport sleeves, bottles of Basic Yellow 40 and gelatine lifters.

Erixon is working on his laptop computer at the other table. The burly forensic technician is wearing white coveralls and a hairnet, a face mask hanging around his neck.

'Jesus of Nazareth,' he sighs, looking up from the screen.

'Far from it,' Joona replies.

'The responding officers forced entry,' Erixon explains with a nod towards the broken front door. 'The killer had screwed it shut from the outside ... We haven't touched anything, just photographed, numbered things and secured prints ...'

Erixon continues, telling Joona that the perpetrator also seems to have taken a sturdy piece of wood from a pile at the rear of the house and screwed it above the garage door, preventing it from opening any more than about twenty-five centimetres.

'We can talk again once you're done,' he rounds off. 'I'll keep working till then.'

Joona pulls on a pair of coveralls and shoe protectors and heads into the house.

Picking his way across the step plates, he crosses a lounge and continues up the stairs.

For some reason, news of the murdered woman in Stocksund had fallen between the cracks, when it should really have reached him as soon as the call came in.

He assumes the delay is precisely because, for the first time, the victim was female.

It wasn't until Erixon arrived at the scene and asked whether Joona had already stopped by that the mistake was realised.

Joona cuts through the kitchen and into the cold bedroom, pausing in the middle of the floor. He turns back to look at the splintered door and listens to the recording of the emergency call.

Ida has locked herself in her room, and the sound of the axe hitting the door is audible in the background as she talks to the operator. She sounds desperate and afraid.

'What do you mean by a madwoman?'

'A woman with an axe, she's broken in.'

The minute the operator understood the seriousness of the situation, he asked for an address to dispatch a car, but the call ended as he was trying to ascertain other, vital information.

The air in the bedroom is the same temperature as outside.

Joona glances out onto the balcony.

There are no footprints in the snow, just small pockmarks from the shards of glass that fell when the glass in the door broke.

The bed has been heaved onto its side against one wall.

Joona opens the door to the linen cupboard and studies the passageway for a moment, then leaves the bedroom and heads through to the nursery.

The large toy cupboard is at an odd angle, away from the wall.

This must be how Ida got out, he thinks.

The killer broke through the bedroom door, realised the room was empty and smashed the door to the balcony.

Joona steps over a small toy crocodile and makes his way back out into the kitchen. There is a broken wineglass on the brown-tiled floor, he notices.

He goes back down the stairs and says hello to the forensic technician working in the lounge.

'The lock was drilled out,' the man says, nodding to the sliding patio doors.

Joona thanks him for the information, turns back out of the lounge and opens the door to the boiler room.

The killer sealed every exit and got into the house via the deck.

Joona moves past the humming ground source heat pump.

The forensic technicians' lights from the garage seep into the room through the cracks around the door up ahead.

In addition to the axe, the killer had a power tool and a drill bit with a hardened tip.

Joona opens the door to the garage and pauses on the first step plate, dazzled by the glare.

Every inch of the room is illuminated, banishing any shadows beneath the bikes with flat tyres, skis and gardening tools.

Erixon comes into the garage with a folding chair beneath his arm. Without a word, he sits down, sighs and looks around the crime scene.

The air is heavy with the stench of blood and faeces.

It is as though time has ground to a halt here.

More than half the floor is covered in blood, and there are also spatters on the walls and across the ceiling, on the stacks of car tyres and a blue roof box.

Dark blood has also trickled down the side of a plastic box full of baubles.

A red-and-blue children's bicycle with pictures of Spider-Man on the frame stands as some sort of mute spectator to the massacre, the tread marks from its tyres visible at the very edge of the pool of blood.

Joona composes himself and forces his eyes to linger on every detail, piecing together the sequence of events in his mind.

The dismemberment that took place here is the most brutal to date.

The woman's head has been severed from her body and chopped into several pieces, and her fingers are scattered across the rough concrete floor, alongside segments of her arm and legs and feet.

The lower half of her torso is lying belly down, with bare buttocks, while the top half is slumped on its side, wrapped in a purple silk robe.

On a segment of leg, stretching from thigh to knee, there are a number of visible cuts and superficial axe wounds.

Joona attempts to read the room, methodically working his way between ragged flesh, blood-drenched cuts, bone marrow, cartilage and brain tissue.

'I'm so sorry this happened to you,' he says as he pulls on a new pair of latex gloves.

'You're still talking to the dead, I see,' Erixon mumbles.

'Sometimes.'

Joona isn't sure why he does it. Perhaps it is simply his way of showing respect to the victim, however cold and clinical the crime scene investigation might be.

He wants to tell Ida that he sees her as an individual, as someone in need of integrity, dignity, and some form of justice.

There is a soft squelching sound as Joona moves forward and gently turns the two pieces of her torso over.

As a result of the sheer amount of blood she has lost, the livor mortis is practically non-existent, nothing but a small, pale cloud where the upper section of her thigh was touching the floor.

She has grazes on her hips, and her blonde pubic hair is matted with blood. Her robe has fallen open to reveal a creamy white breast, and above her belly button, there are two cuts in the shape of a V. A few centimetres of her crudely severed spine are visible, and thick blood is still seeping out of the mangled tissue.

The killer seems to have been overcome by an almost chaotic rage.

It reminds Joona of the kind of atrocities sometimes committed by soldiers after being whipped up into a frenzied thirst for revenge, with the key difference being that this deed has nothing sexual about it. None of the wounds are directed at the genitals, anus, breasts or mouth.

Ida hasn't been tortured, but this time the dismemberment was central.

She fled to the garage, and the door hit the plank of wood screwed to the outside, preventing her from escaping. She tried to crawl through the gap, was dragged back inside and killed almost immediately, Joona thinks as he takes off his gloves.

'Done already?' Erixon asks.

'No, but the case has just taken a pretty sharp turn, and I need to talk to the team before heading over to Uppsala to speak to Hugo Sand again.'

289

Erixon makes a half-hearted gesture to the body parts and blood on the floor.

'You didn't look, but there aren't any defensive wounds on her arms,' he says.

'Of course not.'

'No?'

'She was killed too quickly for that.'

'With a blow to the spine or the back of her head, you think?'

'Her spine,' Joona replies as he leaves the garage.

50

It is almost four in the afternoon, and Agneta and Hugo are driving to the Sleep Science Lab in her quiet Lexus. The pale sun set more than an hour ago, and the sky is now dark again.

The traffic thins out once they pass the turnoff to the airport.

Agneta is in the right-hand lane, behind a white van on which someone has drawn a crude heart in the dirt.

That morning, Hugo called Lars Grind to say that he would like to come back to the lab and that he would be willing to undergo more hypnosis if the police were still interested.

Agneta took a beta blocker and offered to drive him to Uppsala, because Bernard was fired up and wanted to write about Hugo's interview, the intruder and the security cameras. Singing 'La donna è mobile', he headed up to his office in the attic with a handful of ginger biscuits and a whole pot of coffee.

Looking back now, it feels surreal that the three of them sat huddled together in the bedroom until the security firm got to the house. The two guards searched every room and then knocked on the door. Bernard got up to speak to them, and Hugo returned the poker to the stand by the stove.

When the police arrived ten minutes later, they took over from the guards and spoke to the family in the kitchen. The officers checked the security footage and photographed the footprints around the house. There were signs of attempted entry on Hugo's window, and in the corner by the sunroom they discovered that the intruder had drawn a full-sized door on the wall in black spray paint.

It was two in the morning by the time they had the house to themselves again. Bernard swept and mopped the hallway floor, cleaning up the mud and snow the guards and police officers had trampled in. The three of them then slept together in the main bedroom with the door locked, Hugo on a mattress on the floor and Agneta and Bernard in their usual bed.

None of them said anything, but they were all thinking the same thing: that the intruder hadn't been apprehended, and that none of the cameras had caught him leaving the property.

Until dawn, Hugo had been convinced that the axe murderer had somehow managed to break in, and was lying low somewhere in the house.

As she drives, Agneta glances over to the teenager. He has pushed the passenger seat back, and is sitting with his phone in his right hand.

'Dad asked . . . and it's OK with me if you want to stick around for the hypnosis this time,' he says.

'Thank you. But you know . . . this whole thing with the book, I . . . I know you said yes, but you can change your mind if it doesn't feel right,' she says. 'I won't be annoyed. We've barely started, so it's still OK if you want to put a stop to this.'

'No, I think it's a good idea . . . and I'm happy because Dad's happy. I know he'll listen if I say I want to change anything.'

'Of course. Of course he will.'

Agneta indicates, changes lanes and overtakes a transporter carrying seven cars. The turbulence from the heavy vehicle buffets her Lexus, making it shake.

'You know, the police have been trying to get hold of Olga,' she says. 'But she doesn't answer the phone, she's never home and doesn't show up when she's called in for questioning.'

'What do they want with her?'

'I think Joona just wants to ask about the night when you sleep-walked there.'

'Meaningful,' he sighs.

'Do you know where she is?'

'No, we haven't been talking much lately,' he replies, running a hand through his hair.

'OK. I'm sorry to hear that.'

'It'll work itself out,' he says with a shrug.

Agneta pulls back into the right-hand lane, checks the satnav and sees that her exit is in a couple of kilometres.

'Olga works a lot, at a club called Redrum in Hjorthagen,' Hugo says a few minutes later, in a strange tone of voice.

She turns to him just as the headlights from a car travelling in the opposite direction sweep across his face. His eyes look weary, his jaw tense.

'Hugo ... There's something I've been meaning to talk to you about,' she says as she turns off towards Uppsala.

'OK ...' he mumbles, lowering his phone to his lap.

'I wanted to say sorry for New Year.'

'What, why?'

'I shouldn't have said that I wanted to adopt you. It was ... insensitive of me.'

'I just couldn't take it in,' he replies, looking out of the side window.

'Of course, I get that. Your reaction made perfect sense. You've already got a mum and a dad.'

'Except ...'

'And I really would like to adopt you,' she continues, eyes welling up. 'It's not that, but—'

'Do we have to talk about this now?'

'I just wanted to say sorry, because it was all down to my ... pride, if I'm honest. I wanted to be a better mum than Claire.'

'That's not hard.'

'Maybe not at first, when you were little. I mean, you had no option but to turn to me ... and I looked after you, especially when Bernard needed to write. But I've been wondering whether, subconsciously, I also exploited the situation because I needed to be loved too. By you, as though I was your real mum.'

They pass a Maxi superstore and are approaching a roundabout.

'I never thought of it that way, but . . . I don't know, I'm super impressed by you right now,' Hugo says, fixing his eyes on her. 'I mean, it's pretty brave to say what you just said.'

'I'm just sorry things went so wrong,' she says as she turns off onto Dag Hammarskjölds väg.

Tall, straight pines flicker by on both sides of the road.

'I've decided to try to find my mum,' he says.

'Good.'

'I used to be so mad with her for leaving me and Dad, for dropping everything and running away to Québec so she could get high,' he continues. 'But now, I feel like I want to see her anyway. I mean, she *is* my mum, even if she has all these problems.'

'Of course.'

'She used to write to me about getting clean, but nothing ever happened. I don't know . . . I just feel so fucking powerless, because she's going to wind up dead if she doesn't get any help.'

Agneta gives him a quick sideways glance.

'When did you last hear from her?'

Hugo sighs and slumps back in his seat. 'It's been almost three years since she replied to any of my letters.'

'Did you have an argument?'

'No . . . Or maybe, a bit,' he admits, swallowing hard. 'She promised she'd come home for my birthday, but it was just lies like always.'

'What does Bernard say?'

'Dad doesn't want to talk about her. He thinks she's made her choice, and he's learned not to trust her, can't stand it when she gets my hopes up . . . But surely hope is better than just giving up?'

'He's probably just trying to protect you.'

'I know.'

* * *

They leave the car in the small parking area and head inside. Agneta signs in at reception, and is handed a visitor pass on a black lanyard. Hugo then leads her down the corridors to Lars Grind's office.

He presses a finger to the buzzer by the doctor's door, the lock clicks, and the little pink WILLKOMMEN sign lights up.

Lars Grind is sitting at his desk in the cold glow of the computer screen. He is wearing a pale-grey corduroy suit and a white polo shirt.

'Sorry again that I just bailed,' Hugo says, pausing in the middle of the room. 'There was something I needed to sort out.'

'It's OK, you know that. What we have here, it's symbiotic – and voluntary. I try to help you, and we do our research.'

'How did you get on with your jacket?' Agneta asks.

'It's with the dry cleaner. I think it must have been oil, because I'd been watching a tutorial and trying to service my bike before I came over.'

Grind had stopped off at the house with a hamper of food on the first Sunday of Advent. He hadn't been able to stay for long, but had agreed to a quick coffee in the kitchen, and Bernard had noticed that he had a number of dark stains on the sleeves of his jacket.

Lars gets up and gestures to the chairs by his bookcase.

'Coffee? Tea? Hot chocolate?'

'Nothing for me, thank you,' Agneta replies.

'I'll take a hot chocolate,' Hugo says with a smile.

The doctor leaves the room, and they sit down by the coffee table, which is cluttered with scientific journals and annuals.

'What was that about his jacket?' Hugo asks.

'Hmm? Oh, nothing, he just had a few stains on it.'

'Man, that's so stereotypical of a genius, isn't it?' Hugo laughs. 'Not noticing they've got sauce on their shirt, or chalk on their face . . .'

Lars comes back into the room, holding two mugs of hot chocolate with whipped cream. He takes a seat and asks Agneta whether she regrets her choice, but she just laughs.

'We spend about a third of our lives in a kind of trance we know next to nothing about,' he says.

'It's nuts,' Hugo mumbles.

'A quarter of people have trouble sleeping – not like you, of course, but in other ways. They don't get enough sleep, or they sleep badly.

They have nightmares, grind their teeth, snore . . . Someone has to start thinking outside of the box.'

Lars takes a sip of his hot chocolate and ends up with a cream moustache.

'Can Agneta stay for the hypnosis session?' asks Hugo.

'As far as I'm concerned.'

'Thank you,' she says.

Lars Grind's eyes narrow as he studies Hugo. 'But I do have to say I was a little surprised when you said you wanted to do it again. You were so upset last time.'

'Do you think it's bad for me, though?'

'Not really. It's more a question of how much anxiety you can handle.'

'I'll give it one more go.'

'Erik Maria Bark is incredibly good – a legend within the field of psychological trauma. Though he's also been in real trouble a few times.'

'Why?' asks Hugo.

The doctor waves a hand. 'Forget I said anything . . . You do whatever you want to do. For me, personally, it was extremely interesting to be able to get a glimpse of your nightmares from the inside for once.'

Agneta decides that she should look into Bark's background, possibly even request to interview him for the book.

'So what do you think I should do?' asks Hugo.

'I don't want you to feel any pressure. We can still cancel the hypnosis session. I'll call Erik if you want me to.'

'But what if I can help stop a killer?'

'That's the police's job, not yours . . . But if they can't move forward without you, perhaps you should give them another chance.'

'Or else I just do it now, like we agreed.'

'Or else you just do it now.'

51

Agneta and Hugo are in the suite, waiting for the hypnotist to arrive. The lights in the faux windows have been dimmed to give the illusion of dusk outside.

'Erik Maria Bark is super charming, in any case,' says Hugo.

'Handsome too?' Agneta asks with a smile.

'He reminds me of an actor . . . I can't remember his name right now, but he's in that film with—'

Hugo stops talking when someone knocks at the door.

Lars comes into the room, followed by a middle-aged man in a bobbled blue sweater and a pair of jeans. He has a furrowed brow and kind, sad eyes.

'Hi, Hugo,' the man says, smiling disarmingly.

'Hi.'

He turns to Agneta, and she gets up and shakes his hand.

'Erik,' he introduces himself, holding her gaze.

'Agneta.' She feels her cheeks grow hot.

'You know, my first true love was called Agneta,' Erik tells her, brimming with energy. 'I was seven and she was twenty. Nothing happened, of course; she was a supply teacher . . . Sorry, I'm not sure why I'm telling you this, but before I change the subject I should probably point out that I *have* had real relationships since.'

'I was just saying,' Hugo speaks up, 'that you remind me of a handsome actor who—'

'I know exactly who you mean,' says Agneta.

'Either you're joking in an attempt to embarrass me,' Erik replies, 'or something drastic must have happened since I looked in the mirror this morning.'

* * *

Hugo lies back on the bed as Lars Grind attaches the last six sensors to his head. For the second session, the plan is to combine hypnosis with polysomnography.

Erik Maria Bark draws the curtains and dims the lights even further.

'This might be a stupid question, but do you work for the police?' Agneta asks.

'No, I'm a doctor. I have a practice, and I carry out research at the Karolinska Institute, too. But I do also step in to help with the questioning of traumatised witnesses on a fairly regular basis.'

'Using hypnosis?'

'Sometimes, yes, but more often than not, no.'

Grind turns on the monitors, checks the connections, holds up a thumb and says that they have contact with Major Tom.

'Isn't Joona Linna joining us today?' asks Agneta.

'He'll be here soon, but we can start with a bit of relaxation while we wait. I'm just going to go and wash my hands,' Erik replies, turning to leave the room.

On the three monitors, the output from the twenty-two sensors attached to Hugo's body is visible, tracking his heart and brain activity, eye movements and muscle activity during the various stages of hypnosis – induction, suggestion and deep trance.

Erik comes back into the room and takes a seat beside Hugo. He repeats much of the same information as last time, explaining how clinical hypnosis works and then taking him through the breathing and relaxation exercises.

The boy's sceptical, jokey attitude is gone, and he now seems more afraid than anything.

'Hugo, we're going to slow your breathing a little further,' Erik says softly. 'You're safe here. There's nothing to worry about. Inhale through your nose, filling your lungs, and then slowly exhale through your mouth. Feel your eyelids growing heavy.'

Hugo can smell the mild scent of soap on the doctor's hands as he patiently helps him to relax, focusing on his neck and jaw. Erik works through each muscle group in turn, making sure to keep them relaxed and heavy before returning to the teenager's neck and jaw. He gets his body to feel weighty, to sink and press down against the bed.

'You are now deeply relaxed, your heart is beating steadily, and I want you to concentrate on my voice as I count down to zero from one hundred. Ninety-nine, ninety-eight ... You're walking down a staircase made from dark, lacquered wood. With each number you hear, you're going to take another step, and with each step you take, you're going to feel more relaxed and focused on my voice.'

Hugo pictures himself descending a staircase into an enormous vestibule.

'Keep going. Eighty-four, eighty-three ... Everything but my voice should fade into the periphery,' says Erik. 'All you can see is the wide staircase and the soft, red carpet ... You keep moving down, and you feel a sense of calm spreading through you ... Eighty-two, the steps are all the same height and width ... Eighty-one, eighty ...'

Hugo notices the detective come into the room and sit down in the empty chair, just as Erik had said he would, and he feels a comforting sense of order before letting go of the thought completely and continuing down the stairs.

After a while, Erik stops describing the staircase, focusing instead on Hugo's breathing, relaxation and inner concentration.

Hugo realises that the dark wood has begun to sway beneath his feet, that it shakes softly with each step.

'Sixty-five, sixty-four ... Now there is nothing but my voice and the meaning of the words within you ...'

The glossy wood has begun to pale, Hugo notices. It turns to metal, and the great staircase twists into an enormous corkscrew.

'Forty, thirty-nine, thirty-eight ...'

As though in a dream, Hugo is now making his way down a steel spiral staircase in a narrow well. He grips the cold handrail and feels the whole structure shuddering and swaying with every movement.

'Twenty-seven, twenty-six . . .'

Dry earth has begun to fall around the brackets, pattering softly against the metal.

The descending numbers slow, dragging his breathing with them as though he were in a deep sleep. But in his mind, he has started running.

'Nineteen . . .'

His body is incredibly heavy, like he has a number of weighted blankets on top of him, like he has overdosed on promethazine.

'Fourteen . . . thirteen . . .'

It feels as though some unconquerable force is driving him down into the earth.

'Twelve, eleven,' Erik says, his voice soft and monotonous. 'You're going to keep going, but when I . . . when I reach zero, you will be back at Bredäng Campsite on the twenty-sixth of November. The blonde woman is just about to go into the caravan, but before she opens the door, you will see her reflection in the glass. Snow is falling from the dark sky, settling like a delicate halo on the satellite dish.'

* * *

Joona studies the teenager's calm face in the dim light and then turns to one of the screens tracking the gamma waves in his cerebral cortex. The pale light from the monitors flashes in Dr Grind's wide eyes.

'Ten, nine, eight,' Erik says slowly. 'You are perfectly safe here, there is no need to worry . . .'

Hugo's right hand twitches, and Erik places his own on top of it. He notes the boy's steady, even breathing and continues his countdown.

'Seven, six, five . . . In a moment, you are going to tell me everything you can see at the campsite without any fear whatsoever.'

Hugo's eyes begin moving beneath his closed lids.

'The campsite is empty, closed for the winter,' says Erik. 'The sky is black . . . and the snow is falling more heavily now.'

Lars Grind gets up from his chair and looks as though he wants to say something.

'Four, three, two, one, zero . . . You are now standing slightly back from the caravan, watching the woman walk up to the door.'

'Mum,' Hugo whispers.

'I don't think the woman you can see is your mother,' says Erik. 'I think that your mother is part of your dream, and—'

'We need to hide,' the teenager cuts him off, his voice shrill.

Erik places a reassuring hand on his shoulder.

'You're safe here, you're relaxed . . . Breathe slowly and feel the sense of calm in your body as you turn around and look at the woman outside the caravan . . . Do you see the snow? The soft flakes landing on her blonde wig?'

'It's not Mum. I . . . I thought I was following Mum, but . . .'

'Hold on now, Hugo. There's no rush. I want you to breathe in through your nose and out through your mouth . . . Listen to my voice . . . You're sleepwalking, and you think you've seen your mother at the campsite, but it's someone else standing outside of the caravan.'

'Yes,' he whispers.

'Can you see her face?'

'No,' he replies, so quietly that he is almost inaudible.

'I think you can see her.'

'I can't.' Hugo raises his voice and shakes his head.

'He's struggling,' says Grind.

'Relax,' Erik continues. 'Take a deep breath. And once you feel ready, tell me what you see.'

'She's holding an axe,' Hugo mumbles, licking his lips.

'In which hand?'

'The right . . . and she has to twist a bit so she can open the door with her left . . . Oh God, oh God . . .'

'Maybe we should stop now?' says Grind.

'What's happening?' Agneta whispers, a hand to her mouth.

'Look at her reflection in the door and tell me what you see,' says Erik.

'There's no time, it's too quick . . . White cheekbones, eye sockets . . . I don't know, she's already inside . . . I can hear loads of thudding and shouting.'

Hugo holds his breath, his entire body shaking.

'Let the air stream out between your lips and then slowly inhale,' Erik tells him. 'You're relaxed, now breathe out . . . Tell me what's happening at the campsite.'

'I don't know.'

'You're standing outside the caravan, and you hear shouting.'

'Who's shouting?' Joona asks quietly.

'Who is doing the shouting, Hugo?' Erik repeats.

'The man . . . At first he sounds angry, but now . . . Now he's just scared and confused.'

'What do you see?'

'I see . . . shadows flickering over the bright window. I don't know, I . . . I'm walking around the caravan, and I climb onto a breezeblock and look inside right as blood sprays across the window. Oh God . . . I fall into the grass, hit my back on a gas canister . . . but I stand up again, brush myself off and walk around the front, into the caravan . . . I have to get Mum, we need to hide, that's all I can think. I don't care about anything else, I just walk straight in.'

Hugo tenses, sweat pouring down his face.

'What do you see?' Erik asks softly.

'A cop. He's screaming at me, but I don't know why. I'm lying on the floor and my ears are ringing. I can smell gunpowder . . .'

'But what happens before that?' Erik presses him.

'I open the door and go in.'

Hugo stops talking abruptly, and his eyelids stop fluttering.

'What is the first thing you see?'

'A cop with a gun. He's screaming at me, and there's blood everywhere.'

Joona realises that although Hugo is in a state of deep hypnosis, he is not yet deep enough to be able to see the massacre in the caravan. The memories are in there somewhere, but he keeps jumping forward to the moment when the two officers found him asleep on the floor.

'Let's return to the back of the caravan,' Erik tells him. 'Step up onto the breezeblock and stay in that moment, before the blood sprays across the window.'

'God,' the teenager whispers.

'You see a man being killed with an axe, don't you?'

The teenager nods slowly, and the rings in his nose and lip catch the light.

'Hugo ... Listen to my voice. Relax your body and keep your breathing calm. You are completely safe here ... You're going to watch a video clip on your phone now, from the night when the man was murdered in the caravan. Someone has climbed up onto a breezeblock and filmed what happened through the back window ... You start the recording in slow motion, which means you have plenty of time to tell me what you see.'

Hugo takes a deep breath, and when he next speaks, his voice falters.

'The woman has already chopped off both of his feet ... He's lying on his back, gasping for air, can't understand what's happening. The pool of blood on the floor keeps getting bigger and bigger, running along the edge of a brass strip and soaking into the rug ...'

'Keep watching the film,' says Erik.

'I can see the peeling paint on the window frame and my breath on the glass ... Inside, there's a broken red vase ... The floor lamp is on its side, and the snakeskin shade is flecked with blood ... The woman is standing over the man with her back to the camera, leaning forward ... She drags the blade slowly across his torso, and the cut starts bleeding. She changes the angle of it, but the man is screaming, and he tries to sit up ... That makes her really angry, it ...'

Hugo is now whispering, speaking so softly that his voice barely carries, and Joona and Erik both have to lean in to hear what he says.

'She slams the axe into the floor, right by his head,' Hugo mumbles. 'He keeps screaming, so she yanks it back, lifts it again and hits him right in the middle of his face ... There's so much blood, it sprays up onto the window.'

He opens his eyes.

'There's so much blood,' he repeats.

52

Joona is in the car, heading back to Stockholm and the NCU. The light snow swirling through his headlights is a first taste of the low-pressure system currently moving west from northern Russia.

As he drives, Joona thinks about the hypnosis session. About Grind's wide eyes, the look of fear on Agneta's face, the hand she pressed to her mouth. He remembers the moment Hugo woke from the hypnosis, the way his eyes glazed over as he repeated his own words: *There's so much blood.*

Erik had managed to get him to close his eyes and sink back down into relaxation for a moment or two before lifting him out of the trance properly.

'You can look around, but just lie still, taking in your surroundings . . . And once you're ready, you can sit up and have a sip of water.'

Joona knows that Erik was extremely pushed for time, that it's not possible to hold people in their most traumatic moments for too long.

This is uncharted territory, and the doctor has no choice but to feel his way forward, learning more about what works for the specific individual in front of him during every session.

Based on what they know so far, everything points to Hugo having seen the fatal attack during the few seconds when he peered in through the window of the caravan.

It is as though Erik is methodically panning for the truth.

There are certain details that don't quite match the hypothetical sequence of events laid out by Erixon and Nils Åhlén, but that could be because there are still fragments of dream muddying the waters. Still, Joona knows that Erik is getting closer to what really happened with every session.

During their first attempt, Hugo reached the campsite and gave them a brief glimpse of the killer.

In the second, he saw the murder itself, but had no memories from his time inside the caravan. For all they know, he might have come face to face with the killer.

If Hugo is willing to undergo a third session, Joona thinks, there is every chance he will be able to give them a firm description at long last.

*   *   *

Joona parks his car in the garage, takes the lift up to the eighth floor and strides down the corridor.

As he walks, he thinks about the blood in the garage in Stocksund, the spatter on the ceiling from the axe being raised again and again.

Ida's husband has been informed. He was in Tenerife at the time of the murder, but was planning to catch the first plane home. Their five-year-old son was sleeping over at a friend's house, and would stay there until his father could collect him.

The latest murder has turned all their previous theories on their head. There is no doubt it was the same killer – the Widow, as she is now known – but the fact is that Ida doesn't fit the general pattern: she was a young woman rather than a man.

Joona has called a team meeting, asking everyone to return to the station to search for any unsolved or questionable cases involving female victims who might, somehow, fit the pattern.

It can no longer be denied that they are dealing with an active serial killer.

Yet again, Joona's thoughts turn back to the bloody garage. Looking at the scene, he had the sense that while the perpetrator's aim was to end Ida's life, some sort of blind rage took over almost immediately. A fury that nothing but sheer exhaustion could numb, when the killer couldn't physically manage to swing the axe again.

Everyone is already waiting around the table when Joona reaches the investigation room.

He goes straight over to greet Detective Superintendent Bondesson, who has just joined the group. Bondesson is an older man with a thin, wrinkled face, bushy eyebrows and a horseshoe of white hair around his head. He has been a part of the National Murder Squad since it was first set up, and is incredibly experienced, with a firm belief in allowing the slow machinery of an investigation to take its course.

'I don't know about the rest of you,' Bondesson says, nodding to the photographs, 'but my trusty brain always feels an urge to interpret crime scenes like this as chaotic, when really they should be read word for word, as a complete story.'

Joona sits down and takes the team through his latest thoughts following the revelation that the killer does not exclusively target men.

'This time, the victim was a young woman. A mother,' he says.

They go through the sequence of events in the garage in detail, discussing the images from the scene. Everyone agrees that the latest murder is the most aggressive to date, with the caravan coming a close second.

Anna Andersson is studying a photograph of the main pool of blood, a close-up shot of the grooved tread marks left by a child's bicycle tyre.

'Looks like the Widow moved the bike just as the blood was starting to coagulate,' she says with a frown.

'Can I see?' Joona asks.

'Forward a bit, then back a bit,' Anna shows him.

'Strange,' Bondesson mumbles.

'Only a couple of centimetres in both directions.'

'The killer pumped up the tyres,' says Joona.

'Of course.' Anna sighs. 'Damn it. The other bikes all had flats.'

'So you're saying she literally massacred the mother, then stayed behind to pump up the kid's tyres, just to be nice?' Rikard Roslund asks.

Bondesson gets up from his chair, mutters that he needs a cancer stick and gives Joona a lingering look.

The group starts to divvy up the tasks for the new preliminary investigation: producing an updated profile and searching the databases for cold cases involving female victims.

'We still haven't managed to get hold of Olga Wójcik,' says Anna.

Joona stands up, grabs his coat from the hanger and leaves the room.

He heads straight for the lifts, and as he waits, he looks up at the notice board, which is full of invitations to Christmas parties, glögg evenings and a seminar about the impact of the government's decision to ignore the Council on Legislation's advice and introduce a system of crown witnesses.

He takes the lift down to the ground floor and leaves the building via reception. As expected, Bondesson is waiting for him on the other side of Polhemsgatan. The older detective is wearing a long sheepskin coat, smoking a cigarette on the snowy pavement.

Joona crosses the narrow street between the parked motorcycles and walks over to him.

'As you might have noticed, I had a real sinking feeling when I realised I might've made a big mistake,' Bondesson says after a moment or two.

'Everyone makes mistakes.'

'But I had my doubts even then.'

'When?'

Bondesson straightens his arm and drops the butt of his cigarette into the storm drain.

'We turn our backs on the present and travel back three and a half years, tick, tick, tick,' he continues. 'It's high summer, the first week in July, and the station is like a ghost town . . . We get a call from Lund, so I jump straight in the car and drive down there, through the bright night . . . A woman – and I still remember her name, Lucia Pedersen – has been murdered in her own home, a small timber-framed house in Håstad . . . Killed by a single axe blow to the neck.'

'I remember the case.'

'Lucia was in the kitchen, opening a delivery from the pharmacy, when she was attacked from behind. The blade hit the right side of her neck, severing the fifth cervical vertebra from the sixth. She dropped like a rock, dead before she even hit the floor.'

Bondesson lights another cigarette and draws the smoke deep into his lungs. He then exhales, picks a fleck of ash from his lower lip and continues.

'The killer had taken the axe from the chopping block in the woodshed and left it in the sink. There were no prints. They'd cleaned the shaft with some sort of alkaline solution.'

'You saw a perpetrator who didn't take the murder weapon to the scene, who knew there was an axe in the shed.'

'She'd had a number of affairs.'

'A clear motive.'

'The prosecutor's case was built on circumstantial evidence, but it held up in both the district court and the court of appeal,' Bondesson tells him. 'Lucia's husband, Gerald Pedersen, swore he was innocent, but he was sent down for twenty years. And their daughter was handed over to social services and placed in foster care.'

'I know you're wondering whether the Widow might have killed Lucia, but what was it that gave you doubts back then?'

'When he was twelve, Gerald Pedersen and his friends built a pretty powerful pipe bomb, and he lost his right hand . . . But the attacker was right-handed.'

'That sort of thing isn't usually easy to determine.'

'No, you're right . . . *Theoretically*, he could've done it, but he would have had to swing the axe in some sort of high backhand . . . No one would do that in a thousand years, but sure.'

'You didn't have any other suspects?'

Bondesson taps the ash from his cigarette.

'The killer took the jewellery Lucia was wearing, too. A gold cross on a chain, two diamond earrings and a small silver stud with a freshwater pearl that she wore in her bellybutton. But they hadn't searched the house, hadn't touched any of her other jewellery in the bathroom.'

'So the idea that it was a robbery gone wrong was ruled out?'

'The prosecutor thought it was an act of jealousy, that it was Gerald's way of taking back everything he'd given Lucia over the years . . .

None of it was recovered when we searched the place, so the theory was that he'd tossed them out of the car window as he drove away.'

'There's a certain logic to that.'

'Yeah, but what ultimately did for him was the kid,' says Bondesson.

'The kid?'

'The killer gave the girl her asthma inhaler.'

'How do we know that?'

'Lucia had bought her a new one, and the box from the pharmacy was lying in the pool of blood. The ibuprofen, hand cream and tampons were still inside, but the killer had taken out the inhaler, opened it and left it beside the girl in her cot before fleeing the scene.'

'OK.'

'Which is something only a father would do,' he concludes with a troubled smile.

'Where is Gerald Pedersen now?'

'They transferred him to Hall.'

53

Hall Prison, one of Sweden's highest-security facilities, is at the end of the long railway bridge on the outskirts of Södertälje.

It took Joona just thirty-five minutes to drive down there.

He leaves his car in the parking area and turns towards the low administrative building on the other side of the tall fence topped with tight coils of razor wire.

A couple of Prison Service flags strain on their poles.

Joona walks over to the drab grey gates and reports to the control room.

A woman with a lifeless face comes out to collect him, and after leaving his personal effects in a locker, he shows his ID at the security desk, goes through a metal detector and past an eager sniffer dog.

As he then follows a guard with a ginger beard down a corridor in which the doors and walls are all painted the same glossy shade of milky white, he feels an ache in his heart.

Joona will never forget his time as a prisoner in Kumla. The blue vinyl mattresses, the underground tunnels, the long corridors, the dusty yard and the dirty yellow walls.

The air in the corridor smells like cleaning products, and their footsteps sound oddly muffled. Someone has carved a swastika into one of the doors, and Joona hears a man shouting for help through the thick walls.

The guard is talking about the fact that plastic is choking the oceans as they walk down a row of heavy steel doors with tiny windows.

Because all of the other visiting rooms are already in use, Joona is shown into a family room with floral curtains, a birch-bark Advent star, furniture suitable for both adults and children, a round pink rug and a box of toys and games.

He thanks the guard and sits down to wait. After just a few minutes, the guard returns with the inmate.

'Will you come back and get me in ten minutes? I've got a PULS meeting,' Gerald Pedersen asks him before turning to Joona. 'Sorry, but they tell me I've got to attend a bunch of group sessions about "my struggles with violence and aggression" if I want to get out on parole in a few years.'

'No problem.'

'I'm a busy man, y'see. Got a job in the workshop, screwing long screws into really long plastic tubes ... and then there's the big gingerbread house contest tonight.'

'Take a seat.'

'I'd shake your hand, but ...' Gerald says, extending his stump towards him.

'Joona Linna. I'm a detective superintendent with the National Crime Unit,' Joona says once Gerald is sitting down.

'Detective superintendent, huh? Fuck me,' he mutters, getting back onto his feet. 'They said it was my lawyer ... I don't talk to the cops. You can't do this, I—'

'Hold on.'

'Hello! I want to go back to my cell now!'

'I know you didn't kill your wife.'

'What's that now?' Gerald replies, turning to him with a troubled look on his face.

'You didn't kill Lucia, did you?'

'No,' he says, licking his lips.

'Please, sit down. I've done time in Kumla. I know how popular the police are in a place like this.'

'But ...'

'I've spoken to the warden. This will be registered as a meeting with your lawyer.'

'OK, but what the hell . . . I thought this was about me transferring to Fosie,' he says, taking a seat again.

'Gerald, it's going to take a little while to organise your release. It's a process that starts with the prosecutor reopening the case,' Joona explains.

'You think I'll be released?'

'There'll be a High Court review, and you'll be acquitted on all charges.'

'Seriously?'

'Yes.'

Gerald nods slowly as he tries to process the news.

'So I'll get to see my daughter again, tell her that I'm innocent?' he says after a moment, wiping the tears from his cheeks.

Joona gives him some time, allowing him to repress the wave of emotion and compose himself, to put on a hard face again before he continues.

'You'll be exonerated, which is one thing. The other is finding the real killer.'

'Amen.'

'Whoever murdered Lucia must have been to your house before,' says Joona. 'He or she knew that you had an axe in the woodshed and that your daughter has asthma.'

'Could it have been one of her . . . acquaintances?' Gerald asks. 'Lucia was a notorious cheat. She swore she'd stop after we got married, but I don't know how long that lasted. She tried to claim that it wasn't about me, that she was talking to a psychologist, and I thought she'd get bored of it, told everyone that we had an open relationship and that it was good for us.'

'Are you thinking of anyone in particular?'

'Nah, it wasn't exactly like I wanted to be buddies with them,' he says with a sad smile. 'The few times I caught her at it, I just went over to my mum's and slept there.'

'Did you ever see anyone who seemed different to her usual type?' Joona asks.

'I don't know.'

'Not necessarily a man.'

There is a loud knock at the door. The lock rattles, and the guard with the ginger beard comes into the room.

'Gotta go,' says Gerald, getting up from the table. 'Thank you for this, though. I can hardly believe it . . . Don't go getting hit by a bus or anything, will you? I've got to get out of here. I need to get my daughter back.'

* * *

As he drives back to Stockholm, Joona learns that the officers knocking on doors in the neighbourhood where Ida Forsgren-Fisher was murdered have found another dead body. Former Chancellor of Justice Rutger von Reisen was sprawled in a frozen pool of blood on his driveway, killed by a deep axe wound to the back of his head. His black Labrador was keeping watch beside him, and started barking as the officers approached.

In all likelihood, Rutger witnessed Ida's murder while he was out walking his dog that night.

54

The news is reporting that the huge snowstorm is currently over St Petersburg, and that it will hit the east coast of Sweden with full force in just a few days' time.

The sky is dark and the air so cold that Bernard turns around and heads home earlier than usual, before he hits ten thousand steps.

It doesn't matter, he thinks. He is sure he read somewhere that eight thousand is more than enough.

He had been working at his computer in the kitchen for six hours straight – without anything but a cold meatball sandwich to eat – when he pulled on his winter coat and headed out.

Bernard is now almost back at the house. He walks through the gate, down the driveway, opens the front door and turns on the light in the hall. After kicking off his boots, he hangs up his coat and goes through to the kitchen.

He opens the lid of his computer, logs on and reads through the last few paragraphs he wrote before going out.

The pink Post-it note stuck to the top corner of the screen reminds him that he needs to finish his next column for *Expressen*. That type of work always seems so meaningless whenever the idea for a new book takes hold of him, all the interviews and public appearances like obstacles in the way of what he really wants to be doing.

Bernard lifts his hands to the keys, but just as he is about to start typing he hears a series of loud bangs above him.

As though someone is rolling a microwave oven across the floor.

He glances down at his phone, because Agneta promised to send him a message when she was on her way back, but he doesn't have any notifications.

Bernard shudders and gets up. He walks through to the library and pauses at the foot of the stairs. He can hear a sweeping sound from somewhere above, like loose sheets of paper blowing in the breeze.

'Agneta?' he shouts as he starts to climb the stairs.

When he reaches the landing, he peers through the glass door at the end of the hallway to Hugo's old room, where he slept before moving into the guest room.

Bernard turns in the other direction and sees that the narrow door to the stairs leading up to his office in the attic is ajar.

The house is now quiet.

Bernard moves towards the main bedroom, opens the door and goes in. The yellow glow of the lampshade illuminates the bed he shares with Agneta.

She isn't there.

He has just started to turn back towards the hallway when he hears a rustling sound, like a crane fly hitting a window.

From the corner of one eye, he sees something lunge towards him, and he feels a crack on the side of his head.

As though he has just been hit by a golf ball.

Bernard's legs give way, and he takes the bedside lamp with him as he crashes to the floor. The bulb flickers and goes out.

Five empty cans tied to the back of the happy couple's car rattle along the hallway and down the stairs.

He closes his eyes and feels his heart pounding in fear.

The side of his head is throbbing, and he reaches up and touches his temple. It doesn't seem to be bleeding.

Bernard tries to sit up, but is too dazed to manage it.

What just happened? Someone was rolling a microwave, cracked him over the head and then ran away.

His thoughts are confused, he realises.

Five empty cans on strings hanging around a grey woman's neck.

A golf ball hits his temple.

Two black dogs race through the room and down the stairs.

Bernard isn't sure whether he dozed off or passed out when he wakes to the sound of Agneta shouting his name. He may as well stay where he is on the floor, he thinks with a smile. For the drama of it, if nothing else.

'Bernard?' she shouts as she climbs the stairs.

'I'm OK,' he whispers.

Agneta shrieks and runs over to him when she spots him on the floor, and he attempts a smile and holds up a thumb.

'Is it your heart?' she asks.

'No, I fell . . .'

'Are you sure it's not your heart? I'm going to call 112,' she says, rummaging through her bag with shaking hands.

'Really, I'm OK,' Bernard mumbles, closing his eyes for a moment.

'What happened?'

'It's nothing,' he says with a smile. 'It was just a golf ball . . . It hit me right . . .'

Agneta finds her phone and dials the number, quickly telling the operator what is happening, that the front door was open, that he is in the bedroom on the first floor.

'He doesn't have any injuries that I can see – other than the side of his head, maybe. It's pretty red, but it isn't bleeding. He's conscious, but seems quite confused,' she says.

'We'll send an ambulance,' the operator tells her.

* * *

Agneta watches the ambulance pull away up the driveway, then heads back into the house and locks the door. She goes straight to the library, slumps down on one of the bottom steps, and feels like she wants to cry.

Bernard refused to let her go with him in the ambulance, but he did ask her to bring his laptop to the hospital if they decide to keep him in overnight for observation.

She sighs, gets up and climbs the stairs. When she reaches the landing, she turns right, opens the door to the attic and makes her way up to Bernard's office.

'God . . .'

The room is complete chaos, like the bridge of a ship after a hurricane. The desk is at an angle, the chair on its back. The banker's lamp is broken and there are papers and books everywhere, all of the drawers in the desk emptied onto the floor.

The big blue Järvsö cabinet looks like it has been forced open with a crowbar or an axe, and the floor around it is littered with splintered wood and pieces of lock.

Bernard's original manuscripts have been dumped on the floor and trampled, along with his letters, folders, photographs and contracts.

Agneta tries to spot his laptop amid the mess. She moves a hardback book about the criminal code and criminal law and notices a stack of old letters held together with a brown rubber band. The top envelope was postmarked in Québec two years ago. Agneta picks up the stack and puts it on the desk.

She feels a sudden rush of panic – as though she has just been shot with a bullet made of ice – when she realises that it could have been the serial killer who attacked Bernard.

The axe murderer might have seen the interview in *Aftonbladet* and come over here to silence the witness.

Agneta walks down the stairs as though in a daze, imagining the blonde woman hitting Bernard with the broadside of her axe in anticipation of chopping him to pieces.

Perhaps it was the sound of her Lexus pulling up on the driveway that scared the killer away.

The front door was wide open when she got home, after all.

Had Bernard left it unlocked?

Agneta pauses in the hallway, closes the door behind her and tries to bring her anxious breathing under control.

The killer must have come in through Hugo's window the night they saw her on the security cameras, she thinks.

And lain in wait inside the house until today.

Agneta tells herself that she needs to calm down, that it can't be true.

Despite the deep gashes in the frame, the window was intact.

She gazes through the pane of glass in the door to the side of the house they rarely use nowadays, towards Hugo's old bedroom and games room.

A sudden draught around her feet gives her goosebumps.

There must be a window open somewhere.

The thought of the serial killer getting into the house through the door she spraypainted onto the wall flickers through Agneta's mind, and she shudders and starts making her way down the stairs to the library, heart racing.

After eight steps, she stops – at the very heart of the house – to listen. It is so quiet that she can hear the weary snapping of the rope against the flagpole outside.

She needs to ask Bernard what he saw, because if it *was* the killer then she is going to call Joona Linna right away and demand protection.

Agneta glances over her shoulder before she continues down the stairs, crosses the library and goes through to the kitchen. She is relieved to see that Bernard's laptop is on the table. She opens the cupboard beneath the sink and takes out a sponge and a bottle of cleaning spray, then heads out into the hall and pulls on her faded leather jacket and a pair of green wellington boots.

It has started snowing again, and the tyre tracks left by the ambulance are barely visible.

Agneta cuts across the gravel, turns the corner and pauses outside Hugo's window, peering in at his unmade bed and the piles of clothes on the floor for a moment before continuing along the end of the house and gazing down towards the lake.

The islands and holms have vanished in the haze, and the ice on the surface of the water is blanketed beneath a dusting of white snow.

Agneta rounds the corner again and makes her way over to the spraypainted door on the wall: a tall rectangle complete with a doorstep, hinges, a handle and lock.

She wets the sponge and starts scrubbing at the paint with a rising sense of unease. By the time she stops twenty minutes later, dropping the bottle and sponge to the ground, her fingers are aching from the cold. The paint is almost gone, but there is still a faint shadow of a doorway there, as though it were made of smoke.

Agneta hurries back around to the front of the house, opens the door and checks that there are no damp footprints on the floor before going in and locking the door behind her.

She picks up her phone from the chest of drawers and sees that she has a message from Bernard. He will be allowed to come home tomorrow, he writes, followed by three red hearts.

As Agneta makes her way through to the library, she tries calling him, but he doesn't pick up. She climbs the stairs, thinking about the stack of letters again, and with no real plan, she continues up to the attic.

The intruder has trampled on the cigar box containing Bernard's old lucky pens.

She picks her way over to the desk, rights the chair, reaches for the stack of letters and sits down. Agneta takes a deep breath and then loosens the elastic band. Flicking through the letters, she realises that they are all from Hugo's mother, Claire.

Agneta knew, of course, that he got letters from time to time, but she has always made sure to maintain a certain distance from their relationship.

For years, Bernard must have gone into Hugo's room, retrieved the letters from the floor or the bin, and saved them for him.

She reads them in chronological order, starting with the years after Claire first moved back to Québec, written to a small child.

Some of the later letters have been crumpled, and one has actually been torn to pieces, but Bernard must have taped it back together.

Perhaps Hugo got sick of his mother's constant excuses and lies about doing better, about starting various treatment programmes and deciding to get clean.

From his perspective, the whole thing is heartbreaking.

Claire writes that she is working as a translator and that she hopes she will have enough money to travel back to Sweden soon.

Agneta dries the tears from her cheeks and feels a lump in her throat as she unfolds the last letter in the stack and reads:

Älskade Hugo, mon fils bien-aimé,

I spoke to Dad on the phone and he tells me that you're doing well at school, that you're learning to write and that you are incredibly gifted – a wonder boy!!!

I'm sorry to have let you down again by missing *ton anniversaire*. It broke my heart, but the truth is that I finally found a place at a great treatment centre in Ontario. I was in the middle of a detox programme and had no contact with the outside world.

I'm out now, on a methadone programme – methadone mainten-ance treatment – and I'm feeling good, working at a small garden centre.

The hardest part is that my sponsor says I need to cut off all contact with everyone for a while, until I'm strong enough to come back and try to fix the things I broke.

It'll be lonely, but I've got myself a dog – a Siberian husky, because his eyes remind me of yours.

Bluer than robin eggs.

I'll always love you, and I think of you every day. *Câlins et bisous, puss och kram.*

Your mum,
Claire

Agneta folds the sheet of paper, pulls the elastic band back around the stack and gets to her feet. She is thinking about the last letter and the conversation she had with Hugo in the car. He clearly hasn't read it, because it sounds like his mother is genuinely trying to stay clean.

Agneta feels guilty for having often looked down on Claire and her addiction. She leaves the letters on the desk and turns to the window out onto the water.

A shiver passes down her spine when she sees a light come on in the lake house.

55

Hugo has sent six messages to Olga over the course of the day, telling her about the hypnosis session and life at the lab, that he is looking forward to spending more time with her over Christmas, but she hasn't replied.

He has just helped himself to a plate of chickpea stew, and he exchanges a few words with the woman who works in the kitchen before heading into the dining room and sitting down opposite Bo, who is tucking into a hearty portion of meatballs, potatoes, lingonberry jam and sauce.

'Haven't seen you in a few days,' says Bo.

'No, I know, I had to go home . . .'

'To chat to that journalist, yeah.'

'Seems like everyone saw that, huh?' Hugo sighs, spreading his paper napkin on his lap.

'You looked good. The bags under your eyes were *just* dark enough, and—'

'I was an idiot,' Hugo cuts him off with a laugh.

'Nah, man. Sleepwalking and sleepwalkers don't get nearly enough press these days.'

'We're a bit slow, kind of dozy and have trouble communicating, but other than that . . .'

'What's not to love?'

A slim young woman approaches their table carrying a tray. She looks to be around twenty, her face covered in freckles, and she is wearing a clip with an enamel ladybird on it in her straight red hair.

'When I told Bo my name was Svanhildur, he asked if that's why I scream at night,' she says with a smile, lowering her tray to the table.

'It's enough to make your blood run cold,' Bo quips, using his foot to push a chair towards her.

'Seriously . . . It does sound pretty creepy,' says Hugo.

'Sorry. I have night terrors,' Svanhildur explains as she sits down.

She pulls a pill organiser from her pink corduroy bag, takes out three tablets and pops them in her mouth.

'I'm Hugo,' he says.

'Ah, the famous Hugo.' She smiles and pulls on her fingers, making the joints crack.

A thin young man with slicked-back hair comes into the dining room. His tics are plain to see as he stands by the trays of hot food and the sliced bread. He has incredibly pale skin and dark circles beneath his eyes, and is wearing a faded sailor's uniform that seems much too small for him, plus a pair of strange shoes with separate big toes.

Bo jokingly crosses himself as the young man walks past their table and sits down at another with his back to them.

'Kasper, come over here,' Svanhildur shouts over.

The thin young man ignores her, sitting with a straight back as he slices his potatoes and meatballs into four even pieces.

Svanhildur gets up and goes over to his table.

'Don't you want to sit with us?' she asks.

'Whore,' he replies without looking up at her.

'Don't say that.'

'You don't know a thing about me. You're just a fucking whore,' he says, meeting her eye.

'All I wanted to say is that you're welcome to sit with us.'

Kasper mutters to himself as she turns around and returns to her seat. He starts eating again, and Hugo notices that he turns his plate exactly ninety degrees after every bite.

'Little rat,' Bo mumbles in Danish.

'He's just scared of—'

'A frightened little rat.'

The young man eats the last piece of potato, turns his empty plate ninety degrees, finishes the water in his glass, turns the plate another two full rotations and gets up and leaves the room.

'What's he scared of?' Hugo asks quietly.

'Ending up like his mum,' Svanhildur replies, keeping her voice low. 'She was here, at the sleepwalking clinic, when he was little, but she didn't get any better . . . She refused to sleep, and in the end she was so tired that she fell off a ladder and died while she was picking apples.'

'How do you know that?' Hugo asks, biting his nails.

'I met Kasper right after he arrived. He was totally out of it on benzos, and he said way too much . . . He told me his dad had forbidden him from coming to get help here, but he did it anyway the day he turned eighteen. For sleepwalking, too, just like his mum.'

Bo pushes back his chair and gets up.

'I've gotta go talk to Grind. Seems like he wants to change my meds again,' he says as he leaves the table.

Hugo lowers his cutlery and picks up his phone to check whether he has any messages, but there seems to be something wrong with the reception. He closes the app and reopens it, but nothing happens.

'This fucking phone,' he says with a sigh, restlessly bouncing one leg.

'What's the problem?' Svanhildur asks as she spears a meatball on her fork.

'I don't actually know. I never get any messages while I'm in here,' he replies, scratching the back of his hand.

'Want me to fix it?'

She drags the meatball through the sauce on her plate and lifts it to her mouth.

'Fix it?' Hugo repeats with a note of scepticism. 'How?'

Still chewing, she puts down her fork and holds out a hand. He passes her his phone and watches as she pushes a USB-C cable into the charging port and plugs the other end into a small plastic satellite phone.

'Enter the code on the screen when you connect,' she says, handing it back to him so that she can continue eating.

Hugo follows her instructions, and a moment later his phone pings with five new messages.

'Thanks,' he says, taken aback that it actually worked.

'Just eject the device.'

'OK,' he says, passing back her things.

One of the messages is from the dentist, reminding him that he has an appointment coming up. Two are from his father, the first asking how the hypnosis session went and the second telling him that he had a fall, but that he is OK. Agneta has also sent a text to say that Bernard is in hospital following an accident, but that he is doing just fine.

An hour ago, Olga sent a brief response to all his multiple calls and flirty messages:

> You can't keep calling and texting constantly, Hugo. It's really stressing me out, OK? Maybe it's my fault for giving mixed signals, but I need some space, got a load of stuff to sort out. Speak after Xmas. O xoxo

His cheeks are burning as he locks his phone and stares down at it in his hand, trying to work out what just happened. He wants to call Olga and ask what he did wrong, but he knows he can't.

Hugo chews on his thumbnail for a moment, then puts his phone screen-down on the table and looks up at Svanhildur.

She uses her hand to cover her mouth as she chews, smiling as she holds his gaze.

'D'you want to watch a film or something?' he asks.

'I've got a bottle of tequila in my room,' she whispers.

'No way.'

'What?'

'You've got tequila?'

'Shh,' she tells him, pressing a finger to her lips.

Hugo reaches for the salt shaker and drops it into his pocket. He then gets up and carries his dirty plate and glass over to the washing tray before pausing in the kitchen doorway.

'Thanks for dinner,' he says as the woman turns to look at him.

'No problem.'

'I wanted to ask if you had any limes.'

'Limes?'

'Yeah, I've got a real craving for lime. Who knows, maybe I've got scurvy or something,' he explains, tucking a lock of hair back behind his ear.

'We've got lemons . . .' she says.

56

A battery-powered candle casts a warm, flickering glow over Svanhildur's pantry.

The sweaty bottle of tequila is on the table between her and Hugo, alongside two pale-blue egg cups, a lidless salt shaker and a white chopping board covered with lemon slices.

'Seriously, that Kasper guy . . . he's super creepy. Like, what's wrong up here?' Hugo says with a gesture to his temple.

'Yeah, he's kind of weird.'

'Understatement of the year.'

'I've realised he's got a skeleton key . . .'

'What's that?'

'A homemade master key. Because it seems like he can go wherever he wants round here.'

'You're kidding . . .'

'Nope.' She grins.

'You're just trying to make me scared of the dark.'

'I swear, it's true,' she says.

Hugo picks at the label on the bottle and leans back in his chair.

'His mum didn't die here, though, did she?'

'No, at home in their garden,' she replies, holding his gaze. 'I think Kasper was the one who found her.'

'He told you that?'

'There's something about me that makes people tell me things.'

'What do you want to know?' Hugo asks, putting on a robotic voice.

She laughs and looks down for a moment before raising her head. Her eyes are shining, and the tip of her nose is red.

'From now on, let's only tell the truth,' she says.

'A confession after every shot.'

'Great.'

They fill the egg cups with tequila, pour a little salt onto the skin between their index fingers and thumbs, and pick up a wedge of lemon in the same hand.

'To the truth,' Hugo says with a grin.

He watches the tip of her tongue dart out as she licks the salt from her hand, and he does the same, knocking back the shot, swallowing, biting down on the lemon and pulling a face.

'Oof, that's strong.' She laughs.

Hugo refills the egg cups as the warmth of the alcohol spreads through his gut. Svanhildur puts on a playlist of Lana Del Rey and reaches for more salt.

'I'm sure it's a *great* idea to combine the meds they've got us on with booze,' Hugo says with a wry smile.

'You go first.'

He looks her in the eye, and they both do another shot, cough and grin at each other.

'I've got mummy issues,' Hugo confesses.

'What do you mean?' she asks, pouring more tequila.

'My mum doesn't give a shit about me. She moved back to Canada when I was little, and I haven't heard from her in almost three years . . . I'm also seeing a woman – Olga – who's basically twice my age.'

'Definitely sounds like mummy issues,' she says with a nod.

'Seriously, I think my mum might be a junkie . . . That she's in free fall, or whatever. But I've been saving up so I can go and look for her, because I can't just sit around waiting for her to get in touch or die of an overdose.'

'Horrible,' Svanhildur whispers.

They drink again, slamming the egg cups down on the table with a little too much force.

'Your turn,' he says, looking up at her.

'My last date, or whatever you want to call him, was radicalised,' she says, cracking her fingers nervously.

'OK?'

'We were both studying political science, but he started getting sucked in by all this white power, conspiracy theory stuff.'

'Boy, bye.' Hugo sighs.

'Right? Bye bye, on a personal level . . . But at the same time, right-wing populism is more to do with social injustice than anything . . . The sense that people have been left behind.'

'Should be an open goal for the left,' he says, kissing three fingers and raising his hand.

'I know. But I'm not going to waste another minute on him.'

'Good.'

'So you've got a girlfriend? Was it Olga you said? What's the deal with you two?'

'We're not official or anything, but we've got plans . . . She's actually the one who said I should try to find my mum. We've opened a bank account together, to save up for the trip.'

'Does it cost a lot to go to Canada?'

'Yeah, but mostly because we want to be able to stay for a while,' he says, showing her the account balance on his phone.

'Woah . . . That's, like, the deposit for a flat or something.'

With a slight smile, she pours more tequila and reaches for another wedge of lemon. They clink egg cups and drink, slamming them down even harder this time. Hugo gazes into her pale-blue eyes. Her skin is like mother-of-pearl beneath her freckles.

'I think I'm kind of attracted to you,' he hears himself say.

'Oof,' she replies, looking genuinely surprised.

'Sorry, I shouldn't have said that, but—'

'No, no.'

'But it's true.'

'I just wasn't expecting it, that's all,' she says. 'Because you're, like . . . so confident and cool and famous and everything.'

'Ha,' he says. 'Not true, but thanks anyway.'

They drink again, bite down on the lemon and laugh. Svanhildur points to his egg cup with a smile and accuses him of cheating, claiming that there is still some tequila left in the bottom.

'Cheating?'

He turns his egg cup upside down and waits. After a moment, a solitary droplet falls to the table.

'See!' She laughs.

'Turn yours over!'

'I'm a virgin,' she confesses, still laughing.

'Seriously?'

Svanhildur looks down, her freckled cheeks now scarlet. She brushes the last of the salt from her hand, takes a deep breath and meets his eye.

'If we're talking full intercourse, yeah,' she explains, pushing a lock of hair back behind her ear. 'I've done some stuff, obviously. But not, you know . . . It's just never felt right . . . You probably think I'm a total loser now.'

'No, I get it. Guys are always saying that all sex is good, even if it's bad, but that's just . . . not true.'

'No,' she whispers, looking down again.

'What're you thinking?'

'That what you said before made me happy, about being attracted to me . . . Even though you weren't being serious. I mean, we don't even know each other, but still . . .'

They do another shot, and he sees her shudder. The rising alcohol content of his blood is making his lips tingle, his eyes struggling to focus.

'I think I'm starting to get drunk,' he says.

'That doesn't count as a confession.'

'No, I'm just saying.'

'Good.'

'OK, another truth . . . I'm kind of sceptical about the medication they've got me on, and I've tried to talk to Lars about it, but I'm too scared of conflict to actually stand my ground,' he says.

'What are you taking?'

'Zopiclone, obviously, which is fine,' he replies. 'And then Mirtazapine and Tramadol, which both make me sleepwalk more than usual – or that's how it feels, anyway . . . but Lars is convinced that small doses have the opposite effect.'

'I've got it into my head that he comes into my room and watches me while I'm sleeping,' she says in a low voice.

'Why?'

'Because sometimes, when I wake up, I can smell his weird aftershave.'

'Ugh, creepy,' he whispers.

'Yup.'

'I mean, it's different with sleepwalkers, I get that,' he says. 'Obviously they have to bring me back to my room sometimes.'

'Do they?'

'I don't know, I guess so,' he says, refilling their cups.

'OK, listen,' she says, looking at him with a solemn face. 'I've got an idea. I could put a wireless minicam on you, and that way we can see exactly what happens.'

57

Svanhildur is unsteady on her feet when she comes back into the pantry with the small camera. She shows Hugo how to attach it and start the recording, explaining that the lens won't be visible once it is in place.

He catches her hand and feels the heat of her skin, her trembling nerves, then looks deep into her glittering eyes, bends down, kisses her softly on the lips and says goodnight.

'Night,' she replies, unable to stop herself from grinning.

As Hugo leaves her room, he hears her lock the door behind him. He staggers down the corridor, keeping one hand on the wall to stay upright. Her heartbreaking smile is all he can think about, and he makes a promise to himself to look out for her.

He can feel the effects of the tequila as he brushes his teeth, then he takes his pills and calls for a nurse to come and attach his night sensors.

Once he is alone again, he takes out the little camera and fastens it to his pyjamas just as Svanhildur showed him.

The lens looks like a tiny black pearl in the buttonhole of his shirt.

He turns out the light and sees the small green LED from the camera above his bed, plus the dull grey glow of the polysomnographic equipment.

Hugo closes his eyes and smiles to himself as he thinks about his evening.

Sleep has begun to reel him in with its soft yarn when he is convinced he hears someone in the other room, crushing the lines of pistachio shells underfoot.

He opens his eyes and stares up at the dark ceiling.

The cold glow of the full moon is seeping through the blind, and there is a soft clicking sound from the hallway outside.

Hugo gets up, steps over the boxes of Lego and makes his way over to the door. He slowly opens it and heads out.

Through the window in the door up ahead, he can see – beyond the bathroom and the closed door to the attic – into his parents' room.

In the gloom beside the bed, there are two small, pale figures – no more than about thirty centimetres tall – dancing on the floor.

They pause, side by side, and start to tremble.

Hugo blinks firmly and tries to make his eyes focus. Hesitantly, he moves forward, towards the pane of glass in the door, and sees that the two figures are actually bare feet.

Someone is lying flat out on the floor.

From the darkness to one side of the feet, a pile of bones and skulls gets up. Blood drips to the floor.

The door to the attic opens, and Hugo sees his mother tiptoe out into the hallway. She must have been hiding on the stairs.

She is wearing her white silk nightie, and she looks terrified.

Hugo reaches out and quietly opens the door in the hall. He tries to whisper to her to come and hide in his room, but he can't manage a single sound. He doesn't have a voice.

She doesn't see him, just hurries down the stairs to the library.

From the bedroom, there is a series of loud bangs and he sees a couple of sopping-wet towels hit the floor.

Hugo follows his mother to the stairs, puts a hand on the dark railing and shivers as he starts making his way down.

He can hear the dry rattle of loose bones behind him.

The skeleton man has seen him.

Hugo starts running.

He knows that he and his mother need to escape, that they need to get out into the garden, go over to one of the neighbours and call the police.

When he reaches the dark library, he cuts straight across the rug, heading for the hallway.

There are men in the kitchen, mercenaries, shouting at one another and laughing as they pull food out of the pantry and fridge.

His mother creeps over to the front door, pushes her feet into her boots, grabs her coat, opens the door and nips out.

The voices in the kitchen are impatient, accompanied by the sound of bottles from the wine fridge being uncorked and crockery breaking on the floor.

Hugo tiptoes after his mother down the hallway, past green canvas bags full of ammunition and grenades.

The skeleton man is in the library now.

Hugo can hear him dragging a heavy spade behind him as he crosses the rug and the parquet floor.

He reaches the front door just as the skeleton man's spade thuds over the threshold into the hallway.

Hugo turns the handle, but the door is locked. Starting to panic, he fumbles for the knob, but it isn't there.

He tugs at the handle and glances back in the direction of the library. The skeleton man has paused at the end of the hallway.

In the dim light, Hugo can make out the curve of five different skulls on his body, several femurs, a pelvis and a number of strangely interlinked vertebrae.

He realises that there is a plastic button featuring a picture of a key on the wall, and he presses it, hears a faint click, and turns around.

As he yanks open the door, the skeleton man starts charging towards him.

The blade of his spade scrapes against the tiles.

Hugo runs outside, gasping when he crashes into something. He cuts across the raked gravel, but his mother is nowhere to be seen.

He hopes she has the same plan as him: to head down to the fence separating the garden from the common land, and then straight over to the closest neighbour.

When Hugo looks back over his shoulder to the house, he sees flickering torchlights in the windows.

He ducks down as he hurries through the garden, which slopes gently towards the water.

The grass is cold beneath his feet.

He catches a glimpse of his mother down by the lake house, her white nightie and pale skin almost glowing in the darkness.

A rabbit bolts away among the flowers.

Hugo's heart is pounding.

There are raised voices outside the house now, and Hugo lifts a hand to push back the branches of the weeping willow. Up ahead, he can see the silhouette of the lake house against the water.

Hugo is approaching the seating area by the lilacs, and he hears a soft thumping sound, almost like fingertips drumming a table. He slows down a little to listen, but the sound has stopped.

All he can hear is the gentle breeze in the leaves. The lilacs loom dark around the little white garden table.

The gate is just ten metres away.

Hugo is moving more slowly now, trying to spot his mother. He steps over a red frisbee on the grass, notices the heavy flowers on the lilacs and has almost made it past the bush when someone grabs his arm and pulls him back.

It is one of the skeleton man's soldiers.

He knocks Hugo to the ground and presses his knee between his shoulder blades. Hugo tries to get away, but it is impossible.

The skeleton man appears out of nowhere. He must have been creeping behind him the whole time. Together, the two men haul Hugo onto his feet and start dragging him backwards, towards the shouting and gunfire inside the house.

An explosion in the kitchen shatters the windows, causing glass to rain down on Dad's new Volvo.

58

After saying goodnight to Valeria in Brazil and Lumi in France, Joona sits down at his desk and gazes out at the rooftops beneath the dark December sky, at the Advent stars in windows and balconies decorated with fairy lights and spruce branches.

He takes notes as he reads through his colleagues' reports from their interviews with the victims' families and friends, from their door knocking rounds, reviews of the CCTV footage and lists of forensic evidence.

Joona calls Saga, who answers with a subdued hello after seven rings.

'How are you, really?' he asks.

'Fine.'

'I want you to know that I've been nagging Noah non-stop about bringing you in as my partner.'

'Thanks, but I'm OK with it, being on desk duty.'

'Are you?'

'No, but . . . Maybe I'm just not cut out for operative work.'

'Of course you are.'

'I'm not sure anymore.'

'I miss you, Saga,' says Joona. 'Do you have any plans tomorrow evening? I could cook, bring you up to speed on the case.'

'I'm sorry, I can't,' she replies, a little too quickly.

'Another time.'

'Sorry,' she whispers, her voice softer now. 'I just can't handle seeing anyone right now. I can barely stand to be with myself.'

'You know you can always call me.'

'Thanks, Joona,' she says, swallowing hard.

They end the call, and he sits quietly for a moment, thinking about the fact that she struggles to spend time with other people, whereas it is loneliness that eats away at him.

It is late, but rather than going to bed, Joona gets up and locks his pistol in the gun cabinet. He leaves his police ID on top of the chest of drawers, then heads out and takes the lift down to the garage.

There isn't much traffic on the roads as he drives over to Hjorthagen, where he parks the car and walks around the block to join the queue for the Sauna nightclub.

'By four a.m. the dancefloor is so hot that everyone wants to strip off and roll around in the snow,' a famous DJ had written on Instagram.

The people in the queue around Joona are all dressed to the nines, chatting drunkenly, laughing and peering longingly at the doors up ahead.

The area is clearly undergoing a dramatic transformation, but in the void between the traditional industries moving out and the redevelopment work beginning, pop-up venues seem to be flourishing.

The club is in a large building with a windowless brick facade.

Agneta told Joona that Olga Wójcik works at an exclusive members' club called Redrum, which can only be accessed by getting past the bouncer on the door across the rear courtyard from Sauna.

Joona waves when he spots Stina Linton coming around the corner. She has taken off her glasses and tied her hair back with neon yellow bands, applied some red lipstick and swapped her usual outfit for a pair of black jeans and a thin leather jacket.

'Very nice,' he says.

'Any excuse,' she replies with a smile.

The heavy bassline that seeps out onto the cold street every time the door opens is like some sort of irresistible scent.

The line moves forward, snaking around the riot fences in the makeshift holding area and past the doorman.

Joona and Stina reach the front and get inside. They pay at the desk, sign their names on an exclusive members' list, pass through a metal detector and a pat down, and make their way through the throng to the dancefloor.

Joona can feel the pulsing music in his chest as they push past the dancing, jumping people beneath the pink strobe lights.

The air is hot and damp.

On the little stage, there is a golden Christmas tree.

Joona leads Stina around the bar to a dark rubber door that opens onto a row of toilet cubicles.

The black-and-white-tiled floor is wet.

There is a strong stench of urine and vomit, and five women are queuing for the ladies' toilets.

A man with a glittery face is dozing in one corner, a scrap of sooty foil in a red trilby on the floor beside him.

They pass a number of beer kegs, and someone starts pounding on the wall.

Joona opens the metal door at the far end of the corridor, and freezing air floods inside. He and Stina make their way down a metal staircase to a vacant plot of land.

The ground is strewn with bricks, broken glass, car tyres and boxes of wet books.

Behind a heap of concrete and twisted reinforcement steels, a woman is smoking heroin, and by the door to the other building – the one housing Redrum – there is a man in a bulletproof vest, black combat pants and boots.

He is at least six foot five, with a black Colt 933 – a modern assault rifle with a short barrel – in one hand.

'Stop,' he says calmly.

'We're here to see Olga Wójcik,' Joona tells him.

'Nope.'

'Do you know her?' asks Stina.

'You should head back to the party.'

'Could you go and get Olga?' Joona asks.

'Nope.'

'It's important,' Joona explains, taking a step forward.

'You're not coming in,' the guard tells him, switching his rifle to semi.

As he does so, Joona catches a glimpse of a tattoo on the inside of the man's wrist. A dragonfly and a sword.

'Noordwijk,' he says.

'Why d'you say that?' the guard asks.

'Did you train with Rinus Advocaat?'

'I would've given ten years of my life for the chance, but they booted me out before I got that far . . . Hang on, you're not Joona Linna, are you?'

'Yes.'

'Shit,' the man mumbles, fixing his eyes on Joona. 'Everyone used to talk about you.'

'I doubt that.'

'Joona Linna,' the guard repeats, shaking his head with a smile.

'We need to get in.'

'I'll let you in, and I'll let you out, but I have to stay here. They've got my kid sister.'

'What goes on in there?'

'Don't know, and I don't want to know,' he replies, opening the door for them.

Joona and Stina make their way inside, and the door slams shut behind them. The green glow from the emergency exit sign overhead illuminates a corridor with vinyl flooring and peeling patterned wallpaper. Droplets of condensation glisten on the pipe on the ceiling.

Joona feels a brief sting of a migraine behind one eye, and he sees Stina anxiously push back a few locks of hair from her face.

They start walking and hear a muffled scream through the walls.

A bloody sanitary towel has been dumped on the floor, along with a few long strips of toilet paper.

They are approaching a door that has been left ajar, and pale light spills out into the corridor through the gap.

Somewhere up ahead, a man with a deep voice shouts aggressively.

Joona slowly moves over to the doorway and peers into the small control room on the other side. There is no sign of anyone, but he notices a thin column of smoke curling up towards the ceiling from the cigarette in the ashtray, and the large computer monitor is displaying eight livestreams.

Through a grubby window, he can see a studio containing a number of booths fitted with webcams.

In one, a naked boy with a look of apathy on his face is sitting in a pool of blood on a workout bench. His skinny body is covered in bruises, old and new.

'God,' Stina whispers, taking out her phone.

A large man with a tattooed face steps forward and holds a gun to the boy's head as another man starts hitting him on the thigh with a long, thin dildo.

The two detectives continue past the control room as Stina quietly calls command to explain the situation and emphasises that it is urgent.

'Ten minutes. They'll be here in ten minutes,' she tells Joona.

They pass the dented steel door to the studio and a small cloakroom cluttered with trainers, clothes and bags.

The corridor is dark.

Behind them, they hear raised voices.

Against one wall, there are a number of empty wine bottles and a car battery.

Joona meets Stina's eye. She looks frightened.

The next door is propped open, with a rolled newspaper wedged above the bottom hinges.

Joona pops his head inside.

A naked lightbulb illuminates a room with a carpet covered in rubbish, old popcorn and a pair of broken glasses.

Olga is sitting beside a young man on the stained denim sofa.

She is wearing a tight-fitting silver dress and heels, eating salad from a small red tub.

In a flat tone of voice, she tells the young man that everything will be fine, that he will be able to send money home.

Olga glances up at Joona with a spaced-out look on her face. The skin around one of her eyes is bruised and swollen, and her dark roots are showing through her dyed blonde hair.

With her free hand, she reaches up to wipe her mouth.

'Olga,' Joona says as he strides over to her. 'We're from the police, we need—'

'Joona!' Stina shouts.

A stocky man in a pair of sliders, tracksuit bottoms and a sweaty basketball vest straining over his rounded belly has burst into the room and stabbed her in the back.

Joona snatches the fork from the carton in Olga's hand and swings around. He drives it into the man's throat, pulls it out and hits him again.

Blood sprays across the man's hairy shoulders.

He lets go of the knife, sways unsteadily, and crashes into the floor lamp.

Stina collapses onto all fours, spluttering for air.

The man with the tattooed face runs into the room with his pistol raised. There is a loud crack, and the bullet hits the brick wall behind Joona.

Dust swirls around the hole.

Joona pulls the knife out of Stina's back and slams it into the man's chest before he has time to pull the trigger again.

The man takes a confused step back.

Joona snatches the pistol from him and points it at the doorway just as a third man appears.

He immediately holds up his hands and backs away.

The man with the tattooed face slumps to the floor. Beneath the knife, his torso is slick with blood.

Joona keeps the gun trained on the doorway as he helps Stina to her feet. The man with the hairy shoulders is slumped over a Coca-Cola fridge, blood dripping from his mouth and around the fork in the side of his neck.

'Olga, you're coming with us,' Joona tells her.

The young man is still sitting on the sofa, and he turns to Olga with huge pupils as she gets to her feet.

Joona leaves the room, secures the corridor and then waves for them to follow him.

They move as quickly as they can, past the control room and straight over to the door beneath the glowing emergency exit sign.

Behind them, there is shouting and heavy footsteps.

As they emerge from the building, Joona hears the roar of a helicopter approaching.

The bouncer with the semi-automatic rifle stares at them without a word.

They hurry across the yard, and Joona helps Stina up the staircase, dragging Olga behind him. Once they are inside, they pass the toilets and make their way through the rubber door to the crowded dancefloor.

The music is deafening.

Joona keeps the gun hidden by his side as he cuts across the dancefloor to the exit. A tall man blows him a kiss as he passes.

The metal detector starts beeping, but the doorman quickly moves out of the way when Joona points the gun at him.

They leave the club and head out into the cold air, past the long line of revellers.

Joona can hear the sirens from a large number of emergency vehicles approaching from several directions.

*   *   *

While the operation at the club continues, Joona gets into the back of the patrol car where Olga is being held.

The knife had punctured Stina's right lung, and her lips had started to turn blue by the time the paramedics arrived to take care of her.

There are currently at least ten police cars and a command unit outside the club, in addition to four ambulances and a fire engine.

Their blue lights sweep gloomily over the dark brick facades, and a police helicopter hovers overhead.

Joona is thinking about the fact that he killed the man with the tattooed face, causing yet another raven to land heavily in the darkness of his soul.

He runs a hand through his hair and studies Olga's remarkably symmetrical face and bruised eye. She has begun to come down, and her mascara is streaky, her breathing agitated, whistling softly through the piercings in her cheeks.

'Jacek's going to kill me,' she mutters, not for the first time.

'Olga, listen. I'm in charge of a separate investigation, and you've been called in for questioning.'

'Yeah, I know, but I can't talk to the cops.'

'Yet here you are.'

'Do I have any choice?'

She purses her lips, breathing through her nose and the tiny holes in her cheeks.

'When you woke Hugo while he was sleepwalking at your apartment, he started talking about the campsite in Bredäng,' Joona begins.

'Yeah, he was totally manic.'

'What did he say?'

'What did he say? I was in shock, and he was really fucking incoherent. Babbling about my balcony door, the lock, the knife, the snow falling on the campsite and dark caravans. I don't know, I was just trying to calm him down, to keep him still.'

'Did he see the killer?'

'I don't think so. That's not the impression I got, anyway, but he did say something about a bloody tooth. One with a gold crown.'

Olga mutters in Polish as a line of men in handcuffs file out through the doorway, and the ambulances fill up with young men wrapped in blankets.

Joona decides that it is time to hand her over to his colleagues and head home to get some sleep.

The investigation has just taken a significant step forward. Very few people know that the serial killer has extracted teeth from her victims, which means that Hugo really was able to see the reality behind his nightmare and that – temporarily, at least – the detail was stored somewhere in his memory.

59

Following the murder of Ida Forsgren-Fisher, the investigation has been given top priority. They currently have five targeted victims – including Lucia Pedersen – and two dead witnesses.

Photographs of the victims have been pinned up on the wall in the meeting room, alongside pictures from the crime scenes and some of the forensic evidence.

The team has managed to find a blurry image of a pale-blue Opel without registration plates on the E18 close to Enköping and, after scouring the footage from a large number of other cameras in the region, have established that the car doesn't show up anywhere else.

The Widow could easily have crossed the border into Norway by now.

But she isn't done yet, thinks Joona. She is just lying low while she watches her next victim.

He doubts her Opel even made it past Västerås. Most likely is that it disappeared somewhere in the network of backroads between the small, sparsely populated hamlets like Villberga, Grillby and Haga.

Joona is sitting at the table with his boss, Noah Hellman, and his colleagues, Bondesson, Rikard Roslund and Anna Andersson. They are joined by Göran Bergh, from the West Region, and Omar Nasri. Frida Nobel has also stepped in to replace Stina Linton, who will be on sick leave for at least a month.

They began the meeting with the boss taking them through that morning's press conference, explaining that the pressure from both the politicians and the media has risen exponentially. Joona then played the recording from the second hypnosis session, in which Hugo Sand witnessed the murder through the window at the rear of the caravan. Rikard tried to say something about the human aspect of the case, and was so moved by his own words that he had to leave the room to compose himself.

Joona's eyes drift over the pictures of the victims, comparing their wounds, severed limbs, cuts, bruises and livor mortis spots.

'We need to remember that the investigatory machine usually works,' says Omar, running a hand over the table. 'We're following the new guidelines, and the wheels are all turning like they're supposed to . . . just slowly. Frustratingly slowly, it feels like.'

'Yeah,' Anna says with a sigh.

'Let's be bloody honest here,' Göran snaps, getting to his feet. 'It's not *frustrating*, it's fucking torture to be stuck behind a desk when people are having their heads chopped off . . .'

'Let's take it easy, OK?' Noah tells him.

'We're all feeling the pressure, but that's natural,' Frida says, blushing.

'Is it?' Göran replies.

'This is an incredibly difficult situation,' she continues. 'But we really do have the skills and the knowledge to—'

'Oh, come off it,' he snaps, tugging up his baggy jeans.

'Plus, we're still a bit shaken from the hunt for the Spider,' Anna rounds off.

'I doubt that'll ever pass,' Rikard mutters.

Göran takes his seat again, pressing his hands to his face.

'We might have the skills,' says Omar, holding up a forensic report. 'But so far, this case is nothing but loose ends. More and more evidence, but no breakthroughs. No DNA, no fingerprints or decoded messages, nothing that can help us narrow down the perp.'

'Joona, I need more energy here,' says Noah, turning to him with bloodshot eyes.

'This is one of the best teams I've ever had.'

'Then give me a breakthrough. *Anything.*'

'OK.'

'What do you mean, "OK"? Tell me what you've seen,' says Noah.

'If I solve this case before Christmas, you'll bring Saga in as my partner.'

'Sorry.' The boss smiles. 'But you haven't given me anything concrete. The investigation is already up to seven thousand pages. There's no way you're going to solve it in the next week.'

'But *if* I do . . .'

'Drop it, Joona.'

'No.'

'Please. I promise we can have a chat about Saga once this is all over, but right now I need you to show me your hand.'

'*Nuolet,*' he says in Finnish, taking out his phone.

Joona dials Nils Åhlén's number. There is a click, and they briefly hear the professor singing along with 'Stargazer' by Rainbow before the music stops.

'You're on loudspeaker,' says Joona. 'So everyone can hear you tell me that you're not done with the autopsy.'

'Same here . . . so Chaya can hear you tell me you want some preliminary thoughts anyway,' Åhlén replies.

'Do you have any?'

'We're not done with the autopsy yet, but Ida Forsgren-Fisher had unprotected sex shortly before she was killed,' Åhlén begins.

'Any sign of rape?'

'Nope.'

'Her son was staying over at a friend's house,' says Joona. 'And her husband was in Tenerife while she was having sex and getting killed by someone else . . . which fits the pattern.'

'What pattern?' Noah asks, glancing over to the others.

Joona turns to Anna, who is standing by the board.

'What kind of health issues does Ida's son have?' he asks.

'Type one diabetes.'

'Which means?' Noah presses Joona.

'The victims are all people who – in the Widow's eyes – prioritise their sexual pleasure, their lust—'

'One of the seven deadly sins,' Rikard speaks up.

'Over the needs of a sick child,' Joona rounds off.

'Do all of them have sick kids?' Noah asks, his voice a little too loud.

'Lucia Pedersen, Ida Forsgren-Fisher, Pontus Bandling and Nils Nordlund all did,' says Anna.

'We still don't know the real motive, the psychological driving force,' Joona continues. 'But I really do think the Widow uses the kids as a pretext.'

'And you can tell that because four of the victims had children with some form of illness?'

'The Widow shows concern for them,' says Joona. 'Pumping up the tyres on a kid's bike, leaving a girl a new inhaler, and—'

'Joona is the smartest guy on earth,' Göran interjects, feigning admiration.

'I'm really not.'

'Don't be shy,' he teases.

'I'm still on the line,' Nils Åhlén reminds them.

'Could you send us a picture of Ida's torso?' Joona asks him.

'Which half?'

'The one with the scratches.'

'Scratches?'

'Above her navel.'

'No other pictures?' Åhlén asks.

'Not right now.'

'Great, so now we're focusing on a couple of scratches,' Göran mutters, glancing over to the others in search of support.

'You heard what Hugo Sand saw through the window,' Joona explains as his computer pings. 'He described the Widow dragging the tip of the blade over the victim's torso . . .'

The colour printer begins to whirr, and Joona gets up to retrieve the image. He pins it on the wall and reaches for the corresponding photographs of the other victims, so that the four torsos are hanging in a row.

Joona grabs a yellow highlighter and traces over the scratches on two of the pictures. The superficial cut on Nils Nordlund's torso is a vertical line, around twenty-five centimetres in length. On Ida Forsgren-Fisher's body, there are two scratches, forming a small, open V.

'Letters?' Rikard suggests.

'I think they're incomplete arrows, or different parts of an arrow . . . judging by the proportions,' says Joona.

$$\downarrow$$

He repeats the process with the two other victims. On Josef Lindgren's stomach, there is a short, diagonal mark stretching from the left-hand side to the mid-point of his torso. The cut on Pontus Bandling's stomach is almost a perfect mirror image, and together they form another small V.

'The tip of an arrow,' says Rikard.

'OK, great, but what does this mean?' asks Noah.

'I don't know,' Joona replies honestly.

'The clock is ticking, for God's sake, and . . .'

Noah trails off when he sees Frida Nobel hold up her phone to get the others' attention.

'We've finally got a bit of a breakthrough with the wig,' she says.

'Go on,' Noah tells her. He looks like he is almost on the brink of tears.

'Stina has been working from hospital, and she managed to get in touch with the wigmaker, Carl M. Lundh's. It took a while, because the records were destroyed after being digitised,' Frida continues. 'But Stina reached out to one of their retired employees to ask if he remembered who might have bought the wig made from Lotta's hair and he just got back to her. It turns out he'd saved the whole physical record index in his attic.'

'Of course he had,' Noah says with a grin.

'Lotta has sold her hair twice, but it's the first one that fits, timewise.'

'OK.'

'The first wig was bought by a woman called Veronica Nagler.'

'Nagler,' Rikard mumbles, logging into his computer. He runs a quick search and looks up from the screen. 'She's dead . . . An accident over six years ago.'

'Great,' Göran sighs.

Rikard connects his computer to the projector and shows the team the photographs from the police report.

'She's not the killer, but there must be some connection,' says Frida. 'There has to be.'

'Maybe she's an early victim?' Anna suggests.

In the images, a woman with a bald head is sprawled across a ladder on the ground beneath an apple tree. Bright red apples have spilled out of a dented metal bucket. She is wearing a striped cotton nightie, and her brown floral clogs are on the ground by the trunk.

'Are there any pictures from the autopsy?' asks Joona.

'Yep,' Rikard replies.

He clicks a few times, and the first of the images fills the projection screen. A naked woman with grey skin is laid out on the stainless-steel autopsy table. Her eyes are wide open, her dark tongue lolling out of her mouth. She doesn't have any hair, and there is a clear injury to the side of her head. Her torso is covered in cuts and scrapes, from the notch between her collarbones, down between her breasts, to her pubic bone.

'The ladder slipped. She probably got those grazes from the rungs and then cracked her head on one of the rocks there,' says Noah, turning to Joona.

Rikard brings up another photograph in which a deeper mark is visible among all the other scrapes, a cut in the shape of an arrow.

60

Since the early 1970s, four crescent-shaped apartment buildings have loomed by the edge of the motorway in Täby. Viewed from above, the grey blocks resemble an open ellipse, a mandorla.

The snow-covered park in the middle of the complex is criss-crossed with trails left by dogs and people.

Joona gets out of the lift on the fifth floor, steps over a blue plastic sledge and walks through the shabby stairwell.

The wig made using Ann-Charlotte Olsson's hair was bought by a woman called Veronica Nagler, who suffered from alopecia.

Just two years later, Veronica was found dead in her own garden.

Following an autopsy, her death was ruled an accident, despite the fact that she had unusually high levels of zopiclone in her blood. The ladder had slipped on the recently cut grass, and she had fallen and hit her head on one of the rocks laid in a circle around the trunk of the apple tree.

After Veronica's death, her husband Erland and their son Kasper moved from the cottage in Steninge to this apartment on Kometvägen.

Joona stops and rings the bell when he reaches Erland's apartment. He hears shuffling footsteps inside, and a man with a crooked back, slicked-back hair and grey stubble opens the door. The man is wearing a brown cardigan with holes in both elbows over a checked shirt, a pair of trousers pulled up to his waist, and brown leather slippers.

'Erland Nagler?'

'That's me.'

According to official records, Erland is just over fifty, but the man in the doorway looks much older.

The smell of grease and old fabric drifts out onto the stairwell.

On the floor beside a small stool, there is a single pair of men's shoes, a black coat hanging on a hook on the wall.

Joona introduces himself and gives the man a moment to study his badge.

'A detective superintendent from Stockholm?'

'Yes.'

'What's happened?' asks Erland.

'Could I come in?'

Joona takes off his shoes, ducks beneath the low ceiling light and walks through to the kitchen behind Erland. The brown cork tiles are badly worn, and there is a red Christmas curtain hanging in the window. A glass and a plate have been left in the sink, and there is a pre-sliced roll in a plastic wrapper by the breadbin.

'Is it too early for eleven o'clock coffee?' asks Erland.

'No, I'd love a cup. Thank you.'

'I've got one of those newfangled machines now. You just fill it with water from the tap, measure the coffee into the filter and press the button,' he tells him before repeating each step in turn.

'Handy,' says Joona.

'I used to grind the beans and boil it up in a pan . . . And my old man, he had a fish skin for clarifying the coffee.'

As the machine splutters, Joona follows Erland into the living room. The Venetian blinds are closed. There is a rag rug on the yellow linoleum floor and two pink plush armchairs facing the TV.

On one of the pale-brown walls, Erland has a lacquered walnut clock. Through the polished glass, the pendulum swings restlessly from side to side.

Joona takes a seat in one of the armchairs while Erland goes back into the kitchen. The door to the bedroom is ajar, and he can see two small blue hand weights on the floor by the bed.

Erland returns a couple of minutes later, setting a coffee pot, cups and saucers down on the table, followed by two spoons, a box of sugar lumps and a plastic tub of biscuits.

'I don't understand it,' he mumbles to himself.

'What?'

Erland glances up and shakes his head slightly before opening the lid of the tub.

'They *look* like proper biscuits, but they taste . . . I don't know. The boy and I used to bake every Sunday, but nowadays . . .'

'My mother made dream cookies and Finnish sticks,' Joona says, helping himself to a small pink biscuit.

Erland stirs two lumps of sugar into his coffee, then taps the spoon on the edge of the cup and looks up.

'Would you mind telling me why you're here, Detective?'

'I need to ask you a few questions about your wife, Veronica . . . About her wig.'

'Ah, I see,' he says, his voice barely audible. 'I'm not sure I—'

'I know it might be hard,' Joona replies, sipping his coffee.

The clock chimes twice as the hand strikes ten thirty.

'She keeps the time, but she never gets any older,' says Erland.

'Returning to Veronica's wig . . .' Joona reminds him.

'It was like she became shy at first, after she lost her beautiful hair. But . . . I don't know, that wasn't the only tough part . . . As for the wig, it just vanished one day . . . She was buried without it,' he says, his face twisting in grief.

Small black fruit flies swarm around a pot plant on the window sill. The plastic door frame has yellowed, and there is a boxset of *Breaking Bad* DVDs on the bookshelf, alongside a number of paperbacks and old souvenirs.

'Did it ever turn up?' Joona asks after a moment.

'No.'

'What happened to it?'

'Veronica was always losing things. She was so tired all the time . . . So suspicious towards the end, too. She was convinced one of the nurses had nicked it.'

'I know she bought the wig from Carl M. Lundh's and that it was made using the hair from a woman called Ann-Charlotte Olsson.'

Joona places a photograph of Lotta on the table in front of Erland. The picture was taken shortly after she sold her hair for the first time, and she is wearing a shaggy blonde wig of synthetic hair, squinting through her glasses and smiling as though she is embarrassed about her teeth.

'Do you recognise this woman?' he asks.

'No.'

'She lives in a place called Rickeby, not far from Rimbo.'

Erland shakes his head and sips his coffee.

'After Veronica died, I sold the house . . . The boy and I moved here, to a modern apartment with hot water and a shower,' he mumbles.

'Does your son still live here with you?'

'Kasper? Not at the moment, no. But officially, yes.'

They sit in silence for a moment. Joona can hear the ticking of the clock and the hum of a radio in the apartment next door, the subdued sound of the traffic outside.

'We miss that house. Well, I do . . . It was old, but it was right by the lake, with a lawn and fruit trees and a hammock,' Erland says with a sigh. 'I still wake up at five every morning, can't shake the habit . . . Going down to the shed for some logs and wood shavings to get the fire going in the kitchen, so I could have the water boiling before Veronica got up.'

Erland tops up their cups and pushes the tub of biscuits towards Joona. He then stirs another two sugars into his coffee and taps his spoon on the cup.

'No, I don't understand,' he mumbles to himself.

'What are you thinking about, Erland? What is it you don't understand?' Joona asks patiently.

'After everything, when it was just me left . . . I was sitting here, going through her phone, and I found some love letters she'd sent to another patient at the clinic. I don't think she was cheating on me, though. I think it was just part of her confusion.'

'Which clinic are you talking about?'

'You know, the Sleep Lab over in Uppsala,' Erland replies.

61

Hugo woke that morning with a pounding headache and a mouth like sandpaper. He peeled off the wireless sensors, drank the glass of water on his bedside table and slumped back against the pillow.

The lingering clouds from last night's nightmares faded and disappeared.

He thought back to his time in Svanhildur's room, to her eyes and her freckled face, the bottle of tequila and their truth telling game, their innocent kiss – and then he remembered the camera. He reached down and felt the little lens, prised it loose from his pyjamas and put it on the bedside table.

His head felt like a lead weight.

Hugo got out of bed and had just pushed his feet into his slippers when there was a knock at the door. He quickly shoved the camera into his pocket before Lars and Rakia came in with the medication trolley.

'My head feels super heavy today,' he said.

'Did you get a good night's sleep?' asked Lars.

'Yes.'

'Then we might need to tweak your dosage a little.'

Once they had gone, Hugo went into the kitchen and ate two slices of toast with Nutella.

He tried to ring Olga, but his call went straight to voicemail, so he left a message to say that it would be good if they could talk, that he needed to know what was going on and if things were OK between them.

Hugo got up from the table and went through to the bathroom to brush his teeth and take a shower. He then returned to the bedroom and changed into a pair of baggy pink tracksuit bottoms and a yellow sweater with a faded logo from the book fair in Frankfurt.

After that, he went into the living room, slumped down on the sofa with his laptop, and started writing his big school assignment on the Abrahamic religions.

*   *   *

It is almost 11 a.m. when Hugo sends the first part of his essay to Bernard and asks him to give it a read.

He checks his phone, but Olga still hasn't replied.

Hugo gets up and goes out into the hall. A strange sensation takes hold of him as he leaves his suite and heads along the corridor to Svanhildur's room.

It feels as though he is walking down a trail he knows like the back of his hand, bathed in bright sunlight.

She answers the door almost immediately after he knocks, says good morning and flashes him a smile before stepping back to let him in.

'Yesterday was fun,' he says.

'I think so too,' she replies, lowering her gaze.

She leads him through to the pantry, closes the lid of her laptop on the table and fills a pan with water.

'Did we finish the tequila?'

'Pretty much,' she tells him as she sets the pan down on the hob.

Svanhildur is wearing a blue Icelandic sweater, a short black skirt and thick black tights. Her strawberry blonde hair is pulled back in a plait, allowing her freckled face to shine like a shell under water, like Vermeer's girl with the pearl earring.

The faux window in her room is displaying an archipelago landscape today, complete with red boathouses, bare rocks and choppy water.

'Nice view,' Hugo jokes.

'Thanks.'

He takes a seat, pulls the little camera out of his pocket and puts it down beside her computer.

Once the water boils, Svanhildur lifts the pot from the stove, fills two big mugs and makes tea using the same teabag.

'I know I said too much last night . . .'

'Only the truth, though . . . I hope,' she replies, blushing softly.

'Yeah . . . Not that I remember everything.'

She laughs and brings the mugs over to the table.

'Thanks.'

'We both said plenty of stuff,' she says, sitting down beside him.

'Which is good, I reckon. I liked it, anyway. A lot . . . And I'm not going to be embarrassed.'

'Me neither, in that case,' she says, cracking her fingers.

'You know you gave booze to an underage boy, right?'

'Whoops,' she says, sipping her tea.

'It's OK.'

The freckles on her pale skin are like a scattering of tiny crumbs. Her dry lips are naturally rosy, her eyebrows a soft shade of red and her lashes almost colourless.

'Did you sleepwalk last night?' she asks, picking up the small camera.

'I don't know.'

'Shall we find out, then?'

'I dunno, it feels a bit . . . wrong somehow . . . Even though I guess I have more right than anyone to know what I've been up to in my sleep,' he replies.

'There's probably some clause covering this in all the paperwork we signed.'

'But we're rebels.' Hugo grins.

'Exactly.'

Svanhildur moves her chair a little closer to his and opens the lid of her laptop. The keyboard is dusty, and there are fingerprints along the top edge of the screen.

She takes the tiny memory card out of the camera and pushes it into a reader that she then connects to her computer.

'Ready to spy on yourself?' she asks, her face solemn.

'I don't know.'

'Maybe you should be alone for this . . .?'

'Nah, it's OK . . . I hope,' he replies with an anxious smile.

They shuffle closer together so that they can both see properly, and she starts the video. Hugo can feel the heat of her thigh against his leg, and he catches a subtle hint of her perfume as she angles the laptop towards him.

The mute footage from his dark bedroom is surprisingly sharp.

Hugo reaches out and tilts the screen slightly to block out the reflection from the faux window.

In the video, he is lying flat on his back. The camera on his chest is pointing up at the dark-grey ceiling, moving in time with his increasingly slow breaths.

He is asleep.

A green LED glows like the Northern Lights at the top left-hand corner of the feed.

Svanhildur waits a moment or two, then fast forwards through the recording and hits play again.

Hugo's breathing is faster now. The dark ceiling sways forward and back, occasionally jumping slightly to one side.

'I'm dreaming,' he says.

'Do you remember any of it?'

'Just that I was at home. And . . . I don't know, I think I had to run. That's what usually happens, anyway.'

Without warning, Hugo sits up. The camera pans across the bedroom, taking in the curtain over the dark window, the chest of drawers and the armchair.

'So you're sleepwalking now?'

'Yeah,' he replies, his voice barely a whisper.

'This is creepy,' she says quietly.

The camera moves slowly towards the door, where it pauses.

The sleeping Hugo seems to be staring straight at the smooth panel as the world of the nightmare takes over him.

His pale hand appears in the lower right of the screen, and he calmly turns the handle, opens the door, looks around and moves forward into the dark hallway.

When he reaches the main door to the suite, he stops again. His movements become frantic, tugging at the handle and fumbling along the walls beside it with increasing desperation.

'You're trying to get out,' Svanhildur whispers.

The sleepwalking Hugo looks around, takes a step back and presses the lock button on the wall. He then moves forward and opens the door, hurrying out of the suite and straight into the wall opposite.

'Ay,' he mumbles as he watches himself stagger to one side on the screen.

The camera is still for a moment, then starts drifting down the corridor as though it were floating on a dark river, past patient rooms and offices. The row of pale-blue nightlights on the right-hand wall flicker by.

From time to time, Hugo glances back, as though he thinks he is being followed. The camera sways slightly with each step he takes.

In Svanhildur's pantry, Hugo leans into the computer. He runs a hand through his hair and realises he is shaking.

On the screen, a lumpy, dark-grey shadow is visible by the wall at the very end of the corridor. It looks like a heap of sacks full of potatoes and onions.

The vinyl flooring shines in the soft light.

Closed doors with gleaming hardware rush by.

The sleeping Hugo holds out a hand, as though to push back a low-hanging branch.

'What are you doing?' Svanhildur whispers.

'Dunno.'

He sees himself stop and look down at his pale bare feet. There is a dried wad of snus on the floor by the metal skirting board.

Hugo looks up and then slowly starts walking again, past the door to Svanhildur's room.

At the far end of the corridor, the lumpy shadow moves suddenly, and a thin arm becomes visible.

'There's someone there! Did you see that?' Hugo asks, pointing at the screen.

'God ...'

The camera continues past more dim nightlights, floating ever closer to the shadowy figure.

The sleeping Hugo turns towards a red cabinet containing a fire extinguisher, and his frightened face is reflected in the glass.

After a moment, his wide eyes turn back to the corridor.

He holds back something invisible with his left hand, ducks slightly and keeps moving.

Svanhildur reaches for Hugo's hand and grips it tightly.

The dark figure sways and takes a step forward. In the green glow of the emergency exit sign, his face suddenly becomes visible.

It is Lars Grind.

The doctor is staring at Hugo, grinning like some sort of crazed wizard as the camera continues straight towards him.

Hugo doesn't seem to have noticed his presence at all.

The reflections of the nightlights in the locks and hinges flow by like debris in a current.

Hugo anxiously glances back over his shoulder, then keeps hurrying towards Dr Grind, who is waiting for him at the end of the corridor.

'What's *that*? Did you see?' Svanhildur asks, pointing to the screen. 'There, do you see?'

'I've got goosebumps.'

On the floor by the wall a few metres behind Lars, something moves jerkily in the soft underwater glow.

Like a frightened dog, a spider crab.

Hugo holds his breath as he watches himself approach Lars.

The doctor's bald head flashes in the green light, sweat pouring down his cheeks. His eyes are focused and intense, his teeth bright between his lips.

Lars Grind catches Hugo's upper arm, forcing him to stop and pulling him down to the floor. Hugo lands on his side and starts to struggle.

The camera shakes as it films the floor.

There is another patient huddled in the corner up ahead: Kasper. He starts crawling towards Grind and Hugo with nervous movements.

From the other direction, Rakia appears with a syringe. The grubby plaster on her index finger fills the screen as she pulls the protective cover from the needle.

Hugo is still struggling, but Grind has him pinned down on the floor.

A bare foot lashes out.

Kasper crawls over to them, and Grind holds him back with one hand as Rakia gives Hugo an injection.

The camera trembles and turns briefly towards the floor before rolling back the other way.

Kasper seems to have hurt his mouth somehow, because his teeth are covered in blood. He tries to reach Hugo, but Grind is still holding him back.

'This is insane,' Hugo whispers.

Grind and Rakia drag Hugo to his feet, guide him back to his room and put him into bed.

Svanhildur reaches out and closes the lid of her laptop. She and Hugo sit quietly for a moment.

'Did they tell you about the injection?' she asks.

'Nope, not yet.'

'Because they can't just . . . I mean, you're here voluntarily. You should request your full records.'

* * *

Svanhildur accompanies Hugo to Lars Grind's office. They have decided not to mention the camera unless necessary, but feel they need to confront him if they are going to be able to stay at the lab.

Lars answers his door with a surprised smile, says something about special guests and asks if they would like a hot chocolate as he welcomes them in.

'No, thanks,' Hugo replies, noticing that someone has blotted red lipstick on a piece of tissue and thrown it into the bin.

'Please, sit,' says the doctor.

'We need to talk,' Hugo tells him.

'Crikey, that sounds ominous.' Lars smiles.

'Yeah ... I was medicated against my will last night.'

'What makes you—'

'I told you this morning that my head felt heavy.'

'Did you?'

'You have no right to hide whatever's going on from me,' says Hugo. 'I want to see my records, right now.'

'And I want to see mine,' says Svanhildur.

'I understand,' Lars mumbles, rubbing his bald head.

'I'm going to talk to Dad,' Hugo continues. 'This really doesn't feel good, but we need to know what's going on here.'

62

Agneta watches from the doorway as Bernard's taxi pulls up outside the house, completing the circle from the moment he left in the back of the ambulance. He gets out, and the car turns around and disappears up the steep driveway.

Bernard walks slowly towards her, cold air clinging to his body as he makes his way inside and locks the door behind him.

'How are you feeling?' she asks.

'Fine. My back and hip are a bit stiff, but I'm OK.'

He groans in pain as she helps him with his coat.

'Are you hungry? There are some leftovers I could reheat,' she says.

'Please.'

Bernard kicks off his shoes, leaving them in the middle of the mat as he moves forward and hugs her.

They stand in the dimly lit hallway for a moment or two, enjoying the heat of each other's body and their familiar, comforting scent.

'Maybe you could stop scaring me now?' Agneta tells him as they break the embrace.

'Sorry,' he says, following her through to the kitchen. 'I actually got a bit of a fright myself. I was thinking: this is it, I'm going to be beaten to death now, have my head lopped off . . .'

'Did you see her? Was it the killer?' she asks, her voice trembling.

'I don't know. I felt a crack on the head and I dropped like a rock.'

'So someone hit you?'

'Yes.'

'With an axe?'

'I don't know.'

'We need to call Joona.'

'I will. I just need to gather my thoughts a bit first.'

'Sit down. I'll get the food ready.'

Bernard rests a hand on the counter and looks out at the heavy snow falling in the darkness.

'Have you checked that all of the doors are locked?'

'Of course,' she says.

'Good,' he whispers.

Agneta studies the dark bruise on his temple. The blood seems to have seeped beneath his skin, pooling at the bottom of his cheek.

'Do you want us to do it again?' she asks when he fails to sit down.

'I think so.'

They work their way through the rooms on the ground floor, double-checking that all of the windows are closed and the sensors intact. They open cupboards and wardrobes, and Bernard goes down to the basement to fetch a drill.

'I'm going to fix Hugo's window. We can get a handyman out some other time,' he says.

Agneta follows him into the hallway and turns on the crystal wall sconce.

Bernard opens the door to Hugo's room, walks straight over to the damaged window and starts screwing it shut with a handful of sturdy wood screws.

Agneta continues into the living room and glances over to the windows out onto the lake. She can hear the whirr of the drill on the other side of the display cabinet. The disused door behind it dates from a time when parlours and through-rooms were in vogue, but it has been blocked off behind the tall piece of furniture for as long as she can remember.

She peers beneath the sofas around the coffee table, tries the patio doors, checks behind the curtains and then heads back out into the hall.

She is thinking about the last letter from Hugo's mother, about the methadone programme Claire mentioned and her use of Swedish, French and English.

'We should get personal alarms,' Bernard says when he comes out into the library and puts the drill down on the mantelpiece.

'That might feel reassuring,' she replies, remembering that she had been so shaken by the break-in and attack that she was convinced she had seen the light come on in the lake house, when it was nothing but the reflection of the lanterns on the neighbour's jetty in the window.

'I checked the cameras, by the way, but I couldn't see her face,' she says.

'The police will have to take a look.'

They pop their heads into the utility room and the little room where they keep their weights and exercise bike before heading upstairs.

Agneta can tell that Bernard is in pain, gripping the handrail as they make their way up the steep staircase to his office.

'Good grief,' he says when he sees the mess.

'I told you.'

Bernard steps forward into the room, picking his way between books and sheets of paper. He sighs as he takes in the broken cabinet, the empty cigar box and the cracked glass on a framed diploma.

'She took everything of value,' he says after a moment.

'How much cash did you have?'

'Next to none.'

'What about the gold?'

'Eight hundred grams.'

'That's a lot of money . . .' she mumbles.

'I'll have to check if the insurance will cover it. They *definitely* won't pay up for the *DN Culture Section*.'

'She's taken the jar?' Agneta asks with feigned indignation.

'Alas.'

'Well, that's just not on. What a pig!' She smiles.

'Honestly, I could have done with a nice fat joint this evening.'

Bernard sighs as he bends down and picks up a poetry collection with a personal message from Tomas Tranströmer.

'I found some letters from Claire, by the way,' Agneta hears herself say, pointing to the desk. 'I left them over there. One of them had come loose, and I . . . I read it. Sorry.'

'That's fine. I don't have any secrets from you.'

'OK.'

'Did you read the rest?'

'No, just that one,' she lies like a child caught red-handed. 'It had fallen out of the stack.'

'As far as I'm concerned, you can read the lot,' Bernard tells her, putting the poetry collection down on top of a stack of other books on the shelf.

He straightens the shade on the reading lamp, pulls a loose thread from the gold fringing, rolls it into a ball and then looks up and meets Agneta's eye.

'What are you thinking?' he asks.

'No, it's just . . . You never showed her last letter to Hugo, did you? He told me that Claire does nothing but lie and talk about getting clean, but she never actually gives it a chance. But in that letter . . . she sounds like she was really serious.'

'I should have thrown it away . . .'

'You can't do that. Hugo would be so happy if—'

'Hold on a minute.'

'He has a right to know his mum.'

'Just hold on a minute, please.'

'She might be an addict, but she's still his mum,' Agneta says, emphasising virtually every word.

Bernard sighs deeply and looks up at her with sad eyes. 'The problem is that I'm the one who wrote that last letter.'

'Wait, what?'

'Claire hadn't replied to any of his letters in almost two years. I tried to get hold of her, but she blocked me and changed her number,' he explains with a pained expression. 'Hugo used to run home from school every day to check the mailbox. He was crushed, so I wrote that stupid letter, but in the end I couldn't bring myself to give it to him. I just couldn't.'

'No.'

'As a parent, you desperately want to be able to comfort your child. It's damn near unbearable when they're upset, but ... I decided – perhaps a little cynically – that silence on her part might actually be the kindest thing. Or the most truthful, at least.'

'So the part about her joining the methadone programme ... you made that up?'

'I ... She was always talking about it, but she would back out at the last minute every time.'

'OK, I get it. I did think it was weird that she'd used the word "anniversaire" to talk about his birthday when they say "fête" in Canada.'

'Do they? I didn't know that ... I'll have to get you to help next time I need to fake a letter,' he says, attempting a smile.

Agneta sits down heavily on the desk chair and looks up at him.

'What do you think happened to Claire?' she asks.

'Honestly? She couldn't hack life here in Sweden, with me ... All the demands ... I don't know. She went back to Canada, to her messy life there, to the drugs and her old friends ... You can see from her letters that she was trying a bit at first, but that she ... She sort of gets more and more bogged down. It's so tragic, desperately so ... I don't know. I hope ... I hope, of course, that she's in rehab, that she's put the past behind her – myself and Hugo included – in order to start over.'

'But?'

'I don't think she's overdosed. It doesn't feel like she's dead,' he says, dabbing at his eyes. 'But I do worry that things might have taken a turn for the worse for her ... that she's contracted HIV or got mixed up in prostitution, crime ...'

* * *

Bernard and Agneta have made their way back downstairs, and are sitting at the kitchen table in the glow of two candles. As they share a bottle of Château Tour Baladoz, Bernard eats the leftovers Agneta has reheated for him: tagliatelle with steak, lemon, Parmesan shavings and fresh basil.

'Well, the window is a bit more secure now, at the very least,' he says as he chews.

'I actually went out and scrubbed the . . . you know . . . the door off the wall yesterday. So no one would be able to get in that way,' she confesses.

Bernard laughs and splutters. He lowers his fork and wipes his mouth with a napkin.

'The thought crossed my mind too,' he says with a grin.

The circles of light from the two candles flicker in sync across the table, like a couple of hula-hoops.

'Things could have ended very differently, you know,' Agneta mumbles.

'It might've been the sound of your car that scared her off. Or maybe she realised it was me, rather than Hugo . . .'

'You think it was because of the interview? Because Hugo is a witness?'

'I don't know what I think, but I know what I'm afraid of. We can do without a bit of gold, but . . .'

Agneta tilts her glass and studies the blood-red orb of light in the dark wine for a moment before she drinks.

'It's a good job Hugo is at the clinic, then,' she says.

'Which reminds me: we haven't talked about the latest hypnosis session yet,' he says as he picks up his fork again.

'I was there for the whole thing.'

'How was he afterwards?'

'Pretty good, I'd say. A little anxious at first, but I think the whole thing felt OK.'

'Did they give him anything to calm his nerves again?'

'No, there was no need.'

'Good. So what happened?'

'It was crazy . . . and incredibly interesting, too.' Agneta smiles and turns her glass.

'Anything we can use?'

'I wrote it all down as soon as I came out.'

'That's great. We really need it,' he says, topping up their glasses. 'I'm getting excited now. Tell me everything.'

'OK.' She laughs.

'You were there, with Hugo, Lars, the hypnotist and the detective.'

'Joona Linna. He's very attractive, you know ... objectively speaking.'

'Ha ha. What about the hypnotist? Is he as creepy as you'd expect?'

'I'm going to sound insane now, but he was actually really charming.'

'And handsome?' Bernard suggests, pushing his plate away.

'No comment,' she replies with a smile.

A gust of wind blows a flurry of snowflakes against the kitchen window with a soft crackling sound.

'Go on,' he says, hiding his shaking hand beneath the table.

'I don't really understand how hypnosis works – we'll have to look into that – but the whole process took much longer than I was expecting,' she begins. 'At first, I felt like laughing at how serious it all was. The ceremonial aspect of it. He started by counting down, but it all got very suggestive after a while.'

'And that's when you found yourself getting hypnotised too?' he teases.

'I know.' Agneta laughs again. 'It almost felt that way.'

'Sorry, go on,' says Bernard, producing a mechanical pencil from his chest pocket. 'He was counting down ...'

'He started counting down from one hundred, and he kept telling Hugo to focus on his voice. Somehow, he managed to take Hugo back to that night, when he was sleepwalking at the campsite, over to the caravan where he saw the woman with the blonde hair.'

As Agneta takes him through the sequence of events at the back of the caravan, Bernard asks a few follow-up questions and takes notes directly on the table.

'Even though he was under hypnosis, it was like Hugo kept turning away from whatever he saw through the window,' she tells him. 'Erik Maria Bark tried a few times to guide him back over there, but as soon as he realised it wasn't going to work he changed tack . . .'

'OK,' Bernard mumbles as he scribbles, circling and underlining certain words.

'This part was really interesting, so we'll have to make sure it's included in the book,' she says. 'Rather than trying to force Hugo to turn back to the window, he told him to watch a video of the murder on his phone instead, and it actually worked. I wrote everything down. You can read it once I've typed it up.'

Agneta takes a sip of wine, and Bernard leans back in his chair and studies her with a smile.

'Did he manage to give the detective any sort of description?'

'No, but I don't think it'll be long.'

'We're getting closer, aren't we?'

'One more session. That's my guess.'

Bernard picks up his glass, gets to his feet and moves around the table to toast with her.

'I really do believe in this. We're helping the police stop a killer, and we'll be done with the book before the court case is even over. This is going to be great.'

'I hope so,' Agneta replies, getting up.

'You're incredible,' Bernard tells her, putting down his glass.

'Pff. I'm an OK journalist, and I've got a good memory. I can put things in context, and I've got good deductive skills.'

'You've got a good everything. Good mind, good heart, good body. *Incredible* thighs . . .'

They kiss, light-heartedly at first, then more passionately. Agneta wraps her arms around his neck, and Bernard pulls her close.

'What's happening here?' she jokes.

Bernard's warm hands caress the base of her spine, moving down to her bottom and thighs. He lifts her up – says, 'Ow, my back' – and sits her down on the edge of the table.

Agneta laughs and hikes up her skirt. He tugs her knickers down and leaves them hanging around her ankles as he unbuttons his trousers. She leans back on her elbows and parts her legs, kicking her knickers away and sighing as he enters her.

63

The wind roars in the extractor fan as it pummels the house, picking up snow from the expanses of flat roof.

Nina Silverstedt is in her spacious kitchen on the top floor of the villa, with her video camera, lights and reflector all set up and ready. Through the large window, she gazes out across the terrace and the pool area to the frozen bay.

The architect designed the house to be split over a number of levels, and thanks to the angled glass walls and floor-to-ceiling windows, she can see much of the ground floor from where she is standing.

The stovetop is almost invisible on the dark-grey marble island behind her, and her ramen are already cold in the Demeyere pan.

She filmed herself frying the mushrooms and leek in sesame oil two hours ago in order to give her eyes a chance to stop watering before she got started on the rest of the takes.

Nina is in the middle of producing a video for Ten-Green-Min, a fast-growing company that sells easy-cook vegetarian meals made from local and organic produce.

She has written a script in which, as usual, she seems to spontaneously bring up her stressful but luxurious lifestyle. Nina has always been good at planning ahead, particularly when it comes to sponsored posts. This particular video isn't due to go live for another two weeks, the same day she will be attending a charity gala, and she has managed to seamlessly integrate that into the script.

Nina takes a slight step to the left. Through the swirling snow, she sees her husband coming up the stairs from the gym in the basement.

She waves, but he doesn't see her. He has been working out, and his T-shirt is sweaty. She knows he has a board meeting on Kungsgatan in two hours, but he heads straight through the hall to the bar in the lounge to grab an energy drink.

Nina Silverstedt is thirty-five and works as a lifestyle influencer, and has been at the very top of her game in terms of followers and engagement for the past five years.

According to her script, she needs to talk about the dress she will be wearing to the gala with an almost childish sense of excitement, after first telling her subscribers how sweet her husband was when he woke her with a coffee and a red rose that morning.

He knows exactly what she needs in darkest midwinter.

In reality, he was already on a phone call when her alarm clock went off. He never reads her posts and has no idea that she dreams of him giving her a rose.

They have been married for three years now.

Frank is a fund manager and the sole reason they are able to live the way they do. Nina makes a decent amount of money herself, of course, but it is only a fraction of what he earns.

On her social media channels, she presents a lavish vision of her lifestyle, with paid posts about interior design, travel, fashion, jewellery and makeup. But she would never have made it this far if she didn't also share a more intimate, vulnerable side of herself, balancing the more superficial content. She regularly talks to her followers about the fears she has for her son and the deep depressions she sinks into at the thought of not being able to provide what he needs, of not being a good enough mum.

She and Frank were dating when she found out she was pregnant. They got married around the seven-month mark, and she went into labour eight weeks before her due date, during their honeymoon to Dubai. Young Maximus has delayed psychomotor development, and needs help with almost everything.

There are times when she wonders whether Frank's lack of interest in her is down to his disappointment in Maximus. He left his previous wife, and has two adult children that he never sees, so maybe the whole thing is just a pattern. Maybe he is gearing up to leave her, too.

Nina doesn't normally try the sponsored products she promotes, but she made the mistake of giving one of the vegetarian meals a chance the day before yesterday. It was practically inedible, but she is *so* close to sounding believable when – with a laugh – she tells her viewers that she needs to stop filming now, to spare them from having to watch her wolf down the incredible ramen from Ten-Green-Min.

Nina puffs a little smoke across the bowl of soup and checks the set-up on her computer. With the artfully laid table, the window and some of the ground floor visible in the background, it looks great.

The plan is to start the take with her pretending she has just finished a session in the gym, in a white vest and a pair of black trousers from Juicy Couture. In actual fact, she exercised earlier, and will have to do some press-ups on the kitchen floor to get her blood pumping again. She might even have to add a little oil to her skin to give herself that post-workout glow.

She turns on the lamps, checks the computer screen again and measures the light levels beside the carton showing the company's logo. She then pulls a lock of hair down over her forehead so that she can push it back while she is talking, starts the camera, and steps into frame to record a quick test video.

'I swear, this stuff tastes like shit, but that's fine because I'm planning to have a big juicy burger instead – though I'm so fucking scared of putting on weight I'll probably puke it straight up again as soon as I'm done,' she says with a smile.

Nina moves back behind the camera and stops the recording. She presses play and watches the take on her computer, and has just started to wonder if she should adjust the angle of the reflector slightly when she notices a figure in the background, on the steps by the terrace.

She moves over to the window and looks down.

A blonde woman in a shiny padded coat is standing outside in the falling snow.

Nina decides that it must be the girl doing some sort of work experience with Frank, the daughter of one of his business partners.

Whoever she is, she thinks, he'll have to take care of her himself.

She moves the reflector a few inches and turns back to the camera. If she is going to manage to record three takes and edit the footage before she has to leave for a meeting with Tiger of Sweden, she needs to keep going.

Nina's thoughts turn back to the woman outside, and she feels a sudden sting of jealousy.

For some stupid reason, she suspects that Frank is still in love with his ex-wife. They are both major shareholders in one of his companies, and regularly eat lunch together.

Nina often consoles herself at night by telling herself that his ex is a wrinkly forty-eight-year-old, whereas she is just thirty-five and has been voted sexiest influencer two years running. She works out every day, and has a perfect body – aside from a few stretch marks on her stomach, a slight case of scoliosis and a couple of bunions.

Nina decides the filming will have to wait until Frank has seen to his guest, and she turns off the camera and unplugs the cable, then heads back over to the window.

The blonde woman has let herself in, she realises, through the doors by the pool.

Frank clearly doesn't know she is here.

Nina takes a few steps to one side and sees that he is in the dressing room, still naked after his shower. She watches him dry his hair and then drop the towel to the floor like a spoilt child.

With a sigh, she takes out her phone and sends him a text:

Get dressed. You've got a visitor.

He doesn't reply to her message, too busy sucking his stomach in as he admires himself in the mirror.

Frank is a good-looking man, tanned and in decent shape for his age, though he does have a thick rug of hair on his chest and a stubborn roll of fat around his waist. His penis looks small and red from where she is standing, but in truth it is perfectly normal, with a ring of hypopigmentation from where he was circumcised.

She should talk about that on Instagram, she thinks cynically.

The woman starts making her way through the lounge towards him. She is wearing a pair of rubber boots, and her broad shoulders move jerkily as she walks.

Nina tries calling Frank, but his phone is on the charging pad on the bedside table with the sound turned off.

He has started rubbing lotion into his skin.

The woman has paused in the sunken area in the middle of the lounge, and she lowers a canvas bag to the white leather sofa and takes out an axe.

Nina gasps. She can't quite process what she has just seen, and she blinks hard, but the woman really is gripping an axe in her right hand.

Adrenaline pumps through her veins as she tries to come up with a plausible explanation. This must be a joke, some sort of weird event, a psychotic client.

Has Frank made himself an enemy? Is he mixed up in something shady? Has he been buying drugs or gambling illegally?

Nina reaches for her phone with shaking hands, hides behind the curtain and dials 112.

'Emergency, which service do you require?' a woman with a warm voice answers.

Feeling oddly removed from her words, Nina tells her about the blonde woman with the axe.

The call handler seems completely unfazed by everything she is saying, immediately taking her seriously without questioning any of it.

64

A grubby police car is parked with the engine running in one of the icy bays outside Millesgården Museum. The two officers inside are eating clementines, dropping the peel into a paper bag on the centre console between them.

A handful of thujas loom tall behind the stone wall, snow clinging to the side closest to the water.

The sun is shining, and the large windows above the main entrance to the museum reflect the light like the lens in a lighthouse.

The officer in the passenger seat is called Petrus Lyth, though at the station in Lidingö he is better known as Pingu, because of his tendency to make a loud tooting sound to get people to shut up whenever a discussion spirals out of hand. Petrus has been having trouble with his hip lately, so he asked his new partner to drive. He is due to retire in the New Year, and is looking forward to playing golf with his older brother. His colleagues have jokingly started telling him to be careful while he is out on patrol, because cops who are looking forward to retirement have a tendency to meet an early death in Hollywood movies.

Petrus's new partner, Danny Imani Ingmarsson, is still a trainee, which also puts him at risk in the film version of their profession. Danny is young and ideological, full of admiration for his older colleagues, and desperate to be fully accepted as a member of the team. He is muscular, with short hair, kind brown eyes and slanted brows that give him a slightly melancholic air. His father is a car salesman, and his mother fled from Iran following the revolution. She studied in Sweden and now has her own dental practice.

Despite his long career, Petrus has only fired his service weapon once in the line of duty. That was ten years ago now, but he still thinks about it every single day.

The young man didn't even suffer any lasting damage.

He had – like some sort of Don Quixote – been wearing a pan on his head as he roamed around a supermarket with a samurai sword, and it was obvious to anyone who saw him that he was having some sort of psychotic episode.

He had stabbed a watermelon, displayed threatening behaviour, and refused to drop his sword.

The confrontation had ended with Petrus Lyth shooting him in the thigh, and the officer has never forgotten his face, the way his eyes welled up and he thrust out his lower lip like a toddler before collapsing to the floor and screaming in pain.

Petrus looks down at the control unit.

He can't explain it, but he has always been able to sense when an alert is about to come in, as though he can see the dispatcher taking a call at their computer, making a split-second assessment and pressing the pedal on the floor.

As a result, Petrus is ready and waiting when the call comes in from regional command, and he realises that the situation must be serious before the words 'priority one' have even been uttered.

The operator's voice is sharp, with a slight note of stress, as she briefs them about the ongoing attempted murder at a villa on Jaktstigen.

The information also flashes up on the display.

Danny turns on the blue lights and sirens and speeds out of the parking area. He takes a sharp right, mounting the pavement and scraping up against a wall.

'Shit, shit . . .'

They thud back down onto the road, and he accelerates up the hill and takes the next right onto Stjärnvägen. The tyres skid on the tarmac, and the car slams into the grey bank of ploughed snow at the edge of the road, sending lumps of ice flying up over the bonnet and windscreen.

Petrus pushes his glasses up onto the bridge of his nose and focuses on the directions as he talks to the operator.

Both men understand that the call is likely to do with the serial killer known as the Widow, and also that they will be the first unit at the scene.

* * *

Nina feels the heat from her phone against her ear as the operator explains that a patrol car in the area is on its way.

'Should I leave the house?' she asks. 'Or should—'

'Stay on the line,' the operator tells her, quickly adding that she is going to patch Nina through to a detective superintendent.

'Hi, Nina,' says a man with a Finnish accent. 'We've got a car in the area, and there are another two on the way. I've also requested a tactical unit.'

'What should I do?' Nina asks, conscious of her own frightened breathing.

Through the window, she sees Frank open a wardrobe door, pull out a drawer and pick some underwear.

'I understand that you're on the first floor and that you can see your husband and a woman with an axe on the ground floor, is that correct?'

'I don't want to die,' Nina whimpers.

'Are you able to leave the house?'

'I'd have to go downstairs.'

'Has the woman seen you? Does she know you're at home?'

'I don't think so,' she replies, swallowing hard.

'OK, good. I want you to find somewhere to hide and wait for us. Hide in a wardrobe, sit down on the floor and don't make a sound.'

Nina nods, but she remains where she is behind the curtain and peers out of the window. Snow swirls through the air.

The blonde woman has started moving around the room, looking behind furniture and checking potential hiding places as she approaches the stairs leading up to the kitchen.

'Please, just get over here,' Nina whispers to the detective.

Frank has pulled on a pair of boxers and gone into the bedroom. He tears open the thin plastic bag around his dry-cleaned shirt and tosses the metal hanger to the floor.

The woman hears the soft clatter it makes, and she turns sharply and starts striding towards the dressing room. She glances back over her shoulder, and Nina catches a glimpse of a strange, crude face.

*　*　*

Joona was in Takiya Sushi Bar, chatting to the woman preparing his order, when the call came in. He had been planning to visit the Sleep Lab in Uppsala, to talk about Veronica Nagler's time there. Dr Grind wasn't working today, but one of his long-term research assistants, Rakia Dardour, had agreed to meet with him and attempt to answer his questions.

Instead, he ran straight out to the car and turned on his blue lights. As he sped along Surbrunnsgatan to Vallhallavägen and turned off into the long tunnel to Lidingö, the call handler patched him through to the call with Nina Silverstedt.

'She heard Frank. I can see her, she's going towards him now,' Nina whispers down the line.

'You don't have to watch; we're almost there. Just make sure you find somewhere to hide,' he says.

The amber-coloured lights in the tunnel race by as he accelerates to 115 miles per hour. Joona blasts the horn, urging the cars up ahead to get out of his way.

*　*　*

Nina moves her phone over to her other hand and wipes her clammy palm on her thigh. The blonde woman has reached the dressing room, and is currently hiding behind the open wardrobe door.

The axe is still in her hand.

Frank is in the bedroom, doing up the mother-of-pearl buttons on his shirt with a distant look on his face. Nina waves, trying to catch his attention, but he doesn't see her.

She watches as he wanders through to the dressing room and pulls a dark-grey tie from a hanger. He hasn't noticed the woman, who is standing less than a metre away from him behind the door.

The woman slowly raises the axe.

Frank turns back towards the bedroom, seems to realise he has forgotten something and reaches for a pair of cufflinks. His hand rests on the edge of the wardrobe door for a moment, but he leaves it open.

'The first car will be with you in less than five minutes,' the detective says in Nina's ear.

Frank goes through to the bedroom and puts on his tie. He then picks up his phone from the bedside table and sees her message.

Nina manages to switch her phone to silent just before his call comes through, and she quickly tells the detective that her husband is ringing, that she is going to put him on hold.

She can hear her blood roaring in her ears.

'Frank,' she whispers, 'there's a woman with an axe in the dressing room. The police are on their way, but you need to get out. Open the door to the terrace and run.'

'What are you talking about?'

Nina watches the blonde woman rest the axe on her shoulder. She is still hiding in the shadow behind the door, listening to Frank.

'You need to go, right now! Run!' Nina shouts.

'Hey, hey, what's going on?' he asks.

'Frank, listen to me, you—'

'I'll be up soon,' he says, ending the call.

'Frank?'

He puts the phone back down on the charging pad and cranes his neck in the direction of the dressing room. The woman lifts the axe again, getting ready to strike.

'I accidentally raised my voice,' Nina whispers once she is back on the line with the detective.

'Did she hear you?'

'I don't know . . .'

'You need to stay hidden. We're almost with you.'

As Frank turns his back to the dressing room, the woman steps out from her hiding place.

She tiptoes behind him, gripping the axe with both hands.

Frank pauses in the doorway.

Nina doesn't dare shout to tell him to run. Her heart is beating so hard it is almost painful.

The woman takes aim, but she changes her mind as Frank starts moving again.

Instead, she follows him like a shadow.

He pauses, as though he can sense her presence, and has just started to turn around when she swings the axe through the air and strikes him in the upper arm.

Nina clamps both hands to her mouth, almost managing to stifle her scream.

The power in the blow must have been huge, because Frank stumbles towards the wall and hits his head. He manages to stay upright, but his arm has been completely severed from his body. It drops to the floor, and blood immediately starts pouring down his side, spattering around his feet on the white carpet as he staggers forward.

The woman rotates the axe in her hands, following him with what seems like curiosity. She pauses when he pauses and then taps him on the back of the head with the heel of the blade.

'Oh God . . .'

Frank slumps to his knees, looks up and meets Nina's eye through the windows and the swirling snow.

This time, the blade of the woman's axe hits his throat from the front, almost completely severing his neck. His head drops down behind him, hanging against his back like some sort of rucksack as blood spills down over his chest.

'She's killing him,' Nina pants. 'She's killing him.'

'Go and hide, Nina. You need to hide. We'll be there in a few seconds.'

Nina's eyes lose their focus, and she staggers away from the window, throwing up all over herself. She braces herself against the kitchen worktop, blinks hard and goes through to the dark living room in search of somewhere to hide. She whimpers when she hears the woman's furious, guttural scream from the floor below.

65

Danny is driving at almost 125 miles per hour along Askrikevägen, heading in the direction of the marina.

He swings out into the oncoming lane as he overtakes a dirty Tesla.

The blue lights from the patrol car sweep across mature gardens on both sides of the road, glaring in the villas' windows.

'We've lost contact with the caller, and she's not answering her phone,' says the operator.

Around one hundred metres up ahead, a woman pushing a buggy starts to cross the road. She has earbuds in, and is looking down at something on her phone.

Danny blasts the horn, but she doesn't hear him.

On the other side of the road, a minibus stops at the crossing to let her pass. She walks in front of it and has almost reached their lane.

'Fuck,' Danny mumbles, stepping on the accelerator and half-mounting the kerb, speeding past her within touching distance of the buggy.

In the wing mirror, Petrus sees her gesture angrily.

They turn sharply onto Jaktstigen, crossing the strip of snow in the middle of the road and briefly losing control of the vehicle. The back of the car swings out and hits a green rubbish bin, knocking over the fence behind it, and Danny steps on the gas again.

During their anxious drive from the museum, they have learned that the suspected killer is armed with an axe.

They pass snow-covered oaks, flagpoles and expensive cars parked in driveways. Between the exclusive houses on the left-hand side, the frozen bay is visible.

'It's just up here,' says Petrus. 'Pull over there, d'you see where I mean? By the posts with the lights that—'

He is thrown forward and feels the seatbelt cut into his shoulder as Danny slams on the brakes.

The suspect's Opel Kadett is parked just beyond the lamppost, a cluster of air fresheners hanging from the rear-view mirror.

They turn left and speed down the driveway to the house.

'The suspect's car is here,' Petrus reports over the radio. The smell of the clementine juice on his fingers fills his nose.

Danny feels the braking system shudder through the car as he screeches to a halt outside the double garage doors.

They quickly get out and run towards the front of the house.

'We ready for this, Pingu?' the younger officer whispers, a cloud of breath hanging in the air in front of him.

Petrus meets his eye and nods. He pulls his pistol from his holster and loads a round into the chamber.

Danny tries the front door.

'Locked.'

'Get the claw,' says Petrus.

Danny runs back to the car and returns with the heavy tool. He jams the grooved head beneath the top set of hinges and pulls back as hard as he can.

The doorframe creaks and breaks, taking the hinges with it.

Danny moves the tool down to the lower hinges and repeats the process.

'We're going in,' Petrus reports over the radio.

As Danny drops the claw to the floor, he realises his fingers have started to stick to the cold metal. He draws his pistol.

The lock and the strike plate make a loud crunching sound as Petrus forces the door to open inwards. Splintered wood, bent screws and pieces of broken hinge clatter to the floor.

The two officers peer in to the spacious hallway with grey marble floor tiles and modern wooden panelling.

'I'll take point, like normal,' says Petrus. 'You cover my back and the right.'

'Yup.'

Petrus steps inside and swings around to the left, scanning the row of closed cupboard doors.

His glasses immediately fog up, and he yanks them off, squints down the hallway and takes a hesitant step forward.

A blurry figure emerges against the orange background.

His finger trembles on the trigger.

The house is too quiet, as though it is holding its breath.

Petrus pushes his glasses back on and realises that the figure up ahead is just a man in an oil painting on the wall.

'What's going on?' Danny asks behind him as he checks the cloak-room to the left.

'Trouble with the specs, but it's all good now.'

They cover each other, quickly securing the room as they continue deeper into the house.

In one direction, the entrance hall leads to a number of bedrooms, but the other opens out onto a sumptuous, multi-level living room.

A staircase with glass railings leads up to the first floor.

The two officers hear an irregular creaking sound overhead, as though a child is trying to shuffle forward on a rocking horse.

On the far side of the living room, the sliding door to the snowy pool area is open. A trail of wet footprints lead straight over the wooden floor and rug.

Petrus feels a rush of fear for Danny, and he glances over to him. His young colleague is breathing heavily through his half-open mouth, and his eyes look tense and alert. His black pistol – a regular Glock 45, with a scratched barrel – is trembling in his hand.

Petrus moves forward again, then pauses. He has broken out in a cold sweat, he realises as his eyes turn towards the enormous floor-to-ceiling window, and he sees the dimly lit living room reflected behind him.

He and Danny are standing perfectly still, like a couple of wayward guests in a castle made of glass, when he notices a sudden movement from the corner of one eye.

Petrus swings around and hears the heavy thud of snow falling from the roof to the ground.

His heart is racing.

He feels as though he is being watched, and he looks up. Through the glass, he can see an angled window on the first floor.

'Pingu,' Danny says quietly, pointing to the footprints continuing towards the bedrooms.

Petrus lowers his weapon, giving his arms a brief rest as they turn back into the entrance hall.

Somewhere outside, a car engine starts.

Petrus takes the lead again, raising his Sig Sauer as he moves forward into a dressing room with a white carpet, gold-framed mirrors and pale wooden cupboards.

One of the doors is open, blocking his view up ahead.

Petrus realises just how tense he is when he starts thinking that the crazy Don Quixote from the supermarket could be hiding behind the door with a pan on his head.

Face pale, dark circles beneath his eyes, a samurai sword in one hand.

He reaches out and tries to close the wardrobe door, but it bumps up against something, sending a shiver down his spine.

Leaning into the door, he can see a little more of the dark bedroom reflected in a mirror.

There are bloody footprints all over the white carpet.

Petrus composes himself and takes a small step forward, up against the wardrobe door. In the mirror, he can now see that there is a large amount of blood all over the floor and a white armchair.

He backs up and walks straight into Danny. The older officer catches the trainee's eye and gestures to let him know that there could be someone hiding behind the door.

The adrenaline is making every muscle in his body tingle in intense anticipation.

Without a sound, they take up their positions.

Petrus counts them in, and on three they swing around the door and secure the room.

It was just a pile of folded towels that had fallen from the shelf and blocked the door.

The air is heavy with the earthy stench of blood and urine.

Weapons drawn, they continue through to the bedroom, where the blackout blinds are half-closed.

'Jeez . . .' Danny mumbles.

On the floor, a dead man is sprawled in a huge pool of blood. His head has rolled beneath the bed.

Over on the nightstand, his phone screen lights up with a message, and in its sudden glow the two officers see that the room resembles a slaughterhouse.

Blood has sprayed across the furniture and walls, dripping from the ceiling and lampshades and glistening on the fringing on the edge of the bedspread.

The door to the bathroom is ajar.

Danny moves over and opens it. He trains his pistol on the darkness inside, fumbling in vain for a light switch.

In the soft light from the frosted window, he can make out the rough sandstone tiles on the floor and walls. There is a round bathtub, an open shower with two ceiling-mounted heads and an invisible drain.

Danny feels the shock of the scene wash over him, and the gun in his hand starts shaking so much that he has to steady it with the other.

As if in a daze, he hears Pingu talking on the radio, saying that the victim has been beheaded and that the killer has likely already left the scene.

'We think Nina is still upstairs.'

Danny needs to get out into the cold air. He feels like he is about to fall apart, like he might implode from fear.

Petrus glances in his direction, then comes over, gives him a hug and says that the emotions will have to wait.

He lets go of his young colleague and studies him for a moment. 'You OK?'

'Think so. Thanks,' Danny replies, tugging down the zip of his coat.

Petrus hears a soft scraping noise, but he can't quite localise the sound. He turns around, raises his gun, moves back over to the bathroom door and peers inside.

His heart rate picks up as he realises that the sound could have been one of the clothes hangers in the dressing room.

He turns back towards the bedroom and sees Danny bracing himself against the wall with one hand, the other pressed to his mouth.

The low scraping starts again, but this time it doesn't sound like metal on metal. It sounds like metal on rock, like the blade of an axe on rough sandstone tiles.

66

Joona is driving down the narrow roads between the grand villas at high speed, tyres roaring against the frozen ground. Flurries of snow dance in his blue lights.

He reads his colleagues' tyre tracks on the ground up ahead, sees their skid marks and the collision with the rubbish bin, and he eases off the gas, cuts over the snowy patch in the middle of the road and accelerates out of the bend.

* * *

It all happens so quickly, as it often does when a person's fate is sealed. A brief moment of both supernatural greatness and vulgar normality.

Petrus Lyth realises that the scraping noise sounds like metal on sandstone, and has only just had time to follow that thought through to its conclusion when his head is cleaved in two from behind.

He is effectively already dead when he receives a kick to the back and slumps forward.

'Pingu?'

Danny turns around and sees a bloody figure with long blonde hair, and he manages to raise his pistol halfway before the axe strikes his lower arm.

His hand, still gripping his gun, drops to the floor.

Blood sprays out of the stump in powerful spurts.

Danny sees the axe cutting through the air again, and he throws himself back. The blade swings past his face and buries itself in the wall.

He turns and runs out of the bedroom, gripping his bleeding forearm with his remaining hand. He stumbles over the pile of towels, crashes into a mirror and hears it shatter on the floor as he scrambles away.

He staggers out into the hallway, through the broken front door and into the heavy snow outside.

The icy air claws at his lungs, and he has to stop and splutter. His field of vision has begun to shrink, his breathing is much too rapid, and he hurries over to the car and falls to the ground.

'I can't die,' he whispers to himself. 'I can't.'

With trembling fingers, he loosens his belt, wraps it twice around his arm and twists it tight to stem the bleeding.

He can hear footsteps approaching, and he holds his breath until he realises that she has already seen him.

The killer is standing right in front of him.

Danny gets onto his knees and holds up his hand and his stump, pleading for his life with a bowed head.

'Please,' he begs her. 'I haven't seen you, you don't need to kill me. This has nothing to do with me.'

* * *

Joona has almost reached the house when he learns that dispatch has lost contact with his colleagues.

To the left, the low crash barrier races by.

The Widow's car is no longer parked just beyond the lamppost.

Joona brakes gently and turns off onto the driveway as he requests helicopters and roadblocks from regional command.

He pulls up behind the patrol car, reaches for his Colt Combat and loads a round into the chamber as he gets out into the cold air.

A police officer in uniform is slumped on the bloody snow beside the car. His body is still twitching slightly, despite the fact that he has been decapitated.

Joona can hear sirens in the distance.

He takes his gun off safety and makes his way towards the broken front door.

There are flecks of bright blood on the snow that has drifted into the hallway.

With his Colt Combat raised, Joona follows the bloody trail, securing the space as he goes. He crosses the entrance hall and enters a dressing room, opening each of the wardrobe doors in turn. He kicks a pile of towels out of the way and closes the door to the linen cupboard.

On the floor in front of him, another decapitated man is lying flat on his back. His shirt has been torn open, and he has a vertical cut stretching from his breastbone to his navel.

The second police officer is face down on the floor following an axe blow to the back of the head.

Joona goes into the bathroom, taking in the sink unit, bathtub and shower. Behind a near-invisible door in the limestone wall, there is a toilet and bidet.

He repeats the same search process as he returns to the entrance hall and makes his way through to the living area.

Joona gives command a quick status update and then runs up the stairs to the first floor, coming out onto a large kitchen. He sees a video camera, plus several studio lights on tripods.

Outside the house, two patrol cars pull onto the driveway. The wind blows the snow across the spacious roof terrace.

Joona goes through to the living room, where four white sofas are positioned around a grey marble coffee table and a large projection screen on one wall.

The air is heavy with the sour stench of vomit.

Behind the sofa closest to the far wall, Nina Silverstedt is huddled with her knees pulled into her chest, rocking slowly back and forth. Keeping his voice low, Joona explains that she is safe, and soft sobs begin to escape from her lips.

* * *

Joona wrapped a blanket around Nina's shoulders and held her until the trembling started to ease, then led her out to one of the ambulances.

391

They came so close to catching the killer this time.

He is now in his car, driving back to Kungsholmen as he talks to regional command. Thus far, their efforts to trace the Widow's Opel have proved fruitless. The Northern Link motorway is just too big and sprawling. Some twenty police cars are currently involved in the search, three helicopters are still in the air, and a team is busy scouring the CCTV footage.

Agneta rings, and he takes the call over the car's Bluetooth system, giving her a quick update on the latest murder and the pattern of incomplete arrows on the victims' bodies.

'It feels like things are moving faster and faster,' she says.

'Serial killers can be a bit like a wildfire after the wind takes hold of it . . . too big for their own good, uncontrollable.'

'Well, I've spoken to Hugo,' she says. 'He says he's willing to give the hypnosis one last try . . . Bernard has agreed, too, but he wants me to be there.'

'Thank you for your understanding.'

'You have to promise not to put too much pressure on him, though . . . He's already traumatised, and we can't make things any worse.'

'I agree. I'll let Erik Maria Bark know,' Joona tells her.

67

The sky outside is still dark when Erik and Moa sit down at the kitchen table to eat breakfast. They have lit the third Advent candle, and the flames tilt in the draught from the window. It is much windier today, with sudden gusts shaking the trees and picking up old leaves from the ground.

Yesterday evening, Erik cooked Beef Rydberg, with fried pieces of fillet, cubes of potato baked in the oven, fried onions, Dijon mustard and egg yolks.

Moa was wearing a pair of glossy black trousers and a black sequin vest top when she arrived, and Erik realised that she made him nervous – in a good way, he told himself. He had showered and shaved in anticipation of her coming over, but unfortunately, because he had also trimmed his nasal hair, he kept sneezing. He put on a blue shirt, a pair of casual chinos and black socks – leaving his slippers in the wardrobe yet again.

During dinner, Moa told him that she didn't think her ex was even trying to find a place of his own. Erik just had time to unfold his napkin and turn away before sneezing, his eyes watering.

'Bless you.'

'Sorry. I don't have a cold, just so you know,' he had reassured her before immediately sneezing again.

Moa coated her last piece of beef in sauce, popped it in her mouth, chewed with her eyes closed and then lowered her cutlery.

'I don't know. Maybe it's not the end of the world,' she said, fiddling with the gold heart she was wearing around her neck. 'I know Bruno, and he sticks to the guesthouse, playing those games men like . . . Matilda goes down there for help with her homework sometimes, too. But it can't go on like this forever.'

'Not if you don't want it to.'

'No. I *really* don't want him there,' she said, stifling a yawn.

Erik had just got up from the table to open another bottle of wine when a movement out of the corner of his eye made him turn to the window. He attempted to look past his own reflection, towards the fence and the compost heap, and thought he could see a slim figure standing by the apple tree. He told Moa he was going to take the rubbish out, then lifted the bag from the pail beneath the sink, went out into the hall, pushed his feet into his boots and headed outside.

Light snowflakes danced in the gusty wind.

The air was bitterly cold, and the lid to the bin had frozen shut. Erik had to yank it several times before it eventually opened.

Rather than go straight back inside, he walked around the house through the dark garden, gazing towards the bright kitchen where Moa had started to clear the table. Erik turned to the fence. The dead leaves on the bushes behind the overgrown compost heap rustled softly. He kept going and felt a shiver down his spine when he saw the footprints in the thin dusting of snow on the grass by the apple tree.

Someone really had been standing there, watching them.

Erik headed inside and locked the door, drawing the thin curtains as soon as he returned to the kitchen.

They took their wine through to the living room and sat facing each other on the sofa, leaning back against the armrests. Erik put on a Charlie Parker record, and the soft, subdued music made it feel as though they were in a jazz club in the 1940s.

Moa dozed off as Erik talked about the phenomenon of hypnotic resonance, where the hypnotist themselves enters a kind of trance. He tipped his head back and thought about pulling a blanket over her or getting up to load the dishwasher, but when he next opened his eyes it was seven in the morning.

They had both slept all night on the sofa.

'We must've been tired last night,' she says now, pouring herself another coffee.

'I liked that we slept so well together.'

'Just one thing . . . I need to know if you thought I was a bit too "forward" last time,' she says, looking up at him. 'When I basically threw myself at you and started massaging your shoulders . . .'

'What? No. Stop.'

'You yelped the minute I touched you,' she continues, wiping down the table.

'I didn't *yelp*,' Erik protests with a smile.

'Ay!' she imitates him as she hangs up the cloth.

'No, no, it's just that I actually have a bit of nerve damage there, from an old knife wound.'

'On your shoulder?' she asks.

'See?' he says, unbuttoning his shirt to show her the scar.

'Sorry, but that doesn't *look* like a knife wound,' she says with a broad smile.

He turns around and shows her the exit hole on his back.

'OK, wow! What happened?'

'It was a patient. Or rather, a client who wasn't exactly happy with my therapy.'

'What? Was she trying to kill you?'

'It was a he, and I don't know . . . I don't think so. Not really.'

'Did he bring the knife with him?'

'No, it was a letter opener from my desk.'

'OK, I need to see this!'

They get up, and she follows him through to his office. He uses the room to see patients, and it has its own separate entrance. Through the window, the rear of the house is visible, the winter grass glittering.

Erik turns on the Danish desk lamp. The soft glow illuminates the stacks of books and journals, his filing cabinet, armchair and brown leather daybed.

'My dissatisfied client grabbed this,' he says, handing her the Spanish knife from the pen pot beside the computer.

'You're kidding,' she says, weighing the long, slim blade in her hand for a moment before passing it back.

'It went straight through me,' he says, dropping it back into the pot.

'I *knew* you were a badass.' She smiles, her pointed teeth peeping out from beneath her top lip.

'I was pinned to the floor,' he continues, nodding to the gash in the oak parquet.

'Lie down where it happened.'

Erik gets down awkwardly on the floor and lies back. Moa stands with one foot on either side of his waist, then crouches down, straddles his hips and pretends to stab him in the shoulder.

'You're pinned down now,' she says, kissing him. 'You won't get away this time . . .'

She kisses him again, pressing herself against his crotch and unbuttoning his shirt. She has just peeled off her black top when a bell rings.

'There's someone at the door,' he says.

'OK, I'll let you go – but only if you promise we can pick up where we left off later,' she says, pretending to yank the knife out of his shoulder.

They get up and straighten their clothes. The bell rings again, and Erik gives her a quick peck on the lips before hurrying through to the hallway.

He opens the door and finds Joona Linna standing outside. The detective superintendent's coat is unbuttoned, the stiff breeze ruffling his hair.

'Sorry to show up unannounced, but I need your help and you weren't answering the phone,' he says.

'Come in. What is it?'

Joona steps forward into the house and closes the door behind him.

'There's been another murder, and Hugo Sand says he's willing to give the hypnosis one last try,' he says, lowering his voice when he hears Moa's footsteps approaching.

'Right now?' asks Erik.

'Afraid so.'

Moa comes over and says hello. Joona apologises for intruding and tells her that he needs to hire Erik for a few hours.

'You don't have to pay if you promise to take care of him,' she says.

'I'll be back in three hours, tops, if you want to stay. I'd love it if you did. Run a bath, read a book,' says Erik.

* * *

The old friends are in the car, heading north towards Uppsala, when a powerful gust of wind makes the vehicle shake.

'How is Valeria getting on?' asks Erik.

'She thinks she should stay another week,' Joona replies. 'It's been tough on her, but she seems OK.'

'It's good that she's there.'

'I've tried to storm-proof the house and greenhouses as best I can, at the very least.'

'Ah, I've not bothered. It feels as though it's been blown out of all proportion.'

'Ha,' Joona replies, swerving around a ripped cardboard box on the road.

As he drives, he tells Erik about his call with Agneta, and the hypnotist reassures him that he will do his best to prevent Hugo from suffering.

'I spoke to his girlfriend, too . . . What she told me confirms that Hugo sees things in detail, despite his dreams.'

'That's logical, though we can never really be sure.'

'I don't know . . . It's as though his brain shies away from it, as though it's frightened of the fear in his dream world,' says Joona.

Erik explains that research has shown that the interaction between different parts of the brain is markedly reduced following psychological trauma. The right temporal lobe, responsible for non-verbal communication and intuition, is more active in traumatic memories than the left, which controls language and logical thought.

'It's a case of non-verbal fear,' says Erik. 'He's not receptive to reason. He's reliving the fear, nothing else. Like an animal.'

An ambulance races by, sirens blaring. Snowflakes begin to patter against the windscreen.

'This is probably our last chance,' says Joona.

'I'll do my best, but the fact that Hugo's dreams are so intense makes him quite unpredictable. There's always a risk they'll drag him up out of the hypnosis.'

'Focus on concrete things, ideally something we can use – a description, a tattoo, an unusual watch or a piece of jewellery . . . And the car's registration number.'

68

Hugo is lying back on the neatly made bed in his suite. The curtains are drawn, and Erik, Joona, Agneta and Lars Grind are standing around him in the dimly lit room.

He checks his phone as Erik goes over the process for the third time, explaining how hypnosis works and that it is really just a matter of relaxation and focus.

Joona has noticed that the teenager seems more subdued than normal. He isn't his usual defiant, sarcastic self, and seems to have resigned himself to what is happening with an air of melancholy. He answers any questions directed at him, but otherwise he has been sitting quietly, and he also seems oddly curt with Dr Grind.

Erik thanks Hugo for putting his faith in him, then pulls a chair over to the head of the bed and sits down.

'I promised Bernard that Hugo wouldn't suffer as a result of this session,' says Agneta.

'Of course.'

'Because he's had terrible anxiety after both previous attempts.'

'It was fine,' Hugo mutters, putting his phone down on the bedside table.

Erik has dark circles beneath his eyes, but his deep laughter lines mean that his face still looks relatively happy.

'Hypnosis certainly isn't meant to leave any lasting unease – the opposite, in fact . . . But with that said, we *will* be focusing on some particularly difficult memories, at least for a few minutes.'

'I just don't want to think about it beforehand,' says Hugo.

'Which is fine. All I want to say is that I'll be here with you every step of the way, to minimise the risk of any additional trauma. And before I lift you out of the hypnosis, I'll also leave you with some positive suggestions.'

'I'll be here as a kind of referee, too,' says Lars Grind. 'I'll put a stop to things if I think it's having even the slightest negative impact on you. You can trust me, Hugo.'

The teenager avoids the doctor's eye.

'OK, then we're agreed?' asks Agneta.

'Yes. But I also need you all to let me do my job,' Erik replies.

'You're very good at what you do, no doubt about that,' Agneta adds. 'And as I say, Bernard and I are both glad that Hugo wants to help the police stop a killer, but that can't come at any price.'

'Stop. It's fine,' Hugo mumbles, straightening his necklace.

As the conversation peters out and a sense of calm settles over the room, Erik begins the process of helping Hugo to become relaxed and receptive. He takes his time, working through each of the muscle groups in turn, getting the teenager to focus on his breathing and repeating that he is safe, that the bed is comfortable and that his eyelids are growing heavier.

There is a strange smell in the room, Joona notices, like rancid aftershave.

Agneta has wrapped her arms around herself, and is standing with her head bowed, a deep frown between her brows.

Lars Grind pinches his lower lip between his index finger and thumb.

Hugo's eyes are closed, his tongue just visible between his slightly parted lips.

As Erik talks, Joona notices that the teenager's breathing – the rising and falling of his chest – begins to follow the same rhythm.

The hypnotist has taken them down to the seabed twice now, he thinks, and they have found the wreck.

During the first session, they caught a glimpse of the murderer, wearing a wig and carrying an axe. During the second, that was followed by vivid segments of the killing itself through the window at the back of the caravan.

They didn't have enough time for Erik to find an accessible route *into* the caravan. The minute Hugo sets foot inside, he still jumps forward to the moment when the police officer woke him on the floor.

Traumatic imagery, followed by a blank.

In his nightmare – which drives his sleepwalking – Hugo is following his mother, the pair of them running away from a man who seems to be some sort of living stack of human bones.

In reality, he saw a man being murdered through a window and fell back into the grass without waking up.

He got to his feet and went into the caravan in an attempt to save his mother, who only existed in the dream.

The sights he witnessed there were so awful that he was unable to file them away in the usual place.

Episodic memory is stored first in the hippocampus, then consolidated in the neocortex. Most of it is forgotten, though some of it does linger among the nerve cells and synapses.

'You are now deeply relaxed, listening only to my voice,' says Erik.

The hypnotist guides Hugo through a scene in which he is leaving a party and making his way down a long wooden staircase. He starts talking about the light from the chandelier gleaming on the varnished handrail, the red carpet, the brass stair rods, Hugo's soft footsteps and the way the murmur of the guests, the music and the clinking of glasses all get fainter and fainter.

Erik watches the teenager's slow breaths in and out, successively making his voice more monotone.

He counts down from one hundred, talking about the stairs and reminding Hugo to focus on his voice, to let everything else fade like the sound of the party on the floor above.

'Thirty-two, thirty-one . . . You are still making your way down the stairs,' says Erik. 'And in a few minutes, when I get to zero, you will be back at the campsite in Bredäng, in area G. It's the middle of the night, and you are sleepwalking . . . You have plenty of time to stop and look at whatever you want. You're calm, and you're in complete control of the situation . . . This time, you won't see any of the night-mare that brought you here. Your mum isn't here and you aren't being chased by a skeleton man . . . The campsite is closed for the winter, the sky is dark, and it has just started to snow.'

The perpetrator probably wasn't still in the caravan when Hugo went inside, Joona thinks. From his own reading of the blood at the scene, the actual violence was over relatively quickly. Despite the brutal dismemberment of the victim post-mortem, all of the blood – regardless of whether it had sprayed, spattered, been trampled or dragged – was coagulated to the same degree.

Standing quietly around the bed, Joona and the others all find themselves breathing slowly and in unison as Erik continues towards zero. It is as though the whole room is now in a kind of trance, following the hypnotist's diving bell into the dark abyss.

The heat from the radiator causes the curtains to billow outwards from the wall.

Joona studies Hugo's face and notes that it now looks soft and childlike, relaxed.

Erik lowers his voice and leans into the young man.

'Thirteen, twelve, eleven . . . You have now reached the bottom of the stairs, and you can no longer hear the party,' he says. 'Ten, nine . . . You're walking straight down the hall . . . Eight, seven, and through the main doors . . . Six, five, out onto the stone steps . . . Down the last few, four, three, two, one . . . and zero, you are now back in the campsite.'

Agneta rubs her mouth, unable to tear her eyes away from Hugo.

'It's night, and the snow is falling on the grass and the caravans,' says Erik. 'But you can see a light up ahead.'

'Yes,' Hugo mumbles.

'The light is coming from the windows in the caravan.'

'Yes.'

'There is someone there . . . in the darkness outside.'

'A woman . . . with blonde hair,' Hugo says, licking his lips. 'She's holding an axe, and she goes over to the door and opens it.'

'You catch a glimpse of her face in the window,' says Erik.

'No,' Hugo whispers.

'This time you do, because the door opens very slowly.'

'She's looking down, so I can only see a bit of her forehead and eyebrow,' Hugo says, squirming anxiously.

Grind holds up a warning hand to Erik.

'None of this is dangerous, Hugo. You're safe and relaxed . . . You can describe her forehead to me, and there is no need to be afraid.'

'It's white . . . like bone. With a deep groove between her eyebrows.'

'What about her eyes?'

'I can't see them.'

'Focus on her hand on the handle. Can you see any jewellery? Any tattoos or—'

'She's wearing white latex gloves.'

'What about a watch? Does that mean she isn't wearing a watch if—'

'The caravan rocks when she goes inside and closes the door,' Hugo continues. 'The man raises his voice, and I can hear noises . . .'

Hugo's chin has begun to tremble.

'What are you doing now?'

'I'm freezing, I'm shaking . . .'

'There's no need to focus on that – you'll be warm again soon,' says Erik. 'Can you feel it? You're warm now, walking towards the caravan through the falling snow.'

'I step over her canvas bag and make my way around the caravan.'

'You step over her bag and look down at it,' says Erik.

'Yes.'

'What do you see?'

'I see a bag. Made of thick fabric, canvas . . . I see a short crowbar, a roll of kitchen paper and a bloody plastic pouch, but then I look up at the caravan . . . at the shadows moving over one of the windows.'

'Look at the bag again.'

'It's half open, and there's a keyring with a picture of a train inside a big G on the zip. The strap is frayed along the edge,' he mumbles.

'What sort of plastic pouch can you see?'

'A tooth, a bloody tooth,' says Hugo, taking a trembling breath.

Lars Grind clears his throat, catches Erik's eye and shakes his head.

'Could we maybe slow down a bit?' Agneta whispers.

'Just listen to my voice, Hugo,' says Erik, putting a hand on his shoulder. 'If you hear anyone else speak, just focus on my words. You're standing in the snow, and you step over the bag, walk around the back of the caravan, climb up onto a breezeblock and look in through the window. You notice that time is moving more slowly inside the caravan than it is outside.'

'The glass is all fogged up . . . and there's a grey rubber seal hanging loose at the bottom of the window, from the curved corner,' Hugo tells him in a gruff voice.

'I know you would rather not look inside the caravan, but you're safe here, and you can tell—'

'I don't want to,' he whispers, panting for air.

'That's enough now,' says Grind, his voice low. 'Let's stop this before—'

'I know what I'm doing,' Erik cuts him off. 'This fear is bound up in what he saw, but it isn't as traumatic as it might seem.'

'Agneta?' asks Grind.

'Keep going. Let's keep going a bit longer,' she says, swallowing hard.

'Are you sure?'

She nods.

'Hugo, you're standing at the back of the caravan, looking in through the window,' says Erik.

'The man is lying on his back,' Hugo whispers between shallow breaths. 'One of his legs has been cut off . . . It's on the floor, with a plaster on the knee and a black sock on the foot . . . under the kitchen table . . . He's trying to shuffle back, but there's blood pumping out of the stump . . . I don't want to see this, I . . .'

Joona realises that Erik has finally managed to get Hugo to completely bypass the nightmare. The boy has gone from being able to see nothing but his dream, full of bones and skulls, to a confusing double exposure, to this: what he really saw that night.

'He's screaming, trying to stop the blood with both hands,' Hugo goes on, close to tears.

'Can you see the killer?'

Hugo's back arches in a convulsion, and he slumps against the mattress, gasping for air.

'I really do need to put my foot down now,' says Grind.

Erik takes a stethoscope out of his pocket, puts it on and presses the diaphragm to Hugo's chest. He listens to three different spots, then returns the instrument to his pocket.

'He's stressed, but he's just fine,' he says.

'Maybe we should wrap up now,' says Agneta.

Hugo is still panting, and his body tenses again.

'I really would like to keep going a little longer,' says Erik.

'I'm not sure . . .'

Grind tries to reach Hugo, but Joona holds him back, shaking his head with a smile.

'Hugo, you're looking straight at the killer,' says Erik.

'Her blonde hair . . . the blood on it is glistening, and—'

'Hugo?' Grind cuts him off.

'Go on,' says Erik.

'She grabs the man's hair and pulls his head back, then lifts the axe . . . There's blood running down the handle, over her knuckles . . . She twists around so she can hit him and—'

Another convulsion takes over Hugo's body. His head jerks back, and his legs begin to shake, making the bed creak.

'You see her face from the side,' says Erik.

Without warning, Lars Grind rushes forward, grabs Hugo's arm and pulls him up into a sitting position.

'God, what's happening?' Hugo gasps.

'Lay him down again,' Erik says sharply.

'You're OK,' says Grind, hugging Hugo. 'You're still here at the lab. They hypnotised you, but I've just put a stop to it. I'm putting a stop to this right now.'

Joona helps Erik to prise the agitated doctor's arms away from Hugo. The boy's body is red-hot as they gently lower him onto his back.

'What are you doing?' Hugo asks in confusion.

'Just try to lie still,' says Erik. 'Breathe in through your nose and out through—'

Hugo rolls over onto his side, pushes back his hair and vomits onto the floor. The liquid spatters across Agneta's shoes and lower legs.

'God ...' Hugo pants. 'That was the worst, the most horrible—'

'Lie on your back and breathe slowly,' says Erik.

Joona hands Hugo a piece of tissue, and he wipes his mouth and chin before slumping down on the bed.

'Seriously, I didn't want to see that,' he says after a moment.

'I'm sorry, but if I'd been able to wrap up as planned, you wouldn't be feeling this way,' says Erik.

Lars Grind holds out a paper cup of water and a triangular yellow pill.

'I don't want it,' says Hugo, turning away.

'Do you take Atarax regularly?' asks Erik.

'No, just if I'm having a total panic attack ... which isn't very often.'

'What other medication are you on?'

'What?'

'I'd always assumed that your susceptibility to hypnosis had something to do with your parasomnia, but I'd like to make sure it isn't down to your medication or any interactions ... Because your memories from sleepwalking are just so precise,' Erik explains.

'You don't have to answer that,' says Grind. 'He isn't authorised to see your records without your dad's permission.'

'When I'm having an episode, I take zopiclone and a bit of Mirtazapine and Tramadol,' Hugo replies.

'What?' Erik sounds surprised, and he turns to look at the doctor.

'In small doses,' Grind explains.

'OK, but why? I don't understand. Surely they just make him sleepwalk more?'

'Recent research from La Salpêtrière suggests otherwise.'

'Is that so?' Erik asks, holding the doctor's gaze.

'We try new things. It's called research.'

'Hugo, talk to your dad,' says Erik. 'If you and he don't mind, I'd really like to review your medication.'

* * *

Agneta stays behind with Hugo once the others leave the suite. She wipes the vomit from her shoes, sits down in the chair Erik was using and pushes a few strands of hair back from his forehead.

'How are you feeling?'

'I'm OK now.'

'That was pretty intense.'

'Could make a good chapter in your book, though.'

'Remember, it's up to you what we include.'

'Can we scratch the part about me puking on your shoes?' Hugo asks with a grin.

'It'll be tricky . . .'

'OK.'

He smiles and closes his eyes for a moment. Agneta strokes his cheek.

'I'd feel much better if you came home with me,' she says.

'I will, later. But I've got a few things to do first.'

'Things?'

'Someone here, who I . . .'

He trails off.

'What's her name?' Agneta asks.

Hugo blushes, and she laughs fondly and gets up. Before she leaves, she reminds him about the snowstorm approaching from the Baltic Sea.

69

Joona is driving back towards Stockholm along the E4, which runs parallel to the train line. The wind has picked up, coming in waves over the fields and pastures. Powerful gusts from the east rock his car, causing the trees to shake and sending rubbish and debris flying over the road and the tracks.

The fierce snowstorm from Russia is currently surging across the Baltic, and is expected to hit Sweden's east coast later that afternoon. The public has been urged to secure any loose objects, fill jerry cans with water, prepare for long power cuts and barricade themselves in their homes.

As he drives, Joona thinks about the case.

Veronica Nagler's files were all marked private and confidential, but the team has already submitted a request for her medical records from her former doctor at Sankt Göran's Hospital.

After going through the footage from Nina Silverstedt's camera, they discovered that she had inadvertently captured the Widow outside the house, but unfortunately she is too far away and the resolution too poor for it to be of any use.

His thoughts turn to the latest hypnosis session and the fact that it was the closest they have ever come to the killer, that Hugo was just seconds away from seeing her face when Dr Grind intervened.

He understands the doctor's concern and takes full responsibility for Erik having pressed Hugo so hard, to the brink of almost unbearable anguish.

The helicopter search for the Opel in Uppland and Västmanland has been called off due to the worsening weather.

The fact that they have only one sighting of the car suggests careful planning.

The killer likely missed their exit as a result of unforeseen circumstances – a minor accident or temporary road closure – meaning she had no choice but to pass the camera.

Joona hasn't yet had time to listen to his recording from the hypnosis session, and can't shake the niggling sense that he is missing something important.

He feels as though he was just about to touch upon a key piece of the puzzle when his train of thought was interrupted and redirected – just like when the session itself was stopped at the most decisive moment.

The traffic up ahead begins to slow as he approaches Rosersberg Palace, as though hindered by some invisible force. A string of red brake lights twinkle in front of him. On the train tracks to the side of the road, the Arlanda Express is approaching at high speed, and the turbulence makes his car shake.

Joona has just started recapping the hypnosis session in his mind, thinking about Hugo's description of the sturdy canvas bag, the crowbar and the bloody tooth in a plastic pouch, when he remembers exactly what it was that jumped out at him.

Attached to the zip, Hugo had seen a keyring featuring a train and a large G.

A G and a train.

One of the small hamlets close to the road camera that captured the Opel was the former station community of Grillby.

Joona takes the first exit, pulls over to the side of the road by a Burger King and runs a quick search online. He finds the logo for Lokomotiv Grillby, the local floorball team, almost immediately.

A train inside a large letter G.

He contacts the national command centre over the comms unit.

Due to a fallen tree, there are long tailbacks just before Rotebro, so he turns around and heads north again, towards Märsta.

Enköping Police send four officers in unmarked cars to scope out the area, and one of them reports back to say that they have spotted an Opel matching the APB parked outside the large silo before Joona reaches Grillby. He asks the local officers to hold back and put up roadblocks around the whole of the community, then requests backup from a specialist operative unit.

70

Hugo has packed his bag and is standing in the corridor outside Lars Grind's office. He presses the buzzer and waits, but the little WILLKOMMEN sign remains dark. He knocks and tries the handle instead, but the door is locked.

With a sigh, he takes out his phone and rings the doctor's private number, but his call goes straight through to voicemail.

Hugo presses the buzzer again, holding it down for longer this time, only taking a step back when he sees Rakia approaching down the corridor.

He thinks back to the video he recorded, the moment when she briefly came into view before injecting him, oddly illuminated and with wide eyes and a grubby plaster on her finger.

'Can I help you?' she asks coldly.

'Do you know where Lars is?'

'At a meeting with the research centre at the hospital.'

'Ugh, what the hell . . .'

'Why do you need to see him?'

'I was going to head home, but I need more zopiclone to tide me over Christmas.'

'I don't have the authority to give you any.'

'Can't you ring him?'

'He never answers his phone during meetings.'

'So when will he be back?'

'Two at the latest, he said,' Rakia replies as she walks away.

Hugo walks back down the corridor and pops his head into the day room. There are only two people still inside.

Svanhildur is sitting alone at one of the tables, Kasper at another.

Hugo checks the chalkboard and sees that today's lunch is roast chicken, fried potatoes and pickled fennel.

Svanhildur has only a mug of coffee in front of her.

He walks over, says hello and puts his rucksack down on the floor.

Kasper is sucking on a chicken bone, and he pulls it out of his mouth and uses it as a kind of pen, drawing on the table in saliva.

Hugo goes over to the buffet table and helps himself to some food, then sits down opposite Svanhildur.

'You off?' she asks.

'Yeah, as soon as Lars gets back. Just need my meds first.'

As ever, Kasper is wearing his washed-out sailor's uniform and the strange shoes with separate big toes. His face is gaunt. He gives Hugo a flicker of a smile and starts sucking on the bone again.

'You don't fancy celebrating Christmas here, then?' Svanhildur asks.

'Are you?' Hugo replies as he starts to eat.

'Nah.' She grins. 'I'll probably end up going to my sister's place on the twenty-fourth, but other than that I don't know. Meeting some friends on the twenty-sixth.'

Hugo looks up at her, taking in her pink lips, pale brows and the scattering of freckles across her face. She cocks an eyebrow, and he realises he is staring, quickly lowering his eyes and coating a piece of potato in gravy.

Kasper lets out a fake-sounding laugh, and when they turn to look at him he pulls the chicken bone from his mouth and points it at Hugo with a smile.

Hugo points back using his index finger, then reaches for the jug of water and pours himself a glass before he continues eating.

'Are you going to see Olga?' Svanhildur asks.

'Nah, it's over.'

'Oh, when did that happen?'

'Just now,' he replies, fiddling with the coin around his neck.

'Have the two of you talked?'

'Nope, she's stopped replying.'

'And that means it's over?'

'Yeah . . . Plus all the money is gone.'

'What do you mean?'

'I just saw. She's taken all the money out of the account.'

'Seriously?'

'I feel *so* cheated,' he says with a smile.

'You think she's run off with it?'

'Yeah, for sure . . . She must've been planning it all along, and I fell for it.'

'You should call the police.'

'Nah.'

Kasper gets up and points his bone at Hugo again. The sleeves of his sailor's outfit are far too short, the collar dirty.

'Is there something you want to say?' Hugo asks him.

Kasper slowly moves closer, pausing right beneath the ceiling lamp to suck on the clean bone. His slicked-back hair gleams in the light, and he has dark circles beneath both eyes and pimples on his chin.

Hugo twists a little fennel onto his fork and spears a wedge of potato.

'You're really not going to report it?' Svanhildur presses him.

'I mean, it's not illegal. The money was both of ours.'

'But she took it.'

'Yeah.'

Svanhildur chews on her bottom lip and absent-mindedly cracks her fingers before looking up again.

'So what're you going to do? You need to go to Canada and find your mum.'

'I'll think of something. I can always get a job at—'

He stops talking as the lights go out. Neither he nor Svanhildur has time to react before the power comes back on, the bulbs blinking and the ventilation humming again.

Kasper is now just two metres away from their table, brandishing his bone again.

413

'OK, bye,' Hugo mutters to him, a clear note of irritation in his voice.

'What's going on, Kasper?' Svanhildur asks.

He turns to her, jabs the bone in her direction and bares his teeth.

'Come on, man. Chill out,' says Hugo.

Kasper takes a step closer, and the lights flicker again, but this time they stay on.

Hugo leans into Svanhildur and continues talking in a low voice.

'I don't know. I've started to think maybe I should talk to Dad about the whole Canada plan, that he might want to come along.'

'That sounds like a great idea.'

Kasper moves forward again. He smiles and holds out the bone, stretching as far as his arm will allow, but he pops it back in his mouth when Hugo gets up.

'Look, what do you want?' he snaps.

Hugo doesn't get any reply, and he sits back down, puts his cutlery onto his plate and turns away from Kasper. He has just started telling Svanhildur about his mother's family in Québec when he feels something wet on the back of his neck, and he swears and leaps up. Turning around, he sees Kasper standing with the moist bone in his hand.

'Leave me the fuck alone,' Hugo mutters, keeping his voice low.

Kasper backs away, sucking on the bone. He pulls it out of his mouth and points at Hugo, then goes back over to his own table and starts drawing in saliva again.

Svanhildur is trying not to laugh, and her face has turned red. She turns her coffee cup in her hands before looking up.

'Maybe we could hang out over Christmas?' says Hugo.

'I'd love that.'

'Cool.'

'We could open a bank account together,' she says.

71

Just seventy minutes have passed since the Opel Kadett was spotted behind the silo in Grillby, but a command post has already been set up outside the petrol station at the intersection of Länsvägen and Storgatan, with two black vans, three cars and a command vehicle parked by the flagpoles.

Six operatives from the National Tactical Unit and a UAS team are in position.

Behind the shop, two ambulances, a fire engine and four patrol cars are ready and waiting.

Joona has parked his car right to the exit, so that he can make a swift exit if necessary.

Trains first began calling at Grillby in the 1870s, and the service continued for a hundred years. Nowadays, they pass straight through the old station without stopping.

The small community – bisected by the train line – is just south of the motorway, surrounded by an expanse of snow-covered fields.

From a distance, the only thing that distinguishes it from the flat landscape is the tall concrete silo. It looms above Grillby like some sort of damp, brutalist church, with a long nave featuring four half columns on each side and a forty-five-metre tower.

Up against the high barbed wire fence separating the silo from the railway, there is a boarded-up brick building, a hangar-like structure made from corrugated metal and a blue shipping container.

Sandwiched between the silo and the hangar, there are three covered docks that were once used by the lorries transporting grain.

The black-clad operatives from the tactical unit are gathered behind the vehicles, messing about on their phones, tightening the straps on their bulletproof vests and checking their weapons and magazines, stun grenades and breathing masks one last time.

The red flags outside the petrol station strain and flap in the strengthening wind, and tiny snowflakes swirl around the forecourt.

Joona is wearing a black beanie, warm layers and sturdy boots, and he walks over to the group leader, Jamal, to introduce himself with his heavy bulletproof vest slung over one shoulder.

'Thanks for getting here so quickly,' he says.

'No problem.'

Jamal has chocolate-coloured eyes and a small black goatee. His helmet is on the ground between his feet, his Heckler & Koch assault rifle hanging on a strap by his hip. The commander, a white-haired man in a thick coat and a trapper hat, finishes his phone call and comes over to join them. He holds out a tablet and shows them a map of the area, with routes and assembly points already marked out.

The three men quickly agree on a plan for the various stages of the operation.

'Listen up, everyone,' Joona says, raising his voice so that the entire unit can hear him. 'The suspect has just killed two of our colleagues and should be considered extremely dangerous, but is also likely armed with just an axe – though obviously we can't rule out other weapons.'

'Take up your positions and await my order,' the commander tells his men.

'Let's get this bastard!' shouts Jamal.

Joona makes his way over to the UAS unit – two men in puffer jackets and beanies – behind a black car. In the open boot, they have a number of aluminium cases containing spare batteries, transmitters and other pieces of kit.

UAS stands for Unmanned Aerial System – drones equipped with cameras and thermal imaging systems, in other words. The Police Authority made the decision to use the slightly clunky name internally in order to be able to distinguish the drone handlers from other units during operations.

'How's the weather looking?' asks Joona.

'It's not ideal,' says the commanding officer, glancing over to the silo.

'But we'll be OK,' says the other, spitting a wad of snus to the ground.

The four propellors on the drone start to whirr.

'Ready?' asks the commander.

'The airspace is closed,' the other replies.

The drone rises straight into the air, quickly reaching a height of two hundred metres. The little black dot is almost invisible through the falling snow.

Joona takes off his hat and heads into the mobile command vehicle.

Seven people – including the tactical commander – are sitting at computers inside. Joona pulls out a seat and takes a seat beside the coordinator.

Through the police camera feed, he follows the footage from the drone in real time.

Narrow roads, gardens and small houses race by before the drone comes to a halt directly above the silo, rocking gently in the wind.

Down below, the enormous concrete structure is visible beside the hangar, the mossy roof of the brick building, the blue shipping container, trees, the fence and two railway tracks.

The surveillance units from Enköping Police are still positioned around the area, and continue to report that they haven't detected any activity in and around the silo.

'Let's take a closer look, then,' says the UAS operator.

The drone tilts to one side, and the camera zooms in on the closed doors of the hangar, zipping past the silo and over to the brick building.

It slowly turns around.

Beneath the roof of one of the loading bays, the back bumper of the Opel Kadett is visible.

A powerful crosswind knocks the drone, and the camera pans across the villas and a cluster of trees on the far side of the tracks before stabilising.

Jamal comes into the command vehicle to let them know that his team is in position and waiting for the green light.

The drone's camera swings across the junk in the yard and the top of the blue shipping container, capturing the thin dusting of snow on top of the black autumn leaves. It continues around the brick building, to the sloping scrubland, the fence, the tracks and the concrete sleepers.

'Switching to thermal camera,' says the UAS operator.

The image on the screen in front of Joona splits in two. The right-hand side is now dark grey, with the buildings and train tracks visible in black.

A glowing yellow rabbit moves slowly across the embankment.

The drone swings over the area again, past the dark-grey silo, the hangar and the shipping container to the brick building.

An orange shape appears on the screen, like a blob of lava with pulsing blue contours.

'Jamal, over,' the tactical commander says over the radio.

'Jamal here, over.'

'One individual in the house. Get ready to go in.'

'Can we have a more exact position?'

'Close to the south-west corner.'

'Which floor? There are four.'

'We can't see.'

'Can't the drone drop down to check?' the coordinator asks, taking a swig from a bottle of Coke Zero.

'It's too loud,' the UAS operator replies.

'Jamal, get ready to storm the house. Await orders,' says the tactical commander.

Joona puts on his hat, leaves the bus and jogs over to his car. He drives the short distance to the silo and pulls up behind a cluster of trees on Magasinsgatan.

His wiper blades sweep the light snowflakes from the windscreen as he watches the drone feed on the touchscreen of his comms unit.

Six operatives drift towards the building like a handful of bright orange jellyfish.

On the tracks, a long freight train is approaching.

The increasingly heavy snow has begun to settle on the ground.

Through the windscreen, Joona sees two of the tactical unit operatives waiting with their backs to the silo.

'We can use the noise of the freight train to mask the sound of the drone,' Joona says.

'Good idea,' the UAS operator replies.

The drone sinks down towards the gravel in front of the brick building as the train thunders past behind the silo.

Joona pulls his Colt Combat from his shoulder holster, checks the magazine and slots it back into the pistol.

The drone is now hovering around two metres above the ground, clearing the snow from a cross-shaped patch of ground beneath it.

The thermal camera tilts upwards, revealing that the figure radiating heat is at the bottom of the building.

'The target is on the ground floor, over,' the tactical commander says over the radio.

'Roger that,' Jamal replies.

'Await final order.'

72

The men from the tactical unit have put on their breathing masks, and two members of the team are now slowly moving towards the brick building with their assault rifles raised.

On the far side of the hangar, the train thunders by. Car after car jolts as it passes over the switch, as though a slight electric shock is working its way backwards through the train.

Joona studies the brick facade through the drone's video feed, taking in the graffiti and the damp sheets of plywood over the windows.

Someone has pried the front door loose, and it is lying like a ramp on the two steps.

'Moving closer,' says the UAS operator.

The drone glides slowly towards the door, hovering a metre above the ground. A brown doormat emerges from the gloom. There are muddy footprints and empty wine bottles on the floor, a yellow raincoat hanging on a hook.

On the feed from the thermal camera, Joona notices that the blob of lava on the ground floor has started to move. It shifts slightly to one side, slowly spreads out, and suddenly seems to have too many legs.

Thoughts of the skeleton man briefly cross his mind before the orange lump splits in two. A German Shepherd bursts out through the doorway and launches itself at the drone.

The operator makes the unit turn sharply, and one of the propellors hits the overhanging roof, causing the drone to lurch to one side. It slams into the smooth wall of the silo and loses all power.

'Fuck!'

The commander of the tactical unit gives his men the order to storm the building, and the team breaks through two of the boarded-up windows.

They detonate several tear gas canisters, one after another.

Joona gets out of his car and loads a round into the chamber as he runs towards the silo.

The dog has started barking aggressively.

Up ahead, the group of operatives peel apart, moving quickly towards the brick building with their rifles raised.

Three shots ring out in quick succession, echoing around the yard.

Joona rounds the corner of the silo and sees the dog slumped on the ground.

Grey smoke is billowing out of the doorway, and the operatives disappear through it, securing the sides as they go.

Joona speeds up.

The gravelly, frozen ground is so hard it feels like concrete.

As he approaches the brick building, he radios Jamal.

'I'm following you in,' he says. 'I'm following you in, over.'

Joona tears off his hat and uses it to cover his nose and mouth, then raises his pistol and heads in through the doorway.

In the smoke up ahead, the operatives' tactical lights sweep across a large room with peeling medallion wallpaper. Joona takes an immediate right, striding through a mudroom with a shower cubicle. Beside the washing machine, there are two axes in a red bucket. Both are still in their plastic wrapping.

'Freeze, police!' he hears Jamal shout somewhere deeper in the building.

Joona's eyes are burning from the tear gas as he comes out into a shabby kitchen. The sink is full of bloody toilet paper, and there are several empty dog bowls on the floor, a pack of hotdog buns beside a beer can on the table.

He hears heavy footsteps and catches a glimpse of a man with long grey hair dart past the doorway up ahead.

Gun lights flash through the kitchen.

One of the operatives appears in the doorway, and Joona meets his eye and uses a hand to indicate the direction the man ran.

A series of metallic clangs reverberate through the pipes.

Joona turns back towards the mudroom and makes his way into a larger room with a narrow staircase to the floor above.

There are two spent tear gas canisters on the rough wooden floor.

The joists overhead creak, and a trickle of dust falls from the ceiling.

Jamal and another of the operatives come through from the adjoining room.

'He's upstairs,' says Joona.

'Alpha, follow me. Everyone else, stay downstairs,' Jamal says over the radio.

The three men run up the stairs, covering each other as they tactically pick their way between the cupboards, chests of drawers and sofas.

The building is darker on the first floor, the air a little warmer and thick with dust. From the room to the right, they hear a muffled cough.

Jamal runs over and opens the door, swinging around to the left while his colleague takes the right.

Joona hurries after them with his Colt Combat raised.

They catch only a brief glimpse of the long-haired man as he runs through to another room, slamming the door behind him.

His feet thud against the floor.

Jamal stands with his back to the wall, takes off his breathing mask and tries the handle.

The door is locked.

Joona steps forward and kicks it as hard as he can. There is a crunching sound, and the door swings open. Splintered wood and broken metal drop to the carpeted floor on the other side.

The room is empty.

Against one wall, there are a number of old paint tins.

The man has escaped into another room, disappearing down a service corridor and passing them in the opposite direction.

Rather than run after him, Joona turns around and overtakes the man before he reaches the stairs.

'Stop!'

The man veers off into a dark hallway behind a sheet of thick plastic.

The operatives' tactical lights swing across the floor.

Jamal and his colleague come out onto the landing from the same direction as the grey-haired man.

The whites of their eyes glow in the gloom.

Joona points to the plastic sheet, tears it down, and the three men run down the hallway.

The ceiling boards have begun to collapse. One is already on the floor, another hanging down across the passageway.

Up ahead, a door slams.

Joona pushes the loose board to one side and feels a protruding nail catch his arm.

The men pause and exchange a quick glance at the end of the hallway, then move forward and secure the corners in the same way as earlier.

The large room, with a ceiling rose and an arched window looking out onto the train tracks, has two doors.

The one on the left is blocked by a pile of moving boxes.

Joona hears a soft scraping sound.

They stop to listen.

Behind the right-hand door, someone coughs quietly.

Jamal moves over to it and pulls a stun grenade from his belt. His colleague aims his rifle at the door.

Joona lowers his pistol.

Blood from the cut on his arm has started dripping from his wrist.

Jamal pulls the pin, opens the door and tosses the grenade inside, then slams the door and backs away.

There are a series of loud bangs, and the floor shakes. Flakes of paint fall from the ceiling, and there is a bright flash of light around the edges of the door.

The man lets out a guttural scream.

Jamal opens the door and sees him crawling beneath a bed with a filthy mattress.

'Police! Come out!' he shouts, dropping to one knee and taking aim beneath the bed.

His colleague runs in after him, and Joona moves over to the left-hand door to kick the moving boxes out of the way.

Dust swirls through the air, and files and papers spill across the floor.

Jamal pulls the bed back, but the grey-haired man has disappeared through a hole in the wall.

Joona opens the left-hand door and heads through to a large room full of empty bookshelves. He sees the man get up on unsteady legs.

'Police, stop!' he shouts, taking aim at the man's chest.

His dirty grey hair is knotted and hanging over his face, his ears are bleeding following the blast, and he seems to be struggling to see.

The man is dressed in layers of over-sized clothing, and his rubber boots have been mended with silver tape. The sharp stench of sweat and old urine is heavy in the air around him.

He staggers back towards the tiled stove in the corner, blinking repeatedly as he pulls out a knife with a blue plastic handle and brandishes it in front of him.

'Drop the knife,' Joona tells him.

'Go fuck yourself,' he wheezes.

Jamal comes into the room behind Joona, moving level with him and taking aim at the man.

'No one shoot,' says Joona.

Illuminated by Jamal's tactical light, the man lowers the knife. He is breathing heavily now, and his shadow rocks slowly back and forth over the wallpaper and the pale rectangles left by the frames that once hung there.

Joona holsters his gun and holds up both hands.

'Toss the knife,' he says as he slowly approaches the man. 'Drop it, put your hands behind your head and turn—'

The man lunges towards him without warning, thrusting the knife in Joona's direction. Joona twists away from the blade and knocks the man's arm upwards, grabbing his hand as he rams his knee into his chest.

The knife clatters to the floor and skids beneath the empty wood basket.

Gripping the man's wrist, Joona kicks his feet out from beneath him.

There is a loud bang as the man lands on his back, hitting his head on the floor. Saliva and mucus spray across his grubby face.

Joona twists his arm, forcing his shoulder up off the floorboards, then uses his foot to turn him over onto his front and cuffs both hands behind his back.

The man gasps desperately, as though he has just come up for air, and then starts coughing.

73

The yard outside the building is full of emergency vehicles as the tactical operatives lead the suspect out.

Joona notices that one of the grey-haired man's boots has come off in the hallway, and he bends down to pick it up before following them out into the cold air.

Blue lights sweep through the falling snow, over the brick building, the shipping container, the trees and brush.

The tactical commander has fastened the earflaps on his hat beneath his chin. The tip of his nose has turned red, and he has his hands buried deep in his pockets.

'Good work,' he says.

'Thanks . . . though it's hard to believe he's the Widow,' Joona replies, shaking the blood from his hand.

Over by one of the ambulances, the man has been strapped to a gurney, his hands cuffed to the railings on each side.

'Where's Leica? Has someone got Leica?' he wheezes.

A paramedic steps forward to examine the man's ears.

Blue light pulses up the side of the silo.

Joona is having the cut on his arm treated and bandaged when one of the local officers comes over.

'I don't know what all this is about . . .' he says, 'but I think you've got the wrong guy.'

'He's wanted in Stockholm,' the tactical commander replies.

'Right, but Boris never leaves Grillby. That's the main problem with him, from our point of view.'

'Go on,' says Joona.

'It was just a dumb rumour . . . No one knows where it started, but it kept on building, and in the end Boris had to quit his job at the school library. His life fell apart, he started avoiding people. Just stayed home all day, didn't pay any of his bills and wound up losing his house.'

'In that case, it might not even be the right car,' the commander speaks up.

Joona walks over to the forensic technicians and asks if they have any Bluestar to hand, waiting as they open the bottle and fit the spray nozzle.

'Thanks,' he says, carrying it over to the old Opel, which is parked by the silo.

The driver's side window is open, and Joona can smell the pine scent of the air fresheners as he peers inside. The interior of the car has definitely seen better days, but it also looks as though it has recently been cleaned. In the footwell by the passenger seat, there is a roll of kitchen paper and some cleaning products.

Taking care not to touch anything, Joona reaches inside with the bottle of Bluestar and spritzes a few times.

An icy blue glow appears almost immediately on the seams and piping around the edge of the driver's seat, on the floor mat and the grooved rubber pedals.

Blood seems to have dripped down the gear stick, and the back of the wheel is practically quivering with bluish light.

On the windscreen, a couple of bright smears reveal that someone has used a cloth in an attempt to clean the glass.

The entire car is like a fluorescent underwater world.

It must have been completely drenched in blood before it was cleaned.

'Damn,' the tactical commander mutters.

Joona returns the bottle to the forensic technicians and asks them to try to find the car's vehicle identification number as quickly as they can. It has been scraped off the window, but should also be punched into the metal beneath the passenger seat.

He then heads over to the grey-haired man on the gurney. His eyes are bloodshot and his face red from the tear gas.

'Sorry, like,' he wheezes.

'I need to ask you a few questions before you go,' Joona tells him.

'Huh?' The man cocks his head to hear him better.

'Do you know whose car that is?'

'The Opel? Nah . . . Been here years. Probably deregistered.'

'How often do you come here?'

'Every other week, maybe. Never stay long anywhere, me,' the man replies, baring his rotten teeth in a grin. 'I own Grillby. The whole place is mine.'

'Have you ever seen anyone else here?' Joona asks.

'Other than the kids trying to get into the silo or riding about on their motocross bikes, y'mean?'

'Yes.'

'The washing machine was on once, and another time there was a light on in the container . . . When I got here yesterday, the key wasn't in the electric cabinet, and then the door broke.'

Joona walks over to the tactical unit's van, takes out a dark red canister of acetylene and a silver oxygen tank, carries them over to the shipping container and attaches the cutting torch.

There is a steel cover over the sturdy padlock on the container, preventing anyone from breaking in with a hacksaw or bolt cutters.

Joona pulls on a pair of thick gloves and ignites the torch with a lighter.

He directs the surging flame at one edge of the steel cover, heating the metal to over 2,000 degrees before switching to a jet of pure oxygen.

The flame shrinks to a white blade, cutting through the thick metal like butter.

Sparks rain down on the ground, and the cover drops with a thud, hissing as it hits the snow.

Joona repeats the process with the polished steel padlock, then turns off the gas and opens the door.

The shipping container is full of old furniture.

Joona pulls off his gloves, turns on his torch and guides the beam over display cabinets, speckled mirrors, bookshelves, chairs and floor lamps.

Towards the rear, a number of dressers and varnished wardrobes have been stacked right up to the roof.

In front of them, there are two chandeliers hanging on hooks. The crystals are dusty, their plugs yellowed from age.

Behind him, Joona hears Jamal talking to the commander about packing up and clearing out before the storm hits. The wind seems to be growing stronger by the minute.

The beam of his torch sweeps across a secretaire, a sideboard and an open box of tarnished silver cutlery.

At the front of the container, there is a dusty dining table on a Persian carpet.

A number of leaf panels made from the same dark wood have been propped up against the side wall, beside a gold pendulum clock.

Joona points his torch at the rug on the floor and notices a number of indentations.

The heavy piece of furniture seems to have been moved a few centimetres to one side.

He sets the torch down, lifts the end of the table and uses his foot to push the rug out of the way before lowering it again.

A soft clang reverberates through the container.

Joona bends down and rolls back the rug to reveal a square of fibreboard.

He lifts it out and reaches for his torch.

Beneath the board, there is a hole in the bottom of the container, with a narrow spiral staircase leading straight down into some sort of well.

The beam of his torch shakes.

Stale air fills his nose.

He can't hear a sound from inside.

Joona turns around, crawls beneath the table and shuffles into the hole feet first.

His colleagues' voices fade as he makes his way down the stairs.

Each step makes the structure shake, and he grips the cold handrail tightly.

The staircase has been screwed into the walls of the well, and something comes loose and clatters down the shaft.

Joona's torchlight flickers.

Roughly four metres down, the well seems to open out into a concrete-lined space, possibly an old storage tank of some kind.

Joona has just reached the bottom and turned around when his torch goes out.

The stagnant air is heavy with the stench of damp, chlorine and rotten meat.

He pauses and shakes his torch, and the light comes back on.

The gravel crunches underfoot as he takes a step forward, and he hears the staircase creak behind him.

The acoustics are oddly flat.

Everything sounds so close, so intimate.

The beam of his torch wanders across the damp wall, over the thick spiderwebs in the corner, flashing when it hits a couple of glass jars on a rough wooden shelf.

Joona slowly pans back and stops.

There are five dusty jars on the shelf, all filled with what looks like formaldehyde.

In the first, he can see a grey ear wearing a gold earring. The ragged flesh where it was severed from its owner is still pink.

In the next jar, Joona can only make out a couple of coins in a pale sludge.

In the third, a pearl necklace is resting on top of two vertebrae filled with pink bone marrow.

The reflected light dances across the low ceiling, where rust from the reinforcement steels has seeped through the concrete.

Joona hears a couple of tinny shouts overhead, and he moves forward again, swinging his torch in the other direction, where a brownish-red arrow has been daubed on the wall.

It is pointing straight down at a large plastic drum.

The light fades again, and Joona hits the torch, crouches down and shines it on the drum. It is filled with vacuum-packed necklaces, bloody earrings, a rotten finger wearing a diamond ring, stained bank notes and watches.

A number of heavy metallic thuds reach him from the container above.

Joona turns around and sees a dirty mattress in the corner, a bulging rubbish bag in a pool of yellowed water, and some blue plastic bottles of chlorine.

A fly buzzes right by his ear.

At the top of the stairs, the door to the shipping container creaks. Someone shouts Joona's name, and he replies, makes his way back up to the surface, crawls out from beneath the table and gets to his feet.

The commander of the tactical unit is waiting for him in the falling snow, radio in hand. A cloud of pale breath hangs in the air around his mouth.

'The deregistered car and property are both owned by the same person,' he says, sounding stressed.

'Who?'

'Lars Hjalmar Grind.'

74

The fierce wind whistles around the house, making the windows rattle. The rope on the flagpole snaps against the metal in double time, and old leaves and twigs swirl around the garden.

Moa is wearing nothing but a pair of knickers and a black sports bra, and Erik has taken off his shirt.

They had already started kissing and getting undressed when the power went out, and now – giggling – they are in the process of dragging the mattress out of the bedroom, past the bathroom and over to the hearth in the lounge.

They curl up by the fire, holding hands and sipping grappa from small glasses.

The logs crackle, and the warm light pulses through the room like a steady heartbeat, the heat making Moa's cheeks flush.

She sets their empty glasses down on the mantelpiece.

The fire is reflected in the row of dark windows onto the garden.

Moa gives Erik a peck on the cheek, and he turns his head and meets her lips. They start kissing again, slowly building in intensity.

She peels off her bra, runs her fingers through her short hair and straightens the gold heart she wears on a chain around her neck, then lies back and meets his eye.

Erik gets onto his knees, straddling her legs, and leans forward. Supporting himself on either side of her shoulders, he kisses her and starts making his way downwards, his lips grazing her ornate tattoo and her pubic mound.

'You've got the volume on your phone turned up, right? In case the detective calls,' she jokes.

Erik shakes his head and pulls her knickers down over her thighs. She is so aroused that her vulva glistens in the soft light.

The wind howls in the chimney.

Erik kisses her thick black curls and breathes in her heady scent.

The candle on the coffee table flickers, the flame tilting to one side.

He gets up, glances through to the kitchen and hallway, then pulls down his trousers and steps out of them.

The glow of the fire reaches as far as the whipping branches of the willow outside.

A clump of dust rolls across the parquet in a sudden draught.

Erik looks down at Moa, who has kicked off her knickers and crossed her legs at the ankle. Her eyes are glittering.

'What is it?' she asks.

'You're just so beautiful.'

'No.' She smiles.

'Too beautiful for me.'

She reaches for his hand, pulls him towards her and parts her thighs. She kisses him on the lips, strokes his back and lets out a loud groan as he pushes into her.

* * *

Joona is driving north towards Uppsala with his blue lights on in an attempt to make it to Lars Grind's home in time for the raid.

There is a red car up ahead, and he blasts the horn and swings out onto the hard shoulder as he undertakes it.

The fast-approaching storm is already causing trees to bend, branches to break and debris and loose objects to blow across the road or catch on the central barrier.

On learning that the Opel and property in Grillby belonged to Grind, Joona immediately jumped into his car and set off, trying to reach Hugo as he drove.

He grips the wheel with both hands in an attempt to keep the car steady.

Over the radio, he hears that a nationwide alert has been issued for the doctor, along with an APB for his new Tesla.

A tactical unit from Stockholm is currently preparing to storm Lars Grind's home.

Joona first met the commander of the unit, Thor, years ago – in another life – during the search for Jurek Walter in an abandoned house more than fifty kilometres away.

Back then, Thor was dangerously over-confident, and Joona worries that he might not take the threat posed by the Widow seriously enough.

A few snowflakes have begun to flash by in the fierce wind, crossing the road horizontally like tiny projectiles.

Joona hears reports that Storm Eyolf has now made landfall in Sweden, wrecking jetties, dragging small boats inland, breaking windows, tearing tiles from roofs and felling thousands of trees.

The rescue services and emergency hospitals have already declared a critical incident, and the Meteorological and Hydrological Institute has issued a nationwide red warning, urging the public to remain indoors.

Across much of northern Sweden, train services have ground to a halt.

Rubbish and twigs fly through the air, and an SUV travelling in the opposite direction swerves in the wind and bumps against the crash barrier.

On the screen of the comms unit, messages pop up announcing that no planes or helicopters are able to take off, and that one coastal road after another is being closed.

Joona tries to reach Hugo for the fifth time, but his call goes straight through to voicemail.

He needs to talk to the teenager, to get him away from the clinic. To tell him to put on his coat and just go.

Joona doesn't want to end up in a situation in which Hugo is with Grind when the raid takes place.

It doesn't seem likely that the doctor would hurt his patient, but they could easily end up in some sort of hostage situation if he panics.

A large spruce branch skids across the tarmac, leaving a trail of cones and needles as it careens to the other side.

The driver in front of Joona loses control of their car and hits the central barrier. The vehicle jolts back and spins around, crossing the hard shoulder and ending up half in the ditch.

As Joona passes, he sees that the driver is on their phone.

He speeds up again as he approaches a wooded area. The trunks of the trees are bending dangerously low, the last dead leaves being torn from their branches.

Joona attempts to call Hugo again, but there is still no answer.

Something thuds against the side window.

A powerful gust of wind barrels across the fields, pulling up clumps of grass. The bushes are practically flat against the ground, and Joona watches as a hunting stand topples over, the plywood roof flying through the air.

Some of the trees have broken in the middle, and others have fallen with their roots still intact, churning up dark earth and rocks.

Up ahead, two tall pines crash down over the road, breaking the guard cable.

Joona brakes hard, and the back of his car sways from side to side for a moment until the vehicle comes to a halt.

Debris clatters against the side doors.

He reverses towards the ditch, turns around and starts driving in the wrong direction.

He can take the E18 back towards Stockholm, he thinks, then try the 267 to Uppsala.

The driving snow is getting heavier and heavier.

The storm is battering the row of high-voltage transmission towers in the field beside the road, and the arm at the top of one of them buckles and breaks, swinging through the air and completely taking out the next tower.

Joona sees a car approaching, and he sounds the horn and flashes his headlights, pulling out onto the hard shoulder with two wheels and speeding past it with just inches to spare.

75

Thor and his partner Nolan are standing behind their black van in a residential area on the outskirts of Uppsala.

The rest of the tactical unit is currently getting into position, climbing over the low white fence at the edge of Lars Grind's property.

The operatives have familiarised themselves with pictures of the suspected perpetrator – a man who, with nothing but an axe, has killed two armed officers and at least nine civilians – and every member of the unit is wearing a bulletproof vest, breathing mask and helmet.

Thor slots the curved magazine into his automatic rifle and pushes the charging handle and safety catch forward with his thumb.

He has an anxious lump he just can't shift in his throat.

Leaves and debris blow through the air with the swirling snowflakes, and the fierce gusts of wind push branches, broken mailboxes and fallen bicycles along the street.

The flagpoles creak as they bend.

In a garden nearby, a string of Christmas lights has come loose, and is whipping around a tree.

Once everyone is in position, Thor and his partner walk down the paved path to the front door with their guns lowered.

The house is dark.

The storm tugs at the trees and bushes, and one of the men has to duck as a red plastic sledge blows over the fence.

Thor glances down at his watch and gives the order. His men break three windows and toss tear gas canisters inside.

They force the door at the rear of the property while Thor does the same at the front.

Nolan heads in first, with his rifle raised.

Thor follows him in, and their tactical lights sweep through the thick tear gas, over the walls and the coats hanging on hooks, flashing in a mirror.

On Saturday, his wife Kristina left the house wearing nothing but a pink camisole. He realised she must have taken too much of her medication when he spotted her through the kitchen window, feet bright red from the cold, plasters on both knees and dark pubic hair bared for all to see. She got into the car and reversed straight into the hedge, where she got stuck.

By the time he got to her, she had thrown up all over herself, and the white froth from the partially broken-down pills was clinging to the corners of her mouth.

He got her back into the house, and she started rambling incoherently about an old man who suffocated himself with a dildo. Repeating that there is a crackling grey force beneath all staircases, trying to make weak people stop breathing.

Once the ambulance had taken her away, Thor slumped down on the unmade bed and cried in a way he hadn't since he was a boy.

Nolan clears the toilet to the left.

Thor steps over a pair of black rubber boots on the brown-tiled floor and makes his way through to the kitchen, quickly swinging around to one side as Nolan moves past him and checks the other.

The knives gleam in the light from their rifles.

Thor finds himself staring at the reflection of the kitchen in the dark window: Nolan turning without a sound and being swallowed up by the black doorway.

A small blob of gun grease glistens on the barrel of his rifle.

Thor licks his lips, turns around and thinks about the fact that Kristina's frightened ideas often revolve around the underside of staircases.

She has told him about the two young boys who were found suffocated when she was a girl. They were sitting opposite each other beneath a staircase at the end of a bridge, their mouths and throats packed with clay.

He hears the heavy footsteps of the rest of his team, and he follows Nolan into a smoky living room, secures the right-hand side and sees tactical beams sweeping past the stairs to the floor above.

The shadows from the spindles spread like fingers on the wall, and shards of glass from one of the broken windows glitter on the blue carpet.

For a few seconds, in the smoke drifting through the house and the shafts of lights cutting through the darkness, Thor feels as though he has slipped into some kind of alternate reality.

Everything becomes hollow and echoing.

The wooden floor beneath the rug creaks as he moves forward.

On a shelf, gaudy souvenirs cast sloping shadows against the wall.

The door of a sideboard slowly swings open.

Thor tries to swallow his anxiety as he makes his way over to the stairs.

He hears a metallic thud underfoot, as though he has just stepped on a metal hatch or the floor of a construction lift.

Nolan shouts something from behind his mask.

In the corner beneath the stairs, the smoke is twisting like a tornado, a rotating column. Thor swallows, and his mind has just drifted back to Kristina's words about the suffocating forcefield when Nolan runs past him and up the stairs.

As though in a trance, Thor lumbers after him, staring down at the smoke between the steps, the way it is writhing in the corner. He pauses and pokes himself in the mouth, but is dragged back to reality when he hears Nolan fire his Heckler & Koch on the first floor.

Thor breaks into a run, heart pounding. Nolan has just blasted through the lock on the bathroom, kicked the door open and stopped dead.

* * *

The wipers sweep snow and debris from the windscreen as Joona drives at high speed through the dark community, listening to Thor tell him that the raid on Lars Grind's property is complete.

'The place was empty. No sign of anyone,' he says.

Joona asks him to check for hidden rooms or cellar spaces before they head over to the Sleep Lab.

As he speaks, the storm sweeps in from one side with full force, sending a tsunami of snow surging across the road.

Joona can see almost nothing but white, and he slows to a crawl.

The blizzard completely envelops the car, clogging up the windows on the left-hand side in just a matter of seconds.

Joona's thoughts drift back to what Hugo said while he was under hypnosis for the first time: that it was both high summer and darkest midwinter at the campsite.

Snow was falling on the parasols and the sunbathers.

Erik latched onto the brief moment at the rear of the caravan, then began to erase the nightmare from the things the teenager had really seen.

During the second session, Hugo described the killer chopping off both of the victim's feet, something that hadn't happened in reality.

It wasn't until the third attempt that they managed to almost completely bypass the nightmare, and Hugo was able to see the real victim with the straggly dyed hair.

This time, his description was a perfect match for Åhlén's forensic report: the attack had begun with a blow to the head, followed by the severing of one leg – in the middle of the thigh. After that, the victim was beheaded, and the killer got to work dismembering him.

In the white chaos, hazy grey shapes start to emerge. Optical illusions of giants getting to their feet and lashing out around their surroundings.

A powerful gust pushes the car to the side, making it shake as the tyres hit the rumble strips at the edge of the road.

Joona thinks back to the second session, when Hugo stepped up onto a breezeblock behind the caravan. Erik worked methodically to refine that memory, enabling him to peer inside while still blending reality with nightmare.

Hugo described the victim lying on his back, which he had been, but in the dream version both of his feet had been severed. The skeleton man carved the start of an arrow onto his torso, just as someone had in reality, then hacked at the victim's face with his axe.

Joona tries switching to his fog lights, and the swirling snow globe up ahead does look a little different, but it is hard to tell whether it really improves his visibility.

His thoughts turn to the incredibly precise nature of Hugo's dreams. The parquet floor, the blood running along a brass edging strip, the broken vase and the lamp with a snakeskin shade.

With increasing anxiety, Hugo described the chain of events leading up to the fatal blow – including the blood that sprayed across the window.

The wheel jolts in Joona's hands, and the hairs on the back of his neck stand on end as he realises how it all fits together.

The pieces of the puzzle fall into place, forming a perfect picture.

Joona is convinced he has the answer, but he calls the warden at Hall Prison and asks to speak to Gerald Pedersen, explaining that it is urgent.

The serial killer they are hunting is incredibly dangerous, no doubt about that. In addition to his seven intended victims, he has also killed two witnesses and two police officers.

Petrus Lyth was taken out with an axe blow to the back of the head, like a bull. Danny Imani was beheaded while he was on his knees.

76

Snow and debris whirl through Ultuna, over the fields and roads, between the university buildings and industrial units.

The wind sounds like a jet engine.

The tall fence around the dark Sleep Lab is clogged with snow, making it look like a bumpy white wall.

Two black vans are parked on the street outside.

During the drive from Uppsala, as his eyes recovered from the tear gas, Thor reminded his team that it is not OK to *shoot* the lock out of a door.

He is the last to get out of the van, and the snow immediately peppers his grey-flecked beard. He turns his back to the wind and walks over to his team behind the other van.

In the deserted building site next door, a crane has blown over, crushing a loader.

'Listen up,' Thor says quietly. 'There really aren't enough of us for this, given the size of the place, but the comms systems are all down because of the storm . . . That means no backup, but we're here now and we have a job to do before we can head home and give our boys and girls a squeeze.'

The plan is to enter the lab from two sides simultaneously, storming the main door and the staff entrance, searching every room, finding the suspected killer and arresting him. Considering there are patients and researchers inside, they will need to make it clear that they are police officers, and should only use tear gas or stun grenades if they have no other option.

'This fucking weather,' Nolan mutters as he makes his way over to the fence with a pair of bolt cutters.

'There's no such thing was bad weather, just bad clothing,' two of the operatives retort in unison.

Nolan cuts a large hole in the fence, bends back the sharp edges and uses cable ties to hold it open.

Thor turns on the light on his helmet and decides that he probably needs to talk to someone about the impact Kristina's problems are having on him, eating away at his sense of calm and making him see things that aren't there.

'Wouldn't it have been easier just to shoot a hole in it?' one of the men jokes as he ducks through the opening.

Thor exchanges a look with Nolan and points out their approach.

Four men from the team make their way over to the main entrance while Thor and Nolan run across to the staff door.

There is an ominous groaning sound as the wind tugs at the metal roof.

The beam from Thor's helmet light illuminates Nolan's back, making his rectangular reflector badge flash in the darkness.

They round a concrete pillar and continue towards the carport, where four cars are parked beneath the flat rain cover.

A few pieces of white plastic garden furniture skid across the ground.

There is so much snow on Thor's visor that he has to stop and take it off before he can continue, squinting up ahead.

It feels as though he is in some sort of dream world, a pale chaos twisting in all directions, changing speed and causing the laws of gravity to stop working.

The powerful gusts of wind slam against the building, making the snow swirl upwards.

Nolan continues towards the first car.

The drifting flakes have blown in beneath the rain cover, piling up against the wall of the building like a wave ready to break.

Thor feels feverish, and realises that he has begun to fixate on irrelevant details.

He wipes the snow out of his eyes and follows his colleague.

On the ground by a red car, there is a dead magpie.

Nolan runs over to the concrete loading dock and up the steel steps, pausing by the door and taking out an angle grinder.

Thor's back is sweaty, and he feels a sudden rush of fear that someone is about to charge towards him through the haze.

With a whimper, he turns around and raises his rifle.

He hears a loud scraping, screeching sound, and sees sparks flying from the angle grinder, scattering across the loading dock.

Thor lowers his rifle and takes his finger from the trigger. His torchlight bounces off the cars.

Peering into the darkness beneath the steps, he is convinced he can see a black snake curling up.

He forces himself to look away, absent-mindedly wandering over to one of the cars and studying the pretty lace-like frost on the windscreen.

Behind him, pieces of hinge clatter to the concrete.

In the flickering light from the angle grinder, Thor notices a number of footprints on the ground around the car parked at the far end of the port, left by shoes with a separate big toe, like some sort of foot mitten.

The registration plate gleams.

It is Lars Grind's Tesla.

He raises his gun and slowly moves forward.

Through the side window, he can see a figure in the driver's seat. A bald head, throat, shoulders.

A wave of adrenaline surges through him.

It feels as though he is pulsing, like a metal lampshade on an unearthed lamp.

He swallows hard, takes aim at the person behind the wheel and curls a trembling finger around the trigger as he slowly inches closer.

The beam of light from his helmet illuminates the inside of the car.

Thor stops.

Lars Grind is slumped back in the seat with his eyes closed.

His face is the colour of ash, and there are ice crystals on his eyebrows.

Thor opens the door, takes a step back and re-aims his gun at Grind.

After a moment, he moves forward, clamps his right hand beneath his left arm and pulls off his glove. He then reaches inside and, though he already knows the doctor is dead, presses his fingers to his cold throat.

* * *

The metro clanks out of a bend and speeds up. Hugo is almost alone in the carriage, and he feels the soft jolts travel through him.

The woman sitting opposite him looks weary, a couple of bulging Ikea bags by her feet.

Through the reflections in the window, Hugo has also noticed the young man a few rows back, his face hidden beneath the hood of his coat. He has his arms folded as if he is cold, and his thin, pale hands look as though they have no flesh on them.

Hugo sat with Svanhildur for an hour while he waited for Lars Grind to come back, then decided he could do without his medication and left the clinic.

He caught a bus to Uppsala, watching the trees shake and branches break as they drove along the country roads.

Outside the station building, rubbish sailed across the square and around the fountain. The big Christmas tree had blown over, and the flags had all been torn from their poles.

By the time his train was approaching Stockholm, the snow had started coming down heavily, and there were repeated announcements about delays and cancellations.

Hugo headed straight down to the metro and jumped on a red line train to Norsborg.

The young man had nipped into the carriage just as the doors were closing.

Above him now, the lights flicker.

Hugo checks his phone and sees that Lars Grind has sent his records as a PDF file, accompanied by a brief message.

Dear Hugo,

I wanted to apologise and say that you're doing the right thing by reporting me to the Health and Social Care Inspectorate. There is no doubt that I've pushed certain ethical boundaries, largely due to a sense of urgency which – ironically enough – stems from not having had time to check my prostate.

I desperately wanted to leave a lasting legacy, something that could help the next generation of researchers find answers to the big questions.

You have been like a son to me.

My fondest regards,
Lars

Hugo tries to call the doctor, but his phone seems to be switched off. Instead, he gazes out into the blizzard with a deep knot of anxiety in the pit of his stomach.

After a moment, he sighs and starts reading his journal, beginning when he visited the lab for the first time at just six years old.

Behind him, the young man whispers agitatedly to himself.

The train has just passed Liljeholmen when it slows down and stops in the middle of a tunnel. Over the speaker system, the driver announces that there has been a power cut. They have switched over to battery power, and will be able to reach the next station, but no further.

The train will terminate at Aspudden, and everyone will have to leave. Information about rail replacement buses will be provided at the next station.

77

The storm is howling outside, tugging at the eaves and roaring in the chimneys. Snow swirls past in the darkness on the other side of the window.

Agneta is at the PC in Bernard's office, typing up her notes following the latest hypnosis session.

She adds details from memory, makes tweaks to certain aspects and then starts comparing the session with the previous two, noting how, little by little, Erik Maria Bark managed to coax out Hugo's memories.

The lamp beside her flickers, but it doesn't go out.

Bernard put in a large order of books about serial killers, police work and profiling a few days ago, and is currently reading in the library downstairs.

They worked together to tidy up his office following the break-in, straightening the furniture, sweeping up the splintered wood and vacuuming the broken glass. The papers that had been scattered across the floor are in a moving box for the time being, until they can find a moment to sort through them properly.

Bernard carried the damaged door from his Järvsö cabinet down to the hallway, and is planning to send it off for repair.

Agneta turns the page in her notepad, skims through her notes on Joona's description of the killer's modus operandi – the arrows carved into the victim's bodies and the chaotic dismemberment process – and has just started typing when the desk lamp goes out, she hears a click, and the computer screen goes black.

The fan stops whirring.

She gets up and squints out of the window.

It must be a pretty big outage, because all she can see is darkness.

There are no lights on the other side of the water.

With a sigh, she slumps down onto the chair and stares at the computer screen.

She hears footsteps on the stairs, and a flickering light appears in the doorway.

Bernard is singing an old Christmas tune as he comes into the room with a candle in a cast-iron chamberstick.

The soft, swaying glow fills the office as he sets the candle down on the desk.

'It doesn't matter how many weather reports or warnings you hear, it always comes as a surprise when the power goes out,' he says with a smile.

'I was busy writing,' she says, trailing a finger over the keyboard. 'Hope we haven't lost too much material.'

'I know. I'll make a few more notes before I come down, just to be on the safe side,' she says, turning to a clean page in her pad.

A sudden gust of wind makes the roof trusses creak and hurls snow at the window. It feels as though the storm is tugging at the house, trying to test how sturdy it is. One of the brackets on the gutter breaks, and a section of pipe swings up and hits the weather vane.

'This gale,' Bernard says quietly.

'It's mad.'

'I'm a bit worried about Hugo. He said he was planning to come home today.'

'Let's just hope he doesn't head out in this,' she replies, checking her phone.

The network is still down, and not even the emergency number seems to be working.

The section of gutter cracks and comes loose, clattering away over the roof.

'I'll get a fire going in the stove to keep the bedroom nice and warm,' says Bernard. 'And we'll probably have to change our dinner plans unless the power comes back on.'

A couple of roof tiles tumble to the frozen lawn, shattering on impact.

'We could always grill some sausages on the fire,' she suggests.

'Yes, very cosy. I'll go and make some potato salad.'

Bernard uses the torch on his phone to light his way as he heads back down the stairs.

The storm whistles around the corners of the house, making the windows rattle worryingly.

The flame sways, and Agneta notices something catch the light inside the Järvsö cabinet. It almost looks like a small, floating halo.

She gets up, grabs her phone and shines it in on the middle shelf.

At the very back, there is a small loop of darkened iron wedged between the edge of the shelf and the backboard.

Agneta reaches inside. Whatever it is seems to be stuck at first, but when she wiggles it to one side she hears a soft click and sees a section of shelf pop up slightly.

She pulls on the loop, and the lid of a shallow hidden compartment opens.

The smell of old wood fills the air.

Inside the compartment, there is a dark cardboard folder with a black band around it.

Agneta pushes back the urge to shout for Bernard when she realises that the folder might contain more letters from Hugo's mother. Letters that he – for whatever reason – has chosen to hide.

She takes the folder over to the desk, sits down and loosens the band held in place by a small silver clip in the shape of a fleur-de-lys.

Bernard's report card from Year 9 is on top of the pile, along with a swimming certificate and a class photograph from Year 1.

Agneta holds it up to the candle.

In the picture, young Bernard is wearing a brown-and-black-striped polo shirt. He is a skinny little thing, with a plaster on the bridge of his nose and messy hair. Oblivious to the camera, he is laughing at a taller boy, who is pulling a funny face by pushing his tongue against the inside of his lower lip.

Agneta flicks through documents about foster home placements, football diplomas, letters of reference from summer jobs and high school exam results, until she reaches an old colour photograph with dog-eared corners and a diagonal crease across the middle.

A strange sensation takes hold of her as she holds it up to the light.

In the image, a blonde woman in a dirty vest, jeans and a pair of work gloves is standing outside a workshop. She looks to be around thirty, with a resolute expression on her face and piercing eyes, and is holding a heavy wrench in her slim, muscular arms.

Behind her, on the wall of the run-down shed, there is a red neon arrow bearing the words SERVICE – FORD TRACTOR.

On the back of the photo, someone has written 'My poor mum' in black ink.

The next picture is a wedding photograph. It features the same woman, smiling this time, in a white bridal gown. She is standing beside a tall man with a black moustache in a slim-fitting dress coat.

Agneta gasps when she sees the next picture, adrenaline flooding through her veins.

In it, Bernard is around ten, standing on a pebbly beach beneath a pale sky. He is wearing a pair of swimming trunks and black flippers.

He looks cold, his shoulders hunched.

On his wiry torso, he has an arrow-shaped scar, bumpy and red, stretching from his collarbone to his navel.

The same scar she has felt beneath the hairs on his chest.

She hears footsteps on the stairs up to the attic and starts gathering everything back into a pile with shaking hands, catching a quick glimpse of a number of self-portraits drawn by a child.

A boy in floods of tears, a boy holding a black balloon, a boy with an angry dog – all with the same downward arrow on their bodies.

A boy in a coffin, a boy on a train track, and then nothing but arrows. Hundreds and hundreds of red arrows, filling sheet after sheet of paper.

Agneta closes the folder and puts it back into the hidden compartment. She shuts the lid, hears the latch click, and hurries back over to the desk.

Her heart is racing.

The flame of the candle tilts anxiously in the draught from her movements.

Bernard comes into the office, the smell of woodsmoke clinging to his clothes.

'I was starting to think you must have dozed off up here,' he says.

'No, I . . .'

She trails off, panicking as she remembers that all of the victims had incomplete arrows carved into their torsos – just as Bernard had as a child. Like he still has.

'Hello?' He smiles.

'Did you manage to get the fire going?' she asks, conscious that she has broken out in a cold sweat.

'Of course.'

'Great.'

'You seem jittery.'

'Do I?'

'What's on your mind?'

'I don't know. Nothing.'

'Maybe it's just this apocalyptic storm?' he says.

'Mmm, maybe.'

Agneta desperately tries to come up with some sort of rational explanation for what she just saw. Could he be an early victim? Was he part of some sort of weird cult as a child?

But as terrifying and emotionally impossible as it is, there seems to be only one logical conclusion: that Bernard is, in some way, involved in the murders.

She doesn't even need to think back to know that she can't give him an alibi for any of them.

The night one of the victims was slaughtered at the campsite, she had taken a sleeping pill and was out for the count. And on the day of the murder at the tennis club, Bernard had headed into the city for dinner with his Czech publisher.

Agneta doesn't want to believe this. It makes no sense. Why has he been talking about writing a book with her? Why has he been trying to help the police?

In order to gain access to the case and remain one step ahead, she thinks.

'Do you think Hugo will agree to any more hypnosis?' Bernard asks, making a strange swooping movement with one arm.

'No, he . . .'

The flame flickers, causing shadows to dance across the wall.

Agneta looks down and realises that the elastic band with the little silver clasp is still lying on the desk.

'You don't think so?'

'I'm not sure,' she replies, looking away. 'It made him so anxious, both during the session and after, but . . . but he also wants to help the police. And you, with the book.'

'Maybe I should have a chat with him,' Bernard says with an unfamiliar softness to his voice.

'Mmm, maybe.'

Agneta can hear her blood pounding in her ears as she reaches for her notepad, scribbles something in it and then puts it down on top of the elastic band.

'Just to tell him that he's done enough, that he shouldn't feel like he has to do any more,' Bernard continues. 'That he's already gone above and beyond.'

Every one of Agneta's senses is on high alert, and from the slight twitch beneath Bernard's eye she realises she must be acting strangely. She needs to continue the conversation as she would have prior to her terrible discovery.

'Yes, he has,' she says, struggling to keep her voice steady. 'But . . . I mean, he *is* a key figure in the investigation, whether he likes it or not.'

'From our point of view, and the book's, it would be incredible if Hugo's testimony helped stop the killer.'

'It'll be great either way,' she says softly.

Agneta meets Bernard's eye. She has no idea whether he noticed the elastic band on the desk before she hid it.

'The best thing would be if we managed to find the killer before the police,' he says.

'True . . . but I don't think that's something we should be aiming for . . . We should just help them as best we can.'

'So what are you thinking? Who is our killer?'

'I don't know.'

'But what does your gut tell you?' he asks, lifting her notepad slightly.

'Nothing . . . yet,' she replies.

He is toying with her, she thinks. She needs to get away.

'It's just that I've had the sense you're getting close to solving the puzzle,' he says, looking her straight in the eye.

'There are still far too many missing pieces for that, I think,' she says, trying to make herself smile.

'Who knows?' he says, dropping the book.

Agneta might not have the full picture, but she knows that Bernard is involved in the awful murders.

Perhaps he acted alone.

Perhaps he was the one who killed all those people with an axe. Who beheaded, dismembered and carved arrows into their flesh.

Who killed men and women, witnesses and police officers.

'Shall we go downstairs?' he asks, glancing into the empty Järvsö cabinet.

'Let's,' she replies, getting up.

Agneta meets his eye, and it is as though she can see the cogs turning in his mind, trying to work out whether his cover has been blown. She feels like a panicked wasp inside a crushed nest when he smiles suddenly and announces that he is going to open a bottle of wine.

With a sinking feeling, Agneta realises that he wouldn't hesitate to kill her if he knew what she now knows about him.

78

Bernard reaches for the candle and cups his hand around the flame as he makes his way down the stairs.

Agneta can feel her legs shaking as she follows him.

She is thinking about his drawings of boys with arrows on their chests, the swarm of red arrows raining down from the sky.

The stairs creak beneath her feet.

She finds a pack of beta blockers in her back pocket, and she quietly pops out one of the pills, turns her head and swallows it dry.

Their bedroom is warm and filled with the comforting scent of burning birch. The glow from the flames makes it look as though the walls are pulsing softly.

Instinct is screaming at Agneta to run, to flee down the stairs, through the hall and out into the storm, but she also knows she needs to tread carefully. She can't afford to show a shred of fear while she waits for her moment: after he goes to sleep or takes a bath.

Bernard pours two glasses of wine and hands one of them to her. She has to grip it with both hands to stop the dark red liquid from shaking too much.

'Cheers, my love,' he says.

'Cheers,' she replies with a smile, trying to endure him stroking her arm.

She sips her wine and puts the glass down on the bedside table, suddenly remembering the faint pencil arrow on the wall above their bed, behind the Fontana painting.

She had completely forgotten about it until now.

Bernard pulls an armchair over to the woodburner and sits down on the footstool, gazing into the flames.

'Sit down.'

He swirls the wine in his glass and seems a little more relaxed than earlier, his hand resting on her thigh for a moment once she is sitting in the chair.

Agneta feels the heat on her face and tries to avoid looking at the little axe in the wood basket, the one he uses to split logs.

'What is it about mankind and fire?' he asks without looking up. 'I mean, we worship it, but we're also afraid of it . . .'

'Mmm.'

How could she have failed to notice anything suspicious all this time? Is it because she simply looked away, chose not to see what was so obvious?

No, he must have somewhere secret that he goes.

Lars Grind's industrial unit, she realises. The one with the big silo. Bernard used to drive over there from time to time, when he needed peace and quiet to write. She remembers that she and Hugo went out with him once, the last time, to collect his things.

'What do you think?' he asks.

'About what?'

'Fire.'

'Oh, I don't know . . . I used to love going to the spring bonfires when I was little,' she says, aware that fear has made her voice a little shriller than usual. 'My friends and I cycled from party to party, eating sweets and throwing firecrackers.'

'For me, my whole childhood – at least until the age of ten or so – is like a different world. Some kind of strange film,' Bernard says. 'I can't quite believe that boy is the same person sitting here with you now. There are still fragments of him in me, of course – the taste of blood in his mouth, the way he gritted his teeth to stop himself from sobbing in fear, but . . .'

Agneta wonders if Bernard is trying to work out whether she saw the picture of him on the pebbly beach.

She feels guilty for having let him pull the wool over her eyes, for not having worked it out sooner. Bernard has never been violent towards her, not once, but he does have a strong sense of justice, and has always stood on the side of children.

'I think it probably varies from person to person,' she replies. 'I feel like I have a pretty strong sense of who I was then . . . starting from when I was around five, maybe.'

'I know, but I never talk about my childhood . . . And you never ask.'

'I have asked, but I've always had the sense that you don't want to talk about it.'

'What sense would that be, Agneta?' he asks, a new sharpness to his voice.

'It's just something I felt,' she replies, swallowing hard.

With a rising sense of panic, Agneta realises that Bernard must have noticed the elastic band on the desk.

'Do you have any idea why I've never shared all my happy childhood memories with you?'

'You mentioned a bus accident.'

'Yes, a little accident that ended with my mother taking her own life right in front of me,' he says in a neutral tone.

'My God . . .'

'With an axe.' He smiles.

Agneta finds herself thinking about Bernard's scar, that it has always been hidden beneath his chest hair since she first met him. She knows exactly how it feels beneath her fingertips.

She also knows she asked him about it once, at the start of their relationship, and that he said he was in a bus accident as a child.

But that wasn't true.

'Fire is the serial killer's element,' Bernard says, more to himself than anything. 'He burns and spreads like a forest fire unless someone stops him.'

He gets up, refills his wineglass and gazes out into the darkness on the other side of the window before sitting down again.

Agneta knows that she needs to get away from him, no matter the cost, before his rain of red arrows hits her.

'Shall I go and get some more wood?' she asks, as naturally as she can.

'We've got enough here.'

'Not to last until morning,' she says, suddenly queasy.

'We'll see.'

The wind rumbles in the chimney, and the light from the fire flickers over the floor lamp with the grey snakeskin shade.

Bernard dips a finger into his wine and absentmindedly draws a faint line on the table.

'What do you think about the Widow? Are we really looking for a woman?' he asks, taking a sip.

'Almost all serial killers are men,' she replies, hiding her trembling lips behind her hand until she manages to compose herself.

'Loners.'

'Antisocial.'

'Like authors,' he points out with a strange smile.

'No.' She smiles back.

'With a loveless, or violent upbringing,' he continues.

'Torturing animals used to be one of the traits, but . . .'

'I know, who *hasn't* tortured an animal or two? I'm kidding, of course, but I just read the report from the latest FBI convention, and they've taken a step back from the whole bed-wetting, animal-torturing, pyromaniac angle.'

'Mmm, to avoid inadvertently ruling anyone out,' she says with a nod.

A sudden gust dampens the fire for a moment. The windows rattle, and a branch breaks with a loud crack outside.

'Do you think it was the Widow who came over here? To stop Hugo? Who hit me and took the gold and cash to make it look like a break-in?'

'Or maybe it was just a break-in.'

'But if it was the killer, she might come back.'

'Don't say that,' Agneta whispers.

'It's not like we can call the police now.'

'Stop.'

The blizzard is howling around the house with such force that it almost feels like the wind might pick it up and carry it away, like a carousel in a tornado.

'No phone, no internet. Not even any emergency calls,' Bernard says with a smile.

'Could we stop talking about this?' she begs him, eyes welling up.

'Sorry, I just can't help myself.'

'Very funny,' she mumbles.

'You trust me, don't you?' he teases her, putting on a creepy voice.

'Now you're just *trying* to make me uncomfortable.'

'Are you really scared?'

'No, I'm not. It's just tough . . . with the break-in and the fact that Hugo was named in the press . . .'

'And this storm, which is forecast to last several days,' Bernard says, dipping his finger into the wine and using it to complete an arrow pointing straight at her on the table.

79

The road is blanketed in snow, muffling the sound of Joona's tyres as he drives through one dark community after another following the power cut.

He tries to reach Hugo and Agneta again, but the phone network is still down. Even the police comms system stopped working an hour ago. The backup reserve is meant to last seven days in a situation like this, but the Tetranät base stations all seem to have been knocked out, too, probably because of fallen masts.

Despite the stress bubbling inside him, Joona knows he can't drive any faster. He passes an abandoned bus at the side of the road, and a second later it is gone, swallowed up by the swirling white.

When the blizzard rolled in over the fields and meadows, enveloping his car, his mind was cast back to Hugo's hypnosis sessions, to the nightmare-addled second attempt and the stripped-back third.

Just like that, it all seemed so clear.

Heart racing with adrenaline, the thought that he deserved one of his chocolate coins flashed through his head.

At first, Hugo was looking in through a window with multiple panes of glass, then a window with rounded corners and a piece of trim hanging loose at the bottom edge.

But it wasn't a case of nightmare versus reality. In actual fact, Hugo has witnessed two separate murders.

The first took place in his own home, upstairs in the big house, in the main bedroom with its parquet floor, brass transition strip and a lamp with a shade made from faux snakeskin.

Hugo saw his father murder a man through the door in the hallway.

Just to be on the safe side, Joona called Hall Prison and asked to speak to Gerald Pedersen. The inmate was happy to hear from him, telling Joona that he had been contacted by a lawyer who explained that while the process of being released may take time, it is essentially nothing but a formality.

'When we met, you told me that your wife had been in touch with a psychologist,' Joona said.

'Yes . . .'

'Did you mean the relationship column in *Expressen*?'

'That's the one.'

'Bernard Sand?'

'Yes.'

Bernard has used his wildly popular advice column to find his victims. He receives hundreds of letters from people – letters that are revealing, honest and conceited. His readers tell him all about their crises, their problems, their fears and anxieties, not realising that in doing so, they are making themselves and their families targets.

His rage seems to have been triggered by what he sees as betrayal where children are concerned – particularly when they are more vulnerable as a result of illness or other circumstances.

A branch on the road clatters against the underside of Joona's car.

Despite the weak GPS signal on the satnav, the darkness and the snow-covered road signs, he realises he is approaching the bridge to Stäket, high above a narrow inlet of Lake Mälaren.

Visibility is close to zero, but in the brief moments when the storm seems to pause for breath, he catches glimpses of the landscape around him.

The blanket of snow on the road is getting deeper and deeper, covering the tyre tracks from the cars up ahead. Time and time again, he tries to parry the powerful gusts of wind and the slight skids to the side as the snow gives way beneath his car.

Joona needs to get to Bernard Sand's house.

As he drives out onto the bridge, he thinks that it won't be long until Agneta works it out. She is extremely smart and has all of the pieces of the puzzle on the table in front of her.

The moment she puts two and two together, she will be in great danger. In addition to his carefully chosen victims, Bernard has already killed four people who got in his way.

The snow is barrelling down the inlet like a raging river, the wind so powerful that the entire bridge is shaking.

Up ahead, Joona can see five red lights, blinking like lanterns in the storm.

There has been an accident.

Slowing down, he gets his first glimpse of the crash on the bridge. A lorry is on its side, its windscreen cracked and the cab wedged up against the barrier on the wrong side of the road.

Joona drives towards it at a crawl.

The huge trailer is already half-buried beneath the snow.

The dolly is still the right way up, its axel warped.

A lamppost has fallen to the ground, and several cars have collided on both sides of the lorry.

The bridge is completely blocked.

Joona comes to a halt and attempts to back up, but has to stop almost immediately when another car appears behind him. Its dipped headlights slow, and there is a muffled thud. A third car has driven into the back of it, causing its lights to shake and veer sharply to one side. The bonnet breaks through the fibreglass railing and hits the side panel.

Joona gets out of the car and realises there is a line of traffic behind him, stretching right back to the end of the bridge.

He runs over to the cars on the other side of the lorry. Despite having crashed, none of the vehicles seems too badly damaged.

A woman in a padded jacket is standing by one of the cars with a torch, talking to the man behind the wheel.

Joona walks over to her and asks her what is happening. His hair blows in all directions, the wind tugging at his clothes. The woman blinks repeatedly to keep the snow out of her eyes as she tells him that no one is seriously injured. Joona asks her to make sure no one is trapped in any of the cars, then to get everyone to walk over to Stäket.

'Stick to the right and head to the Sisters of Saint Elizabeth.'

Joona runs past the damaged cars to the other side of the bridge. He scrambles down the slope by the abutment and continues along a narrow road, sheltered from the worst of the storm.

He clambers over fallen trees, passing houses with broken roofs and pieces of garden furniture and barbecues.

A trampoline has taken down the power lines, and is caught in the scrub at the side of the road.

Joona makes his way down to a small marina, running past a black pickup outside a small house.

The boats brought ashore for winter have all tipped over, crushing their stands and supports. The ropes tied to frozen water drums are tangled, and the torn tarpaulins are flapping in the wind.

The frothing waves hurl large shards of broken ice ashore.

Very little of the pontoon jetty is still standing.

Joona runs over to two men who are busy trying to haul a large black rigid inflatable boat up a steel ramp with a hand winch.

One of them – a stocky, bearded man in orange overalls, boots and a black hat – has his hands on the side of the boat, keeping it steady on the ramp.

The other, who has a grey ponytail, a black jacket and green trousers with leather patches on the knees, is cranking the winch as fast as he can.

'Go, go!'

'Police!' Joona shouts, holding up his ID.

The man with the ponytail glances in his direction, but doesn't stop. A large wave breaks over the boat, and the man with the beard comes close to losing his balance.

'Control the wire!'

'Listen, I need to borrow this boat,' Joona tells them.

'No chance,' the man with the ponytail mutters.

'It's an emergency.'

'Yeah, for everyone. Come back next summer,' he replies, wiping the snow from his eyes.

'What's going on?' the other man asks, moving closer.

The trunk of a nearby pine breaks and falls onto the clubhouse. Snow cascades from its branches, and broken roof tiles crash to the ground.

'I need to borrow this boat,' Joona repeats.

'Borrow?'

'It's serious; there are lives at stake.'

'Yeah, and who the fuck's gonna pay for it when you wreck my boat? D'you know how much something like this costs?' the man with the beard asks, pointing at Joona.

'It's urgent.'

'D'you think I'm stupid or something?' The man snorts. 'I'm not giving you my fucking RIB. Sorry. Ask someone else.'

Joona pushes the man with the ponytail to one side and releases the brake on the winch. There is a loud whizzing sound as the wire unwinds, and the heavy boat crashes back into the water.

'Hey, what the fuck?!'

'Is the key in the ignition?' asks Joona.

'You are not setting foot in my boat,' the man with the beard snarls, bending down to pick up a spade.

He knocks the snow and ice from the blade on a rock, then adjusts his grip on the shaft.

Joona moves to one side, preventing either of the men from coming up behind him. The boat is floating parallel to the shore, the waves pushing it inwards and the cable straining in the winch.

The bearded man takes a slow step forward, gripping the spade like a baseball bat in both hands. Tiny ice crystals shimmer in his beard, and his eyes are wide. Snow has collected in the folds of his orange overalls.

The man with the ponytail moves round to one side, past the wreckage of an old rowing boat.

'Careful, boys,' Joona warns them.

'People get hurt during storms,' the man with the beard says as he takes aim. 'They disappear.'

'Ronny, just stop,' the other one tells him.

'Fucking pigs.'

Joona steps back and holds up a hand. A ripped tarpaulin flies through the air.

'Let's just stay calm. I promise you'll get your boat back, but—'

'I'll cave your fucking head in,' Ronny snarls.

'If you don't drop that spade, I'm going to break your nose and your shoulder before taking your boat anyway,' says Joona.

Ronny swings the spade at him with a surprising amount of force. Joona ducks back, and the blade passes close to his face. The man loses his footing for a moment, but quickly regains his balance and raises the spade again.

His friend slips in the snow as he tries to get out of the way.

Ronny comes towards Joona again, jabbing the spade in his direction. He takes a quick step, feints a low blow, then swings it towards his head again.

Joona blocks Ronny's arm, twists to one side and jerks his elbow upwards into his nose.

The man's head snaps back, and he drops like a stone.

Joona wraps his arm around Ronny's upper arm, pulls upwards and feels a crack as the bone breaks. The spade swings around, and the edge of the blade grazes Joona's throat, leaving a deep gash.

Ronny lands heavily on his back in the snow.

Joona presses a hand to his neck, conscious that he is bleeding heavily.

The other man has pulled out a hunting knife, and Joona turns to him, taking a step closer.

Ronny gets up on one knee, his arm hanging limply by his side. He roars in pain, spraying blood and saliva into his beard.

80

Hugo almost loses his footing as a gust of wind takes hold of him. He stumbles, slips down a couple of steps and regains his balance, but it feels like he has pulled a muscle in his back.

The snow lashes at his face.

It has taken him almost an hour to walk two kilometres, clambering over fallen trees and ducking to avoid flying debris.

All around him, flagpoles have snapped, and there are broken awnings and solar panels strewn along the street.

When the metro reached Aspudden, there was an announcement telling everyone to leave the train, and the driver locked the doors behind them.

Most people hung around on the platform, but Hugo decided to walk the last few kilometres home, despite all the warnings. He did up the zip on his coat and climbed the stairs. The station doors were broken, and the tiled floor in the ticket hall was buried beneath a thick blanket of snow.

It felt as though he had been hit by a snow cannon as he left the building and headed out onto the dark street.

There was no sign of anyone else out and about.

Hugo is now less than half a kilometre from home, but he has lost all feeling in his face. He hurries along the street, past a fence that seems to have been torn out of the ground outside a large villa. Pink curtains flutter through two broken windows.

He takes cover for a moment against a supporting wall when he sees the cover from a swimming pool careening through the air.

It crashes down onto a car roof nearby with such force that the windows shatter.

The last stretch along Pettersbergsvägen is relatively sheltered, but the tall pines creak as they bend in the wind, and the snow beneath them is full of branches, needles and cones.

In the darkness and the haze, Hugo almost misses his own driveway.

Their green rubbish bins have all blown over.

He picks his way down the slope, battling through the fierce wind blowing in from the lake. He scrapes the inside of his thigh as he clambers over three fallen trees, then runs the last few metres to the door.

His long hair whips around his face.

The ground is littered with broken roof tiles, he notices, and the old maple is groaning.

Hugo fumbles for his keys and opens the door with stiff fingers. He stamps his shoes, hurries inside and locks the door behind him.

Shivering, he brushes the snow from his coat, hangs it up, kicks off his shoes and makes his way down the dark hall towards the kitchen.

The wind is howling in the extractor fan.

He goes through to the library and smells the faint scent of burning wood. His father must have lit a fire in the stove in the bedroom, he thinks.

Hugo climbs the stairs and sees the warm glow in the hallway.

As ever when he reaches the landing, he glances to the left, through the window in the door leading to his old room, before turning right into the main bedroom.

Bernard and Agneta are sitting by the stove, each with a glass of wine. On the sideboard, there is a plate of hotdogs and buns.

'Hugo!' Bernard shouts, getting to his feet.

'The metro stopped at Aspudden, so I had to walk,' he says.

'You were probably lucky; nothing is working,' Bernard says as he comes over to give him a hug. 'My God, you're frozen. Here, sit down by the fire.'

'It's crazy out there.'

'I'm just glad you made it home safely.'

'Hi, Agneta.'

She looks up, nods and gives him an absent smile.

The gale thunders in the chimney, and a sudden downdraught causes sparks to fly inside the stove just as a large amount of snow hits the window.

'Crikey,' says Bernard.

'Have you guys been out?' asks Hugo.

'We're supposed to stay indoors. Come on, sit down.'

Hugo takes a seat on the footstool and holds his hands to the stove. He feels the heat on his face, and his fingers start to tingle as they slowly warm up.

'Would you like a whisky?' asks Bernard.

'Seriously?'

'Special circumstances.'

'I could go for some wine,' Hugo replies.

'Some wine it is, then.' Bernard smiles and pours him a tumbler.

'Thanks.'

'Are you hungry?'

'Starving.'

'Cheers.'

Hugo toasts with his father and tries to meet Agneta's eye, but she is staring at the fire, at the charred wood and flickering embers.

'What do you think? Is it ready for the sausages?'

'Maybe a bit longer?' Hugo replies.

Agneta doesn't speak. She seems lost in thought, absentmindedly scratching at a stain on the arm of her denim shirt.

'You OK, Agneta?' Hugo asks.

'Fine,' she replies, looking him straight in the eye.

'Are you?' Bernard says, giving her a strange smile.

'You two are being really weird. Have you been fighting or something?'

'Fighting? No. It's probably just the storm . . . and because we couldn't get hold of you,' says Bernard.

There is another low rumble inside the chimney. The sound is ominous, like trumpets deep underground. Hugo shuffles back from the stove and feels the cool wine on his lips as he takes a sip from his glass.

'Dad, I know you really like Lars, that you're friends and stuff,' he says. 'But it seems like he's been giving me and some of the other patients meds that actually make us worse, that make us sleepwalk *more*, rather than less . . .'

'He's extremely focused on his research.'

'Yeah, I get that it's all for his research, but it's just so . . . unethical.'

'It's not always an easy line to draw.'

'Would you stop defending him?' Hugo says, both amused and surprised.

'I'm not.'

There is a loud crack outside, followed by a series of heavy noises downstairs.

'God, what was that?' says Hugo.

'Sounded like the maple just fell,' Bernard replies, reaching for the poker.

He jabs at the fire, causing the blackened wood to fall apart.

'I'll go and get more logs,' says Agneta.

'There's no need,' Bernard replies, gripping her wrist.

'For overnight,' she explains, pulling her hand back.

'What's going on, Dad?'

'I don't want her to go out in this weather. I've already brought in all the wood we need; we've got two full baskets in the library.'

Hugo notices that Agneta's face is sweaty.

Bernard spears three hotdogs on skewers with wooden handles.

'I started reading my medical records,' Hugo says. 'You know, from when I was little. It said I had a broken collarbone when I arrived at the lab for the first time. You never told me that.'

'That's right, I'd completely forgotten,' says Bernard. 'You were playing on the rope swing we had back then, and you crashed into the trunk.'

'But I remember I . . .'

Hugo trails off, gazing in at the hotdogs in the stove.

'What? What were you going to say?' Bernard asks, looking up at him with glassy eyes.

81

Joona pushes the RIB up to forty-two knots as he passes Tempeludden, causing frothing white water to spray out behind the two Caterpillar C7 engines.

Other than in the most sheltered bays, the lake is clear of ice, and the surface is the colour of lead.

The bow of the RIB cuts through the tunnel of swirling snow formed by the bright headlights, and the hull slams against the waves.

Back at the marina, the man with the beard had slumped down onto his side, tiny droplets of blood flecking the snow beneath him as he gasped for air. His friend with the ponytail had tossed the knife away when Joona turned to face him.

'I'm taking your boat. Pack his nose with snow and take him to hospital as soon as the storm passes,' Joona told them.

'The keys are in the ignition.'

Before loosening the cable and getting into the RIB, Joona had explained that what was happening was a case of force majeure.

'You or the weather?' the other man had asked.

Joona found a headtorch among the fenders, life jackets and ropes, and he put it on as he swung out onto the water and left the broken jetty behind.

The shaky light from the torch now flashes on the windscreen in front of the steering console, the wipers powerless to keep up with the sheer volume of snow and water crashing against the glass.

Behind him, the two six-cylinder engines roar.

Joona doesn't spot the ice floe in the churning tunnel of light until it is too late, and he sways as the boat hits it with a dull clang.

Mälaren is the third biggest lake in Sweden, stretching from Köping in the west to Stockholm in the east.

Viewed from above, its countless bays, channels, islands and skerries resemble a tangled web, as though a child has blown droplets of watercolour paint across a sheet of paper.

Despite the patchy GPS coverage, Joona tracks his progress using the electronic nautical chart, convinced he has found the best way to reach Bernard's house under the circumstances.

Time could be running out.

Bernard is in an intense phase of killing, displaying near-senseless violence.

He has mercilessly executed witnesses, purely to avoid being caught, and his drive is all-consuming. Nothing seems to be able to stop him.

* * *

Hugo's mind starts to wander as he sits by the hot fire, eating his second hotdog. The sausage is charred on one side, cracked on the other.

Bernard coats his last piece of hotdog in Dijon mustard, pops it in his mouth and helps himself to more potato salad.

Agneta's untouched plate is on the floor beside her armchair. She doesn't look well, with a greyish tinge to her face and beads of sweat glistening at her hairline.

The wind is still howling down the chimney, and there is another loud crack outside as a branch breaks.

Hugo turns to the window and watches the swirling snow. The memory he touched upon a few minutes ago comes back to him: as a child, while sleepwalking, he had climbed out of the window in this room and fallen into the large rhododendron outside. All he really remembers is how upset his father was afterwards, interrogating his mother about what happened, going through the whole thing over and over again and demanding to know why she hadn't reacted to the alarm.

Bernard had made her cry when he said that Hugo could have died.

'You never said what you'd remembered,' Bernard reminds him, tossing his crumpled napkin into the fire.

'Huh?'

'I mentioned the accident on the swing, and you said you remembered.'

'He was only a child,' Agneta speaks up.

'I didn't ask you.'

'Dad, what's going on? Are you drunk or something?' Hugo asks, watching the napkin catch fire and turn black.

'I'm just interested, that's all,' Bernard replies, forcing himself to speak softly.

'I remember falling off the roof and you being mad at Mum,' Hugo says.

'She was supposed to be looking after you. I was away, we'd had motion detectors fitted in your room.'

'It was an accident.'

Bernard's eyes drift to one side, and Hugo follows his line of sight over to the lamp with the grey snakeskin shade.

In the pulsing light from the stove, it almost looks like it is breathing.

Adrenaline courses through Hugo's veins as fragments of the hypnosis session come back to him. He doesn't notice that he has dropped his glass.

In his mind's eye, he is a child again, bathed in pulsing pink light as he stares through the window in the door in the corridor.

His father has fashioned a kind of poncho out of the black shower curtain from the bathroom in the basement, the one with a pattern of skulls and bones.

Hugo's stomach turns, and he swallows hard repeatedly.

Skulls, thigh bones, ribs, knees and fingers.

A tangle of quivering images dart by, racing around a corner and getting lost in the darkness.

Hugo's fingertips are tingling.

He notices his glass on the floor, droplets of wine flecking the pale boards, and he mumbles a quick apology, bends down to pick it up and mops up the wine with his sock.

'You fell off the roof,' says Bernard. 'Is that OK?'

'It wasn't her fault,' Hugo replies.

'Maybe not.'

'I need to use the toilet,' Agneta whispers, getting up on unsteady legs.

'Sit down,' Bernard tells her.

'But I really need—'

'Not now,' he snaps, gripping her wrist again.

'Dad, cut it out.'

'I was away, and Claire was meant to be looking after you. We'd had motion detectors fitted, but you still managed to fall off the roof,' he replies, letting go of Agneta. 'The next time I was supposed to go away, I decided to stay behind instead . . . In the basement.'

'What have you done?' Hugo whispers.

Bernard gets up, grabs the axe from the wood basket and follows Agneta out into the hallway. The bathroom door closes, and the lock clicks.

Hugo forces himself to stand up and slowly turns around. He goes out into the hall and sees his father lurking in the darkness by the bathroom.

Outside, the storm is still raging.

Hugo tiptoes across the worn parquet floor, over the brass edging strip, and gazes towards the door in the hallway behind his father.

He takes in the reflection of his father's back, the axe hidden behind him, and his own silhouette in the bright bedroom doorway.

'What did you do to Mum?' Hugo asks, anxiety writhing in his chest.

'Nothing,' Bernard replies without looking at him. 'I just got the truth out of her.'

'She never went to Canada, did she?' Hugo whispers, overcome by a dizzying sense of surreality.

'Of course she did. You know that.'

'I was sleepwalking, Dad, but I saw everything.'

'You were dreaming. It was just a dream,' Bernard says, turning to look at him.

A sudden jolt, dark as death, drags Hugo back to that moment behind the door as a child. He glances into the bedroom and sees his father's face flecked with red spots, as though he has chickenpox. He sees blood running down the skulls and bones on the shower curtain, dripping from the axe in his father's hand, a severed foot on the floor in front of him.

'I saw you kill a man, right here in the bedroom,' says Hugo, licking his lips.

'You really think I would—'

'What did you do to Mum?'

'This isn't how I wanted it to be.'

'What have you done?'

'You don't understand,' Bernard says with a strange smile. 'I honestly think you'd be dead if I hadn't intervened before—'

'Stop!' Hugo cuts him off.

'I can't stop,' says Bernard, bringing the axe out where Hugo can see it.

For a brief, shuddering moment, the house is completely silent. Any sense of surreality is gone, and sheer panic has taken over, ferociously pulsing through Hugo's chest.

'Dad?' he whispers, taking a step back.

'You know I'd never be able to hurt you, don't you?' Bernard says, looking down at the axe.

'We can work this out, Dad. It's going to be OK.' Hugo rubs his mouth with a shaking hand.

'It's going to be OK.'

'We'll talk to the police, just you and me.'

'Yes . . .'

'You don't need the axe. You're done with all that.'

'But Agneta will never understand.'

'We'll talk to her. It'll be OK. She'll keep quiet for my sake,' says Hugo, conscious that he has begun to tremble all over.

'I don't even think *you* will keep quiet,' Bernard says coldly.

'Of course I—'

'But that . . . No, it's by no means certain, not at all, though it's a choice you have every right to make. I have no intention of letting Agneta stop me, nor the police, nor—'

'Dad, listen to what I—'

'No, *you* listen.'

'OK, I'm listening.'

Hugo's back is drenched in sweat. He has no idea what to do, hasn't quite managed to put all of the pieces together yet, but what he does know is that the murder in the bedroom was real and that it was his father who killed the man in the caravan.

'Bringing a child into this world is a great responsibility, and not one you can just shrug off,' Bernard says, running his free hand through his hair.

'I agree,' Hugo whispers.

'Did you know that my father abandoned my mother and me for a circus girl? Can you believe that? A real-life circus girl from Bulgaria,' he continues with a smile. 'What can I say? I was left all alone with my mother, and that didn't go so well . . . But I survived. Against all odds, I might add.'

'Why don't we go back to the bedroom?'

'You don't understand. This has to be done. It's what's right,' says Bernard, looking down at the axe in his hand again. 'Perhaps I've gone too far, but I was doing it for the children. I almost felt like a superhero at first.'

'Let's—'

'No, hold on, damn it. Let me explain . . . It's all connected. You were so small, sleepwalking,' says Bernard, knocking impatiently on the bathroom door. 'All your mother had to do was take care of you, go to your room when she heard the alarm, make sure you got back into bed and didn't hurt yourself, but she couldn't even manage that. She was too preoccupied.'

'I can see why you were angry.'

'I tried to tell myself that it was a one-off, that she'd learned her lesson. I mean, it was so serious. You really could have died . . . But when she did the same thing again two weeks later, it was like it lit a fire in my belly. It was unbearable. All I knew was that I had to put a stop to it, right there and then,' he says, pointing down at the floor.

'For my sake.'

'For your sake, for mine, for all those who . . . I don't know. I'm not done yet, far from it . . . That fire is still burning brighter than anyone else's,' he says, pounding on the bathroom door.

'Leave Agneta alone.'

'Open the door!' Bernard shouts. 'No one is going to read whatever you write on your phone, surely you must see that? I'll delete whatever statement or little farewell note you've written.'

'I don't want you to talk to her like that,' says Hugo, moving towards his father.

'No,' Bernard sighs, taking a step back.

'What's done is done, Dad, but it's over now,' Hugo continues in a soft tone of voice, positioning himself between Bernard and the bathroom door.

His heart is beating so hard that he can feel it in his neck and nostrils.

The lock clicks, and Agneta opens the door. She steadies herself against the doorframe for a moment, then moves past them into the hallway.

Bernard lifts his head and looks straight at his son.

Agneta's breathing is ragged and shallow as she starts making her way down the stairs to the library.

Hugo holds up both hands and takes a step to one side to block Bernard from following her.

82

Joona chooses the shorter route, on the inside of Lambarön, keeping the boat steady as the swell surges back on itself and following what is left of the channels cleared by the ice breakers prior to the storm.

He turns the wheel and hits a large wave.

The boat becomes airborne for a moment, and the engines rev loudly before the fibreglass hull slams back down and water crashes up over the windscreen.

* * *

Agneta makes her way down the stairs on shaking legs. The beta blocker she took earlier has started to take effect, but her heart is still beating uncomfortably fast. Behind her, she can hear a tearful Hugo trying to convince his father to give up, to put the axe down.

The wind tears around the house.

'Let's just stay here and talk about—'

'You stay,' Bernard barks.

Agneta hears a loud noise upstairs, followed by someone crashing to the floor. She breaks into a run, losing her footing when she reaches the polished floor in the library and landing on her shoulder. Agneta gasps and scrambles up when she hears someone on the stairs, and she staggers out into the hallway, past the kitchen and towards the front door. The frame seems to have buckled slightly, and the door is tilting inwards.

She quickly pulls on her boots and reaches for a coat from the hook before turning the key in the lock. Agneta tries the handle, but the door won't budge, even when she puts all her weight against it. Something must be blocking it from the outside, she realises, possibly the old maple.

'I just want to talk to you!' Bernard shouts from the library.

Agneta turns around and tiptoes through to the kitchen, carefully pulling the door shut behind her. She drops her coat in the process, but doesn't stop to pick it up, hurrying past the dining table to the other door to the library. After pausing to take a deep breath, she heads through into the dark room and hears heavy footsteps down the hallway to the front door.

She should have grabbed one of the knives, she thinks, but it is too late now.

Moving as quietly as she can, she makes her way past the foot of the stairs and has to make a real effort not to scream when she notices a dark figure standing by the fireplace.

It is Hugo, and he is gripping a black poker in one hand.

Bernard tugs at the front door, turns around and meets Agneta's eye.

She and Hugo cross the library and hurry down the hall towards his bedroom and the lounge.

The crystals on the wall sconce jingle as they pass, as though to give them away.

It is hard to see in the darkness.

Bernard sets off after them, practically growling with each breath.

Agneta breaks into a run in her heavy boots.

Hugo pulls her into his room, tosses the poker onto the bed, locks the door and runs over the window to try to open it.

'He screwed it shut after the break-in,' she whispers.

The storm rumbles through the house.

Hugo takes out his phone and uses the weak torch to illuminate his room. The window is completely covered in snow.

Agneta gasps in fear as Bernard turns the handle and starts pounding on the door.

Hugo runs over to the armchair blocking the disused doorway into the lounge and pulls it away from the wall.

The rice-paper lampshade sways in the draught.

The hallway outside is now quiet.

Hugo grabs his phone and turns on the front camera, then gets onto his knees and pushes it beneath the door to the lounge.

On the display, they can see the underside of the china cabinet.

An icy draught blows through the gap.

Holding his long hair back, Hugo tilts his phone as far as he can, enabling him to see a little more of the room on the other side.

There doesn't seem to be anyone there.

Agneta exchanges a look with him, presses her ear to the door to the corridor and listens carefully.

She can't hear a sound.

She gives Hugo a shake of the head.

He tiptoes over to her, gets down onto his knees and repeats the same process with his phone.

On the screen, the bare wood on the bottom of the door becomes visible, followed by the ceiling in the hallway. Right then, Bernard comes into view. He is standing in the gloom by one side of the door with the axe in his hand and a blonde wig on his head.

Hugo has just had time to process what he is seeing when Bernard swings the axe into the door, and he reels back and drops his phone.

Agneta grabs a chair and attempts to wedge it between the handle and the floor.

Hugo runs over to the other door and opens it, but the china cabinet is blocking the passageway.

Bernard has started kicking the bedroom door, and the wood groans with each blow.

Agneta holds the chair steady with one hand and presses the other to the door.

Hugo picks up the poker from the bed and gets down onto the floor.

Bernard kicks the door again, and Agneta feels the power of it shudder through her palm and shoulder.

Lying flat on his back, Hugo has begun to crawl out from under the china cabinet.

Without warning, the head of the axe breaks through the door, and Agneta screams. The blade has left a deep gash on her palm, and she backs away. Blood immediately begins spurting from the wound, and she grabs a T-shirt from the bed and wraps it around her hand.

Bernard swings the axe again, and more of the blade smashes through the wood. It gleams in the light as he works it free, then he yanks it back and kicks the door again.

Hugo's feet disappear beneath the cabinet.

Agneta crosses the room, trying to protect her injured hand as she gets down onto her back. She has to turn her head and press her cheek to the floor to be able to get beneath the cabinet.

Bernard has started hacking at the door again, shards of wood falling into the room.

Agneta pushes her right arm through to the other side and grabs the front of the cabinet, pulling herself out as she tries to find a foothold.

Her breathing is ragged.

There isn't much room, and the cramped space is claustrophobically tight against her ribs.

The floor is freezing cold beneath her.

Her bloody left hand is throbbing.

Hugo grabs her denim shirt and pulls her towards him slightly before losing his grip.

Agneta looks up and sees the ceiling in the lounge.

'Help me,' she whispers between quick breaths. 'I've hurt my hand.'

He tries again, but one of her boots is caught on the back of the cabinet.

Agneta manages to kick them off with a cramping sensation in her calves.

Somewhere in the house, a window breaks.

Hugo lets go and hurries away, out of view.

Agneta tries to push herself the rest of the way through the gap, but her knees knock against the underside of the cabinet.

She hears heavy footsteps approaching.

Turning her head towards the hall, she sees Bernard in the doorway. He is wearing a blonde wig, and his lips are pressed so tightly together that they have turned white.

She uses both hands to pull herself clear of the cabinet, screaming in agony.

Bernard rests the axe on his shoulder for a moment, and has just started walking towards her without a single shred of emotion on his face when Hugo appears in the doorway behind him.

The teenager swings the poker as hard as he can, hitting his father on his back and lower neck with a sickening thud.

Bernard falls headlong and then lies motionless on the floor.

Hugo stares down at him with a hand to his mouth.

Agneta wriggles clear, rolls over onto her stomach and gets to her feet, leaning against the china cabinet to steady herself.

She has bled through the T-shirt around her hand, and the blood has begun dripping down onto her socks.

Bernard's right foot twitches a few times.

Agneta is struggling to think clearly. She is in a great deal of pain, and she looks around the room in astonishment. The storm has torn open the patio doors, and a large amount of snow has blown in over the floor, sofas, coffee table and lamps. Two crows have taken refuge on top of the mahogany bookcase, and the crystal chandelier sways in the wind.

Hugo drops the poker and leans back against the wall with his eyes closed, drying the tears from his cheeks.

Agneta is in shock, blood dripping from her hand. She sways to one side and feels something grip her leg. Looking down, she sees that Bernard has his hand around her ankle. His mouth is bloody.

'Hugo,' she mumbles.

She tries to shake him off, but Bernard's grip is too tight, and she drags him across the floor.

Agneta takes a deep breath and manages to pull her foot free, stumbling slightly and breaking her fall against the snowy sofa.

One of the crows spreads its wings and caws.

Bernard gets onto his knees, spits and reaches for the axe.

As though in a daze, Agneta staggers towards the doors onto the garden. The snow is churning through the air outside, blowing parallel to the ground.

Bernard lets out a low groan and tries to stand up, his bloody wig hanging over his face.

Hugo grips Agneta's arm and guides her out of the house. Moving as quickly as they can, they make their way down the slope in the deep snow.

83

Joona is racing across the open water at a speed of forty knots. Huge waves crash all around him, and the fierce wind throws the foam up into the air.

Snow patters against the windscreen.

The two motors roar and churn up water behind the black boat.

The GPS signal is still weak and patchy, but Joona has memorised the nautical chart and is trying to use the searchlight to orient himself.

He passes frozen inlets, beaches where the diving towers are lying on their sides, wrecked marinas and dark waterfront properties.

Drottningholm Palace isn't visible through the snow, but he knows it must be somewhere up ahead.

Joona swings to port side, cutting across the waves and parrying the worst of the gusts before turning off into a new channel in the ice.

The swell washes back towards him with surprising force, surging over the side of the boat and knocking it off course. The rubber floats on the side of the RIB thud against the edge of the ice before Joona manages to regain control and picks up speed again.

He swerves to avoid a sofa floating in the water, and the broken ice clatters against the bow.

Up ahead, he spots the dark Nockeby Bridge through the blizzard.

* * *

Hugo and Agneta trudge down the slope towards the icy bay in a strange world of darkness and furious power.

The wind tugs at their hair and clothes, making it hard to walk in a straight line.

Snow swirls in from the right, and debris and branches bounce across the ground.

Agneta glances back over her shoulder, but there is no sign of Bernard.

The house is nothing but a looming shadow.

Hugo loses his footing and slips down the slope, leaving Agneta with no choice but to attempt to follow his tracks.

A lifebuoy rolls past her feet, and is swallowed up by the snow and the darkness beyond.

Behind her, she hears Bernard roar.

Agneta knows she is following Hugo, but she still feels confused. Out of nowhere, she starts to worry that she is retracing her own steps, and she is just about to shout when she spots the teenager up ahead.

He is waiting for her, and he wipes the snow from his face, grabs her good hand and pulls her after him.

Agneta's breathing is much too shallow, and she attempts to protect her bloody hand against her body.

She catches a glimpse of the lake house straight ahead, but it quickly vanishes from view.

A sheet of corrugated metal sails through the air, hurtling in the direction of the common land.

Hugo drags her with him.

Agneta feels as though she is no longer in control of her feet and legs.

There is a loud crack as one of the birches snaps and crashes to the ground, branches shaking.

She has lost a lot of blood and knows she won't be able to go much further. Her knees are about to give way beneath her, and all she wants to do is curl up and go to sleep.

When they reach the lake house, they take cover against the wall and squint back up the slope, trying to see through the flurries.

Black shapes emerge from the haze only to disappear again a moment later.

'Come on,' Hugo shouts, pulling her inside.

The wind catches the door and slams it back against the wall, making the little window shatter.

Panting, Agneta slumps down against the wall.

Hugo manages to pull the door shut, muffling the sound of the storm slightly. He gets down onto his knees in front of her and starts brushing snow from her socks.

'We can't stay here,' he says, pushing a pair of tennis shoes onto her feet. 'He'll follow our tracks. He'll find us.'

'I just need to catch my breath.'

'There's no time,' he says, pulling life jackets and fenders out of a large plastic box.

'Give me a few seconds,' Agneta whispers, her eyes on the door.

'We need to get out onto the ice and head for the yellow house,' he says as he rummages for a rope. 'I know them.'

'I'll wait here,' she replies as he ties the rope around her waist and checks the knot.

'We can help each other if we go through the ice.'

Hugo hangs a pair of ice claws around his neck and pulls Agneta back onto her feet, making her groan in pain. As he wraps a blanket around her shoulders, he asks if she is able to stand.

*　*　*

Joona reaches the end of the channel in the ice and speeds out onto the open water again. He heads straight for a huge wave, and the RIB briefly glides through the air, slamming back down and breaking through the next wave.

Water cascades over the bow and windscreen.

In the bright searchlight, the swirling snow makes it look as though the world is twisting like a screw, and for a few seconds, Joona has the sense that the boat is upside down, that his hair is trailing through the water.

*　*　*

Agneta staggers forward across the ice behind Hugo as the wind batters them from the side. He has tied the other end of the rope around his own waist, and is carrying the looped slack around his forearm.

She hunches over as she follows him, trying to keep the blanket pulled tight around her shoulders, but a sudden gust grabs hold of it and tears it away.

Agneta loses her footing and drops to one knee, but quickly manages to get up again.

Ripples of snow dance across the dark ice.

Bernard is still bellowing behind them, but she can't make out what he is saying.

Hugo uses one hand to push back his hair, squinting through the blizzard in an attempt to get his bearings.

Agneta has lost all sensation in her face and no longer feels the cold. Her lips are icy, but her bloody hand is burning.

The tinny sound of an engine reaches her through the gale, and in a sudden lull in the storm, she catches a glimpse of the open water up ahead. Frothing waves break over the thin edge of the ice.

A faint light flickers above the rough water, then vanishes into the haze.

'A boat!' Hugo shouts, dragging her further out.

Agneta stops and turns her back to the wind. She needs to rest, and can feel the hot blood from her hand seeping through her shirt, running down her torso and leg.

'We need to keep going!' Hugo tells her, glancing back.

'I can't.'

Her breathing is quick and shallow, her heart pounding uncomfortably hard, and she realises she is probably on the verge of circulatory shock.

'Come on, I'll help you.'

A dark figure emerges from the gloom behind them, and Bernard comes into view. His blonde wig has blown away, and his mouth and chin are smeared with blood. He is gripping the axe in his right hand, and he uses the left to wipe the snow from his eyes.

Hugo gets in between him and Agneta, holding up both hands as he tries to catch his father's eye.

'Enough now, Dad . . .'

Bernard jabs the axe out in front of him and hits Hugo square in the chest. The blow knocks the wind out of him, and the teenager drops to his knees for a moment before slumping onto his side and trying to catch his breath.

Bernard takes a step towards Agneta and severs the rope between them on the ice. He then stands tall and looks down at her with a sad smile.

84

Joona turns off into the bay at a sharp angle, moving parallel to the ice. The searchlight on the RIB sweeps through the blizzard, towards the row of lakefront villas, flashing in broken windows and illuminating exposed beams, fallen trees and the debris of broken garden furniture and boats.

Aggressive clouds of snow blow across the dark ice.

He spots Bernard's house up ahead, followed a moment later by three figures on the ice. Joona reaches for his pistol and tries to get a clear shot. The bow of the RIB breaks through another wave, and water crashes over Joona before the hull slams back down.

* * *

Bernard adjusts his grip on the axe and starts moving towards Agneta. She backs away from him in confusion, swaying when a gust of wind hits her.

He comes to a halt and raises the axe, studying her without emotion, like a predator watching its wounded prey.

Without warning, he swings the axe towards her. Agneta instinctively throws herself back, and the blade passes close to her face. She loses her balance and falls heavily onto the ice. Something in her neck cracks, but she immediately starts trying to scramble away.

Hugo has grabbed one of Bernard's legs in an attempt to stop him from going after her.

Agneta turns around and supports herself on her good hand, but she quickly realises that she will need to use both if she is going to stand any chance of getting up.

She whimpers in pain as she presses her bloody hand to the ice.

A searchlight cuts through the snow.

Bernard kicks Hugo away from him without so much as a glance.

Agneta tries to straighten up, but her bloody hand has already frozen to the ice. She screams in agony as she desperately tries to pull it free, but it won't budge. She is stuck.

Bernard is getting closer, the axe hanging by his side, and she raises her free hand in an attempt to ward him off.

'Please, Bernard! You don't have to do this!' she begs him.

Agneta knows that he is going to behead her, and she finds herself hoping that he knocks her unconscious first.

She closes her eyes and makes one last attempt to pull her hand free, but it is still frozen solid. The pain is so bad that she is about to pass out, and she rests her forehead against the ice and starts whispering the Lord's Prayer to herself.

Bernard moves up beside her and has just raised the axe like an executioner when Hugo charges towards him. He tackles Bernard, and they both fall headlong. Their combined weight makes the ice break beneath them, and father and son plunge into the freezing water.

*　*　*

Joona steers the RIB straight towards the ice, but he can no longer see the three figures. The hull slams into the biggest waves and glides over the rest, and he tilts both motors up out of the water and sits down with his back to the steering console.

The bow rises as the boat slows.

There is a crash, and the back of Joona's head slams into the console as the boat mounts the ice. It skids for around twenty metres before coming to a halt and tilting to one side. Joona jumps out and immediately starts running.

*　*　*

Hugo and Bernard break the surface, gasping for air and struggling to pull themselves out of the water.

Frigid waves wash over them, and the ice cracks and breaks.

They disappear in the dark, churning water.

The rope tied around Hugo's waist starts to ripple past Agneta, over the edge of the ice and beneath the surface.

She tries to grab it, but it is too far away.

Agneta lies down and stretches her legs as far as she can. She manages to catch the last loop of rope on her foot, and she pulls it towards her and quickly winds it around her good hand.

A moment later, it pulls taut, yanking her arm. Whimpering, she grips it as tightly as she can, and feels the tugging movements on the other end.

* * *

Joona runs across the ice with the wind behind his back. In the swirling tunnel of light from his headtorch, he spots Agneta up ahead.

She is on her knee with one arm outstretched. There is a rope around her wrist, pulled taut over the edge of the ice into the water.

'I can't get him out!' she shouts.

'Don't let go!'

A sudden jolt pulls her forward.

The line has begun to fray where it is rubbing against the edge.

Joona's eyes follow the line, and he sees the shadow of the rope cutting in beneath the ice.

'It was Bernard, he killed them all,' Agneta tells him.

'I know.'

Around five metres away, Hugo's limp body is visible just beneath the ice. His long hair is billowing in the water, and his eyes are closed.

Bernard is floating on his back beside his son, gripping his wrist.

The rope Agneta is holding is all that is stopping the current from carrying them away.

Bernard refuses to let go.

Joona moves directly above them.

The cold glow of his headtorch illuminates Bernard's wide eyes and the small bubbles of air escaping from his nose.

Joona takes his Colt Combat off safety, gets down onto one knee and presses the barrel of the gun to the ice above Bernard's torso. He then looks him straight in the eye and pulls the trigger.

There is a sharp crack, and shards of ice spray upwards. Joona shoots again, then again.

The third bullet breaks through the ice and hits Bernard in the heart.

A bright red sea anemone of blood unfurls from his chest.

Bernard's mouth starts to tremble, and bloody water seeps up through the hole in the ice.

His grip on Hugo's wrist loosens, and Agneta staggers back, pulling the boy away from his father. Bernard is swept away on the current, leaving a trail of blood behind him.

Joona rushes back over to Agneta and grabs the rope. He reels it in, then gets onto his stomach, shuffles over to the edge and reaches down into the cold water. He manages to grab the boy's coat and drag his lifeless body up onto the ice, away from the edge and over to Agneta.

She clutches him to her, and her face breaks into a smile as he begins to splutter. With her arms wrapped around him, the scene is like a joyful Pietà in the middle of the blizzard.

85

It is the day before Christmas Eve, and the fields and meadows are blanketed beneath a thick layer of shimmering snow.

Joona and Valeria are eating dinner at the table in her kitchen.

After the storm, a solemn calm descended over the country. People came together to restore and repair their communities, to take care of those who had been injured or bereaved. The roads were ploughed and cars dug out. Masts were raised, the power restored and communication made possible once again.

In anticipation of Valeria's return, Joona busied himself getting ready for the holiday. He bought food, wine, beer and snaps, put up the Christmas decorations, chopped down a tree and wrapped the presents.

Valeria got home late yesterday evening. They took a shower together, made love, and she then slept for thirteen hours straight.

They have just finished the last few preparations ahead of their family arriving for the holidays: Lumi and Laurent, Valeria's sister, her husband and their three daughters.

Joona went out to buy mussels that morning, and he cooked a simple spaghetti vongole – a contrast to all of the heavy festive food that awaits them over the next few days.

As they eat, Valeria tells him about her trip and how grief found its place in their everyday routines. Her mother had taken a chair to the grave and spent every day sitting there, giving her husband admonitions and advice to take with him to the afterlife.

They clear the table, take out the box of chocolate coins, sit back down and pour a couple of glasses of wine.

Valeria's amber eyes have a ring of bronze around the edge of her irises. She has lost weight during the trip, but says that it is Joona who seems thinner.

Joona has placed the only decoration he still has from childhood on the window sill. It belonged to his father: a snowy landscape featuring a red cottage with a yellow cellophane window. He has lit a tea light behind the little house, creating a cosy glow in the window.

Valeria sets the two glasses down on the table and holds Joona's gaze as she asks what he has been up to while she was in Brazil.

'Just the usual.'

'You've eaten two of the chocolate coins.'

'I waited to have a third until now.'

They both smile as the chocolate melts in their mouths, and Joona then leans into Valeria and starts telling her about the complex hunt for a serial killer that became world news when it emerged that famous author Bernard Sand was the perpetrator.

Using the material Agneta found in an antiques cabinet, Joona has been able to piece together a fairly detailed timeline of Bernard's journey from vulnerable young boy to compulsive axe murderer.

As a child, Bernard lived with his parents on a farm outside of Gislaved. His mother and father ran a car and tractor repair service there, and Bernard suffered from the same sleepwalking issues his son Hugo would later exhibit.

'Is sleepwalking hereditary?' asks Valeria.

'Apparently.'

His father came up with a primitive, yet effective system to avoid any accidents. At night, Bernard was tied to a rope that allowed him to go as far as the bathroom, but not out into the yard or over to the stove in the kitchen.

'Wow,' Valeria says with a sigh.

After his father abandoned his family for another woman, his mother entered a period of instability that quickly spiralled into schizoaffective disorder.

492

One day, she picked up an axe, carved an arrow into Bernard's chest, told him to get back into bed – that it was all his father's fault – and went outside.

'The boy was tied to the rope, but he could still see out of the window . . .'

Bernard watched as his mother turned the axe around, pressed the sharp edge to her forehead and then ran into a concrete wall, cleaving her head in two.

'I feel sick,' Valeria whispers, pressing a hand to her mouth.

With his father gone, Bernard ended up being taken into care and spent time in a number of different homes.

'That was his original trauma,' Joona continues. 'But he seemed OK, did well at school. After he graduated from high school, he was awarded a scholarship and enrolled at Stockholm University. He was only twenty-six when he got his PhD and became a professor, and just three years after that he started writing romance novels and had a huge amount of success.'

'Was he romantic?'

'Yes, he was . . . which is a key piece of the puzzle,' Joona replies. 'He met Claire, and they got married and had a son. Hugo.'

Bernard's second trauma took place when he discovered that his wife had been cheating on him while Hugo sleepwalked over to a window, climbed out and fell from the roof.

'She should have heard the alarm. He couldn't understand how she hadn't, and he grilled her, but she denied everything.'

Claire continued to deny everything, but she walked straight into the trap Bernard set for her when he pretended to go on another work trip two weeks later. He fashioned a poncho out of the shower curtain in the basement, grabbed an axe, took his wife by surprise in the bedroom and started dismembering her lover while he was still alive.

She fled down the stairs in terror and was running over the grass towards the gate when Bernard caught up with her. He tackled her to the ground, beheaded her and wrapped her body in the shower curtain before dragging it over to their beach house and burying it beneath the floor.

'Bernard told Hugo that Claire had abandoned them and moved back to Canada,' Joona goes on.

He wrote letters from her to Hugo and quickly came up with an alternative narrative about drug addiction to explain why the two could never meet.

Several years later, Bernard happened to cross paths with a patient at the same sleep lab as his son. He learned that she was cheating on her husband, and that lit some sort of dark fire in his belly, an icy blaze. Bernard grabbed his axe, drove over to her house by Lake Mälaren and hid among the trees until he spotted his opportunity. When the woman came out of the house and carried a stepladder over to one of the apple trees, he ran over and hit her on the back of the head with the flat side of his blade. She fell to the ground, losing her blonde wig in the process, and died of intracranial bleeding on the grass beneath the tree.

'So that was the moment he became a serial killer?' says Valeria.

'Yes.'

After the third murder, a new hunger took hold of him, a fire that helped to soothe his trauma but which also needed feeding far more frequently.

Wearing the blonde wig, he resurrected his own mother, but this time he turned his fury on the man who had abandoned her and her child.

'It wasn't that Bernard thought he *was* his mother, but the wig gave him some sort of protection and strength . . . almost like a kind of mask.'

Following that murder, it was primarily Bernard's relationship column in the newspaper that triggered his anger, people asking for advice and telling him about their complex lives, moral dilemmas and longing for change – such as when Nils Nordlund's jealous wife wrote to him and asked what she should do about her husband cheating on her every time he went to a conference.

'Bernard watched his victims, planning every step and setting traps for them . . . He became increasingly active, increasingly violent . . . It was as though the punishment he meted out was never quite harsh enough, because the void inside him . . . it refused to be filled. The more he fuelled the fire, the hungrier it became, which is – I think – why he also robbed his victims. He thought they should *pay* for what they had done, too.'

Joona trails off for a moment, thinking that there are many reasons why a person might repeatedly kill – all more or less explicit – but that the shadow the perpetrator casts is always roughly the same if you put the victims in a row: barren loneliness, a lack of empathy and a dark energy.

'No one can single-handedly create life, but there are some people who get high on death,' he says.

Joona and Valeria sit quietly for a while, sipping their wine and gazing out at the snow in the light from the kitchen, the vast darkness beyond.

'Go on,' she says.

'Do you want me to?'

'I won't be able to sleep otherwise,' she replies, flashing him a smile that makes the tip of her chin crease.

Joona gives her a brief overview of the Sleep Lab and Lars Grind's particular role in the investigation, explaining that for a brief time, he was their key suspect. But Dr Grind had no idea that Bernard was using his property or his deregistered Opel. He committed suicide once he realised that his less-than-ethical methods would be exposed. His secret research had been focused on the interaction between sleepwalkers, and the effect their medication had on their approach to various rules and regulations.

'The way Bernard managed to avoid drawing any suspicion to himself is remarkable,' says Joona. 'No connection was ever drawn between the murders. The first two – Claire and her lover – were seen as separate disappearances, the third as an accident. I haven't gone into detail about the fourth yet, but it happened in the south of the country, and the wrong man took the blame . . . It wasn't until the murder in the caravan that a wider investigation was actually launched.'

'After Hugo ended up in jail?'

'Exactly.'

Joona tells her that the victim had arranged to meet two prostitutes – women who didn't know each other – in a caravan at Bredäng Campsite.

'You might question his judgement,' Joona says with a wry smile. 'He had a beautiful wife and a young son at home, but he arranged to meet both a woman who made a habit of robbing and assaulting johns *and* an active serial killer.'

At eleven that evening, after Agneta had fallen asleep, Bernard drove out to the silo in Grillby, picked up an axe and Lars Grind's old car, and drove to the campsite. He then walked home to get changed.

Wearing a padded coat and a blonde wig, he returned to the campsite, entered the caravan and knocked the man to the floor with the broadside of his axe. Rage took hold of him, and he then chopped off one of the man's legs, beheaded him and began the rest of the dismemberment process.

What he didn't know was that the female robber was also at the campsite, and that she turned around and left when she heard the victim's screams. Nor that his son had followed him while sleepwalking, and had witnessed the entire murder.

Once he had finished dismembering his victim, Bernard walked over to Grind's car, shoved his bloody clothes into a couple of rubbish bags and drove back to the silo. He cleaned the car, burned the bags in an oil drum, left his trophies in his underground room, washed himself with chlorine and then got dressed and drove home in his own car.

'Following the second murder – that we knew about, anyway – I asked Saga what she thought.'

'How is she doing?'

'Much better. My boss has agreed to let her join the team with a view to eventually bringing her back into operative service.'

'That's great news.'

'I've told him I want her as my partner.'

'And what does he say to that?'

'That it sounds like a nightmare.'

'OK.' Valeria laughs.

'But he didn't say no.'

Joona explains that he had described the first two murders to Saga, and that her immediate reaction was that they sounded like medieval punishments.

'Aggravated capital punishment, as it was known. When death wasn't considered harsh enough.'

'Always so smart,' Valeria says.

'She was right, and that led me to the real question . . .'

'Of what they were being punished for.'

'Bravo. That was the question we needed to answer in order to understand the killer,' says Joona. 'The punishment is obvious, but as for the *crime* . . . that was only visible in the murderer's head.'

'Buying sex, infidelity . . .'

'Right, a kind of selfish lust – and one that impacts upon a child who is already suffering for whatever reason.'

'But didn't he think his death sentences were a bit over the top?'

'He identified with the children, and he punished the victims for all of the pain *he* had experienced. Everything that made him into the person he was.'

Joona takes a sip of wine and turns towards the little yellow window in the Christmas decoration as he tells Valeria about Pontus Bandling. His sister had written to Bernard's column in an attempt to explain her dilemma. She was convinced that her brother was cheating on his wife with a woman called Kimberly, and that it had all started a few years after his daughter was diagnosed with schizophrenia. The sister felt a powerful sense of loyalty towards her brother, but she also couldn't accept his behaviour and therefore wanted Bernard's advice.

'But what she hadn't realised was that Kimberly didn't exist, that she was just part of a game between husband and wife.'

'Oh God.'

Joona moves on to the book Bernard and Agneta were writing together.

'I don't know,' he says. 'It felt like they were really trying to help me stop the killer.'

'Isn't that strange?'

'To Bernard, it was probably just a way of trying to gain access to the investigation, of staying one step ahead of us,' Joona replies. 'But in the end, it proved to be his downfall.'

'How so?'

'I couldn't stop thinking about the fact that Hugo had been sleepwalking, that he'd had his eyes open . . . but that he didn't remember anything other than fragments of his nightmare. At the same time . . . the axe, the blood, the caravan – those weren't insignificant things, they should have been fresh in his episodic memory, even if he didn't know how to access them.'

Joona describes how Erik used the hypnosis sessions to gradually wash away the nightmare, enabling reality to emerge.

In his dreams, Hugo was being chased by a skeleton man while he followed his mother to the campsite.

'But even in the first session, he gave us a glimpse of the murderer.'

During the second session, Hugo had described what he saw through the window at the rear of the caravan, but the violence he recounted didn't fit with the forensic evidence. In a state of extreme anxiety, Hugo had talked about seeing the killer amputate both of the man's feet before killing him with a blow to the face.

'It wasn't until the third session that Erik finally got him to talk about the murder in the caravan.'

Driving through the snow in his car, it had dawned on Joona that Hugo had actually witnessed two murders, one in his own home.

In the second session, Hugo had been looking through a different kind of window. He had mentioned a parquet floor, a brass edging strip and a lamp with a snakeskin shade.

As a child, during a bout of sleepwalking, he had seen his father kill his mother's lover while wearing a shower curtain featuring a pattern of skulls and bones. He followed his mother through the house, out into the garden, then lost her in the darkness.

That subconscious trauma had then found its way into his nightmares about the skeleton man, programming him to always follow his mother in his sleep.

In his nightmare on the night of the murder in the caravan, Hugo had been following his mother in an attempt to save her from the skeleton man, but in reality he was following his father in a blonde wig.

'For Hugo that night, Bernard was both his mother *and* the skeleton man.'

'I understand.'

Joona swirls his wine and wraps up by telling Valeria about Bernard's habit of carving the arrow from his childhood trauma onto his victims' bodies. Occasionally, he only managed a single line before another impulse took hold of him and he turned his attention back to the dismemberment.

'But what do you think those arrows symbolised for him?'

'They were a part of him. He carried them with him, physically, on his body, and they appeared on hundreds of his childhood drawings. I think they probably meant something like "this is the moment your fate is sealed".'

'And the arrow is always pointing downwards? Towards the earth, the underground. Towards Hades?'

'Away from heaven,' Joona mumbles.

Epilogue

In June, Hugo and Agneta travelled together to Canada for Claire's funeral in the small hamlet of Le Grand-Village. Her skeletal remains had been found wrapped in a shower curtain beneath the floor of the lake house, buried in the sand.

The ceremony took place in a simple wooden church, Église Baptiste de Saint-Augustin, just off route 367.

Eight relatives attended.

The closest was Stephanie, a cousin who had played with Claire as a child. Her hair was just as blonde as Hugo's mother's had been, and she wore thick glasses and a faded T-shirt with the words *Jésus sauve* on the front.

Hugo was the only one who cried.

When her ashes were buried two days later, Hugo and Agneta were the only ones present.

He took off the coin he wore around his neck and placed it inside the urn before it was lowered into the ground.

* * *

Hugo has found a French restaurant in Québec, and he takes Agneta for dinner two days before they are scheduled to fly home.

It is a warm summer's evening, and they are sitting on the terrace with views out across the calm river. The sun is about to set, and the red, yellow and blue lanterns in the trees start to glow.

Hugo looks down at his phone and sees that Svanhildur has sent around three hundred hearts in reply to his message about coming home earlier than planned.

Joona Linna has also been in touch to let Hugo know that Olga Wójcik has been remanded in custody on suspicion of trafficking and procuring, and is facing up to ten years in prison. She is suspected of having, over a number of years, forced asylum seekers, undocumented migrants and vulnerable young men into hardcore pornography and prostitution.

There is evidence to suggest that she herself was groomed when she was sixteen, by a man called Jacek Jeżak who then forced her into blindly doing whatever she was told.

Jacek was the one who came up with the idea of approaching Hugo and getting him to pay money into an account that Olga had access to. She tried to convince him to borrow or steal money from his father, but when he failed to do that Jacek broke into the house and took anything of value he could find – before being surprised by Bernard.

'How do you feel now?' Agneta asks, taking a sip of her wine.

'I really don't know,' he replies, pushing his phone back in his pocket.

They no longer talk about Bernard and everything that happened last winter, but Hugo opens up and tells her about the coin. The silver dinar had been in his hand when he woke one morning as a child, and after the police investigation revealed that it had belonged to his mother's lover, Hugo had asked Joona if he could keep it.

Since he arrived in Canada, Hugo has spent a lot of time thinking about the fact that his mother never did manage to return to her homeland, that all of the letters were actually from Bernard. She was never an addict, and she didn't abandon Hugo. Her leaving, and choosing the drugs over him, was nothing but a lie to help explain her absence.

The waiter arrives with their food, and Hugo decides that he can't wait any longer. He puts down his cutlery and looks up.

'Agneta, I . . . I just wanted to say that I'm sorry for being such a dick towards you,' he begins, swallowing hard. 'I'll be eighteen in October, but I was wondering if . . . I . . . I wanted to ask if you were still interested in adopting me, because I really, really want you to . . . You're the best mum I could ever have, and . . .'

Agneta immediately starts crying, but despite the tears running down her cheeks, Hugo realises that he has never seen anyone look happier.